EDISON MARSHALL'S
Exotic Desert Adventure...

From the moment the young officer held her in a wild Romany dance, he knew the colonel's beautiful daughter must be his bride.

With that single desire he sealed his fate, betraying himself to the wild fury of the savage hordes of Asia and Africa—and the ruthless passion of a silken slave girl.

"Top-notch, lusty adventure"
Library Journal

"Enchanting, torrid, delightful . . ."
St. Louis Post-Dispatch

"Edison Marshall has excelled his own high standards! Vivid, topflight . . . thrilling adventure!"
Atlanta Journal

EDISON MARSHALL
GYPSY SIXPENCE

AVON
PUBLISHERS OF BARD, CAMELOT, DISCUS, EQUINOX AND FLARE BOOKS

Dedication:
To the Lady of the Lake,
Frances Cates of Burke County, Georgia,
In constant gratitude
For an enchanting studio in the Piney Wood.

AVON BOOKS
A division of
The Hearst Corporation
959 Eighth Avenue
New York, New York 10019

First Avon Printing, May, 1969
Third Printing

Cover illustration by Vic Livoti

Printed in the U.S.A.

While I was looking up a reference in the *Encyclopaedia,* my eyes happened to fall on the biography of an eminent man of Victorian times whose works were already known to me. He served in the secret service in India; he made a pilgrimage to Mecca disguised as an Arab; he translated *The Arabian Nights;* and his explorations in East Africa won him a knighthood and a place in history.

The article in the *Encyclopaedia* said of him:

There were even those, including some of the Romany themselves, who saw gipsy written in his peculiar eyes as in his character, wild and resentful, essentially vagabond, intolerant of conviction and restraint.

The conception of this novel, its main character suggested by, but by no means patterned after, that of Richard Burton, occurred at that moment.

BOOK ONE

CHAPTER ONE

The Fortuneteller

STAR-BRIGHT EYES OF BOYHOOD! Mine had seen more than they ought, including much that Queen Victoria would not countenance in her handsome universe, ere I shed my milk teeth. With them dropped away my innocence, for by disposition I had no fondness for it, and by my fate, already moving, I could not afford it. Helping me in this good riddance was an old, fat Gypsy woman.

I remember the year, 1830, and almost the summer day, for, having celebrated my twelfth birthday, I was puzzling over a weighty question—whether I was yet a man. Still I had not confided my perplexity to my foster brother Gerald, as different from me as a young watchdog from a fox. Of the eame age—so we were told— taller, manlier on many counts, finer by my own ungrudging counting, he would be above or ashamed of such matters.

Gerald and I, perched in our pony cart, had overtaken her on the road to Hungerford, below Ilsley, as she made for the encampment by the river. Gerald was driving—Papa had told him he might, save when he let me spell him—and I was busy looking. Instead of slowing up, he whacked the nag to a brisk trot and was fifty paces past the granny before I could grab the reins and pull up.

"Let's drive on," Gerald cried, shivering in his breeches. "Gypsies steal children—"

"I don't reckon she could handle us both," I answered. And my childhood was lost that day like something fallen out of a wagon and left on the road.

"Mamma says so, and they're thieving and dirty—"

I did not doubt the latter charges, but felt no moral indignation and, instead, some envy. I had often lusted to steal Gerald's belongings, even though Papa had told me, a little shamefaced, that I must not mind them being better and more numerous than mine. Most of them were gifts from Mamma, bought with her own money. Since I was only her foster child, not hers and Papa's flesh and blood, of course she loved Gerald most. He had told me, too, that although I was distant kin to him, I must not expect him to give me equal gifts. Truly, I did not mind in a painful measure. As for the Gypsy's being dirty—I got along well with dirt, detesting the deal of washing, bathing, combing, and brushing that Mamma ordered for me. There seemed a greater portion than she personally bestowed on Gerald, but perhaps I needed the lion's share. In lieu of fine playthings, real things close to earth came close to me.

That was being shown this moment. The fat Gypsy woman was coming closer to me and not just with her legs, while the nearing view of her made her ever more an alien to Gerald. He could not really see her; he could only look at her. Having an avid appetite for new experience, of course I was enchanted with the old wanderer in her gaudy kerchief, her red-and-green dress, jangling bracelets, and necklace of gold coins. No other Gypsies had visited our country lanes in my remembrance. Something more than the strangeness of the sight was exciting me, though—and in a strange, strong way. There was a warm welling in my heart and a mystery in my brain. It was as though I had dreamed of Gypsies traveling on a road, although in an opposite direction somehow—retreating instead of advancing— being able to see their backs and not their faces. Maybe that dream had been invoked by reading about them, and envying their wild, free life.

She overtook the cart, and I saw her swarthy, wrinkled, undoubtedly dirty face. She glanced into my eyes, then quickly fixed her gaze on Gerald. I might have thought she had already divined he was cock of the walk—more likely to have a shilling in his pocket—except for what had happened in the brief interval that our eyes had met. What had happened was an extraordinary lack of anything. She had stopped in her tracks, her eyes had stopping gleaming and changed to black stone, and the set of her features, which gave her a cunning, greedy expression, remained fixed but utterly expressionless.

"If you'll cross my hand with silver, little gentleman, I'll tell your fortune," she blathered, looking at Gerald. If her mind was on her words, my instincts—maybe they were just a batch of fox-sharp senses—had lied to me.

"I don't want my fortune told," he answered. "Drive on, Rom."

Those words had astonished her—stonied her, as our fathers would say—and I could not imagine why. A wild, almost frightened expression whipped across her face, and the knuckles of her brown hand, clutching the arm rail, showed white. I had a sense of the uncanny, the familiar details of the scene—the hedge and the sheep grazing in the field and a distant farmhouse set among trees—having the aspect of things seen in dreams.

Very slowly her eyes wheeled to mine. I could not see into them; a film had come over their lustrous black.

"What a pretty name you have, little gentleman," she said.

"It's short for Romulus, ma'am," I answered, excited and barely able to steady my voice.

"Romulus?"

"Yes. He was the one who was suckled by a wolf and founded Rome."

"You are a clever little gentleman, with good learning. Will you tell me your last name?"

"It's Brook, and his name is Gerald Brook."

"Yet you do not look like brothers. He is so fair—pretty as a picture—and you so dark."

"We're only foster brothers, Grandma, although we're

9

kin. I was born in America, the child of Papa's second cousin, and since I was an orphan, Papa adopted me."

"What were your real mother's and father's names? I can tell your fortune better—"

"My real father's name was Harris, Papa told me. He never told me my mother's name. Both died with plague when I was a baby."

"Will you cross my hand with silver—or even with red money?"

"Give me first a sample of your wares."

"Your real father—maybe you have seen his picture —had blue eye and fair hair."

"My foster father has 'em, so maybe his cousin did."

"You are very fond of music, and like to dance."

"I've neve been to dancing-school, but I like dance tunes, if they're real lively."

"He found an old fiddle in the attic," Gerald broke in, "and can play a tune on it already. But I'm going to be a soldier."

"I see that, little gentleman. Without looking in your hand, I see it." The witch turned again to me. "You love to take journeys, and you always wonder what's around the bend in the road."

"I'm going to travel all over the world some day." I fished a sixpence from my pocket. "Here's your wage, and if you can tell me any more—"

She took the coin, spat on it neatly, and, her lips moving, rubbed the spittle in well.

"What if I should give it back to you?" she asked, her eyes searching mine.

"He don't want the dirty thing now," Gerald protested.

"Yes, I do, Grandma, if you want me to have it."

"I want you to have it and keep it for a good-luck piece, but will ask a gift in return."

"I'll give you anything I've got—"

"Only a lock of your hair. It is black and coarse, not fine and pretty like your foster brother's, but I may have use of it, which will do you no harm."

I fetched out my clasp knife, opened and handed it to her. Gerald flinched as though she might cut our throats with it; but I trembled, too, I did not know why, when

10

she cut off a strand of hair from the very crown of my head. This she put inside a kind of locket she wore on her necklace.

"Good-by, Rom," she told me.

"Aren't you going to tell my fortune?"

"Your fortune was told you long ago. Perhaps you will remember it, when it comes true. It is full of the great things—love and hate, danger, beauty of women and of mountains, and great change. It will seem a stranger fortune than your half-brother's—"

"He's my foster brother, not my half-brother, Grandma."

"You told me so, but I am old and my memory fails. But to you it won't seem strange, because it comes out of you. Good-by— *P'ral!*"

With that strange salutation, she walked away from us, and it seemed the second time I had seen that. Gerald took the reins from my hand, and we were a half mile down the road before I wakened from a kind of dream. He had made some remark to me, and I had answered him, without remembering a word that had been said.

"Don't tell Mamma I talked to the Gypsy."

"Why not?" he asked.

I could not think of the real reason. "Well, she says they're dirty and thieving—"

"I won't, if you give me that sixpence."

"I thought you wouldn't want it, after she spit on it."

"Well, I don't. How could her spit bring anybody luck?"

"You'll have all the luck anyway. Mamma loves you, and she hates me."

"How can you say such a mean thing?"

"She does. I've never thought about it before—but it's true."

"Papa loves you."

"I think he'd like to, but he's afraid." I said that without knowing its meaning. Then, cold and empty from fear and loneliness, I had to speak again, looking straight ahead. "Do you love me, Gerald?"

"Yes, Rom."

"Are you sure?"

"Cross my heart and hope to die, I do."

"Will you promise not to tell Mamma about the Gypsy, even if I don't give you the sixpence?"

"Not if you don't want me to."

"I love you best of anybody. You're all I have."

Until this moment I had thought that I loved Pa best, for caring for me with good care—no matter how small the end of my horn compared with Gerald's—when I was not his son.

At the first opportunity after getting home, I searched Papa's excellent library for all I could learn about Gypsies. A book entitled *Etymology of the Balkan Peninsula* had a short article about them, but I could find no reference to *p'ral*, the Gypsy word she had used. Then the short hairs rose on the back of my neck. I read:

They call themselves the Romany people, and employ the word "Rom" to mean a Gypsy man.

CHAPTER TWO

The Past Revealed

THE TYPE SWAM BEFORE MY EYES. I closed the book quickly, as though it were a closet door I had opened on a frightening scene. The room was suddenly haunted in a dim, eerie way, the curtains and furniture looking almost but not quite the same. My skin prickling, I hurried out, a silence closing swiftly on my heels, to the big parlor where Papa was reading a newspaper, the pale woman whom I had called Mamma was sewing, and Gerald was sorting over his beautiful collection of birds' eggs. Gerald and Papa glanced up in a friendly way, then their gazes made a V of which my face was the point.

"What's the matter, Romulus?" Papa asked quietly, with a reassuring smile.

The woman looked up from her sewing. Her eyes appeared too full of other thoughts to attend immediately to the present matter.

"Nothing, sir," I answered, pretending to be puzzled by the question.

"Well, you look a little pale—"

Then the woman fixed her calm eyes on my face. Papa stopped talking because of that. He was waiting, with an anxiety he could not conceal from her—like that he had often concealed from me but could not any more—for her to speak.

"Why, Frederick," she said slowly, "he seems in good color to me."

"Oh, well." Then Papa went back to his newspaper, Gerald to his birds' eggs, the woman to her embroidery. I could never go back to what I had been doing, or thinking, or feeling, or being before.

13

For the next few weeks I could not go anywhere. In a very real sense I had lost my way. I did not seem to be living in this house—the large, comfortable villa, known as Yew Gate, part of the woman's estate—but only queerly visiting here, knowing well I should be bustling about, packing up to leave, but unable to take the first step. Sometimes, after sitting still a long time, in deeply troubled introspection, I seemed to have no right to the body that belonged to a boy I wasn't any more—Gerald's cousin, Romulus Brook. In my nightly dreams Gerald's mother became miraculously mine. She would be petting him while I stood back in cold shadows, then she would call me to her to receive an equal share, while my heart burst with joy. But one dream, just before dawn, began with me on her lap, her kisses warm on my face and throat; then when Gerald had called me "Rom," she flung me away and spat in my face. Even so, it did not end in the icy paralysis of nightmare. I was fighting hard someone or something, in hope of victory.

Often I caught myself building air castles, wherein I saved Gerald's life at the dreadful risk of my own—saved the house from burning down—saved the Queen from an assassin—and was rewarded by the love and gratitude of my foster parents. Such daydreams conflicted with going to my foster father and demanding, as my right, the story of my birth and adoption. Suspecting the truth, I feared that his telling it would cause a permanent rift between us. But when I was fourteen those very suspicions served me as a weapon. The occasion was shortly after Gerald's departure for Rugby—I was still going to a day school in Berkshire, and being treated to a spell of evil temper by his doting mother.

She had wrinkled her nose a little as I came in from a long walk through the fields, and bade me take myself to the bathroom for a good scrub.

"Ma'am, I had a good scrub just this morning," I replied. "If you please, I've got to do some studying."

"You heard me, Rom."

"Yes, ma'am."

"You propose to disobey me?"

"Yes, ma'am."

14

"I advise you to change your mind, before I speak to your father."

"Speak to him if you care to, ma'am, but I think he'll tell you that the dark color and the smell won't wash off."

The words sprang from a desperate heart and a painfully dry throat, but the instant they were out of my mouth, my heart leaped, and I almost laughed aloud. The reason was the expression on her ugly face. Indeed, I had never before realized its ugliness, with which I had lived as long as I could remember—sharp-boned, dull-white in color, with a sour mouth and spiteful eyes. Now her eyes had opened to show their whites under their cold blue irises, and I knew she was afraid.

"What do you mean, Rom?" she asked, her weedy-looking neck working.

"Why, nothing, 'cept from now on I'll bathe when I please, and go dirty when I please. I'll obey him, but I won't obey you 'cept when I feel like it. If you want to complain to him, go ahead. But I doubt if you will, for although you like to hint around, you don't really want to be told the truth. It might cause trouble in our happy home."

She sprang up, but I had not the least notion that she was going to Papa.

"This truth you speak of. Is it something your father told you?"

"No, but it's plain as the nose on his face."

"You're an unspeakable little beast."

As she swept out of the room, I laughed with a boldness, perhaps a wickedness, I had hardly imagined yet, and the surprise of it was still on me when I made an important discovery. All the time I had been defying her, my hand had been in the side pocket of my trousers, my fingers toying with a smooth silver coin.

That night I hung it on a stout cord to wear around my neck.

I dreamed no more of the woman's kisses. Sometimes I had dim, far-distant dreams of being kissed by a younger woman, with a darker face and warmer, lovelier lips. In the next year, I got almost entirely rid of daydreaming, confronted the future, and began to prepare for it in small, solid ways. So Papa was surprised at my declining his offer to send me to a new-found, inexpensive school in Wales. He readily accepted my excuses for studying at home for a year or two more, then going to school on the Continent.

Among his most intimate friends was a stout, gray-headed man, named Graham Byrd, who had lost a leg in a hunting accident in India, and gained a sunburn too deep-dyed to wear off. He had always treated me with particular kindness, so on an evening that I found myself alone with him in our library, I ventured to seek his advice as to my education.

"I've decided to make a career in India," I told him.

"That's what I call a full-size decision," he answered, with a quiet smile. "Will you tell me how you arrived at it?"

"I think I can do a lot more out there than in England. I heard you say once that very few Englishmen understand the natives, and I think I could be one of 'em. I kind of look like an Indian I saw in London, and I'm mighty interested in the country. I thought maybe you could tell me what preparations I could make, while I finish growing up."

"Well, you must read all the books you can find that deal with the East—not only India, but Arabia and Persia and what we call the Northwest. They're all interbound. You'd expect me to tell you to learn the Hindustani vernacular. More than that you should become an expert in both Hindi and Urdu. But maybe you'll be surprised at the language I'd advise you to master before either of those. I refer to Arabic."

"Well, I will, if you think best."

"It's a big order, but it's also the key to a real knowledge of all the nearer Orient. It's as necessary to an Orientalist as Greek to a classicist. It's the root of scores of Eastern languages—the speech of the conquerors of East Africa—really the great bridge between India and the West. Mighty few Englishmen out there ever go to the great labor involved—they'd rather play polo. The few that do reap a tremendous advantage."

"I'll go to London and get some books and start right away."

He looked at me curiously, wondering if this were a boyish whim soon to be forsaken. I could assure him that it was not. All childish things had to be put away —this was my intensely vivid, unmitigated realization.

"Of course, you've got to know French, too, you know," he went on. "That's the language of the courts and the password throughout Europe. I mean, if you're after big game."

When I thanked him, he made one long-remembered observation. "Being dark as you are—and having perhaps some of the traits that go with it—may be either a great asset or a great liability, depending on your strength of character. Most English men and women live only in the façade of India—a gay and pleasant life, a bit on the swagger side—but a few go behind that and find—well, you may see for yourself, someday. By the way, you needn't go to London for your first books. I'll send you some tomorrow."

He kept his promise, and I had no intention of breaking mine. I think Papa was rather gratified by my studying French, thinking it a move toward social prestige, but was mystified and worried by my determined attack on such a strange, alien language as Arabic. I could not help but grin inwardly at him as he glanced uneasily into my swarthy face. I had become an apprentice in the vocation I meant to pursue, as definitely as though bound to a master. I was, in a sense—the master being my own driving ambition.

The only person who expressed any curiosity about my doings was Nora, the upstairs maid, seventeen or so when I turned fifteen, and with whom Papa exchanged many telltale glances. I found her one morning in my room, gazing round-eyed into a copy of Jamil's poems.

"Can ye read this 'ere, Master Rom?" she asked.

"After a fashion."

"Ain't English books good enough for ye? They're good enough for the Master, and Master Gerald."

"Well, Nora, I'm not like either of them. I was born in America, and my real father—so Papa told me—was a distant cousin of his named Mr. Harris."

Something about my tone made her glance up. "I don't see nothin' funny about it."

"I'm not being funny. I'm telling you what he said. Of course, I can't help but wonder what my real parents were like. One of them must have been mighty dark, with hair and skin like mine. But my eyes are hazel, aren't they?"

"I don't want to look at 'em."

"Why not? I haven't got the evil eye, I hope."

"I'm no ways sure ye ain't. Anyhow they're the brightest, strangest eyes I ever saw in a yonker's head. And them high cheekbones and eagle nose—"

"Yet there's a family resemblance between Gerald and me, don't you think? Quite marked, for third or fourth cousins."

"Yes, and to blazes with ye."

"Why, what's the matter? It's not so marked that anyone would think we were closer kin. You can see that Gerald's much better born. I wonder if I'll take after Papa's family in liking to travel. His cousin, Mr. Harris, went out to the States. Papa visited there at least once—the trip that he found and adopted me. Had he ever been there before?"

"How do I know?" Nora stood as though her back was to a wall. "Why don't ye ask him?"

"I'm asking you, Nora."

"'Pears like I heard someone say he'd been out there once before, while the Missus was carrying Master Gerald—"

"And she cranky and sour the whole time. I reckon Pa had to take a vacation to stand it. But it's a long journey—he must have been gone at least four or five months. Do you suppose he sowed some wild oats out there?"

"I'm not going to say that about the Master, and ye can't make me."

"Supposing he did, Nora, how do you fancy she looked?"

"Well, ye asked me and I'll tell ye, ye young devil. Mind ye, I won't say the Master did anything amiss, but if he took a woman out there—I've heard the like of gentlemen—she was wild in the face as a ferret. She had wild eyes and a wild, wicked heart and was headed

18

straight for hell. Like enough she was a Red Indian squaw."

"I don't think she was a Red Indian. And she might have been nearly as pretty as you, Nora, in a different way."

Nora had a far from phlegmatic temperament. The weather of her heart was ever April. She glanced quickly into my eyes, vilified only a moment before, and, deciding I was not mocking her, she gave me a provocative smile.

"Ye never said I was pretty before, Master Rom. I thought ye took me for plain."

"And no one could have a prettier figure," I went on, coming a little nearer. It was partridge-plump, small-waisted, stout-thighed, finely rounded calf.

"Well, ye ain't as tall as Master Gerald, but ye're fashioned sturdy enough."

"Where is everybody?"

"Why, the Missus has gone out—she won't be back till lunchtime—and it's Lucy's day off— Oh, the blessed saints!"

It was not a difficult victory—Nora being bighearted, red of blood, in her Irish springtime, and well-schooled in surrender—but the most gratifying and delightful of my days. I could not take it lightly, had I been blind or knavish enough to try. Its very force caused me, through an operation I did not clearly understand, to make a decision that she might think was caused by its being ineffectual.

"Master Rom, was this the first time for ye?" she had whispered, her face in rosy bloom, and with a confiding smile.

"Yes, Nora."

"I don't know how I guessed it, when ye was so good a man."

"I wish we could meet often. I'd like to come to your room every night. But we can't—ever again."

Her color deepened, and the joy rushed out of her face, and her incredulous expression changed to one of deeply wounded pride.

"Please don't look that way, Nora! You're real sweet, but for us to keep on wouldn't be fair to Papa."

19

"I don't understand ye, Master Rom!" Her eyes that I had seen long and lustrous only a few minutes ago had grown round and glistening.

"You know. I can go and find some other sweetheart, but he can't. He's too old and respectable. And he's mighty fond of you."

"Why, I never—"

"I couldn't give you the money you send home every month. He treats us both very well, and we mustn't mistreat him"

"But it's not for his sake ye're turning so hard and cold. A body'd think ye didn't like me. Was ye puttin' on, like a whore 'tis said, the sweet way ye was treating me?"

"I do like you. You gave me a real treat. But I'm glad to have Papa get some joy out of life, and you give him a lot."

"Ye've got some other reason for wanting the Master to stay with me. I can see it in your wicked eyes. It's something to do with the Missus—"

"Hasn't she—the way she treats Papa and you—something to do with you and him?"

"It eases my conscience, like. She knows chalk from cheese, but she can't prove nothing, and she's too top-lofty to try."

"Why, that may worry her more than catching you!"

"I don't care a whit, when she's so mean. But I wouldn't cut off my own nose—"

She started to say more, but thought better of it. Anyway the wound to her pride had been suddenly healed. I saw that, and something else far more significant—willingness growing to gladness that we would not meet again in this way, but for reasons of her own. These reasons I did not want to plumb. I knew only that she drew away from me as though frightened.

With Papa's consent, given with such readiness that it smacked of gratitude, within four months I was pursuing my education across the Channel. I chose France for my first training-ground, and for half a year was in the nominal charge of a brilliant, slightly drunken Oxfordian, who kept a kind of boarding-school outside Paris. When my remittance was cut down—Gerald was on his way to Sandhurst, and must live in style—I took off happily for Marseilles, where francs went farther than in the North, where the sun and the maidens were more benign, and ships from Smyrna docked.

It lay just around the corner from Toulon. Free as a peregrine falcon, I was soon in Genoa, and after a while, and better yet, in Trieste. Here I could have had my fill of Austrian Gypsies, had instinct not warned me to steer clear of them. The long way I must make could not be traveled in a Gypsy wagon. It was a wonder how easily my tongue, long adroit in French, caught on to Italian, the latter so akin to Spanish that I would not have hesitated to take Don Quixote's road. Instead I took off across the narrow seas to Tunis, there to strengthen and humanize my halting, bookish Arabic, which ever more clearly promised to be the keenest tool in my kit. On leaving there I could match curses with a dragonman. Although yet a neophyte in the elegancies of the great, noble language, I was turning quickly into something rare among English youths, common on the Continent, and thick as fleas in the Levant—a real linguist. I was discovering that the term meant more than the ability to speak and understand several tongues. It was a subconscious perception of the function of speech, whereby all the tongues the linguist knows become aspects of one, his mind taking a different bent and color with the expression of each. A curious but no doubt natural consequence was, every successive language could be learned with a progressive ease.

Actually my pride in the achievement was dimmed by a sense of fate. I had to learn, as I had to eat, for strength to meet it. The great boon was, I was beginning to love the excitement of learning. Looking eastward, I proposed to master Hindi and Urdu before long, a pleasant as well as a relatively easy task for an Arabic scholar.

Meanwhile I was tasting every experience that came my way. A few had a touch of the sublime, the greater part were the come and go, give and take, of spirited living, and some were base. To supplement my remittance, I made a few ducats as a dispatch carrier, a tutor, a spy, and once—not greatly to my shame, since all parties profited well—a procurer of an ambitious virgin for an amorous duke.

It so chanced that at eighteen I fought in a minor holy war in Albania. I had got into it without hardly knowing it, siding with some Slavic Christian rebels against the Turks, and in six months was out with a whole skin, but in the interim I had seen men die as dead as at Waterloo, had tasted sweet little victories and big, bitter defeat, and had been made a subaltern of horse.

The next year I was at Oxford, of all places. Kicked out with great dispatch—the word was "rusticated"—I was seeking a commission in the pay of the East India Company when word came that Papa had been gravely injured in a hunt-meet accident and I must come home at once.

There I found Gerald, a full-fledged officer of the Queen, and we talked awhile before Papa sent for me. Great God, I thought, how blood told! He was three inches taller than I, althought of about the same weight, and remarkably handsome. Rather humorless, he seemed to me, also innocent. Tall and lithe, he was a superb horseman and a dead shot, had a commanding presence, and, being fearless—a much braver man than I, who always took anxious care of my own neck—would undoubtedly make a reputation as an officer. He could not lie, I thought; he could not flatter or scheme. I would always let him precede me through a door.

I wanted him to say that he still loved me. I ached to hear him say it, and without shame; save for pride, I might have tried to get him to. In my heart, though, I did not believe it. It was against reason that he should, even if he did not surmise, by now, that I was his bastard brother. So be it, he would do his duty by me. He was doing it now, in making me feel at home.

When Papa summoned me, I found him flushed with fever, rational, and very sad. He did not want to die so young, but saw no way to dodge it. For a moment I wished strangely that I could die in his stead. If I were God, I would decree it—not only erasing Papa's sin of spilling his seed in the womb of an Egyptian, but turning it into his salvation. It would be such a godlike gesture of generosity it would put earth kings to shame. Only by some such divine stroke could I fetch dying—so I thought crazily amid these lowering shadows. It would take more than His mere consent—instead His unsheathed sword. I felt my life flaming within me, fierce and bright from inexhaustible oil, unextinguishable in any wind. Its lamp, my body, was adamant as iron. I was most strangely cursed.

"Have you anything to tell me before I die?" he asked, in a low, clear voice.

I started to tell him, why, he would be walking about in another fortnight, visiting London to see Gerald parading before the Queen ere the leaves fell, but the lie stuck in my throat.

"Yes, Papa. I want to thank you for everything you've done for me."

"Romulus, you cut me to the quick. If you only knew—"

"I do know," I broke in quickly, unable to endure the anguish on his face.

"You—know?"

"For years now."

"Yet you thank me?"

"You went back and got me, in spite of your fear of Mamma. In spite of the danger of people's guessing, and your losing the repute you prize so. You would have done more for me, if you hadn't had to live the lie that I was only your cousin's son. Even though Mamma knew it was a lie—and you knew she did—still you let me stay."

"Maybe I did wrong. Mamma hated you—and Juvena loved you."

"I think you did do wrong, but you thought it was right. And I thank you for another favor—naming me Romulus. It showed you weren't ashamed of lying with my mother."

"It was a little joke we made up together, beside the fire, before you were born. We didn't think you would ever find it out. You were to be an English gentleman—"

"You were wrong about that, Papa."

23

"I know it. Gerald is a gentleman, as fine as they come, but that makes your lot harder—"

"You're wrong about that, too. I love Gerald, and he's my greatest pride."

"That's the Gypsy in you, like the rest. They're the only truly humble people on the earth. Do you know why?"

"I've heard the story. They turned away the Virgin and her Child from their tents, when she sought shelter there. For that they must wander over the face of the earth forever, knowing what they've lost."

"Juvena told me by the fire, my head in her lap. No one loves fineness as much as the Gypsies, and though they can't have it, they never deny it for their pride's sake, knowing they lost it through their own blindness." Papa's throat grew dry and his breath short. To revive him for a little while, I poured him a glass of wine.

"I swear to you, Rom, that I thought you'd be like Gerald," he went on, a trace of his old vigor in his voice. "Darker of skin and gayer of heart, of course, but a true Englishman. I'd come and get you before you picked up their ways. But I delayed too long. Maybe if I'd snatched you from her breast, even then 'twould have been too late. I've made poor amends, but the best I could with Mamma looking on. I've left you half of what I have, and she'll despise me for it in my grave."

"You needn't have left me a penny," I told him, choking.

"That I know. You'd never have blamed me, or blamed Gerald. There's the Gypsy again. I had to leave him half—besides what he'll get from Mamma, entailed to sons of her blood—even if I didn't want to, which I did. He's my first-born, and my pride."

"And I'm your shame."

"No, I swear before God. I've pride in you, too—a strange, joyful, defiant pride. Only after she conceived, proud as a robin of her first egg, did I see what I'd done. Before that, when I was running after her, my eyes were blinded with passion."

"Passion," I said aloud, after thinking what I was too proud to say.

"I had never dreamed such passion as she waked in

24

me. I was out of my mind all that summer. But what's that I see in your face?"

"Just a wish that failed."

"What was the wish? Maybe I can grant it yet—"

"It's too late for that. It doesn't matter, I reckon. I'd wished that you loved her—a little."

"A little!" Papa rose on his elbow, his eyes burning.

"Hell's fire, I loved her out of the world. If God sends me to hell for my unrepentance, I'll love her still."

CHAPTER THREE

A Marked Man

I HAD SHRIVED Papa, almost without his knowing it, and on the following night he died in peace. I was his chief mourner, too, since Mamma had hated being his lawful wife—not quite the same as hating him—and was glad to have him in a hole from which he could not extricate himself to seek some warmer and more pleasant bed than hers. Maybe there was another mourner beyond the waters. Perhaps in a dream Juvena had felt him pass. I did not think she, too, had died, for I had not felt her pass in any dream or vision. It stood to reason—reasoning in terms of human realities, not a mess of scientific pottage—that she would have loitered briefly in my doorway, ere she journeyed on. Quite likely she was hardly thirty-five. Had she been much older than fourteen when he had kindled her, she would have been married, in which case her Rom would not have so lightly yielded up a blooded colt caught in his trap. Maybe Papa had paused in his flight to stand in her doorway, and then she had told her husband and her tribe, encamped on some Yankee road, that her tall, white lover, for whom she had borne a man-child, had struck his tent and gone, and the crones sang a death song, and the fiddles wailed.

Mamma's time to weep was a year later, when Gerald, gazetted to a Cheshire regiment, sailed for India. I was already India-bound—I had been ever since my voice changed—although I had not yet picked my route or packed my trunk. I was still packing my head with the equipment I would need on my arrival there. Having no strings to pull, and smelling slightly disreputable because of my irregular education, I appealed in vain to the East India Company for a post to my liking—with a tether long and light. The only alternative was service in its military establishments. With General Napier's bloody prophecies of Indian mutiny blasting its ears, it was glad enough to count my guerrilla warfare in Albania as qualifying me for a subaltern's commission. Of course I did not try for one of the old, aristocrat regiments, to command beef-eaters, and be foremost in the fray. At age twenty-two I managed to be gazetted to a sepoy rifle regiment barracked at Bombay, a green and not greatly trusted rabble whom I thought would smell the battle only from afar, until I had completed my studies and could find more welcome employment.

Before our fine P. and O. steamer had passed the Gates of Hercules, my fellow officers knew me for a bounder. Instead of breaking bottles with them in the canteen, I studied Hindi and Urdu and practiced it on homeward-bound Hindus and Moslems above and below decks. They addressed me as "sahib," in due respect for an officer of the Queen, but after studying my countenance with their quiet, wise eyes, and finding in mine no disdain, they led me down fascinating paths of their minds. At Cairo I boarded a camel for the journey to Suez. *Good Lord,* I thought, *the ill-smelling brute is my brother!* We were both fated to kick and bite, to cross dreary deserts, and to thirst long ere we drank deep. I was wonderfully happy on his back, sensing his capacity to survive in a deadly region. I would always make use of such experts, whereby to flourish. My fellow riders cursed their rough, ungainly mounts, but I made truce with mine. The sandstorm that we buffeted angered and hence harmed us less than any other alien and his beast.

Despite my low-born lust to shine among my betters, I did not speak one Arabic word on these Arabian sands. The sahibs would have respected the learning, since it would seem to be useless in India and no push toward promotion, but I concealed it like an extra weapon, for a time of need. The dragomans and camel tenders greatly enriched my working knowledge of the tongue, and entertained and enlightened me by their

27

lurid, lewd descriptions of the sahib travelers. I was not spared, and indeed more discussed than the rest.

"His rogue of a camel serves him well, though I would swear before Allah he has never before set rump on hump," said a drover captain. In lieu of the rhyme he employed a fine, alliterative obscenity.

"Then a Bedouin bedded his mother," returned his fellow. The pun employed was much more pointed.

"Was he born in Hind, like some of the others? Is there purple at the base of his nails? I would swear no lotus-white memsahib gave him that darkness of skin and luster of eye."

"Bah!" cried an old nomad, puffing a hooka. "He's a Christian Frankistan, and I, for one, will not look twice at his foreskin ere I cut his throat, on the day of jihad [holy war]."

Meanwhile I was learning how they sipped coffee, smoked, spat, gestured, and invoked Allah. Some day I might make a pilgrimage to Mecca in their company. The world was wide and wonderful, and it was obligatory upon me to see much of it—and gather many of its pleasant fruits—in this so little time.

After being baked on the desert, we travelers were boiled in the swelter of the Red Sea, ere the ocean breezes cooled us. I took another chilling at our new-won town of Aden, my fine plans for a quiet, safe year in Bombay having gone wry. Orders were waiting there for our ship to dock first at Karachi, in the troubled North, and there to discharge some casual troops and officers, including me, not direly needed elsewhere. The Mohammedans of Baluchistan, on India's western frontier, were up in arms, according to rumors flying about the Head. There might be some pretty fighting, and maybe a massacre.

From Karachi we were marched upcountry, making for Hyderabad in Sind, from where the resident, General Outram, had sent a call for help. Midway the journey I heard news that changed most wonderfully my whole outlook on the venture. It was that Gerald's regiment, the 22nd Foot, was likewise Hyderabad-bound. That in itself was no great wonder. General Charles Napier had mustered every British soldier he could lay hand on. To me it seemed a stroke of fate to make a real soldier of me.

The expedition was no longer the concern only of the Queen, the bigwigs of the Company, and some battle-hungry troops. I was no longer its chance conscript, blown along by a desert wind, and worried about my skin. I was not sure that I loved Gerald any more, and quite confident that he did not love me, but he was some great, necessary underpinning of my walls. All that I should be, he was in my stead; I, from the same loins, had escaped from the Law and the Love. My reverence for him was at once my mockery and pride. Amid the desperate brilliance and low-born grossness of my mind, it was my only jewel.

Our last day's march turned into a thirty-mile charge. What had wrought the change, marvelous to me, was the response of every English heart to the rumors and reports brought by native runners from the front. Every successive word was worse. General Outram's little garrison of Hyderabad had been treacherously attacked by ten times its number of howling Baluch hillmen. By God, he had fought them off! Now a horde of thirty thousand had come down to cut every white throat in Sind. Nothing stood between them and the slaughter but Outram's handful of survivors and old, gray Charles Napier's hastily rallied force of twenty-five hundred white and native foot soldiers. When the English with whom I marched took thought of their prospects, how could they vision any save death? The thrilling wonder was they calmly expected, by lending a hand to their hard-pressed countrymen, to share in a great victory!

They were only three hundred or so—one company of tommies, some casuals and new recruits, and a dozen officers. The news that spurred them forward would have turned back a Baluch force of many thousand. The hillmen were not cowards—their favorite death was in battle, praising Allah—but also they were not fools. Yet charging with the English were several sepoys and native baggage handlers whose lives were dark, short, and cheap. Perhaps they considered them a cheap price to pay for the brief glory the tall men lent to them.

Our little band joined Napier's meager force at sundown, February 16, 1843. Able to speak Hindustani, but never having smelled a British battle, I was given a command somewhat larger than a junior subaltern's due, but the last pick of the army. It consisted of three English sergeants, some half-caste corporals, and a motley band of camel drivers and cooks enlisted the week before. That the villainous company should have a place in a British line would shock the War Office. Huff-and-puff generals of the old school would get apoplectic seizures. Charley Napier cared little for that, if the knaves could stand up to fire!

Gerald's company was quartered only four furlongs from our fires. I did not go to see him, though, partly because he would worry about me in the soon-breaking battle, mainly because his high principles might worry and restrain me. Our army—we called and even thought of it as that—rested until the pre-dawn hours, then roused and marched. I thought surely we were making for prepared entrenchments, there to form our square and hope to stand firm against the Baluch charge. Instead it appeared that General Napier's mind had been deranged by our desperate situation, and, with illusions of Napoleonic grandeur, he was going to attack eleven times our number on their own ground!

At half past eight in the morning, the vultures wheeling high, the heat waves beginning to shimmer, we caught sight of the vanguard of the Moslem host. We had come close to the bank of the Fullailee River, steeply raised above the plain, and over its summit loomed a long row of turbaned heads. Under each was a starry gleam of sunlight on a gun barrel—a pretty row of glitters—but its very neatness was a comfort to Sergeant Willis.

"The beggars 've got their bloody matchbooks at dead rest," he told me, " 'spectin' to make sure. They ain't 'alf as dangerous such wise, as if they had 'em handy across their chests."

We formed our lines, our officers looking neat and debonair, and the pale tommies able to joke, swear, and sigh for beer. When we were advancing at quickstep, a shout rose in our van, and the Cheshire Rifles rushed toward the river. At the same instant our gunners lashed their teams, dashed up the slope at one side and ahead of our column, and began massing our cannon— a total of twelve—on broad, almost level ground full on the summit and no doubt commanding the river bed beyond. The cannoneers and their wise beasts, stencil-sharp on the sky line, toiled in an eerie hush within thirty yards of the nearest ambushed tribesmen. Every second that I expected to see them blown to bits, or swallowed up, or hurled down the hill, passed in strange peace; the only sound was the gathering, loudening shout of the charging infantry. No dust or smoke rose on the summit. The Baluch were waiting for the bayonet charge.

Running to keep closed with the attackers, our rear guard was halfway up the hill when the first Baluch volley woke its thunders. Gerald and his Cheshire brethren-in-arms had rushed within fifteen yards of the waiting matchlocks. Even so, the Baluch moved too soon in bringing flame to powder, in some way misjudging the distance or the speed of the attackers, because the charge never halted, and only scattered helmets dipped and disappared from the front line. A stiff line, almost as straight as though dressed for parade, it moved like a red scythe over the crest, then appeared to check briefly. Since no new volley had been fired and the Baluch swordsman had not yet met the charge, none of us watchers from below knew the reason for the almost imperceptible pause.

The fleet arrest was by wonder. At that point in their advance our dry front ranks had come into view of the whole wide, deep, dry bed of the Fullailee. Therein the Baluch horde seemed at durbar rather than at war, well-ordered save for its front rank of musketeers who had been balked and shamed by their futile blast. The smoke of the volley had dispersed, and the desert air was yet clear. Of nearly thirty thousand Baluch, every one stood poised and, in one sense, posed. Each knew his pride and declared it with haughty eyes, by the size and hue and style of his turban, and by the multicolors of his garments. The Cheshire regiment that had seized the ill-guarded summit had become one will, one brain, it seemed one body, with six hundred deadly tubes. Below them, the vast hollow was filled and overflowing with individual swordsmen, each in extravagant knightly quest of glory or death. Each had adorned himself for the rite, and the welter of color in contrast with the tawny desert dizzied the mind.

But this was not the Field of the Cloth of Gold, where bedizened knights strutted and jousted and drained flagons. The desert men raised their big black shields and, brandishing their swords and shouting the glory of Allah, charged the British line. I caught one clear glimpse of what seemed a rainbow-hued wave, just as it broke against an invisible beach of flying lead. Every bullet coolly aimed and fired from the bristling row of rifles cut horrid gashes in the dense, howling mass. Surely such human mewing must have sickened God's sight, but a heart bounding wildly as mine could not feel pity. Gerald was one with the tight line holding our front. I exulted at the heaps of dead that for a moment seemed bloody earthworks raised against the still surging-forward foe.

Smoke and dust had set the gaudy array at naught as the second volley roared over the heads of the calm heroes in front, who had dropped on one knee to reload. Ever the horde pressed on, but the cruel grape hurled into the billowing swarm, or the mewing fire of veterans who had somehow found time to reload, or a new windrow of enemy dead behind which our tommies had a brief respite from the countless swords, staved off defeat for one more nick of time.

Again and again the howling warriors rushed our guns, to be blasted and blown away in batches. More than once they breached our lines, but the cursing, grunting tommies, remembering their training and minding their officers, methodically cut them down. Some thousand were crossing the bed farther up, no doubt to attack us on the flank, or rear, and a body of Baluch horsemen, apparently late arrivals, rode up and down the plain balked by milling bands of foot warriors. It was then that my scurvy band did a good turn for Gerald's platoon.

Part of the line had been turned by a swarm of

Rohela fanatics, and he was under hard attack. Our clumsy charge gave his panting tommies time and room to re-form. I thought he caught a glimpse of me in the smoke and dust, and certainly I saw him, tall and fine, his complete self-control not stiffening him but lending him something like grace, amid the raving storm of battle.

Then the enemy mass debouching on the plain caused our General to strengthen his right wing. In the movement, I lost contact with my commanding officer, then my bearings, and then, it seemed, my mind. Giving the wrong order, I found my platoon hanging like a broken limb from the main trunk of our battalion, and before I knew it we had been torn off by a thousand tribesmen who had come from God knew where. Then, according to the Code of War, we could be shot for cowardice. Our choice had been to try to break back through the horde, our lives sold cheap, or to sneak off—an easy choice for me and my mongrel pack. But we had not quit the battle, and were merely absent without leave until we could find our way back.

The dust cloud, like a sandstorm on the desert, concealed us until we could find shelter in a dry watercourse. Peeping over the edge, I was wondering how we could conceal our shame, when a hard-riding Baluch horseman, taking a short cut to overtake the *lashkar* I had seen before, suddenly vanished from sight. No doubt he had fallen into a steep-walled nullah crossing the open plain.

Our shallow watercourse led in that direction, and the nullah bed might provide a safe path back to our lines. Beckoning my men to follow me, I led the tortuous way. Sometimes on hands and knees, more often flat on our bellies, we finally found our vanished rider and his mount. Both were lying on the bottom of what had once been an irrigation canal, now a dry ditch twenty feet wide and half as deep. The horse's neck was broken and his rider groaning and incapacitated from the hard fall.

I dropped down and ran the length of the ditch. It was perfectly straight and steep-walled for a distance of two hundred yards; then it petered out in what was once the bank of the Fullailee, long since changed its course. Farther on the plain it had either been filled in, or the project of its digging abandoned.

Then a chance struck hardly before I could wink, let alone think. The body of Baluch cavalry, after much aimless and futile galloping about, were finally surging forward, their charge to pass close to the upper end of the ditch. I yelled to my knaves to show their rascal selves to the foe. They did so, their black eyes and white teeth shining. Looming up only a second or two on the far bank of the canal—obviously a band of stragglers from the British lines—we were belly-down again before Rohela sharpshooters could find their aim.

Just as I had visioned, as through Juvena's sybil eyes, the whole passel of charging tribesmen swerved in their course. Each spurring to be first to wet his spear, the race of the fifty foremost was remarkably close. Neck to neck the horses thundered over the plain, and a gambler would be hard put to it to pick the winner; a thruster from the frenzied mass behind might push into the lead. Suddenly their howling vanguard sang another tune. No more they shouted the glory of Allah, and their noise turned strangely shrill. No more they laid on whip and spur, but hauled on the reins.

The horses tried to stop, their hoofs sliding and throwing dust and gravel. Blind, frantic might behind them heaved them on. The first fifty dropped out of sight with a curious neatness and dispatch. An equal number struggled ere they toppled, and no few turned somersaults into the pitfall. Then a score or so of riders catapulted over their horses' heads, beards and garments flying—the finest sight of all for my wolf-eyed watchers. The ranks close behind were thrown into disorder, milling and plunging on the bank, and now the main body, balked and bemazed, was under a mowing fire from Brown Bess. Having no heart to surround the ditch in a leaden hailstorm, the crippled *lashkar* wheeled and made off.

Their dust had hardly settled when my exultation came tumbling down. It fell before I knew what had pricked its bubble. The field was much quieter than a while ago, and vision much better. The Baluch hosts on

34

both banks had dissolved into ragged bands backing and filling, their numbers ever swelled by larger mobs streaming out of the hollow to join them. Although our cannon still roared, the scared vultures had come back and were wheeling high overhead.

All this had prevailed longer than I thought. Indeed the thunders of battle had dwindled to mere noise before our measly company had strayed far from our lines.

There was a long pile of dead and wounded horses in the ditch. Among them lay perhaps a score of lousy hillmen, kicked to death or with broken backs or necks; an equal number stirred or groaned; the rest of the fallen had escaped by way of the river. These were not the flower of the French Army spilled into the sunken road at Waterloo. The battle of Meeanee was assured of an honorable, minor place among the great battles of the age; generals had fought like tommies, and the 22nd Regiment of Cheshire Rifles had won undying fame. But the victory had been won before we had laid our trap!

I began to lead the way back to the British lines. At first we squirmed along in fear of stray bullets; then in sick revulsion I stood erect. Although without witch charms to guard them against wild-flying lead, my *jangal-wallas* sprang up behind me. In what my superiors would have to call good order, considering our kind, we double-quicked it to our place.

Some English officers, still utterly pukka in their coating of dust and soot, looked at us curiously. I found the major in command of our battalion, and saluted him.

"So you're back, Lieutenant Brook." His eyes had a cold shine, his tone was the amused one he employed when, having ordered whisky, a native servant brought him gin, and his lips curled in a faint smile.

"Yes, sir, I am."

"Well, you saved something like six hundred cutthroats, by breaking the necks of a hundred of their horses. Good stock, too, those nippy Baluch *ghoras*. You see, Brook, that *lashkar* had run amuck—the beggars often do, when they've lost a battle. We would 've sent the whole passel to Paradise."

"They'd 've sent a few Christians to heaven, sir, before they went."

The Major thought this over. It was in the way of a junior officer bandying words with his superior, but it also happened to be true. It was neither a quite pukka or quite soldierly reply, and indicative of the wrong attitude, but, after all, war and cricket were two different things. Changing the subject and his countenance, he told me that written report would be required to explain the absence of my platoon from its place in the lines. Meanwhile we could assist the stretcher-bearers in getting our wounded to a field hospital.

My spirits would have risen a little now if my meeting with Gerald were not still ahead of me. I found him before long, unscratched but with a bullet hole through his cap, and there was nothing but brotherly welcome in his somewhat boyish, handsome face. He told me I had given him the surprise of his life by my sudden appearance on the battlefield. I had proven myself a "stout feller" when the foe had attacked his flank.

"When I saw your johnnies pop up in the field, I knew you were up to a dodge," he went on, his fine eyes glowing. "Do you remember the time you trapped old Crandall's pheasants? Better yet was the way you paid off the Kennet Hunt for riding over our tenant's crops —though it was a bit cruel. Gad, I wish I had your quick wits."

"No, you don't, Gerald."

"I fancy I know what you mean. They're Yankee wits that would be wasted on me. But I'm jolly grateful for the good turns they did me. We must see all we can of each other out here, old boy."

My shrunken heart swelled. I might have known that Gerald would stand up! Perhaps he stood taller in my sight because he had not overplayed his brotherly hand. Of course, he had not mentioned his promotion on the field from senior subaltern to captain, won by efficient leadership and quiet courage. When I did so, he seemed embarrassed.

Almost an equal comfort was in the pointed comment made by one of our sergeants, after we had shot all the crippled horses in the ditch and given what aid we could to a few wounded riders.

"We won't get no medals, Lieutenant," he told me, in a more familiar manner than he would dream of addressing Gerald. "I could've told you the bloody battle was won, before that lousy *lashkar* come bent on suicide. But by now they're braggin' that 'cept for bein' dumped into that there ditch, they'd won the battle. They'll remember it, no fear. 'Twas the kind of sell that strikes their 'eathen fancy. Sir, you're a marked man 'monst 'em from this day for'ard."

CHAPTER FOUR

Jealous Rivalry

THE VAST TERRITORY OF SIND, big as all England,
where rolled the wide Indus from Kashmor to the sea,
became British territory. Britishers proclaimed it so after
our defeat of its previous owners at Meeanee. It broke
upon me with a slight shock that this was the real reason for the battle, the design of masterly minds had
been accomplished. The "treacherous attack" of the
emirs on General Outram was their barbarous way of
objecting to him and General Charles Napier taking
over the governing of their richest domain.

The slight shock passed off. It was not a soldier's
business to ask the right and wrong of his killing people,
or being killed by them. The foe was the foe, and the
Queen was the Queen, and orders were orders. After
the victors built roads and bridges, where before were
only cart tracks and dirty, dangerous ferries, their subjects could use them by paying toll, and travel much
faster up and down the country. After they laid down
their law, the old rulers could no longer cut their subjects' heads off or their tongues out at their mere whim.

Gerald, a cavalry officer by rights, was appointed
Captain to the uppercrust Tatta Lancers, barracked at
Hyderabad, capital of Sind. I was set to loafing there,
with the dismal feeling that I was again to be "rusticated," perhaps more politely than before, but as definitely. Then to my inward upheaval, a Colonel Jacob
from Delhi, the guest of the General, invited me to his
quarters in the former palace of the emirs, within the
labyrinthian fort wide as a farm.

He was a small, spare, quick-moving man, almost as
brown as I, and not as completely pukka as I had

38

feared. He talked a while of the battle, highly praising Gerald's part in it, and predicting a brilliant future for him in the Service. As to my escapade—it was not the sort to appeal to the military mind.

It was coming now, I thought, but why by word of mouth from a high-ranking officer, instead of a terse communication from an adjutant?

"As it happened, the C.G. hadn't been informed of that disused canal," Colonel Jacob remarked. "There'd been no time for proper reconnaissance. That *lashkar* was the palace guard of the Emir of Kalat and in the same fix. How did you come to know of it?"

"I saw one of the beggars fall in."

"A cat climbing a fence showed Tamerlane how to storm the Raghistan." Colonel Jacob pronounced the well-known Arabic saying in the Arabian language.

He did not look at me. It was my first inkling that he belonged to the Indian Survey. The outfit, like most secret organizations, had its little vanities and an excuse for histrionics. In this case they amounted to a thrilling challenge. He was not trying to find out if I spoke Arabic. A sack of rupees to an anna-piece, he already knew. He wanted to know if I loved, and could play, the kind of game of wits that delights Orientals. If I had a cold, grown-up heart to such trifling, making a flat-footed direct reply to his indirect inquiry, I would be forever an alien in India.

"I beg your pardon," I remarked in English after a long silence. "I was thinking of King Bruce's spiders."

"Arabia is the hub of the East," he went on joyfully. "One spoke extends to Turkey, one to Egypt, a third to East Africa, and a fourth to Persia and India. Of course it is not a very useful language here in Sind—"

"It is the mother and father of Urdu," I told him in that tongue. Then, whipping to Hindi, "And there was an Arab in Kali's woodpile." Which was to say that the latter tongue contained many Arabic words.

All Orientals are show-offs. Jacob was boyishly delighted. "We've been wondering where to put you for training," he remarked. "There's no better hide-out for an individual than in an army uniform, and you'd have it lively here in Sind, with border raids, uprisings, and so on for the next few years. Policing with small detachments would be enjoyable and informative. Spare time can be well utilized in the holes and alleys of Hyderabad. So, if you like, you can be attached to Brigade Headquarters as a reconnaissance officer, with special duty under Colonel Webb. For convenience you'll be billeted with the Tatta Lancers. Reconnaissance covers a multitude of sins."

"I would like it very well indeed, but perhaps I would find more time for study if billeted with strangers. Gerald and I find each other very good company."

It was a lame excuse, and if Colonel Jacob took it at face value, it might well annoy him. I wished I could reveal my real reason for not wanting to mess with Gerald, that I would be in some fashion in his way, and he in mine. Maybe I had revealed it, without meaning to. The Colonel had sharp, black eyes.

"The Tatta Lancers are the senior regiment in the Brigade and will have the best service," he said. "It happens, too, that Colonel Webb's adjutant, Major Graves, has a connection with the Survey and will appoint you interesting duties. No one else is to know of your connection—not even your brother Gerald." He paused.

"Yes, sir."

"Subtlety is not his long suit—this is true of our most successful generals and administrators. It is not a pukka English virtue, if you follow me; its very absence impresses the natives and may be one of the main reasons for our success out here." His tone changed slightly. "I agree with you that close relatives should not always serve together. My first cousin, a full-blooded Englishman, is a highly competent official with the Company at Calcutta. I, politely called a 'boy of the country'—at other times a quarter-caste—find it expedient to take a different path."

"Thank you, sir." Perhaps that was an odd thing to say, but it said itself.

"This arrangement is necessary, and I know it will be very pleasant."

He proved an excellent prophet, as far as the work and my association with Gerald was concerned. But of the other officers, only Major Graves honored me with fellowship, itself never close because of the difference in our ranks. The rest accepted me as Gerald's foster brother, never as one of their own, my skin was too swarthy and my features too alien to fit the sahib mold. These I had tried to account for by claiming some Irish blood, which has been undependable ever since Armada castaways hit it off with colleens, but their first glances of surprise and suspicion were ever after reflected in a distant manner toward me.

Of course I knew what they suspected—inevitably in India. Before long, I caught one of my messmates, a ruddy-colored Londoner named Clifford Holmes, glancing covertly at my fingernails, plainly hoping to find blue or purplish moons at their base. Pure-bred Englishmen in India believed these to be God's way of branding a Eurasian and exposing his base pretensions. Actually the sign failed as often as narrow-set eyes fail to be a sign of meanness. Then he began to question me in what he thought was a sly fashion.

Disliking the fellow for the most human of all reasons —because he disparaged me—and happily better able to see through him than vice versa, I could not resist a little game of cat-and-mouse.

"I dare say you've noticed I'm a good deal darker than Gerald," I said in an uneasy tone.

"Why, yes." His sharp face colored a little. "But that isn't surprising, since you're not real brothers but only distant cousins."

"Well, Lieutenant Holmes, I fancy you've guessed the secret."

He leaned forward, his eyes glistening. "I'm not sure I know what you mean."

"I'm really proud of it, if you must know the truth. I have some Irish blood—but—well—let's say a spot of Indian."

"Fancy that! I must say I thought it might be the case, because of your appearance—I'm rather an expert at spotting Anglo-Indians. Mind, it's nothing to be ashamed of. Some of them have served the Empire wonderfully well. You did the sporting thing to come

41

out with it. But you know, old man—you'll have to tell the Colonel."

"What concern is it of his?"

"Dash it, someone—Gerald was the right one—should have explained that to you. There are a good many Anglo-Indian officers out here, but there are some regiments—ours is one—that have only European officers. It's a sort of tradition, you understand. It can't be that your foster brother doesn't know it!"

"Well, he never mentioned it."

"I can jolly well understand that."

"And since I'm only billeted here—"

"That's true, but—how am I going to put it? You're messing with a regiment that everyone assumes to be pure white, members and guests alike. Gerald hasn't been out here very long, and I suppose he reckoned that if it was just a touch—"

"That's all it is. You see my great-grandfather—but I don't want to bore you with unimportant family history."

"You're not boring me. I'd better hear the straight of it."

"Well, it's been handed down—possibly a romantic yarn—that he married Broad-in-the-Butt, the daughter of Big Chief Loose-in-the-Bowels."

"What in the Devil do you mean?"

"If it's true, I'm part Anglo-Indian. Actually they're not so polite out in the States where I was born—they called 'em 'breeds' as long as it showed. You've heard how even a drop of native blood will sometimes cause a throwback. Often I have the impulse to scalp people. If you think I'd better tell the Colonel—"

"You think you're damned clever, don't you?" White with anger, Lieutenant Holmes stalked away.

At once I cursed my cleverness. Holmes was not the right man to make game of. He had a great deal of money, which made mares go even in the Tatta Lancers, notwithstanding sentimental legend to the contrary. Although fairly civil after that, he was waiting his chance to get back at me, a chance that I reckoned would never come. The other officers gave me my due in the field, but could not quite hide their relief at my avoidance of the social whirl, always busy and sometimes dizzy among English exiles in new-won native cities. When it would presently boil over with the arrival of the Colonel's daughter from London, I intended to be chasing border thieves. Despite the temptation to defy their sahib conventions, I did not want to embarrass Gerald by seeming to need his defense.

When he and I were in the field together, I was unreasonably and somewhat ashamedly happy. His icy, nerveless courage at once thrilled and chilled my spine. Sometimes my pride got in the way of my instinct, causing fever in my brain; then my soul went from me and looked inside a Gypsy wagon, visited the filthy tent that had shut its door to the Virgin and her Child, and returned and faced its kismet.

On those excursions we were boys again in the woods and fields of Berkshire, playing the best game yet. Since we looked at everything from a different standpoint, I was able to help him without seeming to, too much, to my joy that I could keep within sensible bounds. When he questioned a village headman or mufti, I could catch overtones in the replies or read double-meaning riddles that are the natives' delight. Sometimes the Rind tribesmen, who claimed to be Arabs, discussed our business in front of us in a bastard Arabic, a *lingua incognita* to every British officer who had ever passed their way. I could understand enough of the atrocious lingo to give Gerald tips. Occasionally, though, one of them would stare at me hard and then pass a signal to his fellows to mind their tongues. Apparently he had guessed that I was Lomri Sahib, who had broken some horses' necks at Meeanee. The name had been given me by a Hindu sweeper in our train and meant "fox"—plainly it had taken the tribesmen's fancy and had carried far.

I was never recognized during my increasingly bold excursions in native dress. These were part of my training and testing—if I demonstrated a flare for the masquerade, I would be ten times as useful to the Survey. From the holes and corners of Hyderabad I was already bringing trifles of news to Major Graves, and by wisening Gerald—he believed that I had a garrulous servant

—furthered a trifle his great ambition to be the military governor of Sind.

To keep him unashamed of me, I stayed out of ditches in the field and of native women's beds as far as anyone knew. When Major Graves pressed me to attend a party—an invitation I could not refuse—I waltzed sedately with the wives, not even tempted to some wilder dances captive in my legs. Highly vulnerable to brandy, I could not compete with my fellows in the canteen, but could dodge drinks smoothly. To further my own ambitions, I sometimes kept a secret overhead, and, riding far with a handful of troopers, changed the minds of one or two would-be rebels.

Once a pocket piece rubbed with a Gypsy's spit almost overworked its charm. A venerable-looking Rind hadji, captured hands-down astride our Lieutenant Colonel's favorite mare, proved to be Kambar Melik, a cutthroat of some note, and a real thorn in the regiment's side. At mess that night, Gerald was put in the shade by his bastard brother. That night, too, I was given a strange character reading by a messmate, Lieutenant the Honorable Henry Bingham, the younger son of a peer.

Henry's position in the regiment was much higher than junior subaltern. Colonel Webb was especially pleased when he distinguished himself, and a little of such distinguishing looked bigger, and was made more of than was common. His wit was wittier and his remarks at mess more clearly heard than most. Truly, though, his title of Honorable was deserved. In that, he reminded me a great deal of Gerald, his best friend.

Happily the Colonel had gone and the ceremonies done, when the memorable incident occurred. The officers had pushed their chairs back from the table and were talking in groups; the port was no longer being passed; our *khansaman* was serving brandy and coffee. Henry had drunk more deeply than we had yet seen. His highbred countenance was flushed and his hands unsteady. Sitting close, with an effect of hovering over him, was Clifford Holmes. At its outer edge sat Gerald, quiet tonight, but quite sober. It came to me that he, too, took pride and pleasure in my exploit, but had been made a little self-conscious by his temporary eclipse.

Major Graves, primed almost to the muzzle on brandy and champagne, was making too much of the incident. I had tried in vain to change the subject, and again had patiently insisted that I had not recognized Kambar Melik previous to his capture, that I had only spotted the stolen mare, and that he had surrendered as tamely as a low-caste bazaar thief.

"You're being unduly modest, Rom," Holmes commented in a clipped tone. "No doubt the fellow recognized you, and thought, 'What's the use? The same indomitable sahib who, almost singlehanded, broke the charge of the Emir's *lashkar!*'"

"I saw that charge, Cliff," Graves broke in. "I don't believe you had the pleasure. Don't make the mistake of underrating anything about it, including Rom's contribution. A real gift for this trade of ours isn't always easy to spot. He's a real *Jangi sawar.*"

"And besides that," Henry Bingham added, speaking slowly and distinctly, his glazed eyes on mine, "a subtle, scheming, sinister son of a bitch."

CHAPTER FIVE

Dance of Passion

IN A REGION OF MY MIND like a cool, deep well under a burning house, I wondered what Henry expected me to do. If I did not watch out—with most rigid vigilance— I would be driven by those expectations to perform it, regardless of unknown and perhaps disastrous consequences. If Clifford Holmes was hoping I would funk it, I must take utmost care not to let that hope force me to lash out. The most powerful and dangerous element of the scene was Gerald's hopes, trusts, and expectations. With a deliberate act of will, I took command of both his and my futures, as far as this matter went, on the bold premise that what would be best for me would be best for him. I did not look at him or regard his wishes.

That victory won, I did not care about the glitter in Holmes's eyes or the sudden sobering manifest in Henry's.

The silence appeared to crackle like tinder about to break into flame. I broke it as softly as I could.

"You're not in your right mind, Bingham, just now."

I drained my glass—that seemed a necessary gesture —and rose. As I turned to go out, I heard the scrape of Gerald's chair as he, too, started to rise, but I did not want him to follow, an overt act of championing me, and told him so with a glance and a suggestion of a shake of my head. Then I went to my quarters to wait the next move in the game.

It was Henry's move, and every man knew it. In the end he would have to make his word good or confess to a drunken lie. Whether it was really a lie was outside the point at issue, and I did not bother my head about it. Its maintenance was up to Henry.

There was no sound from the mess hall. I took it that he was waiting, with growing anxiety, in case I should return. No such fool, I gave him an hour to put in an appearance, then undressed for bed. Shortly thereafter I heard someone going out the front door. Since any officer going on watch would certainly go out through the orderly room, and none of the rest would have business on the parade ground, I reasoned that it was Henry, about to take a solitary walk. I went to sleep listening for his return. I would continue to listen amid my dreams—one of my Gypsy gifts was a kind of alarm clock in my brain that ticked away, keeping track of time, waking me at any hour I had set, or for any contingency I was waiting on.

It grew toward dawn. I continued to slumber at the usual depth, since no parade had been ordered for this Sunday morning. With the first blue-gray glimmer through the window, Henry came to my door. He touched it lightly; I rose, lighted a lamp with a friction match, and let him in.

His boyish face was drawn, but his eyes were shining in sign of some notable victory.

"I dare say you know what I've come for, Rom," he began.

"I have a notion that I hope is true. It may not be, though."

"I've come to apologize, of course. I wanted to hours ago, but couldn't quite fetch it then. When I finally decided to, God, I was happy! And it's so much easier than I ever hoped."

"I accept it with deep thanks. Have a chair and a pipe."

He sat down, his hands on his knees, gazing at the floor. "Of course that doesn't square it," he went on presently. "I'm going to apologize to the whole mess."

"For the Lord's sake, don't," I burst out. "The Colonel had gone—the mess was not in assembly. Besides that—I want to say this just right—I don't want to make you say what you may think is a lie. I wouldn't profit by it, in the long run. Your only offense was expressing an opinion which, if you'd stayed sober, you'd have concealed."

"I had no right to that opinion. You've never harmed anyone that I know of—you've been a brave, able soldier—you've done everything you can to push Gerald. My God, I insulted your mother, too!"

"Behudgi!" The word meant an extreme form of twaddle. "You employed the English form of 'Your mother had no nose,' perfectly good bazaar invective. I flatter myself that I do have a certain subtlety and am certainly of a scheming disposition. Sinister means, as, of course, you know, the left as opposed to the right. I think I am on the left side of life—in the shadow instead of the sun."

"Are you serious—or laughing at me?"

"I wouldn't laugh at you for anything. The really pukka, *burra* British sahib is a slightly comic character to us left-siders—I suppose because he's so romantic in a tough, real world—but we revere you no end. We're no end grateful for you, for being in the world. You not only demonstrate the existence of God to us—the only kind of God we can imagine, the most pukka and *burra* of all sahibs, but somehow you relieve us of doing our duty to Him. With such as you shining before Him, we can be schemers and thieves or whores or ruffians, without worrying about making Him ashamed of His handiwork. It's true we get drunk sometimes—on notions of equality and other rubbish—and go berserk and kill you off. When we go hungry, we're likely to blame you— sometimes you are to blame—and, turning against God, take it out on you. Sometimes we take out on you our own low birth, our being His second-grade turnout, or even His culls. But on the whole, and in our hearts, we worship you from a distance."

I was showing off, of course, although more for my own admiration than his. Also, having kept a whole skin, I was in that state of exultation to which we off-white people are liable. His boyish mouth gaped a little. His scattered faculties presently rallied to deal with one phrase I had used.

"You said 'low birth.' Gerald's got good breeding

written all over him—he's the highest type of English gentleman. You said you were his cousin—"

"I'm what might be called a poor relation."

"Look here. If it's on account of my rank, such as it is, that you're going to take what I did to you—" He stopped and turned red. "I mean—if *you're* being a gentleman—"

"I can never be a gentleman, Henry. God forbid I should try."

"I mean, that silly code that a gentleman can't have it out with anyone but an equal—"

"You mustn't fight me, Henry. If it were necessary in order to win, I'd knee you in the groin and be forever disgraced."

"Good God!"

"Maybe I wouldn't. I'd scheme that the disgrace would be more of a calamity than a good beating. I can assure you, sir, that your rank would make me more likely to fight you, than less likely. If a drunken ruffian in a bar called me that—of course he wouldn't use those adjectives, let alone the fine alliteration—I'd not even hear him."

"You're a queer card, Rom."

"No, just a fish out of water in the Tatta Lancers."

"Well, I've already apologized for what I called you —the name I mean—and I'd like to take it back. I know it isn't so."

"Thanks, but I'm not at all sure."

"If you say so, I'll ask the Colonel to have me assigned somewhere else, for the good of the regiment."

"If you were out to smash my career in India, that would be the surest way. 'The rotten little cad who got Bingham shipped out.' Gerald would feel dutybound to stand up for me, so he'd be done in, too."

"Right you are. Not the least damned doubt of it. Well, how am I going to get my towel?"

"I don't know what you mean."

"My ribroast. I've got to have it or be a stinker. Oh, dash it, Rom—you never went to public school."

"No, sir."

"What you admire in the British sahib is mainly a

well-dusted jacket by a headmaster. You obey the rules or you catch it. By Gad, I've got it."

His roving eye caught sight of a Malacca cane leaning inside the open door of my closet. He fetched it and handed it to me.

"One lusty lick across the shoulders, if you please."

"No, thanks."

"I mean it, Rom," he told me with a grave voice and tone. "And a real stinger, not a token. There's more to this than meets the eye."

"Very well." I struck him hard.

He stretched, shivering a little. "Are we friends, now, old man?"

"I tell you!"

"If I may say so, I'm damned glad I haven't got you for an enemy. Maybe that was what didn't meet the eye —yours and mine, too—the real what's what behind my fine contrition. I wonder! I do indeed. In any event, I made a mistake."

He grinned and waved and went his way.

I would go mine shortly, I thought. It would not be with Henry Bingham and Gerald and the other gentlemen of the Tatta Lancers. With the other adjectives Henry had employed, "secretive" and "solitary" would have gone well. When, soon thereafter, I told Major Graves that I would like to be detached for full-time operation in the Survey, he replied that I was quite eligible and he would arrange it when the border quieted a little more. Until then, the C.G. could not spare me. Actually he had been quite gratified by my arrest of Kambar Melik—I had the makings of a good reconnaissance officer and I would come in handy if and when the Baluch rode again.

One Baluch bandit would not raid again. In the night before he was to die, I saw him hanged in a dream, the sly, subtle, scheming son of a bitch, and wakened knowing I could not watch the real thing, even if cashiered for cowardice. At reveille I sent my servant to report me sick, with symptoms of dengue fever. The doctor came hurrying, and truly my pulse was fast and my breathing hard. The wise, kindly fellow did not take my temperature, only prescribed quinine and a morning's rest in bed.

"It's not dengue," he told me, smiling. "It's related to a serious condition that the Romans called *locus poenitentiae*." Dr. Haines loved to air his Latin.

"That sounds bad."

"Do you remember the quotation:

> " 'Thou rascal beadle, hold thy bloody hand!
>   Why dost thou lash that whore? Strip thine own
>   back;
>   Thou hotly lust'st to use her in that kind
>   For which thou whip'st her.' "

"I'll give you some more of it, Doctor.

> " 'Through tatter'd clothes small vices do appear;
>   Robes and furr'd gowns hide all.' "

"They weren't small vices, Rom. The fellow did slay and burn."

"If I were a lousy lungi and had to salaam to an alien conqueror, I'd slay and burn, too."

"Oh, hell. Neither of us is properly educated for the military life. What're a few hangings, if the country's going to get civilized thereby? You'll learn, my buck, the prodigious folly of ever looking at anything from the enemy's viewpoint. When you do such a damn-fool thing, you lose sight of his horns and tail. Take the enemy straight. Don't sickly him over with a pale cast of thought. The General will pick him out for you—then you go for him."

"That's good advice."

"It will be a lot harder for you to take than it is for the pukka sahibs. I'm medically interested in those eyes of yours, and that mouth. They're not Irish, let alone Red Indian. Do you know what they are?"

"When my mother was carrying me, she was scared by a wolf that had escaped from a circus," I answered, looking him in the face.

"You do know, don't you? Damned interestin', I bet you. Well, Rom, you'll get over this indisposition.

There'll be other attacks but of decreasing severity until you're completely cured."

He grinned and went out. I stayed in my room until certain that Kambar Melik had been efficiently and completely hanged. Then I was ashamed of my panic, so at odds with my resolution to thrive and advance. If need be, I would quote with a pious air, "Render unto Caesar the things that are Caesar's," the stand-by of every little Caesar as well as everyone ambitious for the part, and of landlords and moneylenders throughout Christendom.

My recovery was furthered by Major Graves's report that a high compliment had been paid me.

"Better than Henry's?" I asked.

"Of the same ilk, but coming from the enemy it's a tribute. His nibs Nazir Khan has unofficially put a price on your head." Nazir was Emir of Baluchistan.

"I hope it's not piddling."

"A hundred cattle was the figure I heard. All his chiefs are competing. Your head is to be sent to the Colonel Sahib with plums in your eye sockets."

"A pretty touch."

"Another triumph. Your *izzat* has riz a good deal in the regiment since the Bingham incident. The feller sings your praises."

"I'm flattered more than's good for me," I told him, when I felt my heart swell and my face flush. "I might begin to believe I had the makings of a pukka sahib."

"I wish you could get detached. Meanwhile the C.G.'s going to give you carte blanche to discover the various rendezvous of the Rohelas, when they gang up to raid. You can bivouac with a squad well west of the river, then scout the hills alone with a good glass."

"That will be jolly," I told him, imitating Gerald.

"Try to save Nazir Khan that hundred head of cattle."

I enjoyed the lonely sport and regretted cutting it short to be present at a parade in honor of a dignitary who had escorted the Colonel's daughter, Miss Sukey Webb, up from Bombay. Fresh from school, egg-fresh out from England, she was to be honored with a regimental ball, to take place in Nazir Khan's former throne room within the fort. The scandalous rumor that Sukey had been an ugly duckling—freckled and gawky with butter-colored hair—could not reduce her importance as soon mistress of the widowed Colonel's house, and hence the first lady of the regiment. Her name, suggestive of a bossy-cow, despite its honorable antiquity among English names, was to be treated with great respect.

She would have to be a real fright not to dazzle the regiment. Middle-aged wives could not drop in at our clubrooms without being surrounded by half a dozen officers with moony eyes. That she would receive one or more proposals in her first month at the station was a safe bet. The odds against her capturing Henry Bingham should not be long, although Colonel Webb had no connections to justify an alliance with authentic English nobility, and his sock was not long enough to bridge the gap.

I had intended to stay away from the ball, and might have done so if I had not heard a scrap of talk in the guest parlor. The speaker was the wife of our second-in-command.

"I hope he has the grace not to come," she mouthed to the majors' wives.

I need not think she was referring to me, even while I knew it. Indeed, I was more than half convinced that she had meant for me to hear. But I had wanted to go anyway, after my first glimpse of Sukey.

The ugly duckling had not grown into a swan. Although her figure was fine and tall and her stride long and light, she stood in such awkward positions that "gawky" was the right word for her still. Her hair was the color of yellow butter from grass-fed cows, too far from red, even too smooth-looking to deserve the description "golden." Far from ugly, indeed striking-looking from a distance, she would be called moderately pretty by a disinterested observer. There was nothing remarkable about her oval-shaped face, with blue eyes of ordinary brilliance and nose a little stubbier, a trifle less delicate and high, than most noses on English ladies. After being presented to her, ere the trumpet sounded for the Grand March, I found myself interested in her mouth. Of no marked beauty of shape or color, it was the clue, perhaps the giveaway, to a character different enough from that of most colonels' daughters—complex enough to interest an odd fish who liked to think he could look deeper than the skin.

Without being very full, her lips hinted sensuousness. Their smiles were almost painfully bright, I thought; she seemed very anxious to please. When she was not smiling, they were slightly pursed, giving her countenance not a petulant but a wistful expression. It came to me that she was inordinately shy and doing her utmost to conceal the fact. Her laughter was nervous and a little harsh; she flushed frequently and not very becomingly, since her white skin became uniformly pink—her face and throat and the no little I could see of her quite fine bosom, up her arms, and presumably up long, nicely tapered legs that my mind's eye saw. During the Grand March played by one regimental band, the Colonel often whispered frantic instructions, and gave her not very subtle thrusts and tugs.

This ought to have fed my cur-dog malice, hungry on this night. Instead I resented the knowing glances between some of the other women, especially middle-aged tabbies who were "second mothers" to Henry. I was pulling for her, without knowing why, and was pleasantly surprised when three or four of our very best seemed greatly taken with her. One of these was Henry, and another Gerald. At first Clifford Holmes had buzzed about her because she was the Colonel's daughter; now that he could sniff the wind of his betters' approval of her, he became her most ardent courtier. The wonder was that the ardor appeared, even to my jaundiced eye, completely real. I could almost hear him sigh as he gazed at her. Perhaps it *was* completely real. How little I knew of the workings of other men's hearts and minds! Even less than the piddling little knowledge of my own!

With good partners, Sukey danced awkwardly at first, then moved with grace and beauty. I was proud of the couple that Gerald and she made, both so tall and fine. To my dismay, she danced best in the arms of Clifford Holmes, partly because of his notable skill, and partly, alas, as eager response to his male vigor; for ballroom dancing, sure as the Devil, is a polite and approved form of sexual intercourse. I found myself jealous of him, the jealousy aggravated by spite. I had not had a white girl in my arms, even when they were sleeved, since setting foot on India's strand—and long-legged, shapely Sukey would be a fine armful.

True, my turn with her was coming. Our programs had provided full sets of partners for the numbered dances, every bachelor having at least one trip-it with the guest of honor. However, I had been awarded a minuet, the least intimate of dances, instead a ceremony that reminded me of the bowing courtship of owls—well adapted to knee breeches but on which my talents in terpsichore would certainly be wasted.

These were real enough talents, among a stiff-backed, stiff-mannered people such as upper middle-class English. A buffalo compared to my mother's tribe, Salomes every one, and a dancing bear in contrast with Albanians, Hungarians, and even Italians, by nature and nurture I had been grounded in their art; hence in their peculiar style of caper, I could dance circles around any man here. That style was frowned upon by the Queen. Those circles would not raise me in regimental esteem. I had gained pukkahood by my capture of Kambar Melik, since no one knew it had been accomplished by unpukka traits and training. Now I contemplated losing this hard-won ground and again being branded as an alien, by obeying one defiant, disreputable impulse.

But the night was hot, the throne room garish, and the wine heady. Our beefy regimental band played marches, quadrilles, and minuets, but in between these a civilian orchestra of drums, flutes, and fiddles, led by a quite remarkable half-caste harpist, played extra waltzes and wildly popular polkas with great verve. I might have resisted the temptation if my spit-on pocket piece had let well enough alone. It bumped me up against Gerald, at the same time reminding me how he fancied himself as a minueter. Before he knew it, I had offered him my turn with Sukey if he had an "extra" with her to give me in exchange.

He did have, to his boyish joy. The charm continued

to work when I questioned De Silva, the orchestra leader, as to his repertoire. When he mentioned "Arkany," the Devil came forth from behind me, bold as brass. While technically a Hungarian galop, suited to the burly, innocent galloping popular in England, it inspired Magyar peasants to all sorts of didos, and had the fiery beauty of a Gypsy tune. When the time came, he announced a galop, at which the eager couples bustled to the floor. Little did they know what they were in for!

Although not in the least aloof, Sukey was tongue-tied when I led her out, and at first she lived up to her name in its more homey connotation. Her long legs were loath to limber, or her big feet to follow mine. However, she knew the step, and there was witchery even in the opening passages. Some couples who had expected only hard, healthy, pleasant exercise left the floor. The witchery began to take hold of my hitherto proper partner. I was helping it along by my own restraint—dancing as well as I could while minding my manners.

She flushed, gave one worried glance at the spectators, then unpinned her bones. They became wonderfully nimble and her bound muscles thrillingly lithe. Her body's surrender to the barbarous music began to effect a change greater than this—one that I had divined but not consciously foreseen. There was waking in her a vitality out of place in this staid society, and of which she was frightened and ashamed. Her attempt to repress and conceal it was, of course, the real cause of her gawkiness. Her shyness was nothing else than fear of being herself. I knew, too, that her previous partners had been affected by it, unconsciously, perhaps, and yearned to have her back in their arms.

Her personality was revealed as far richer than it had seemed, with a wider and deeper range of feeling, and hence her countenance became more meaningful, I could not tell if it were prettier—perhaps it had lost a superficial prettiness to gain an exciting individuality. She was suddenly equal to all this experience offered. Following me joyously into the variations of the steps, she was soon expressing their lovely meanings. As for me, I forgot where I was. We were dancing the Arkany

56

as might Albanian mountaineers, late at night under the harvest moon.

There, after such dancing, the couples frequently stole away to dance to another tune. It is a curious fact that while a dreamy waltz may excite English youth and maiden to a like desire—the satyr Lord Byron complained of it, strangely enough—the more lively dances leave them sweating but serene. Not so south of the Pyrenees and east of the Carpathians. The most impassionating dances that ever lighted Hymen's lamp are some of the violent, stamping rhapsodies of southern and eastern Europe; that was the reason for their existence. Gradually I became aware that this had turned into a passion dance, as eloquent an expression of that force as the posturings and leapings of an East African n'goma.

I was making love to her in a profoundly primitive way, whether or not the onlookers knew it. There were many onlookers now, and their number was increasing —some of the more proper couples had stopped dancing to watch what they vaguely felt was a scandalous display, and the rest, as well as the wall sitters, had eyes for no one but the guest of honor and her swarthy partner, dancing as wildly as dervishes in dreams of Paradise. I felt their gaze, but a flood of stronger feelings set it at naught. Sukey felt it, too, and knew what was happening; still she did not stop. The reason was she could not.

She was caught up in that flood and transported by it. On her face was the same ecstasy I had seen waked in nautch girls by abandonment to their ancient, lascivious art. She was not expressing herself, Sukey Webb, but her Mother Eve; she would have reminded Colonel Jacob, deep student of Indian cults, of a Dravidian priestess dancing before a phallic pillar of stone.

Truly we did credit to the beautiful invention, if, indeed, we did not change it into something new. I was too lost in it to think how strange and wonderful this was. The witch's brew was perfectly measured and mixed—an Eurasion orchestra, happily gifted, playing for us alone, inspiring and inspired by our fervor, the great, gaudy room, the heat of India, and, in some fash-

57

ion, my darkness and her blondness, symbolic of the East and West which, when rubbed together, give off sparks. We two were in conflict, and so was each of us within himself, and so was the pair of us with the assembly. We might swear we had forgotten where we were and who was watching us, but it would not be wholly true. We had thrown off their yoke and gloried in it. We defied them and their little gods.

"Arkany" meant "lasso" in the Hungarian tongue, and its strains seemed to dart and spiral and undulate. It ended with a vision of a Tartar drover leaping in and out of his whirling coil at ever mounting speed, the rope hissing, his lean limbs flying, his howls resounding—a scene of dynamic life. At the last crashing chord I swung up my partner and kissed her on the mouth—as though this were a Magyar carnival—and her lips burned mine. But now we must pay the fiddler, and perhaps the fee was more than a Gypsy and his stolen queen could raise.

Two faces among the throng stood out from the rest. They seemed to, because my gaze went searching for them in unseemly haste. It moved on quickly, lest I betray the guilt and fear that shamed me, but I saw both as in rifts through cloud. One was Gerald's. Inevitably I should look at his first; if he was smiling, I would not care about any of the others for my own sake. He was —but I had rather he had frowned! A frozen smile, for all the others to see, was like a grimace on his pale face. The Colonel's big, broad face was florid, and the flush on his bald dome could well have reminded me, bitten even now by the perverse humor of the damned, of a snow peak at sunrise. As yet he was only embarrassed to a degree that I never had been or ever could be, my dignity being so much less dear. Very soon—perhaps in a few seconds—that heat would start a fire.

I was walking toward him through what seemed a brittle silence, Sukey's hand on my arm and her head high, when Clifford Holmes spoke in low, biting tones.

"You're quite a dancer, Rom."

"It's that dashed squaw coming out in me, Clifford."

At that instant Henry Bingham stepped out from a cluster of officers standing near the Colonel.

"Colonel, may a mere subaltern make a remark eminently called for?" he asked in a clear, cheerful voice.

"Why, certainly—"

He turned to us. "Then I want to speak for the whole assembly in thanking our guest of honor and my friend and messmate, Rom Brook, for the greatest delight of the night. As you know, a military ball is likely to be deadly. This one could not help but be a success, with such an inspiration as Miss Webb, and now she has multiplied our pride many times. Rom, old trooper, seeing you harrying the heathen, I never dreamed you could so distinguish yourself in a ballroom. Ladies and gentlemen, give me the honor of leading you in applause!"

Two or three officers clapped loudly, with cries of "Hear, hear!" and *"Rung ho!"* Most of the rest of the applause was a frightened flutter. All the spectators believed that he had leaped into an "imminent deadly breach" to save everybody's face. That could be expected of a scion of the nobility and the pride of the regiment. Only I, perhaps, seeing his lighted eyes, wanted to believe that he was not prompted by *noblesse oblige,* merely by a boyish delight in the performance.

CHAPTER SIX

Sign of Ill Omen

I STAYED AT THE BALL just long enough to show flying colors, then made for the canteen, where a couple of misanthropes sat sipping rum. Presently Major Graves joined me there, grinning from ear to ear.

"You won't get shipped—straight off," he told me.

"You could lay plenty of bets on that."

"Partly for that very reason, you'll be among us a good while yet. Our good Colonel can hardly maintain that some high-stepping in a ballroom will militate against our quieting the border. Also the C.G. is a good old sport with his own fame to look to. When the word trickled from here to Burma, as it would in this gossip-starved empire, that a brigadier general shipped out the capturer of Kambar Melik for prancing about with a colonel's daughter, he'd never hear the end of it. Brigadier generals may seem omnipotent gods—but they ain't."

However, he went on to say, if I applied for transfer, say within six weeks, I would doubtless receive a good hearing.

His opinion, usually sound, was remarkably pleasant to hear. My defiance of the Colonel's stuffiness had cooled—I dreaded public rebuke in the form of transfer —and there might be another reason for my joy. I did not look for this, instead looked away, yet it appeared and disappeared in the deep of my mind like an underwater shadow that might or might not have solid shape. After waking from a procession of wild dreams in the last hours of the night, I could no longer doubt its reality.

Juvena's bastard pining for a memsahib mate! The

demented joke would fit so well into the grotesque pattern of my fate. A swarthy foster son in a Victorian home—a horse-trader's trick in a scientific British battle—a Balkan peasants' dance at a regimental ball—a Gypsy passion for the Colonel's daughter! There would be a kind of perverted logic in those sequences, and there were other ministers in this world than those of grace.

My next glimpse of her was at a distance, as she rode with Henry Bingham. What happened was amazingly trivial for me to note so carefully and remember so long—merely his seeing me first, calling her attention to me, the quick, perhaps eager, turning of her head, and her high-spirited wave. I looked for, instead of tried to overlook, signs of her unobtainability. Henry's delight in her was one—what the likes of him wanted was by nature unavailable to the likes of me. The way she rode, the way she dressed, the way she acted now that the ice was broken, all said the same. Unlike the fox, I took refuge in the grapes hanging so far out of reach that I need never wonder whether they were sweet or sour.

At my next sight of her she was having tea with Clifford Holmes, in our guest parlor. Other officers and guests were coming and going; it was an opportunity to see her at close range and perhaps dispose of my infirmity. I had no fear of Cliff's thrusts and would revel in a wicked retaliation, but I was stung by the glow of her countenance and her deep rippling laughter, and did not go near them.

The next day I saw her playing skittles with Gerald on the green laid out in the Emir's garden. His fatuous busying about her invoked my ribald grin. He trotted to and fro, sparing her all the exercise possible, exclaiming over her mediocre shots, chivalrously looking away when her bending down to throw raised the back of her skirt and neatly outlined her fine, round, natural enticement. The whole silly ceremony was Mother Nature's work. I could hardly believe she would stoop to it, for her gross ends—she who caused Adonis's docile stallion to rise against his master at the smell of a mare, and stags to fight nobly in the forest, and Lochinvar to steal a lovely bride. Perhaps Sukey knew what was afoot—

her treasure being hunted in this weird fashion. Deep in Gerald's imagination, perhaps, was a vision of rough conquest; but he was much too gentlemanly to look in that direction.

Here lay my cure, I thought. Gerald's amorousness might well be satisfied in due course; how much funnier was my futile own! But when I strolled to the edge of the green, the scene ceased to be laughable. Sukey gave me one of her too-bright smiles and her next throw was stiff and awkward and went wide of the pins. Gerald appeared to catch her embarrassment and talked rather feverishly. I snatched in vain at my old, trusted down-to-earthness, a quite different thing than cynicism, that had saved me so many falls. The sky was much too blue, the flowers too gaudy, the wistfulness of her expression too lovely.

Sukey, do you repent your fling with me? Do you see the enormity of it, now that the Colonel and the Mrs. Grundies of the post have drawn long faces? Have they hinted that sterling young officers, with private means and good connections, are not prone to offer hands and hearts to young women who make shows of themselves dancing with rakes? Do you not know that young ladies must be especially careful in India, where goats are likely to become mixed with the sheep? Has the offense grown in your mind as might another, committed by a village lass on May Day in the woods, that did not seem too wicked at the time, but the consequences whereof grew alarmingly?

What has embarrassed you, Sukey? Did you tell your good advisers that you did not co-operate in the dido, only acquiesced with a guest's politeness to one of her hosts? Is all not beer and skittles with the Colonel's daughter, now I have shown my swarthy face?

But as I gaze at your face, Sukey, my mockery turns inward. It was never more than a shabby bulwark of my pride. I am seeing you through a kind of haze that I cannot rub off my eyes. I have the illusion, which will not crack, of you turning beautiful. It could be called a trick of my imagination, but what reality has excited it? What is real save what is in the mind? All that we call beautiful is the symbol of an often unrecognized desire.

Well I know what ails me, wan and woeful knight-at-arms! No, I am still Rom of the Open Road, my freedom paid for by exile, desperately crafty or defiant lest I starve.

"Sukey, you skipped better than you skit."

Even now, I was proud of my clever tongue and of the casual tone that made the insolence all the more marked. Merely calling her by her first name was a barbed reminder of a secret intimacy. It stung Gerald in a tender spot; he stiffened and smiled a sickly smile. But I could not understand Sukey's response. It was as though I had fired at point-blank range and missed. Her color rose a little and she made a sound that could only be called a giggle. Perhaps it was a nervous giggle, but I would have taken it for a happy one.

"Romulus, don't you dare mention that scandalous affair again," she said, looking me full in the face. "I almost got sent back to England."

Maybe she was an able actress, in a pinch. I laid aside a load of some sort, felt a real grin on my face, and answered in pleasant kind.

"I wonder why I wasn't sent to Timbuctoo?"

"Oh, Daddy didn't blame you. He said you'd been a perfect gentleman, if I hadn't led you on. Then he remarked—after a little fuming—that when he was a young man in the Peninsular War he cut quite a figure dancing the Spanish bolero."

I was quite sure this was an ingenious lie. For whose benefit it was told, Gerald's, or mine, or her own, I could not decide. I was too excited to think clearly. Despite the failure of my present enterprise, I felt dizzy elation.

Suddenly it came to me that the lie was told to Gerald, for my sake. When I glanced at her with raised eyebrows, she showed me crossed fingers, the children's sign of a white lie, as a crossed heart is sign of solemn truth.

"But it would be cool and nice in England," she went on, wiping away a little sweat. "Gerald, if I play any more, I'm going to melt. Will you get me my parasol? It's in my rickshaw."

Gerald seemed relieved to run the errand. He was

barely out of hearing of her low tone when she turned wide eyes to mine and spoke tensely.

"It *was* your fault, wasn't it?"

"Yes."

"You started it, anyway. Why did you?"

"I don't know."

"It was pretty mean, if you knew how far it would go."

"I don't think I knew. I don't remember any motive other than trying to beat out Clifford Holmes."

She drew a deep breath. "You've made no effort since. You're not interested, and that's all right. I'm not either, particularly; no other man at the station would be mean enough to work that *pooja* on me." *Pooja* was a Hindustani word meaning "witchcraft." I was a little surprised that she knew it and amazed by her use of it in this way.

"No, the others are too gentlemanly," I answered.

"But you might speak to me around the post sometimes. I don't like to remind anyone of a girl you've ruined to find out if you could, and then cast off."

"Great God!" But it was not only the bold expression, bloodcurdling to a proper Victorian, that staggered me. All my figuring had been wrong and I had to start again.

"Swearing won't help matters," she told me, with a touch of anger.

"No, but maybe if we could have a talk—"

"What about?"

"About us. I have a feeling it's important. Anyway it would be interesting."

"When and where?"

"When you haven't an engagement and can run into me somewhere."

"In plain words, you're asking me to meet you on the sly."

"I'll meet you on the church roof, if you say so. I was thinking that if we made a formal engagement—and your father found out about it—you wouldn't keep it. If he found out about it too late, he wouldn't like it. Isn't it agreed I'm to be kept at a distance?"

"Why ask such a silly question? You're to be completely ignored. Well, here comes Gerald—"

"Can you go sight-seeing to the Nirum ruins tomorrow morning at ten? The section's policed and perfectly safe."

"I'll be in ruins if I'm caught," she told me, her eyes suddenly dancing.

Gerald appeared with the parasol, opened it as though the feat was beyond her strength, and hoped she had not caught sunburn. Sukey looked a little ashamed of herself, I thought, and perhaps wondered why I did not. One night, long ago, I had dreamed I broke faith with Gerald and had had to kill myself. But I had deceived him countless times, in the maintenance of faith. If he fell in love with Sukey, her conduct, not mine, I thought, would prove its requital. I did not think she would even keep our rendezvous.

Merely settling on that beforehand would save my face before my soul, when she did not come. That was a good trick; a better one, played at the scene, was the excited interest I was taking in the ruins. It did not matter now whether she came or not; I almost said so aloud, to reassure my palpitating heart and to settle my stomach.

On a hillside, in a densely populated section of the city, the ancient rubble had been undisturbed as though cursed by an afreet. I saw remains of Mohammedan graves under shabby cypress behind a walled court, and their veneration long ago might have built up a taboo. Not even the pariah dogs ran and left sign, for there was not a scrap of *roti* from a beggar's bowl to draw them here.

A hired doolie, with unliveried bearers, turned in the tumble-down archway. Out of it came Sukey; and if I had expected her to be changed back from the way she had looked last, I was a fool. I might be looking at her through rosy spectacles, but it seemed with freshly washed, wide-open eyes. They saw her move and stand and walk in a new way. They rejoiced in every little thing about her, from her smooth, thick, saffron-colored hair flowing from under her helmet, to the swing of her large feet under her lifted skirt, and the buoyant bobbing of her parasol. Pretending to act demure, she wore a droll, small smile.

I led her through a queen's gate of long ago into the ruined court. We sat down on a stone bench I had dusted for her. I wanted her to think from my actions that I was greatly pleased to meet her here, but not very excited, certainly not bewitched. A low murmuring with an occasional thin shout reached us from the street. She had something to tell me; I could see a minute furrow in her forehead.

"I should confess to somebody that I've no business coming here, but obviously you're not the one," she began.

"No, since I'm your partner in crime."

"I should also have some sort of excuse, but I can't think of any. If I got caught, I wouldn't have a leg to stand on. All Papa's worries about me would be proven justified."

"What worries?"

"That's a deep family secret. Now I want you to tell me something. Why is it—and this isn't as easy as I thought—why is it I have to meet you on the sly? All Papa said was—you aren't our sort. Of course you knew he felt that way, but it might hurt your feelings to have me come out with it—"

I laughed at her, entirely real laughter.

"Oh, I'm glad you did that," she went on. "I can talk so much better. But, Rom, I want to know *why* you aren't our sort. If you don't tell me, I'll have to go at once."

"I suppose you, too, know I'm not."

"Well—I suppose—I do. But I don't know why. You're the best educated man on the post—Henry told me so. You're Gerald's kinsman, and he's the acme of respectability. You're a very successful officer—Papa admitted that. Clifford Holmes hates you—I know that from what he said after we danced. I tried to work it around to get him to tell me why, but he didn't, being very ethical and gentlemanly. He did correct me, with some hauteur, when I mentioned you as one of the officers of the regiment. He said you were only billeted with it. Do you know why he hates you?"

"In some fashion I reduce his opinion of himself. I'm in the way of his conceit."

"Well, are you going to tell me what you've done—or who you are—that makes you not our sort?"

"What do you think?"

"I thought the first thing that would pop into the head of any girl who was born in India."

"Pardon me a minute. I didn't know you were born out here."

"I was, and lived here until I was eleven years old."

"What popped into your head was that I am a 'boy of the country.' Well, I'm not. I was born in the States."

"I'm relieved. I couldn't possibly have engagements with a Eurasian. If I lived in America, or even in France, it would be different, perhaps, but it's been bred in my bones—" She was too glib, I thought.

"No, fed into your mind, but it amounts to the same thing."

"You've got some kind of foreign blood, though."

"One of my ancestors may have come from the Balkan Peninsula. You know all kinds of people settled in the States. Also, I wasn't born with a silver spoon in my mouth."

She considered a long time, then shook her head. "If that's all it is, I might disagree with Papa. I was raised differently. I don't dislike foreign-looking people or men who make their own way. But that wouldn't have made us dance the way we did. It was a wicked dance, and you know it. It wouldn't account for you trapping the *diwana* [crazy] *lashkar* in the ditch."

"Who told you about that? It's not often mentioned at the post. It wasn't cricket, and the battle was already won."

"My ayah told me. And Rom—you'll probably think I'm a fool—I'm not sure it would account for your capture of Kambar Melik. You caught him defenseless, on a stolen horse, and you hadn't even recognized him—so you said."

"It was a little too lucky, wasn't it, to happen to one of your sort?"

"That's what I mean. The real truth was you used

67

imagination and cunning and maybe wicked trickery you didn't dare confess; and for certain reasons—maybe Gerald—you refused to take any credit you might deserve. Well, that, too, might have been the cunning of the Devil. Anyway you're not just his poor relation with some foreign blood. It's much—worse—than that. It may be—something—so awful—"

The trouble was not with her breath or her voice but with her tongue. It was becoming curiously tied. There was a strain in her face as when a traveler tries to employ a little-known language.

"For instance what, Sukey?" I asked.

"For instance"—whipping to Hindustani, her words rolled free—"thou hast sold thy soul to Shaitan."

She could not have said this in our guest parlor, even in the vernacular. She was at once ashamed of having said it here, and began to smile as though it were a jest. But I was not in the least surprised. The mastery of any language so that one thinks and dreams in it amounts to mastery by it—the capture of one's mind by the mind of its natives. I was quite a different person when I was thinking in French—at once more rational and emotional. I was not yet capable of full possession by Arabic, but when employing it I was aware of faint, exciting, in some way delicious change. Arabic had helped my progress in Urdu; my advance in Hindi by leaps and bounds I could not explain. By now I knew it just well enough to surmise—from that single sentence—how completely and perfectly it had mastered Sukey through some strange childhood experience. Truly, not nominally, it was her native tongue.

The present scene was favorable to her self-emergence. Within this court Buddhist and then Hindu kings had walked, pondering the mystery of God, ere the sons of the Prophet, certain of His love and law, harried them from their thrones. Also, I was a favorable communicant, although she did not know why. Quite likely she would not have revealed her mastery of Hindi to any other officer at the post.

"This is the nineteenth century," I said in English.

Suddenly she was flushed and awkward. "I was pulling your leg, Romulus."

"Nay, thou wert speaking of a mystery which the English do not understand. Long ago they did, but they have become Caesars, to whom half the world is rendered, and the mysteries and wonders are forgotten. But thou art English in every drop of thy blood. What dost thou know of Shaitan?"

"Only what my ayah told me when I was very little. She said that the Devil does not come to one as in the tale of Fou-ist Hakim [Doctor Faustus], but always one goes to him, perhaps in a dream, or when heartbroken as a child. What she meant was a turning away from Good, to live with and at last to love Evil. The line between being ashamed of evil deeds and proud of them is very narrow. Thousands cross it almost without knowing it. Natives know their own minds and hearts better than do the English; thousands of them, such as the Yezedi peoples, have no god but Shaitan. If you are one of his own—the old saying is in English, too—you know it and glory in it. Speak, sahib."

There is a diabolical quality in Gypsies. Witches and warlocks are common among them. On the night that they turned Mary and her Babe from their tents, and then the heavens and the earth shook, perhaps they called on Satan in their terror, and broke bread with him.

"Nay. It be true I know him well, and often do his work. I may be doing it even now. But I am yet in the other camp."

"It is only idle talk—*khel kud.*"

Sukey's vocabulary was over my head. I thought that *khel kud* meant "amusement."

"Thy tongue is too swift and cunning, Princess, for one of my dull wits. Wilt thou speak in my native tongue, yet not hide your thoughts from me?"

"If you like, Rom. But I'm afraid I can't say Hindi thoughts in English. They sound so silly."

"They won't sound silly to me."

"I hoped they wouldn't. I'll try not to be embarrassed."

"What made you think I might be among the damned?"

"Your appearance, I suppose. Eyes—mouth—the

bones of your face. At times they're pretty wicked-looking. And you danced wickedly. You did—you know it. A girl raised in England wouldn't know it. I was raised by ayahs all around India until—I was eleven." She was speaking in low tones, her eyes deep and still. I wondered what she had started to say instead of "I was eleven." Probably it was the English equivalent of *"jab tak ki jawani."* If so, in remembrance of her pride equal to a native girl's in the great event, she had quickly minded her English P's and Q's.

"I know what it is now, Sukey," I told her. "I was marked for the Devil, perhaps—he does a lot for me and I do a lot for him—but when I'm tempted to sell out to him, I can't. There's someone in the way."

"Gerald?"

"Of course."

"Does Gerald know it?"

"Of course not."

"His love for you?"

"Oh, no. Heavens no. My love for him."

"I should have known that. A thousand people can love us without changing us a particle. It's our loving them that does the trick."

Her mind took a long leap. I could see it in her face.

"I'd better tell you something. I'm going to marry a completely pukka sahib. That's why I'm in Hyderabad. If I don't land one here, I'll visit from post to post until I do. That's a settled thing. It's my kismet—it has been ever since—well—almost as long as I can remember."

"Do you think I could possibly interfere with that?"

"I'm positive you couldn't. No one in the world could." She considered carefully. "But you might have an effect on my attitude toward it—and therefore on its success."

"For good or ill?"

"How could I mean anything but ill?"

"Well, I once looked at an old book with wooden covers, in a shop in Marseilles. It seemed to be a medical book. Actually it was one of the most remarkable pieces of *double-entendre* I'd ever seen. It was a work on black magic by a medieval heretic. It might be 'tother way round with me. Instead of reducing your chances for future happiness, I might increase 'em."

"In other words, sow my wild oats and get them over with."

"I didn't say that."

"It's what you meant, though. You wouldn't dare say such a thing to—a girl raised in England. Remember I *am* the Colonel's daughter."

"I thought we could dance a little more. I would expect to fall in love with you, without the least notion of your returning the compliment. It would be a compliment, wouldn't it? I've never been in love. Until now I didn't know it was possible. In fact, I intended to avoid the malady, because it might cripple me. It wouldn't cripple me to fall hopelessly in love with you. It would strengthen me."

"You're either lying—with awful wickedness—or you don't know what you're saying." There was a working of the muscles in her throat.

"I'm not lying that I know of. I'd gladly stand the pangs; and wouldn't it give you something that you need for a successful marriage with a pukka sahib? Confidence—or content? You've got a wild streak in you, Sukey—otherwise you wouldn't be here. You rebel against your Pa and all he stands for. That caused you to be attracted to a vagabond like me. In a sense you would sow your wild oats, with no harm done, and find out how foolish and profitless it is. You'd find out that the pukka sahibs are your best bet ten times over. I've got a little something they haven't, but they have all the best things. You'd marry one and be glad you'd got him and never look back."

"Rom, that is the damnedest—or the most damnable, I don't know which—invitation I ever received."

"It's mad, of course."

"If I accepted it, there would be more method in my doing so than you know. But how could you be sure I wouldn't return the compliment?"

"Because there's Henry—and Clifford—or possibly even Gerald. You can spread it pretty thin among 'em, and still be safe."

"It would be—quite exciting." Her eyes, deep and

still a moment ago, began to glow strangely and beautifully. "But you've got to have one, too."

"One what?"

"An excuse for the affair. It could be very good for me, but it must be good for you, too. You've already sowed enough wild oats to plant all Sind, so it can't be that."

"I'm going to sow some tame oats, Sukey."

"That's very clever, Romulus."

"The Colonel's daughter. An absolutely pukka memsahib, except for speaking Hindustani too well."

I stopped because her expression changed. I might have known it would, by the reduction and hardening of my heart. This was the old malice, the mockery, the cur's bite which I carried like a dagger and used in moments such as this, defending I knew not what—only that it was not worthy of defense.

"Yes, it's very clever," I went on. "I'm a remarkably clever fellow, as Henry once pointed out, but sometimes I get tripped up. One of my tricks is to tell the truth in such a way that it serves as a lie. If you please, I'm going to be honest."

"All right."

"I had my first woman when I was fifteen. She was a housemaid. Since then I've had a good many. Some were barmaids or bumboat girls who went with me in the joy of life—and sometimes a little money to help them along. Only a few of them were bad women—harpies and traitors. Many were kind and good and will make good wives for men of their own station. I didn't try to have girls with whom I might fall in love. I had a long way to go, and was content with brief, happy adventures on the road."

I paused. Sukey had moved her hand and had laid it on my arm. She was breathing slowly and deeply. "Is that all?" she asked.

"It is, if you understand what I want. From you I want mystery—and wonder. I want to enrich my life; because it's very poor. All I have of any worth is Gerald. I haven't any other loyalty, and my struggle has no meaning. I want love in my heart for you. Do you understand that, Sukey? It will be by your gift to me.

That gift is your beauty that you let me see—the rest of the memsahibs have hidden theirs from me. It is your fellow humanity with me, which you didn't stint me. When you told me that I couldn't possibly have you, I believed you. I didn't want to believe it, but every instinct tells me it's true, for some greater reason than the one you gave, although I don't know what it is. But that won't stop me from loving you. I want to love you with all my heart—and I will."

It was as though the whirling loops of the Arkany were around us again. I was caught up in that exultation native to the South, to which off-white men like me are so subject. Sukey was responding to it, and a wonderful thing might happen. What did happen was so strange only because it was so mundane.

A native youth wearing dirty rags came into the court, his hand outstretched and cupped. "Baksheesh, Protector of the Poor," he whined. "My mother is sick, my father is starving—"

"Bas karo [enough]!"

I had tossed him an anna-piece and was about to shout, *"Jao* [begone]!" when Sukey addressed him with what seemed unnecessary harshness. Apparently she was angry over the interruption—a good omen to me. *Ek gadha jis ke dum nathi,* could mean only a "jackass without a tail," but no doubt was a comprehensive insult to a native of this caste.

"Be merciful, memsahib," he went on, almost weeping. "Bid your husband give me five—three—one anna more, that the gods may swell thy womb with a man-child! The sahibs on the street gave me nothing but angry words. Ask them, for they will be here in a little while. But he is a rich man—"

"What sahibs are coming this way? Speak quickly."

"The book reader, with the great beard, and an officer of the Rani. They have stopped to look at the Mosque—"

The bearded bookman was obviously Dr. Ludlow, a German archeologist touring India, at present a guest of the Resident. I had hoped to meet him, but not here and now. It was partly a lack of foresight, mainly sheer bad luck, that we had come here when the learned gentleman was peering and poking into the history of Hyderabad. I hoped that Sukey did not believe in signs.

I gave the native three annas—more than that would have fastened him upon my neck like the Old Man of the Sea—and sped him on his way. Sukey had already lifted her skirt to run. She took time, though, to show me that she did believe in signs, by giving me one. As though pausing in flight, she threw one arm around my neck and gave me a brisk, cheerful, but unmistakably ardent kiss.

CHAPTER SEVEN

Wicked Gifts

SUKEY WAS A FREQUENT VISITOR to our guest parlor, tea tables, and skittles green.

There, squired by our bucks, responding prettily to their attentions, butter would not melt in her mouth. She received and returned my polite greetings, and showed the company that, although she had made a mistake the night of the ball, she had learned her lesson. The days went by without our having even a moment's private conversation. Such opportunities as I tried to make she airily ignored. Meanwhile she was reveling in the ardent wooing of Clifford Holmes, the boyish homage of Henry Bingham, and occasional romantic squiring of Gerald.

About a fortnight after our meeting, I looked for her in our clubrooms, caught her gaze, and firmly led it to the door of the cubbyhole we called the library. My gesture in that direction was reckless enough to worry her. While I stood among the dusty, battered books, wondering to what lengths I would go when she failed to come, she burst in, pretty and gay and smiling.

"Rom, this is a bit ticklish," she told me cheerfully. "I can only stay a minute—"

"First, I wanted to ask you if you'd seen any more of that native that followed us into the Nirum ruins."

She looked startled. "Why, no."

"I have. I caught a glimpse of him on the road, and got the impression he was following me. He'd changed to a Mohammedan and was better dressed."

"I fancy he was off duty. Mohammedan beggars often dress as Hindus, to cover the field. Possibly he was following you, intending to tip off some beggar friend of his and split the take. The three annas you gave him were quite a windfall. He'd expected only a few pice."

"I thought he might be hoping for a little blackmail, and had dropped a hint to you. When he mentioned seeing the sahibs that day, we thought it was a lucky accident, but he wouldn't have had to be very cunning to realize we were meeting on the sly. If we were caught by Doctor Ludlow and Major Graves, his valuable cat would be out of the bag."

"My word. Do you mean he passed up immediate reward, hoping to catch us later in a more compromising situation? It's possible, since he's something more than an ordinary Hindu beggar. It's a good thing we had sense enough not to try to meet again."

"I didn't have that much sense, as you call it. I haven't now. When and where can we meet?"

She gave me a small, quite lovely smile. "I don't know when, if ever."

I nodded, as though I had expected this reply—that I understood—that it was probably for the best. Her eyes big, she started to open the door. But I could not let her go without fighting for her. What did I care for the false pride of half a sahib, or any other tin god that had never helped me? She had come into my life pretty and gay as a spring shower and had settled its blinding dust so that I could see, and made seeds germinate in its sterile ground, and made a rainbow in my sullen sky.

"So you're not going to be foolish or run any risk of a slip-up in your campaign," I said.

"That would stand to reason, Rom. It's going quite well. I'm almost certain of landing Clifford, even if Henry gets away."

"How about Gerald? Isn't he in the running?"

"No. If you think otherwise, you're mistaken."

"Yet you met me here, to hear what I had to say. I owe you something for that."

"Well, I owe you something for making me popular. You did it, whether you know it or not—by indirect means you didn't intend and wouldn't understand."

"So we're even, except for one debt. You may want to forget it, but no person who puts someone in debt can honorably refuse payment."

"That's quite true," she said thoughtfully, her eyes on mine.

"Well, here it is."

I put my arms around her and my mouth against hers. She did not resist the action, only stood still as though waiting. When the gentle pressure of my lips was prolonged, she was still resolved to remain serene. Yet she could not help but stiffen and finally made a quick, light acknowledgment, as though to complete a ceremony and be allowed to go her way. Instantly she realized her mistake. I had another debt to pay, according to the game we were playing. It was paid while her lips were still parted, and she knew, now, what a dangerous game it was. I had a great ally whose power she had defied.

Then we were kissing in hunger and deep thirst, all else paled into eclipse. I did not doubt this was the first burst of her fountains. By the sudden freeing of their long, aching curb, they leaped like geysers. But to me, too, a libertine, with sensuality stamped on my swarthy face, this was an unknown journey. Sukey was racked by the sharp pains of frustration, but I knew the laughter of the gods. They were those gods from whom the Hindu hides, sitting very still when he is happy, lest they turn his joy into sorrow; poets, drunkards, and outcasts knew them well. Foolish starvelings parched by the Southern sun, we cut such comic figures with our drawn faces, immense pupils, darting tongues, and heaving breasts—lusting so fiercely and so in vain.

Someone might open the door! An officer's boredom or a gossip's nosing could turn the trick. I thought of this and perhaps saw it in a vision; then Sukey thrust at my breast and flung out of my arms.

"Will you go across the room?" she asked in that truly breathless tone between gasps.

I went on the other side of the reading-table. She stood facing the door as her hands moved quickly at her hair and the ruffles of her dress. Her beauty was so apparent to me now, involved with her hair being yellow instead of gold, with her nose too stubby and her mouth too changeable, with her unbecoming flushings and with vestiges of freckles she had once hated, all these highlighted by her intense vitality. It was like the sudden blossoming of a deep-rooted plant in perfect weather.

Then her voice flowed quietly, bearing a little sadness but no reproach.

"You *are* a cur, aren't you, Rom?"

"In a manner of speaking, yes. But I'm not sure in what way you mean."

"You found out my weakness, and took advantage of it."

"Perhaps I found out your strength, and took off its chains."

"You're very clever with words. You make things seem the opposite of what they are. But strength means self-control. Weakness means the lack of it. You can't fool me about that." She paused to steady her voice. "Anyway you've shown where taking off chains gets us. You and I can never be on the same side of the table again."

"Even if we find out we love each other?"

She put her hand on the edge of the table, its tendons visible under the tight-drawn skin. Proudly she drew it away.

"I don't want to find it out. I don't want it to happen. I don't want the kind of love that you can give me. If I do want it, in my heart—in my flesh, I suppose I mean—I renounce it. I'll take the kind of love Gerald could give me—that I think Henry does give me. It doesn't lay traps for me. It doesn't try to make me bad. It wants to honor, not dishonor, me."

"In my heart—no, I mean in my best judgment—I believe you're right. You should renounce me and all the love I might give you. My heart must be a liar and it's a poor thing at best. But I want you to remember what you said just before this happened—that I had made you popular. You said it was by indirect means I wouldn't understand. Did you mean that I'd given you confidence?"

"I dare say I did mean that—partly."

"Did you mean, too, that I'd made you beautiful?"

"Rom!"

"You look so frightened. You needn't—it wasn't witchcraft. Or are you afraid to have me know it?"

"How could you make me beautiful? That's more of your trickery with words. It doesn't make sense."

"Is it true, Sukey?"

"Whatever you did, it was not for my good. It was for my ill. What any good person would know is for my ill. The dance—and all the rest."

"I gave you beauty, Sukey, and I gave you bliss."

"They were wicked gifts. You gave them for wickedness's sake."

"Can't you remember the beauty and bliss you felt only just now? They're still on your lips. Do you deny it?"

"No, but I renounce it."

With her eyes deep and still on mine, she drew the back of her hand hard-pressed across her mouth.

CHAPTER EIGHT

Assassin or Informer?

ONE OF THE STRENGTHS of the English sahib was his gullibility. He took himself and his world for granted, and had a schoolboy sense of right and wrong, being his obedience or disobedience to a pre-established, relatively simple code of conduct. He never challenged Authority. Least of all, he never doubted the authenticity of his own sentiments and emotions. If disappointed in love, he took one of several lawful courses. One was to get and stay drunk until so sick that he disgorged the whole matter. Another, rarely resorted to, was to nurse a broken heart with a mellowing melancholy that in time came to be as comforting as old shoes or pipes. The best course was to lose oneself in work and seek consolation in its rewards. In very rare instances, yet by no means unheard of, a perfectly pukka rejected lover sought death in battle.

In my case, there was a temptation to drift with the tide of defeat—a pull on my mind toward apathy. Why not get into Moslem dress and vanish down the road? By first going to the proper bother of resigning my commission, I could disappear into the limbo of gone-native white men, without causing Gerald or the Indian Government any great trouble. I had always used Gerald as a stick to beat back the Devil. It came upon me, with deep pain, that I had also used his neck on which to hang a millstone. Against his conscience, he might be glad to have me off his world.

Love has been called the greatest of self-deceits. If so, my heaviness of heart persistent as a toothache, the dismal grayness over everything, and the loss of appetite at mess, were most strangely vivid illusions. Partly to test the theory, mainly seeking some sort of reassurance, I tried an experiment that no doubt millions of clay-footed lovers had essayed when suffering similar pangs. The degree of its failure was frightening.

Haunting, rather, like specks before my eyes, was my failure to apply for immediate transfer to the Survey or to some distant regiment. A squirmy disgust with myself underlay all my thoughts and hopes. So it was with a surge of gratitude that in a crowded bazaar I again caught a glimpse of the native youth who had followed Sukey and me into the ruins. Plainly he was devoting to me determined and expert attentions that had nothing to do with blackmail. With the bounding up of my self-esteem, every vista had a new and brighter aspect. I fixed my attention on this matter like a dog's on a bone.

It seemed quite possible that the rather handsome young native might be a hired assassin. One hundred head of Nazir's best cattle, delivered at Hyderabad, might be worth two thousand rupees; even his scrub stock might bring half the amount. Common murders could be arranged in India for as low as fifty rupees— five English pounds—and two hundred could settle the hash of a good burgher—so, after all, this was a princely sum! Major Graves ventured the opinion that the fellow might not be a mere professional murderer, but a trusted agent of the Grand Vizier to Nazir Khan, Emir of Baluchistan.

"I don't quite believe it, though," Graves said thoughtfully. "The ditch episode, along with catching Kambar Melik with his *jangiya* down, is growing into a legend—you could expect nothing else on the desert— and if the hillmen could come on you in the field, they'd cut your throat before you could cheep. Every serdar [chieftain] is eager for the honor. But Nazir Khan is known to have sporting instincts, and I fancy he wants you alive until you can be done in with some éclat. By the way, Brook—you haven't raided any harems, lately?"

"Nary one."

"Or mortally insulted some influential Mussulman?"

"Not that I know of."

"It may be a big thing. Anyway, a jolly interesting

job for you. You're to find out who the johnny is, what he's up to, who hired him, and so on up. The trail might lead to some big hakims who pretend to be our friends. *Rung ho* and be careful."

A good trailer, the spy seemed interested in everything I did while off duty. After two cautious night excursions with Graves in his all-but-invisible company, we failed to keep an appointment he had heard us make. In Mohammedan dress, ready as an actor in the wings, I fell in behind him, when, discouraged, he wandered off. It was no trick to dog him to a near-by coffee shop where he drank and smoked and gossiped with some familiars. I dared pass behind his bench only once, despite the smoky dusk of the room, and the venture yielded only one small gain. One of his fellows had addressed him as Hamyd.

After loitering awhile on the street, I was again his unseen escort when he took a puzzling course. He seemed to be making for our regimental quarters. Turning into the postern gate, he was challenged by a sepoy sentry. Evidently he knew the password, for he continued up the cart road toward the family bungalows. I decided to risk recognition by following on, because I had business with him if my present angry guess proved true. That guess was he was neither an assassin nor a dangerous spy, but a professional informer put on my trail.

At the gate I gave the password and told the guard I was a new *khadim* of Graves Sahib. Then I lost sight of Hamyd in the tricky moonlight, only to see his shadow flick in an alleyway as he passed a watchfire. My breath caught, and went out in a long sigh. Obviously, now, he was making for the big bungalow at the head of the row, the quarters of Colonel Webb. That was the kind of sahib he was. That was what I got for serving in the Tatta Lancers. Tonight I had business with Hamyd. Tomorrow I would shake their damned spit-and-polish off my Gypsy feet.

I crept a little nearer, to complete the business. The spy had encircled the house and rather stealthily, I thought, had entered the compound. Was the pukka Colonel going to meet him in the dark? He spoke briefly to a sweeper or chokidar, who disappeared inside the house. Presently a rear door opened narrowly, as someone came out. The figure was too slender to be the Colonel's, and the lamplight in the doorway limned yellow hair.

Sukey was not merely carrying a message from her father. As she and her spy whispered together, their very postures indicated mutual confidence and friendship. Hamyd touched his forehead and hurried away. Now was my time to be gone, before I made some sickening mistake. I was not in any state to think clearly and act intelligently. Instead I waited five minutes, dripping sweat, then approached the same chokidar squatted with a cheroot at the gate of the compound.

"I come from Hamyd," I told him in Hindustani. "I must see the memsahib at once."

He shrugged and entered the servants' door. Sukey emerged with breath-taking promptness, and, happily, the servant did not follow her, no doubt because he had been ordered out of hearing when she had business with her spy. Standing in the shadows I cupped my hand.

"Baksheesh, memsahib," I whined in low tones. "I am Hamyd's friend, and my mother is sick, my father—"

"What trick is this, thou father of lies?" But she did not cry, "*Jao jaldi!*" and she spoke softly.

"Dost thou not know me, Protector of the Poor?"

The sound that she made then was hardly more than a grunt. I thought her lips shaped the native exclamation "*Wah!*" as could be expected of one whose native tongue was Hindi. She stiffened with the curious effect of bracing herself, and her face looked grayish-white in the weak moonlight. I did not know how mine looked, save for its sneer.

"Yes, I know thee now," she murmured after a long pause. "But I have no anna for a dog, only my spit."

"Yet I must be a dog of rare sort, that a memsahib of thy glory should seek to know of every tree where I lifted leg."

"With thy mocking, thou has staled upon all my garden."

My scalp prickled and crept. No pure-blood Indian girl could have said this, at least unless she were a high

83

shahzadi [princess] speaking to a faithless lover. A low-caste bazaar girl trying to express the same thought would have sounded obscene. In the history of India there could have been only a few pure-blood English girls so steeped in Orientalism that they could conceive the dramatic metaphor.

It came forth in a low monotone, as she held her head high—causing the indictment to slash and burn. I *had* made a sickening mistake, probably the most disastrous of my life.

"Great God, Sukey, what do you mean? Of course I assumed you were only trying to find out all you could against me. I didn't try to think why. Maybe to help get you over what you thought was a shameful infatuation. Maybe you wanted all the reasons you could find for despising me. Remember what you said and did the last time we met—"

"I already knew enough against you, Rom. I wasn't ashamed of what you call infatuation."

"Then why—"

"If you don't know—if you are that blind—if you are so base as to accuse someone you thought you loved—"

"I am blind, Sukey. When I'm base, it's because I can't see straight. It's not my fault."

"I'll tell you this. I was raised with Hamyd. He was my playmate as long as I can remember. He's the only person whose loyalty and love I can always trust."

"Sukey—"

"I'm not going to say any more."

"He was posted on guard the day you came to the Nirum ruins. Since then—but I can't say it either. No, I've got to look out for my *izzat!* The fall it would take, if I'm wrong."

"Since then, Hamyd has supposedly been on a visit to his kinsmen. That accounted for his absence from the compound."

"He's an accomplished spy. He could find out a great deal not only about me, but anyone interested in me."

She nodded almost imperceptibly.

"Anyone interested in winning the price of a hundred cattle—" I went on.

"I don't want to hear you say it, either. He won't bother you any more. Good-by." She turned to go.

"Wait for one second more. I did think I loved you and I never stopped thinking so. I know now that I do, and with full cause. Such poor love as I can give you."

Standing still, she heard me out. Then raising her head as though someone had called her, with great beauty of movement, she walked away.

CHAPTER NINE

Tangled Fate

SOMETIMES IN MAY, when the land is as parched as a man's throat in a sandstorm, and the wild camels die on the desert, clouds gather only to dissolve. When the herdsman longs for baptism from the skies as for the Moon of Ramadan, the cruel sun bursts through the rack again. Sometimes he forgets his rage and anguish in pity for the rain that so longs to bless his pastures and tries in such agony to fall.

Sometimes in a man's life, when all its tides stand still and his little affairs have fetched up in a cul-de-sac, he feels that his fate struggles in vain to move. I half forgot my travail and remorse to stand off and watch it, beating against adamant barriers, at loggerheads with sullen circumstance. I had made all the *pooja* I knew that it might break free. For woe or weal, I wanted to get out of this slough of futility. I had performed the rite of penning a score of letters to give to the flame. I had lingered by the doors that Sukey might pass through, only to see her come nearer, then retreat, like Gypsies down a road. In her face was sign that she saw me and perhaps had something to tell me, but I had to let her go.

Happily it was now the cold season—days only a little warmer than Italian summers'—affording the hillmen long, cool nights on which to ride and raid. The regiment was pleasantly busy in the field; and I ran some interesting errands to the western villages. In mid-March, when the temperate sun began to blaze again, Graves sent me to an ancient tower not far from the left bank of the Indus to watch through a spyglass for a certain bunder boat suspected of transporting stolen firearms to Lahore.

The edifice conjured my imagination partly because of its seeming uselessness. No muezzin's call could be heard, save by the desert foxes; there was no sign of a dead city; it guarded no road or pass. Yet it was of bastion stoutness, its stones carefully fitted, and had a narrow, wrought-iron staircase from its terraced floor to balustered roof top. Perhaps a mad king had built it, as a place to watch for the coming of Azazel, the Destroyer of Delights.

My *sais* [groom] swept and garnished my eyrie before he left me to my solitary vigil. Two saddle blankets under me tempered the stored heat of the stone. From the baluster hung two water jugs, Sybarite luxury on the desert, since they were baked of porous earth, whereby their contents kept cool as amid the shadows of a deep well, a process known to camel drivers for thousands of years but its scientific principle unknown save to a few wan-faced savants who rarely saw the sun. Wrapped in leaves was my supper, superbly chosen for a desert repast—rice balls flavored with saffron, chapatties fried in ghee, a jar of strained honey, golden-brown half-dried dates, and an earthen flask of arrack. I watched my *sais* ride away, leading my horse, to wait for me out of sight in the nearest wadi. Like him, I hoped the watch would be long. That much of a native now, I welcomed solitude as a fresh slave girl in a stale harem. Like two-faced Janus I, too, wanted to muse on the past, dream about the future.

Over the knee-high balustrade I could see a great coil of mile-wide shallow Indus burning-glass bright in the sun. Like fine embroidery on the border of a scarf, a caravan of a hundred camels showed minute but sharp on the sky line. I was thinking that, after all, the tower was nobly raised if only for revealing the face of the desert, wonderfully wrinkled, unconscionably old, unmarked by sojourners amid the wastes. Time might get turned around, amid the dunes, and Alexander's legions come marching out of the West. Ere Time found his bearings, a lame Tartar might come riding ahead of a Tartar horde. They would see no difference in the land, in the aloes and mean, thirsty shrubs, in the foxes racing with their clean-cut shadows, and the vultures wheeling far above. Yes, by Zeus—or by Allah—the river had shifted its bed in the night! Where the crocodile had slept on a mud reef, a hyena rolled and romped about a skull.

In the direction of Hyderabad, there was a puff of dust. I glanced at it now and then, noting that it was coming nearer, but did not raise the Devil's spectacles to discover its cause, and thus cheat myself of pleasant speculation. A spyglass was one of the worst of cheats. It was the enemy of curiosity, and of mystery, two of Allah's greatest blessings on his children. It played hob with dreams. It could even be called profane, because it turned his afreets going about their business on the desert into little whirlwinds, and made light of his other wonders.

Before long the vague shapes of two animals appeared and disappeared in the swiftly approaching cloud. They were not wild asses that had come out of their fastnesses for a look at the city and were now heading home, they loomed too tall for that. They could be camels, but they showed too short to have riders. Well, they were two horsemen. Since they were making straight for the tower, I was forced to conclude they were couriers from the Brigade. That two pilgrims should visit the lonely tower on the same afternoon would change lawful coincidence into chaos. They did not look like couriers, but they must be.

I had never seen a courier use a sidesaddle, as the foremost rider appeared to be doing. I had never seen one with yellow hair spilling from under his helmet. But I could be quite mad now. Any unbelievable thing could happen. The dust cloud began to settle as the riders slowed to a walk and revealed the solid-looking wraiths of Sukey, her white mare, and Hamyd acting as her *sais* on a Baluch pony. My hair had rustled up on the back of my neck because it was all true.

I stood up and looked down at her, some fifty feet from the tower. By instinct establishing solid ground, I called, "Hello?"

She answered, "Hello!" and waited.

"Come on up, while Hamyd waters your horses at the river."

"Perhaps you'd better come down. I want to talk to you a minute."

"I can't leave my post. I could be court-martialed for it. The stairs are just inside the arch."

She had lowered her face cloth. Now she removed it and wiped away some dust from her temples and around her eyes. At her low-voiced order Hamyd helped her off with her duster, revealing her white muslin dress. She gave him some other instructions before he rode off, leading her horse; but she paused an instant before entering the narrow arch, and stood what seemed a long time at the foot of the stairs. Gazing down the stairway well, I could barely make out the glintings of her hair in the shadowy chamber. Then she took the first hesitating step and was either saved or lost, depending on the good or evil of her fate.

There were narrow ports haphazard in the walls of the tower. When she passed one of these on her upward climb, her dim form and face lighted up, only to half fade again in shadows. Not once did she lift her eyes to the big, bright star of the egress onto the platform. I took it that she was being driven up the stairs, by forces beyond her control, against her better judgment. I did not stop breathing nor did my heart stop beating; but my head swam and my stomach churned. When I reached down to take her moist hand it felt fevered because mine was so cold.

She came out on the terrace and at once gazed back toward Hyderabad. The view must have strengthened her in some fashion, because her head rose a little, and she turned and gazed far across the desert. The deep breath she drew caused her dress to draw tight against her breasts, outlining them and revealing their shape as beautiful as the Kashmir maidens'. The Indian sun had begun their rounding and outward thrust, forced growth in her first springtime, and the fogs of England had not blighted them.

"Won't you sit down, Sukey?"

"I might as well. This will probably take longer than I thought."

I folded a saddle blanket to serve as a cushion. She sat with crossed legs like a fakir. Her hands lay still in her lap, and there was no longer any strain on her face. Evidently she had crossed a wide river.

"The first question that would come to your mind," she said, "is how I knew where you were."

"No questions are crossing my mind," I answered. "I'm too full of wonder to be curious."

"I wish your tongue wasn't so clever and quick. What little English raising I had makes me suspicious of it. Well, Hamyd didn't spy on you. Nobody did but me. I shouldn't 've, of course. I went into Major Graves's office on an errand for my father. An order was lying on his desk, and your name stood out from it. When he turned his back, I read it."

"Well, I'm glad of that."

"I didn't decide right away to ride out here. I never did really decide—just came. I wanted to talk to you—and this is a wonderful place."

She looked about her and spoke on. "It's completely Indian. That's all right. I can't leave India out of anything I think or do. I've got to give it plenty of rope—it would take it in the end, anyway. This—between you and me—is an Indian affair." She paused.

"I was afraid it was over."

"Well, it's not—quite. You know now the main reason I had Hamyd follow you. But in addition to guarding you, he told me everywhere you went and what you did. So I *was* spying on you. It was an unpardonable—people would think so—intrusion into your private life."

"Do you think so, Sukey?"

She appeared not to hear me.

"For instance, I knew about your visit to the half-caste girl on Pushta Road," she went on. "I led Hamyd on to tell me everything that happened—until the light went out. I wanted to know because I was jealous."

"You—jealous of a Eurasian girl?"

"Some of them make me look like a mud fence, and you know it. I was more jealous of her than I would have been of an English girl. She would have more to give you—you being the kind of man you are."

"Did Hamyd stay till the light came on?"

"Yes. He told me that you appeared to be both disappointed and ashamed. I almost clapped my hands with joy."

"Do you know why I went there?"

"Hamyd told me why. He told me he did the same, when he'd been jilted by a hill girl in Assam that he was in love with. Then I felt so relieved."

"Relieved! Any other English girl would have considered me a rotten—"

"Other English girls weren't raised by Parbati—and didn't have Hamyd for a playmate."

She mused a moment, while I marveled over her yellow hair, blue eyes, and pink-and-white flesh colors.

"You asked me a minute ago if I thought spying on you was unpardonable. I didn't answer because it would sound so awful. Anybody the least pukka knows it is, but to me it seemed perfectly natural. Everything you did concerned me. That's because I'm not an English girl of the right kind. I can say some of the right things, but I never think the right thing. I'm more native really than half-caste girls. They are in perpetual conflict with themselves. I'm in conflict mainly with my present environment. It's almost—completely foreign."

"How did that happen, Sukey?"

"I told you I was raised by natives. There's a lot more to it that I can't tell you now—probably never. Under the circumstances, it was almost inevitable that we—you and I—should become involved with each other. We're in the same boat."

"How did I get there, do you suppose?"

"I think I know, but I might be wrong. You remember that I once asked you if you were a Eurasian, meaning part Indian. You said you weren't. I think you lied —Gerald would want you to, even if you hated to. Then I lied—saying I couldn't stand having anything to do with a half-caste. Actually I wouldn't have the least objection, if he were proud of it instead of ashamed of it. When I came through Bombay on the way here, Colonel Jacob called on me. I'd known him when I was a little girl. I might have tried to get him to marry me, if he hadn't already the most beautiful wife in India. I didn't mind him being thirty years older, and his high-caste native blood made him fascinating. He told me a little about you—how I was going to meet you—and—this was a secret between him and me—you had Asiatic blood. He said he could have told it without looking into your face—by the way you spoke Hindi. Yet he couldn't to save him put his finger on the inflection. Poor man, he's been itching with curiosity ever since he met you. He said it was faintly suggestive of the Hindi spoken by low-caste criminal tribes in the Punjab. He said he would bet that some dialect rooted in Sanskrit was your native tongue."

"Well, I may tell you about that, if the time comes. I'll say now I never was in India until two years ago."

"Anyway—you're not an Englishman. That's why I say we're in the same boat."

Sukey was not talking at random. She was preparing the ground for some extremely important proposal. There passed across my memory another scene of late afternoon, the red sun tumbling down, the shadows long, I, hidden in babul scrub behind a cattle byre, waiting for a raiding leopard. There were sounds that seemed random but were not—dry twigs cracking at long intervals, the all but imperceptible creak and rustle of underbrush, the excited clamor of birds, and the sudden flight of rock grouse. They told a connected story and were preparing my heart for its stunning climax.

"I can marry a sahib and cut quite a swathe in Indian society," she went on. "Since I'm not very well fitted for the life, it would be very interesting—a challenge to all my abilities. I revere the sahibs in somewhat the same way you do, and would be proud to have children by a real *burra* one. Actually I'd rather marry Gerald than either Henry or Clifford, not just because he may go further than either. In idolizing him the way you do, you're inclined to overlook his humanness. I could fall deeply in love with him, if he'd give me a chance. He has depths that I'd never plumb."

"Well, are you going to marry Henry or Clifford?"

"I might not marry either of them. If we were

enough in love with each other, and you wanted me to,
I might marry you."

She spoke as offhandedly as if proposing we eat supper. That did not surprise me and seemed proper in this
scene. We were as alone as though visiting an uninhabited planet. At the top of this ancient tower, the silent
sentinel of the desert, we had escaped from the world
and the fear that makes it go round. Only a few mortals
get so high that they are no longer afraid of being
wounded where no wound ever completely heals—in
the soul. We had done so, for this hour, by a kind of a
magic. It was as though we were fakirs who had thrown
up a rope, climbed it, and drawn it up after us.

Calmly I replied, "That would be quite a departure
from your program, Sukey."

"Departure! It would be throwing it to the vultures.
Such a thought never occurred to me until the night
after I'd called you a dog to spit on—when you tore me
to pieces with that sneer—and then it knocked me silly.
Suddenly I was free to think of the life I might have
with you! You won't be a governor—you won't be a
general—it seems to be that you're so delicately bal-
anced that you may be a vagabond. But if you can stay
fairly sane—and I could help with that—you'll certainly
have an exciting, perhaps quite a notable life. I'd take a
chance on it, Rom, if I wanted to bad enough."

"You say 'bad enough.' It's a child's saying. But I
wonder—"

"I know what you mean, I think. Something like—if
I want to *be* bad enough. I do have a feeling it would
be a bad—almost a wicked thing to do. I can't explain
it entirely on the grounds of hurting Papa. And it
would be a tremendous hurt, greater than you can
imagine without knowing the whole story. But maybe
that feeling of guilt will go away."

A low bank of clouds in the west glowed with manifold flames, and a reach of the river between looked like
the Styx. She was gazing there with what seemed frightened fascination.

"Is the main question whether you love me enough?"
I asked.

"Whether we love each other enough." Her eyes filled with reflections from the elemental fires as they slowly turned to me. "You see, Rom—it's got to be an awful lot."

CHAPTER TEN

Empress of the Night

SUKEY SEEMED RELIEVED to get this said. She sighed as a child might, and stretched her limbs.

"It's a hard seat," I said. "Aren't you tired?"

"Heavens, no. That's one thing of value that I got from my raising with natives. I slept on a grass mat on the hard floor. If I had a pillow, it was a low block of wood. I got used to it before I can remember anything. When Papa came to visit me, Parbati had to stick me in a real bed, where I tossed and scratched all night. Of course in England, in that cold climate, I became quite civilized, but have reverted to savagery since I came home. When the door's locked—kerthump, I hit the floor."

I was picturing her there, on a hot, windless night, and was fearful of what she could read in my face.

"There weren't any chairs in the part of the bungalow where I lived," she went on. "I squatted for hours with Parbati and her numerous relations. It's a wonder I didn't grow those hard bunches of muscle you see on so many native women."

"Well, then, if you're not tired, are you hungry?"

"Ravenous."

She rejoiced over the supper that we shared, especially my flask of arrack. It appeared that she had been given a small ration, diluted with coconut milk, whenever Parbati could get hands on a bottle. We took turns at the glass my servant had provided, and apparently she did not notice that my sips did not reduce the quantity as much as hers. The sun was under the mountains by the time we had finished the solid food, and the river was orchid-color. She proposed we mix some water and honey with the fiery arrack and make something like mead, which was altogether the finest thing obtainable in England. I was doubtful of the experiment, but when she had stirred the beverage with her finger—we had no spoon—and then licked it, she pronounced it delicious. No doubt, like all natives, she doted on sweets.

"Do I seem to you awfully different from pukka memsahibs?" she asked anxiously.

"I've never known any. I suspect though that the main difference is you do and say what comes natural to you, and they don't dare."

"That's terrible, Rom."

"I don't mean downright natural. A head-hunter's daughter in the Aka hills doesn't do that. But your second nature is less cluttered up than theirs; and you have more faith in it. I might think that you had more faith in the God Who made you. Lots of people make a religion of trying not to be what God made them—by resisting every natural impulse that they can, and regarding as wicked many of those they can't resist."

"For instance—they make love behind God's back?"

"That's very keen, Sukey."

"What's keen about it? It was exactly what you were getting at. The whole speech was deliberate—flattering, and reassuring. It's on a piece with your just pretending to drink the arrack, meanwhile putting down me all I'll take. Almost every move you make is crafty."

"Is that a new discovery?"

"Heavens, no."

"Why did you come here, then?"

"Well, I was interested in the purpose behind it all. You see, I'm not in the least scornful of craft itself—have you heard native women laugh with that high-pitched glee when they see it work? Also, I wanted to see if it was good or evil craft. A tiger's very crafty—he has to be to survive. I don't hate him for that. Do you have to be to survive?"

I stopped and thought. "No."

"Is it evil craft?"

"I don't know."

"Why are you trying to ply me—that's the term you read in the books—with arrack?"

"I suppose to put down as many of your guards as I can."

"Well, I might think that was the quintessence of viciousness if I wasn't trying to do the same thing. That's why I let myself be plied. But maybe I wanted my guards down for another reason than yours. I wanted my own truth to come out."

"Aren't you afraid of it?"

"Terribly so—but I've got to know what it is, the sooner the better."

It might be very soon. The glow in the west had died and some pale-blue stars were turning white and beginning to twinkle. The river glimmered wanly, and we had the illusion of being able to see a good distance yet across the desert, but that was because near things looked so far. Before other stars could light up, great magic was in store. There was a silver thread along the eastern horizon.

"Once you weren't crafty," she went on quietly. "It was when you called me out that night. You were beastly. That's another reason I came."

"When do you have to go?"

"When I want to."

"I can't figure that out."

"It's really very simple. Papa thought I was going riding with Gerald. I sent Gerald a chit that something had come up and—" She paused, her eyes wide in the dusk.

"What's the matter?"

"The expression on your face. It was in your body, too. Well, I dare say I don't mind. Of course you think no one has any right to break engagements with *him*. He only asked me out of common politeness, and, anyway, something very important had come up—you being sent to this tower. Papa was away when I left, and when I get back, I'm going to tell him that I was with you. I'll have to let him think you invited me. If it turns out that it's for the last time—which I'm almost sure it will be—I'll tell him so. He'll be furious that I went with you at all, but it won't last when he sees I'm a good girl from now on."

The fine silver thread between the eastern plain and

the sky shortened rapidly, gained brightness, and began to bulge upward a little. The whole weight of the sky seemed to resist the movement; instinctively the watcher held his breath, to sigh with relief when the arc formed. Upward, with power and glory, surged the gigantic moon.

Since her brilliant ascension and majestic decline last night, she had come full circle. This was her night of nights in her swift sweep around the world; since her last resplendence, she had sickened for one quarter of her journey, sailed blind for another quarter, and then, appearing no more than a fragile bow of silver slung on the side of the sun, she had become transfigured to the empress of the night. It seemed that she reigned by right of beauty only, but her soft and silvery beams were of mighty potence. All life came to full circle and resplendence at her zenith, the tides of the seas most high, those of the blood most sparkling in their most dynamic flow; fishes fed ravenously or spawned fiercely, and the bitch jackal ceased to whimper in proud heat.

A tidal wave of moonlight rolled out across the plain and inundated the darkened river. It revived and shone again, and the breeze stirred as from the same impulse, hunting everywhere for something, wandering off across the whispering sands, only to return, chill in our faces. The tower flung a long shadow, sharp below us, growing dimmer as it thrust across the silvery plain, and vanishing in the dusk without revealing our own shapes high aloft. But perhaps these things would not seem signs and wonders, if a hyena were not sobbing and wailing from his sand-dune watchtower.

"It's only the full moon," Sukey murmured, as though in fear of being overheard.

"I dare say we've seen it as big and beautiful plenty of times."

"You could expect to be sent here on the day of the full moon, so you could put in a long watch."

"But it was a chance in a hundred—a thousand, I suppose—that you saw the order."

"Let's not be any more superstitious than we can help. We're supposed to be English."

"Do you notice how cold it's getting?" My voice,

pitched too low, would not hold steady. "The warmth of the stones feels good."

"The desert's always cold as soon as the sun sets. If you partly unfold my blanket, we can both sit on it and throw the other over our knees."

When we were seated so, I drew her slanting across my breast. Therein she poured her intense life, which she could not withhold from me. But in greater self-conflict than I, not nearly so well oriented or as firm a fatalist, Sukey was possessed by Good and Evil. She was whispering something, her lips brushing mine.

"Maybe this is the Dark Tower."

My imagination vaulting wildly, I could not at once understand her.

"You remember," she went on. " 'Child Rowland to the dark tower came.' I don't know what it meant. I don't know whether the tower was evil, as well as dark. I suppose he went there to find out—"

I stopped her lips with mine.

"When you do that," she told me when they were fed and free, "I have trouble caring whether it is or not."

It is part of the function of poetry to haunt the mind in moments of high sensuality, its imagery the only means of capturing and wholly realizing superb experience. The lover who knows none is sadly bereft. My mind was haunted by voluptuous Arabian poetry, and I would woo my Hindi maid as a swarthy son of the desert his new-caught slave girl. I was becoming one with the scene, with a tingling sense of kismet brooding over the tower. And the sunburned Arab must love kismet for woe or weal—both with the passionate love he gives the newest-comer to his harem and with the solemn love he gives his *saki*, who has borne him a man-child. If they conspire together to mix death apple with his bread, he must cut their silken throats but love them still.

"I wish I could make you as happy as you're making me." Maybe she fought off the happiness, being so young and innocent. I would disarm her and then instruct her.

"I'm too happy. That's the trouble. It's great trouble."

"Your face is so beautiful in the moonlight." But its beauty was only a tittle of what I would behold, when the moon climbed higher.

"It's going to be daytime by and by. We've got to remember—"

"We'll have these to remember," I told her. For our kisses were more deep and strange than ever before, and now there was no enemy outside the door, no danger of our ecstasy being surprised and punished; there was no fear disguised as guilt.

"I love them, Rom, and maybe they're only passion. We both feel that so strong but if that's all it is, this is terribly wrong—"

"I love you, *Cobah*." I had meant to say "Sukey," her English name, but instead my lips had shaped the Oriental tribute to female beauty, "Morning Star." Perhaps she would not catch any inference. Perhaps she would not wonder what tricks were being played within my mind, to make our carnal delight the justification of her seduction when I hed no real faith in her love for me, and no real hope of a shared future.

"I don't know what you mean by love."

"I mean I want you now and always."

I might have her very soon and for an hour. Under her dress her silky shoulder flowed slowly upward from my descending palm. The moon rose higher, and so did every tide. The stored heat of the sun pouring up from the stones through the blanket under us was confined, glowing, by the one above, their rough touch making more blissful the humid, satin touch between.

She grasped my hand, whispering, "Why don't you fight for me, instead of against me?"

"I'm fighting for us both." That, too, might be trickery.

"You would if you loved me. You'd protect me against my love for you. You know nothing can come of it, except evil done in the dark—"

"If it's evil, why did you come here?"

"The reason is—I wanted it to happen. I rode by this tower with Gerald and saw it all—what's happening now—in evil imagination. It wasn't just chance that you were sent here today, and it wasn't your fine kismet you dream about. It was a woman's scheming."

"It's too late to be sorry or afraid." But when I tried to move my hand, pinned against her sinuous, naked waist, her nails drove through the skin.

"You know you're to blame," she told me, no longer with troubled breath. "You made me fall in love with evil. That's why I wanted to meet you here—give myself to you at this savage place—"

She broke off, a tremor ran over her body, and her eyes grew slowly round.

"Did you hear what I said?" she whispered.

"You said 'give myself to you.' I'll give myself to you, too. We love each other."

"I said 'savage place.' A while ago I spoke of the Dark Tower. Neither of these came from my conscious thoughts—they were from poetry that had haunted my imagination, and they came up out of the deep of my mind to tell me what's happening—and to warn me."

"The mind works that way, I know. But I still don't remember any quotation—"

"I don't know the exact words. 'A savage place—as —lonely?—and enchanted—' "

"I know now. Kubla Khan. He may have built this tower. 'As e'er beneath a waning moon was haunted—' "

" 'By woman wailing for her demon-lover!' "

"Sukey, your imagination has carried—"

"Of course it has. It's been aroused along with every nerve in my body, every inch of skin, and drop of my blood. You did that by arousing all this passion. You're not a demon-lover, but there's something demonic in your face—I saw it just now—and you may be a wickedly false lover. I tell you, Rom, there's evil around here. It was about to take both of us. I don't know if there's any escape from it, except by breaking off this minute and going home. But if what we both crave to do comes from loving each other—" She paused.

"I think we love each other with all our hearts."

"But we've been afraid to put it to real proof, because it might interfere with our giving way to lust. Isn't that true?"

"We've been shutting our eyes to something. I don't know what—"

"You wanted to take my virginity first, and find out afterward."

"Perhaps that was it. I don't know."

"That's what I wanted you to do. I didn't want to look into the future, until this awful hunger was satisfied."

"Well, we will look into it."

"That is what I mean by proof of love."

CHAPTER ELEVEN

The Woman's Question

WE LEANED AGAINST ONE OF THE BALUSTRADES, Sukey in the hollow of my arm, and our hands clasped.

Our passion had not receded, but seemed for the moment an inert force. I could contemplate Sukey more calmly and forthrightly than myself, and was aware at last of her uniqueness. An English colonel's daughter, living in India and almost altogether with Indians until she flowered, would certainly turn out a rare sort of young woman. But there were other factors and forces in her life I was yet to learn.

Every personality on earth is more complex and enigmatic than we assume. No one knows another like a book; all expression in words, looks, and behavior is subject to too many outward influences to portray the naked soul. Truly every soul is as different from every other as, under a magnifying glass, are peas in a pod. But Sukey's variations from the run of the human mill were far greater. There were many apparent reasons why, moving in proximate ways, her rare and beautiful being might come close to mine, but there were some unknown.

"I'm glad that a woman schemed for us to meet here," I remarked. "How did she work it?"

"It was a pretty good trick. I heard Papa mention the bunder boat suspected of carrying rifles. I'd already seen the tower and was wondering how to get you here, so I led him on to describe her pretty well. Then I got one of Hamyd's friends, a boy I could trust, to carry a rumor to Major Graves that such a boat had been hidden in the mangroves in the Delta and would pick up some cargo at Kala Weir late this afternoon. But if there were any sahibs about or soldiers, the boats would be warned in time to hide the contraband. So the only way to catch her would be to post a lookout at about this point on the river, watch her load through a field glass, and search her at Kotri ferry." Plainly Sukey had a native's love for trickery.

"Of course Graves would figure it that way. This tower is the only good lookout. But how could you be sure he would send me?"

"He's always putting you forward—and I knew why."

"I dare say you know that a sahib policeman and a whole squad of sepoys are standing a dull watch at the Kotri ferry."

"What does that matter in an affair as important as this? They got out of some harder duty."

She had not covered the risk of our being surprised by Colonel Webb. After counting noses at mess he might make discreet inquiries. All I could do about it was on no account to mention it to Sukey, and to think about it as little as possible in respect to my own nerves.

"Well, we'll look into the future," I told her. "We'll judge our chances of sharing it in honor and happiness."

"Rom, is there any real reason that you know of why we mustn't marry?"

Cunning failed me for a moment, and I hesitated longer than was prudent before I said no.

"You had to think that over, and there was something the matter with your voice."

"If you were any other English girl in India, I couldn't have said no."

"You *are* a Eurasian after all?"

Briefly I recited the events whereby I was the son of a well-off Englishman and a Gypsy woman, and Gerald's half-brother. The words were plain and by little pauses, as though taking thought, I concealed lack of breath. There was nowhere to take my face out of the moonlight to hide its little, bright, cold beads.

"So you see, Sukey, when I told you one of my ancestors came from the Balkan Peninsula, the gateway the Gypsies used into western Europe—"

"It was quite true, Rom." Sukey did not try to manage her voice, and her hands in mine felt cold.

"Well, I've never told anyone before, and you see my lack of practice."

"Does Gerald know it?"

"I think he may suspect part of it."

"Did Gerald's mother live with your father after he brought you home?"

My head reeled strangely. "I—don't know. They slept in different rooms. When I was a little boy—just finding out about things—I assumed they did. But they never had any more children."

"Did she hate you?"

"Yes." Then there was an upward surge of strength within me, and I wiped my wet face. "Is it worse than you thought, Sukey?"

"An awful lot worse."

"You wish I'd turned out a half-caste?"

"You have. A half-caste beyond the pale. I heard someone—not Colonel Jacob, some other scholar of Indian history—say that the Gypsy's original home was North India, not Egypt, and they belonged to the sweeper caste. So Colonel Jacob was right. Your native tongue is an ancient Hindi dialect. No wonder you picked up Hindustani so quickly. No wonder he was puzzled about your inflection."

"My father wasn't ashamed of having a son by a Gypsy girl. They had a fine little joke about it—my name. Rom, short for Romulus, means a Gypsy man."

"That was fine."

"Would you be ashamed to have a son by a half-Gypsy?"

"No."

"Will you try for one tonight, and marry me tomorrow?"

"Did you put it that way—bluntly, to say the least—on purpose?"

"I suppose so. I've been put on the defensive."

"I'm sorry you are. No, I can't do either. I can't ever have a child by you, or ever marry you. I want to do both—I think I'm very deeply in love with you—but there isn't one little chance. I'm going to marry a sahib

105

just as soon as I can. For both our sakes, you'd better get transferred."

She was speaking in low tones. It seemed queer that such little sounds could convey such heavy meanings.

"You said you wouldn't be ashamed—"

"Of course not. You're a well-gifted man and will go far."

"Don't you think you owe it to me to tell me why—"

"I intend to. I was trying to shape it clearly as possible. You give your name as Romulus, a Roman name, but really it's Rom, meaning a Gypsy. I was christened Sukey, an old English name that's come to be a pet name for a cow. I don't know whether the Indians know that or not, but they gave me my real name— Bachhiya—meaning a heifer—a lovely name by Hindu thinking. If they did know, it was a fine little joke as well. Have you ever noticed that people live up to their names?"

"That's Oriental mumbo-jumbo, Sukey."

"Perhaps so. But I've lived up to a native name. My soul and my heart are almost wholly Indian. Being raised by Indians wouldn't have had that much effect if I'd fought against it, but I fought for it. I had to be an Indian—or nothing. In my impressionable years they were the only people I had. The only ones who loved me or whom I could love."

Sweat beads glimmered on her face. When I handed her my handkerchief, she laughed strangely and wiped them away.

"My God, Sukey, we're both going mad—"

"Oh, no. This is just an old tower on the desert. We shouldn't have picked it as a place to reveal sordid family histories, but we'll get them over with and go home. I was Papa's daughter by his wife—but he wouldn't let her have anything to do with me. She wasn't allowed to touch me—she couldn't even lay eyes on me except when we had company, and then only to conceal what was going on. You can't blame him—brought up as he was—living by the code he did. He's stern—unimaginative—stubborn. If later he wanted to forgive my mother, she wouldn't let him. She spited him—taunted him in every way she could—made him think she despised me because I was his child, and I thought so, too. But he couldn't know—even now he won't let himself realize—the dreadful thing he did to me by separating a baby from its mamma."

Her eyes, glimmering in the flood of moonlight, looked dry as stones. I felt her heart hammering her side. There was nothing for me to do but wait.

"You're wondering, of course, what awful thing she'd done. When I finally found out, I made up my mind to condone it as far as possible. I made light of it, you'll think, when I spoke to you in a joking way about a family skeleton. I wouldn't have done so, if I'd dreamed you would ever know the truth—I was just showing off. No one alive in India knows it but Papa, Hamyd, and I. Papa doesn't know that I know it. Parbati told me against his strict orders. Our other servants knew only that my mother was in some strange kind of purdah [female seclusion] and were scared to mention it even among themselves. Well, what she did wasn't so awful from a realistic point of view. There are a lot of domestic tragedies among English exiles in India—the hot climate, the new way of life, the time on people's hands all help bring them about. If he and Mamma had separated, and I hadn't eaten its poison with every mouthful of bread—but I've gone over that a thousand times. Well, I know now I never did condone it—its effects had been too terrible. It wasn't hard to tell Hamyd—but my throat's dry—and I want to cry and can't—"

She sat up straight and faced me.

"Papa was only a junior subaltern, living at a cantonment near Calcutta. Mamma was beautiful but not his social equal. When she began carrying me, Papa chivalrously slept in another room—maybe some silly doctor told him it was best—and I suppose she was very passionate and could hardly stand it. Anyway before long Papa came home suddenly from shikar, and caught one of his own sergeants in bed with her." Sukey stopped, her throat worked, and she added in proud jest, "I dare say it gave him quite a nasty jar."

"Did he kill the sergeant?"

"No, his behavior was completely pukka. He told the man that he was less to blame than Mamma and that

107

he could apply for discharge and go back to England, but if he ever breathed a word of what had happened, he'd whip him to death."

"Well, it's no wonder both of us are lost sheep."

"I'll tell you the rest, the little that's left. My mother couldn't stand it and died. She'd taken malaria and wouldn't fight it hard enough. I was not quite six years old, and I put my hand on her cold face—the first time I could remember touching her. Papa didn't get away from it that easy. It's still with him, and I pity him. So of course my marrying you was only a crazy dream. It's a good thing I woke up from it in time. I'm going to marry a sahib and be true to him and have English children by him—not dirty little *bachchas*. That far I'll atone for what Mamma did to him, and for what both of them did to me."

"You've changed your tune, since you first came here."

"I was singing a love song then. But I did tell you—pretty soon—that there wasn't any real hope for us."

"Sukey, we found each other—"

"That seems like fate to you, Rom. India such a big country, and both of us so out of luck. Actually there are thousands of people who've had to live with hate instead of love. If it was fate that we met and fell in love, the old girl came a cropper. Don't misunderstand me, Rom. Calling this quits is only a little for Papa's sake. Mostly it's for my own sake—my health and happiness, made up of dignity—safety—peace. You said a moment ago we were both lost sheep. Well, I'm going to find a fold. In any case I'm not going to be a black sheep."

When I could not reply, she took my hand between both of hers. "Rom, does this hurt?"

"It doesn't tickle!"

"Good for you! And it's going to hurt worse—both of us—when the drama's over and only the emptiness is left. You know you are a black sheep."

"Yes."

"Your father and your foster mother made you one, but you were good material for it to start with. The Gypsies are real outcasts. Untouchables in India are respectable members of society compared to them—at

108

least they're under the Hindu umbrella—the castes recognize their existence. Gypsies are witches and warlocks
—thieves—fortunetellers—baby stealers. Why do they
steal babies? They don't hold them for ransom. They're
at the bottom of the human barrel and a white baby's
worth a dozen of theirs. Their music—their dancing—
their second sight all belong to the Devil. When I said
you did, I was right."

"That's *behudgi*. They're just poor damn vaga-
bonds."

"Would you try to tell *me* that big a lie? Have you
forgotten already that I'm not an English girl, but
mostly Indian? Anyway, Rom, imagine a marriage between you and me. A black sheep and a lost sheep.
We've both got to find our way back. You marry the
nicest English girl who'll have you. If you can find a
good, middle-class beef-eater, she'll think you're romantic and never discover what you really are. Have children who'll marry other beef-eaters, and so on until
your descendants have blue eyes and fair hair and
curtsy to the Queen. Stay out of native clothes. Stay out
of towers and all haunted places. As for me, I'm going
to marry Henry if I can. Neither Clifford nor Gerald
are as safe—you won't believe me, about Gerald—but
can you imagine me refusing either of them to take
you? You wouldn't love me, Rom, if I were that much
of a fool. Now let's go home."

My response was not, to my knowledge, deliberate. I
kept her eyes on mine for a few seconds by seeming
about to speak. It came to me that she wanted me to
speak, but if I did, she would have a ready answer, and
the more we spoke, the wider the gulf that we must
speak across. In those seconds my fingers dipped between the buttons of my shirt and touched a silver coin
hanging between my collarbones. It was an unconscious
invocation made only a few times before. Yet it happened that when she started to rise, a little tug at her
hand, entreating her to stay, upset her precarious balance and fetched her body backward across my lap. My
arm was in the way of hers as I bowed down.

"Sukey, did you think I'd let you go?"

"Don't, Rom—"

"You looked at it backward. Every reason you gave for us to part was that much more reason for staying together. That's what we're going to do. We're going to be together always. This is the sign of it—"

"Let me go."

"You don't want to go. There's no strength in your arms. But feel this strength. It's what we make together. Your nails sting, but they'd hurt worse if you'd rake 'em. Why don't you, Sukey? Because you can't. My flesh is too dear to you to make bleed. It's becoming your own flesh—"

"I don't want to go, but won't you help me?"

"I'll help you, never fear— Wasn't that a big help?"

"Don't mock me."

"I'm not. I'm only replying to what you're telling me. You're speaking to me with every cell of your body and inch of your skin. Words lie, but they tell the truth. This is the truth—"

"No, I don't want to go, and you're taking advantage of it."

"I don't know which of us is taking the most advantage of it. It's a close race. I was ahead, but you're catching up."

"I want this. But it's wrong."

"If so, I'm afraid it's going to be a lot wronger."

"Don't stop making love to me, but stop taking that wicked attitude. Admit we're wantons, and stop glorying in it."

"It's hard not to glory in—whatever it is. I don't think it's anything but being deeply and passionately in love."

"Even if it's right, we'll be terribly punished."

"Well, then, we'll catch it together."

"We may be separated. I think we will be— We'll want each other always."

"We'll be hard to separate, after this. That's the real reason it's happening—to stick us together so tight we can't be pried apart. They're going to have their hands full, I tell you."

"I love to have you say that." Her hand no longer imprisoned mine, but, with exquisite hesitations, guided it. "It makes me love you like an Indian girl. She can't

110

wait to surrender. She doesn't know any pain or sin except failing to please her lover." Sukey drew an ecstatic breath and then whispered something in Hindi. I thought it was from the prelude of the nuptial ceremony in one of the cults of Indra, and it meant, "I declare, my lord, my virginity."

"I now bear witness."

"But, thou, Rom, art a Gypsy! How may I entrust thee with it? Wilt thou go away in the night? Will I wait in vain, hearing the mocking laughter of the women? I charge thee, Rom, if I give thee my maidenhead now, wilt thou marry me before witnesses, that I and my babe may bear thy name in honor?"

For a moment I thought her use of Hindi was instinctive and unconscious, caused by her transports. One glance into her face told me that I had underestimated her self-control. Its rapturous expression had been briefly arrested; holding fire, she had asked the Woman's Question in the tongue in which she could be both eloquent and humorous, while being perfectly plain.

"Will you marry me, Sukey?"

"Yes, and then if you want to go, you can."

She put her arms around my neck and kissed me with great beauty and tenderness.

"I remember now the word I was trying to remember about the savage place. I was afraid to remember before. In the poem it wasn't 'lonely.' It was 'holy.' Isn't that right?"

"Yes."

"Does it fit?"

"Yes."

She touched the blanket. "It's awfully rough."

"That fits, too, doesn't it?"

"Horse blankets on the stone in the moonlight. Yes, it's a wonderful fit. Hurry, Rom, because I'm so cold and empty."

CHAPTER TWELVE

A Gift of Love

THE WORLD MOVES IN THE TRAIN OF THE SUN, but the moon is in our train. Men may worship the great sun, by whose potency and light they live, but they may feel kinship with the moon, a friendly bond, since she shines only by his far-darted light, and illumines our darkened skies by his sufferance and, whether shining or extinguished, she is our close, constant companion. She had never treated me cavalierly. She never seemed too high and aloof to bother with me. When my spirits were gray, she did not mock them with her glitter, but appeared to put on a gray, melancholy mien, and sail sadly on her lonesome way. When they were bright, she was a radiant, cheerful, adventurous voyager among the stars.

When I could look at her a moment again, I had never seen her so beautiful and blithe. Only a few large stars, far-scattered, signaled feebly from their posts. One might imagine one of the little stars so put out by its eclipse that it had plummeted to earth, and was yellowly flickering on the desert in its death throes. There was a small flare, sometimes concealed by smoke, in the nearest nala. Hamyd and my *sais* had built a cheery fire of babul scrub, to comfort their long, chill watch.

"If I could get a message to Papa—" Sukey began thoughtfully. Then she laughed nervously but irrepressibly at my riveted attention.

"To bring out the regiment in force?" I asked.

"It's a little too late for that. My idea is—if I send him word that I'm all right—not captured by the hillmen, that is—we needn't break our necks getting back."

"Can't you write a chit?"

"Yes, if you'll send it by your *sais*. I can't send Hamyd. He just wouldn't go. It would be against his principles, even though there's no real danger this side of the river. Anyway I want him with us when we start home."

"I'll send Abdullah. He'll be delighted to deliver the chit, then attend to his affairs at the teahouse."

I fired my horse pistol, the signal I had arranged with the groom, and both he and Hamyd, leading our horses, soon took shape in the middle distance. Sukey and I climbed down to meet them, and when she had written a chit on the pad that she carried in her duster pouch, she instructed Abdullah to deliver it without fail to the chokidar, then quickly *jao*. On no account was he to meet the Colonel Sahib face to face. Then she bade Hamyd follow her into the shadows of the low dunes, where I did not doubt that she told him of our betrothal. Some minutes later they returned walking hand in hand, such a sight as I never expected to see in India. When she came close to me, the probing moonlight in her eyes showed them but recently dried of many tears.

"Hamyd will get the blankets," she told me. "Let's walk to the fire."

We did so, with a kind of humility—a token atonement for our exultation—leaving our footprints in the cold sands with those of the hyena and rock grouse. We had gained hardly half the distance when Hamyd dashed by us, leading both our horses, and it seemed to me there was fierce pride in the way he rode. Then we saw the fire dim smokily only to blaze high and bright. When it had guided us to its warm yellow ring, Hamyd had spread the blankets clear of its smoke and was gone.

"He's got his saddle blanket if he gets cold," Sukey told me. "We can stay till the fire burns down."

It was burning in a little wadi between high sand dunes.

"Until then, is he likely to—"

"We can do anything we like. He won't come till we call him."

The tough wood would still be glowing an hour from now. We looked at each other in wonder and triumph.

We could afford to sit awhile, telling our happy stories of falling in love. So we intended, at least with half a mind, until the first thought of tomorrow. Even then I was a little ashamed to be so greedy, since I could make my bride only a Gypsy bed by a desert fire—until she taught me to be proud. Only then did I fully realize what great fortune had been poured into my hands, without rhyme or reason. I was passionately beloved, not by the Colonel's daughter, but by a daughter of the sun, who in more epic times might be recognized as an avatar, and in whom the clear-eyed Indians might behold manifestations of Rada, the ravishing beloved of the cowherd Krishna. If my soaring imagination was making *pooja*, it was well inspired and the enchantments strangely real.

This communion was the fulfillment of our bridal adventure. We could have renounced each other, when we had first descended from the tower; now we were interbound by the common miracle, the profound mystery, of marriage. Solemn rites and lawful testaments would be its declaration to the world—the same as with more than half the marriages on earth. I was trying to express such of its meaning as I could grasp when, its carnal beauty realized, I asked Sukey to close her eyes, while I gave her something.

When she opened them, there was nothing to see but a small silver coin, hung on a cord around her neck. But perhaps she saw something in my face, for her eyes grew big with wonder and a touching expression came into her face.

"It's not just a good-luck piece," she murmured, deeply moved.

"I think it's a real talisman." I told her about the Gypsy woman Gerald and I had met on the road.

"Rom, it's a wonderful gift, but—"

"Sukey, you look frightened!"

"I am. For you." She seized my hand. "Rom, do you realize what an awful thing—in the sight of my father's world—we've done?"

"I suppose I do—but I haven't seen to it, yet."

"Not joining our naked bodies without a marriage ceremony. You know I don't mean that. If that were all, we could conceal it. If the pressure against our marrying became too strong, we could give each other up. But you've made me your wife. I've made you my husband. No one can come between us. You—Rom—and I —Bachhiya."

"Not Romulus Brook and Sukey Webb?"

"You didn't have a chance to be Romulus Brook. This talisman kept you from it. Do you see what I mean? It's hard to put it in English words. When you hung around your neck a silver coin on which a Gypsy woman had made *pooja*—sympathetic magic that you and I both know works, if you believe it strongly enough—you renounced Romulus Brook. You went across the line with your mother. You become a renegade from your father's people, and now Gerald is the only real link between you and them."

"That's quite true. I never thought about it exactly that way—perhaps because I didn't go to live in a tent."

"You did go to live in a tent. It's amounted to that. But Rom—I did have a chance to be Sukey Webb. Instead—I married a half-breed Gypsy."

"Good God!"

"You've read *Othello,* haven't you?"

"Many times. It was a favorite—"

"You know why, of course. Every person can find his own story in Shakespeare. Well, do you remember what her father said to Othello, in the Duke's council chamber, after he and Desdemona had eloped?"

"He charged him with 'practices of cunning hell.' Well, I didn't win you in such a simple, natural way as Othello won Desdemona, but I didn't use any drams or mixtures."

"Do you think the sahibs will believe that? They're not broad-minded civilized Italians of the sixteenth century—they're nineteenth-century Englishmen."

"Othello was black. At least he had a rich-chocolate color," I went on, smiling a little.

"They don't know you're a Gypsy. They know only that you're more alien to them than a half-caste orderly. They won't blame me—I've been tricked into the ditch at Meeanee. But you need all the Gypsy luck that ever was."

I started to make a light answer, but it stuck in my throat. The fire was burning low, and the ring of shadows leaped more boldly than before, and some of them took grotesque shapes. Hyenas had been howling, far and near, ever since dusk, and now a little fox yapped at the moon.

"I give that luck to you, Bachhiya."

She put her arms about me and kissed me with deep love. "I'll share it with you, Rom, good or bad."

She took a brand from the fire and threw it high in the air, the old desert rider's signal to his clansmen. Soon we heard the muffled thud of horses' hoofs. When Hamyd dismounted in the moonlight, I thought the moonlight in the fire's ruddy ring had the strange effect of paling his brown, handsome face. Then I glanced at Sukey, and the usual process of a seeming fact proving to be an illusion was reversed—a seeming illusion was proved a fact. Both he and his mistress were pale.

"I waited until thou came, to speak of the matter to Rom Sahib," Sukey told him.

"Aye, memsahib."

"Thou art still of the same mind?"

"Aye."

She turned to me but continued to speak in Hindi, for Hamyd's understanding.

"My lord, there came upon me, atop the tower, the wish and the need to give thee a noble gift. Of this I spoke to my servant Hamyd, apart from thee. Mark that the time was before thou gavest me the talisman from off thy heart. That be proof that the gift is not given in payment of debt, or in duty, or in gratitude for anything, but is given from within my heart, in token of love."

"I mark thee well," I answered.

"I give unto thee, for as long as ye both shall live, the service of my dearly beloved servant, Hamyd Din."

Her voice had trembled and she looked at me through a lovely moonlit mist of tears. Hamyd stood quietly, sideways so that I could see his profile, a pos-

116

ture of great significance among the Mohammedans of India, and indicative of great pride.

"I entreat thee, Bachhiya, to reconsider," I replied. "Surely we will be parted many a day and night, and perhaps for many moons, thus parting ye both."

"Lord, if thou didst remain every hour at my side, of what good would be the gift? It is because thou wilt be gone from me so long and far that it is worth the giving." She turned to Hamyd. "Thou shalt be his ears and his eyes and his hands. Thou shalt follow him across all the waters and the deserts of his fate. If he should put me away, and take another wife, thou shalt follow him still. Hamyd, is it met?"

"Aye, memsahib, it is met."

"It is also meet. Thou art a youth of great strength, of many manly gifts, the grandson of a great sheik, and schooled in cunning. It is not meet that thou shouldst any longer dance attendance upon a memsahib. Following the *burra* sahib, thou shalt come into thy birthright as a doer of strong deeds, a challenger of many dangers, and a traveler and warrior of renown."

Sukey turned to me. "My lord, wilt thou accept my gift?"

"Aye, Shahzadi [Princess]."

"Then, Hamyd—thou hast my leave to go."

CHAPTER THIRTEEN

Unspoken Warning

WE LEFT THE MOONLIGHT ON THE DESERT, the tower standing forsaken as before, the river glistening, the hyenas laughing and sobbing. As we rode into the warm, ancient city, we did not try to hide our fears from each other or count them too little or too much. She did not instruct me in what to say or how to act in the soon meeting.

Several lamps burned low in the big bungalow. I saw a shadow cross a window curtain as Colonel Webb rose from his chair. He must have delayed a few seconds, perhaps to steady himself, before answering the door; when it opened, our sense of inert waiting instantly changed to one of swift-moving event. We beheld a scene, and almost instantly that scene changed.

I was a little behind Sukey on the dark veranda, and at first glance her father did not recognize me. Indeed he did not look at me, and no doubt mistook me for Gerald. His face and bald dome were flushed with anger over her long and worrisome absence, so thoughtless of him, but his lips were close pressed, lest he say too much in rebuke of her inconsiderate but not-to-be-offended escort. There was time for a dart of wonder through my mind that he could be so deceived. Indeed on the homeward ride I had half expected to meet him on the road. Evidently he had not asked what bearer had delivered Sukey's note, and Gerald had happened to be absent tonight from mess.

He saw that I was not Gerald. Between then and his seeing who I was there was an indescribably brief lag in which he did not believe his eyes. Then, if I had struck him full between them with my fist, he would not have looked more stunned.

"Papa—" There was compassion in Sukey's cry, but I did not think there was guilt or remorse.

He made a brave and partly successful effort to rally. He had done the same, no doubt, that shattering moment that he had entered his wife's bedroom, after returning unexpectedly from shikar. He thought upon his dignity and his righteousness. He was the Colonel of the Tatta Lancers. He spoke in his military voice.

"I don't quite understand, Sukey. I thought you were with Captain Gerald Brook—"

He stopped. There was a flash of hope in his face—perhaps Gerald had met with a minor accident, and I had merely escorted her home.

"No, I've been with Rom. And we've got something to tell you."

He cleared his throat carefully. "It's very late, Sukey. I'll hear it in the morning—"

"I think you'd better hear it tonight. It's very important, and I want Rom with me."

He stood very straight as he considered her request. His strength had come back to him, bringing with it danger to us both. His eyes had resumed their normal shape and, it seemed, an accentuation of their normal blue color. That might be an effect of their glistening whites.

"Very well. Please come into the drawing-room."

He paused at the door of the big stately room while first Sukey, and then I, entered. Something more than a sense of ceremony had caused him to listen to us here, instead of in the more informal library. Over the mantel was a big portrait of an officer with shining epaulets, holding a bear-skin of Wellington's Foot Guards. Colonel Webb held a chair for Sukey, designated one for me half the length of the room distant, and, after turning up two of the lamps, seated himself by a massively carved table. There he would be a fine study for a portrait painter, I thought. No one who saw it would mistake his place and pride.

"I am ready to listen," he said slowly, "to what either of you has to say."

119

"I'll speak first, Papa," Sukey said quickly. "I am sorry it has to come as such a surprise to you. I've been seeing Rom occasionally ever since I came here. It wasn't his fault that we met in secret. I was sorry to have to do that, but I didn't have your consent to receive his attentions."

"That is quite true," he said when she paused. "You did not."

When she started to speak he interrupted her.

"In fact—as I suppose you told him—I expressly forbade you to do so."

"Yes, sir, she did tell me," I said.

"Yet you paid court to her anyway, Lieutenant Brook?"

"Yes, sir."

"It is not a very auspicious beginning—but please continue."

"Tonight I rode out to the tower where he was on watch, and we became engaged." Sukey spoke clearly, turned to smile at me, then leaned back in her chair. I looked at the lamp glow in her hair and eyes; it outlined the delicate, exotic molding of her face and picked up the warmly alive tints of her skin. That beauty was now mine, and I knew its reality and the realness of my possession, which I would not yield. It was the sense of my own strength of possession.

Colonel Webb leaned forward in his chair, about to speak with fury and great force. But he held his tongue in deliberate silence. The silence grew long and very heavy, perhaps he thought it would expose weakness in us. Instead we smiled at each other and waited.

"Before I make my reply," he said at last, looking at me, "I would like to ask a few questions. They may save my making extensive explanations. However, you're not at all obligated to answer them."

"I'll answer as many of them as I can."

"I hadn't expressly forbidden you to pay court to Sukey, and her connivance in it appeared to justify you. But you were aware of my objection. And it might be that you knew things about yourself that would make your courting her a despicable offense. In that case, you deserve to be horsewhipped."

"Sir, I knew nothing that would make my courting her an offense in my own eyes. I was in love with her."

"We shall go into that. And I shall assume for a moment you're both in love and not merely victims of an unfortunate infatuation. But the sooner lovers who are unsuited to each other find it out, the sooner they can set about serving and seeking more suitable partners. I wish to be perfectly fair. I'll begin by asking you a question I would ask of any young man seeking permission to marry my daughter. Would you be able to maintain Sukey in her present position in society?"

"No, sir, but I intend to make my way in the world, and make my wife proud of me."

"We had better talk plain. What are your monetary means, in addition to your salary?"

"I have four hundred pounds a year from my foster father's estate."

"I would not consider that nearly sufficient, allowing for any amount I can sensibly expect you to make in the next few years. Your speaking of your foster father suggests an equally—indeed a far more important—qualification. According to report, you are the adopted son of Frederick Brook, Gerald's father. Will you please state the position in society of your real father?"

Hours ago, it seemed, I had foreseen him sitting here, uncannily as he sat here now, asking that question. Unable to decide how to answer it, I had lamely put it off. Sukey looked to me with big eyes. Her face was telltale pale. Suddenly I knew that anything I told him, as little as I could, or as much as I must, must be true.

"I have reasons to believe that my real father's position in society was quite high. But I stand as the adopted son of a highly reputable Englishman, and as an officer in the English Army."

"Of course you know your real father's name," he said after a brief pause.

"Of course." The thin ice crackled, but not yet—

"Is he still alive?"

"No, sir."

"Is your mother still alive?"

"As far as I know. My real father and she were sep-

121

arated. It was agreed that she should not communicate with me. I was no longer in her life."

Despite my fear of him, growing every moment, I had made shift to look straight at him in replying to his questions. Lately I had seen color returning to his face, in evidence of his rallying strength—tried and trusted strength, buttressed by place and power that all men recognized and honored, and with mounting hope of another victory in its wake. But suddenly his sunburn and graying mustache and brown eyebrows appeared actor's make-up, painted or pasted on sickly white skin.

My scalp tightened with the effect of creeping. I could almost hear the Small Voice telling him that this was his retribution for taking Sukey out of her mother's life. But his hand went, unhurried, to his pocket, brought forth a handkerchief, and carefully wiped away the sweat beads on his face. The straight hard line of his lips never wavered. A muscle flexed and quivered under the taut skin of his jaw, then became invisible.

"I wish to inquire further into your history, Lieutenant Brook," he went on in a low unruffled voice. "It should be evident that I have every right to do so. From what walk of life did your mother come?"

"I have reason to believe that her father was a horse-dealer."

"What was your father's calling?"

"He lived on the income from his property."

"Did you inherit any of it?"

"Yes, sir."

"I understood you to say that your present estate came from your foster father."

"I did say so, sir."

"Then I may presume you haven't it now?"

The thin ice cracked at last.

"I decline to answer that question, sir."

His expression did not change. He merely paused a few seconds. Sukey clasped her hands, then dropped them on her lap.

"I must say, I cannot possibly fancy your reason."

"It has to do with my relations with my foster brother Gerald. And I request that you don't repeat to him or to anyone anything I tell you of my own history."

122

"Was your father born in America?" Colonel Webb went on.

"I believe he was born in England."

"Indeed! But he spent most of his life there, I suppose."

"If you please, I won't answer that question."

"Fancy that! Well, I told you you needn't answer any of my questions. However, I have a few more. Did he ever live in America at all?"

"He was there twice. I don't know for how long."

"Did he live or visit in India—or anywhere in the East?"

"No, sir."

"Did your mother ever live in the Far East?"

"Not that I know of, sir. She might have been born in Europe. She was living in America when I was born."

"But perhaps her parents or ancestors lived in the Far East."

"Perhaps they did. I don't even know their names."

"Speaking of names—what was your real father's name?"

"My foster father told me that it was Harris."

"Were you well acquainted with him, and was his name really Harris?"

"I'll answer neither of those, if you please."

"I don't see the slightest use in prolonging this interview. You have too much to hide."

"To tell it would do no good to Sukey and me, and might do harm to others." For suddenly I was not afraid of him any more, at least with the personal, instinctive fear I had felt before. Fear is curiously wedded to uncertainty. I knew where both of us stood.

A malicious but strong hope gleamed in his cold eyes. "If you please, I'll ask one more question. Answer it or not as you choose. Sometimes young lovers in the first flush of their passion don't bother about inquiring into each other's lives. Did you tell her what you refused to tell me?"

"Yes, sir."

He set his jaw more firmly than before.

"And it didn't make a speck of difference to me," Sukey broke in calmly.

Colonel Webb rose. He was very tall and powerfully built. But Sukey was tall, too. I noticed it as she walked toward me. We stood side by side, facing him.

"I shan't ask her your confidences," he said. "Such facts as I have discovered speak for themselves. Lieutenant Brook, I refuse my consent to an engagement between you and Sukey. I forbid any further relationship between you. If you are gentleman enough, whatever your origins, to obey me in this matter, you may continue your duties in the Brigade until the General sees fit to transfer you elsewhere. But there is an unwritten law in our Service that no officer of my rank need retain under or attach to his command any officer who is *persona non grata* in his home. For your brother Gerald's sake—and in fairness to you—I must warn you against any act detrimental to your military career."

"I thank you, sir, but that won't have the slightest effect on my engagement to Sukey."

"You insufferable—" But the Colonel Sahib remembered where he was, and pressed his lips tight.

"Yes, it's my turn," Sukey said, when he turned to her. "Papa, I know your strong mind. I know you're capable of doing all you threatened to do—if you can. To save you the trouble of forbidding things—to save us all the embarrassment of your making any more threats—I'll tell you now where I stand on this. I'm not going to ask your consent to marry him or discuss it at all. I'll just go ahead and do it. We'll wait two weeks, should you decide on a pukka wedding that will save you all the face possible. If by then, you still oppose it, we'll be married by a missionary or by the Hindu ceremony or by common law."

Her father stood so straight, his arms so rigid at his sides, that he gave the impression of standing at attention. Actually he had struck the pose in which he could retain the greatest possible self-control. But his face was livid, and only in battle had I ever seen such a lethal gleam in human eyes. I thanked my stars that we had already been married by common law.

"Sukey," he said evenly, "I'll try not to hold this against you. I refuse to believe that you're to blame."

"Tricked into the ditch in Meeanee? I told Rom you'd think that."

"I don't know who this man is. I believe him to be a Eurasian. But I do know you're not in your right mind. I'd be justified—"

"You'd be justified, you think, in shipping me off at once to England. Well, I won't go. You can ship Rom off on some duty. Well, I'll follow him. Anyone who knows India like I do can get any place he goes. You succeeded in separating my mother from me, but you can't separate me from my husband. For that's what he is. I consider myself his wife."

I did not know what to expect in the next second. I was poised on the balls of my feet, every muscle ready to move. But what that second brought was almost beyond our credence.

The powerful arch of his chest receded, and he took a backward step and spoke in a tone that seemed to be deliberately dull.

"I accept your proposal to wait two weeks. Lieutenant Brook, I beg your pardon for anything I may have said in the heat of anger that did you an injustice. Since I am greatly shaken by this experience, please find your own way to the door."

But halfway there, at a point where Colonel Webb could not look into the eyes of either of us, I turned to gaze at Sukey.

"Good night, sweetheart."

"Good night, my Rom."

Those were our words, safe enough for him to hear. But the expression on her face told me something else. *Beward! Beware! Beware!*

CHAPTER FOURTEEN

Confidences at Midnight

HAMYD HAD PUT UP THE HORSES while I was in the bungalow, and was waiting for me with a puzzling bit of news.

"Did the sahib leave a lamp burning in his room when he went forth today?" he asked in formal Urdu.

"Nay."

"There is a light in the window."

"I will see to it."

I could not imagine who my caller might be at this late hour, or what his mission. My nerves on edge, I opened the door narrowly with a flexed forearm, ready to close it swiftly, only to be instantly ashamed of the absurd precaution. Gerald was sitting in my one easy chair, wearing a lounging-robe and enjoying a pipe. But there was no doubt of the importance of his visit. I knew his face well enough to know that he had not been to bed. Too, I knew from the wick of my lamp, which had needed trimming at its last burning, that it had not been lighted long.

"Sit on the bed, old man," he told me. "Since it's this late, we might as well make a night of it."

"Didn't you find my bottle? It's in the corner of the cabinet."

I poured two drinks, and my heart glowed as always when we touched glasses. He gave me a salaam.

"That's particularly appropriate tonight," he said.

"News must travel fast."

"None has traveled that I know of. I've got a confession to make, Rom. You know we all do damn-fool things—pretty rotten things sometimes—when we think no one need ever know. Well, I was put out with Su-

126

key's fishy excuse for breaking an engagement with me this afternoon. I'm quite fond of her and had planned a rather nice outing. Of course I thought she was going out with Clifford, whom we both know is a cad. Riding along the old canal, I caught a glimpse of her making out Kil Sarak. I was stung enough to follow her as far as the *pahari* and then watch her through my field glasses. She made straight as a crow for the old tower."

I nodded, wondering at his hollow eyes.

"It offers interesting possibilities as a rendezvous, you know. I hadn't realized she was thick enough with Clifford to meet him at such a place. Well, when I wandered back here, Clifford and Henry were fixing for a sundown chukker. It happened they hadn't seen me, and when I thought of something, I deliberately didn't let 'em. What I thought was how you'd mentioned being ordered to watch the river this afternoon for a gunrunner. Of course it came to me in a flash that you and Sukey had made a little deal that neither of you wanted anyone to know."

"That was a reasonable assumption," I said.

"Of course I wanted to back your play. I didn't understand it, but I figured I'd better say out of sight, so the chaps—maybe his nibs, too—would assume our engagement hadn't been broken and she was out with me. I didn't appear for mess, and in fact didn't show my shining face hereabouts until you two were safely home."

"That's what I mean by a brother."

"Thanks, Rom. Perhaps I saved you two from interruption—the Colonel might not have taken kindly to his daughter and a subaltern roosting half the night so far from chaperonage. But I'd put Jamrud on guard—you know I can trust him—and his report made it look serious. He said the Colonel was waiting up—that he'd answered the door in person—and you'd gone in to *bukh* with him. Frankly, I was a little worried. Since I was up that late, I thought I might as well hover about until you came home. Old man—are you in trouble?"

Any trouble I was in had become suddenly a great deal less. The very tone he had used—largely matter-of-fact but with a cheerful rather than solemn inflection —reduced it, and so did his every lack of a long face. Maybe he was only doing his duty by me, I thought; even so he did it with such grace! I had never known what the word "grace" meant before. It meant giving without thought of incurring obligation. But maybe he had a deep affection for me.

"In a way," I answered. "But it's the most wonderful trouble I could imagine."

"My word! That sounds as if—"

"Look, Gerald. It would be ghastly trouble if you wanted her for yourself. For God's sake, tell me you don't—if you know it's the truth. She said you didn't— you haven't given any sign of it—you remarked that you were 'quite fond' of her, and I was convinced from the start that was all."

Gerald smiled without removing his pipe, puffing comfortably. Finally he took it out and watched the upward-wreathing smoke.

"Compose your mind in that regard, Rom," he said. "I *am* fond of her—I must say I found her exciting, too —but tastes differ—and she wasn't what I was looking for in the way of a wife. Do you mind my saying that?"

"Heavens above!"

"You know I'm a bit of a stick, old man. I was raised that way and can't help it. I'm a typical middle-class Englishman and Sukey is too—unconventional—what a hell of a word!—too dashing for such as I. I wouldn't be sure I could hold her. I'd be worried about her not being 'proper'—I mean, the way she says and does what she damn well pleases. But she'd have been a perfect match for Henry Bingham—and if she's picked you, he's in for a nasty jar."

"Have another drink?" For I needed a minute to think this over.

"Right." He poured one half the usual size.

"With that last, you told me two things I didn't know. If she's too unconventional to make the right wife for you, I'd think the same would apply to Henry." Actually I did not think so, but the differences between the two men were not clear in my head.

"He's a real aristocrat, Rom. Born one—bred one.

What in the hell need he care for Mrs. Grundy or any of her works! There are only two classes who are free to be happy. The way up and the way down. It's we middle fellows who get it in the neck."

Apparently he sucked in a slug from his pipe, for he made a disgusted face, rose, spat out the window, wiped his lips, and blew throught the stem.

"She would have been a sensation in London," he went on, after musing. "That gawkiness we both saw—that painful shyness—were just signs of extreme sensitivity. But once she found herself among her own kind—the real nibs—people who can appreciate her—people who dare be natural—she might have made history." He stopped and turned his glowing eyes on me. "What was the other thing I said that surprised you?"

"That Henry was going to—"

"Rom, didn't you know he's head over heels in love with her?"

"I didn't know it."

"Didn't Sukey tell you he proposed to her last night?"

"No."

"Well, he told me. He made no great secret of it—and she'd tell you anyway, in time. He told me that until he actually popped the question, she seemed highly agreeable. He thinks she intended to accept until that very moment. Then her eyes got big and she told him he would either have to take no or to give her a little time, because she might be—she didn't know yet for sure—in love with another man."

My throat felt tight from some emotion that did not make itself comprehensible. "Did she say who the other man was?"

"No. Henry flattered me by thinking I was the lucky fellow. I don't know how he got such an idea. When I told him how wrong he was, he decided it was Clifford. Clifford is quite effective with the ladies, you know. But I wasn't convinced it was he. I had the vaguest kind of inkling that it was—you."

"Incredible as it seems, you are right."

"There's nothing incredible about it, Rom. You're a very powerful man. You have a way of getting what
129

you go after—I've seen that all my life—and also you seem to be extraordinarily lucky. Of course you've been meeting her all the time that we three fools—Henry and Clifford and I—thought we were competing only with one another."

"Not often, but occasionally."

"And making more hay in those infrequent meetings than all the rest of us combined. If she wasn't sure last night—but of course she was. She was just a little reluctant to let Henry go. She's been completely sure at least since that day you ran into her in the club library, weeks ago."

That was the day we had kissed in such frantic hunger. "I don't remember you being in the rooms that day—"

"I wasn't. She mentioned finding you there. That is —she pretended to mention it—meaning a casual remark—but really she spoke of it deliberately, with her heart in her mouth. I suppose she was trying to find out if you'd told me about it."

"Then it wasn't altogether a vague inkling—"

"That was all the evidence I had, and was put off by the impression she was seeing red. Well, maybe she was, and I wasn't clever enough to know how serious that was. I don't understand females very well. I'm a frightful dub around 'em. To be frank—we've got to be, you know—I took it you'd tried to make pretty free with her in the cubby, and she'd resented it. You're supposed to be a satyr, among other things. There was other evidence if I'd had the brains to see it. Even that incident —the first week she was here—when she sent me for her parasol. You had the inside track even then."

He had been speaking in a calm tone, his eyes full of thoughts. His smile at the end was not even bitter, only wry.

"I dare say there were little difficulties, as usual, but you ironed 'em all out tonight," he went on.

"Yes, we became engaged and are going to be married in two weeks."

"Pretty short notice." His voice betrayed no great surprise. "But since you're both passionately in love—why wait?"

"How about drinking to my wonderful luck? I can take another stout'n without risk to my weak head."

"How much of it was luck? Some. That's always the case in everything big. Rom, do you remember that day in the pony cart—and the old Gypsy woman spitting on the coin you gave her, and giving it back to you? You kept it as a good-luck piece, didn't you?"

"No fear!"

"I remember asking you to give it to me. Of all the cheek!"

"I remember you standing by me just the same—as you did tonight."

"Well, it was plain as a pikestaff that the old man wanted her to take Henry. That was natural enough—Henry being one of the biggest catches in India—money—maybe a peerage before he's done. And, knowing what a highhanded old snorter he is, I thought he'd raise a row."

"Well, he did."

"But gave you his blessing in the end?"

"You know better than that, Gerald. Sukey told him blessing or no blessing, we were going ahead in a fortnight. I wish you could have seen her—standing up to him. My God, it was thrilling—"

His expression, as though looking through me and beyond, made me pause. "I knew she would," he said quietly.

"But Gerald—you meant more than the Colonel's ambition for her to marry well. You knew—you couldn't fail to know—that he'd rather have her go unmarried all her life than marry me."

Gerald sprang to his feet and walked quickly to the window. I saw his back straight as a broom. When he turned, he was deeply flushed.

"I beg your pardon, old boy, for that show of emotion."

"I wish I could tell you what it meant to me."

"Rom, if he feels that way—do you know *why*?"

"Of course. Infinitely better than he does." And then, coming upon me so quietly and naturally that I did not even feel surprised, the moment had arrived to break a long and aching silence. "Gerald, do you know, too?"

He looked at me as though in profound amazement, hesitated, and then slowly nodded.

"As soon as I did?"

"A little before, I think. I knew years before that you were Papa's real son. I felt it in my bones—or divined it somehow by the way Mamma acted toward you. I knew, too, you weren't like me—like any English boy I knew. Do you remember those high mountains in Yorkshire, Papa took us to, when we were about nine years old? The highest was Mickle Fell. I thought of you as coming from over Mickle Fell, from some wild, strange country beyond. I found out what country it was, the day we met the Gypsy."

"Did your mother ever know?"

"You told her yourself about the darkness not washing off. But she knew long before that, that your mother wasn't a—white woman. Do you mind my speaking of her that way? It's the way we speak of Indians, although God knows they belong to the white race the same as we do."

"Of course not."

"I don't know when it dawned on her that your mother was a Gypsy. The only reference she ever made to it was in her last, bitter, half-mad letter to me, two weeks before she died."

My hair brushed up as from an icy breeze through the window.

"Gerald, why didn't you tell me that Mamma—your mother—had died?"

"I couldn't, Rom. I felt I ought to—then I remembered how she hated you—and how—because of that— you came to hate her. I got the news of it on the very day you captured Kambar Melik. That was why I couldn't join in the celebration. I decided not to tell anyone."

Gerald rose, poured a small peg, and downed it in one quaff. I had no heart to remind him that his next drink was to have been to Sukey's and my engagement. Then we sat as still as though all our main business was over, but we both knew we had only prepared its ground.

"Colonel Webb thinks you're a Eurasian, doesn't he?" Gerald asked, suddenly and rather briskly.

"Yes. A rather charitable view of me, don't you think? Don't most of the fellows say, 'If he's not a half-caste, he's something worse?' "

"Not to me they don't, by God! But I know what they think. Your best friends, Major Graves and Henry Bingham, believe there was some hanky-panky one or more generations ago, whereby you're part Asiatic. Apparently they credit you with not knowing it yourself—or at least not being sure of it."

"Otherwise I wouldn't foist myself on the Tatta Lancers. No gentleman, knowing he wasn't a real white man, could do such a thing."

"Oh, come, Rom. There's a lot of poppycock about this sahib business—"

"Certainly, if he knew the taint, he wouldn't pay court to the Colonel's daughter." I felt an old familiar smile, if it could be called that, beginning to curl my lips, and quickly straightened them. "What about my worst enemies?"

"You have only one—Clifford—that I know of. Well, perhaps I should add Colonel Webb who never forgave you for that dance. They, too, think you rose out of the Asiatic swarm—that you know you did—have been cunning enough to conceal it—and got where you are by Asiatic cunning. What in the Devil kind of Asiatic they can't figure out—something God-awful they can be sure —and you're halfway, whatever it is."

"They're quite correct."

"They've never made a downright issue of it for a lot of reasons, the main one being they haven't any evidence. Another is lip-service democracy—liberalism— the real word is politics—of the powers that be. Colonel Jacob's very powerful, and he's a quarter-caste. Regimental snobbery is very unpopular at home. All the records show you're a hell of a good officer, and this is a great country for gossip—all the big fellows are scared of a question in the House."

"I wonder if it would be better—or worse—if our fellows knew the truth."

"I don't see how such a thought could ever cross your mind."

I could not keep from flushing. "Forgive me. I need a poke in the jaw for that mental lapse. The exposure of one's father's wenching with a Gypsy woman, and the betrayal of his lady-wife! You see, Gerald, a bastard can't possibly regard his father's sin the way other people regard it. He has to thank God for it—otherwise where would he be? No wonder real bastards—not merely the illegitimate children of kings and dukes and so forth, but what our forefathers lumped off as whoresons—were always considered base."

I knew what I was doing—trying to take a look off Gerald's face by this abstract discussion—but I could not stop.

"Actually the word 'bastard' isn't derived from 'base,'" I went on. "It comes from the old Provençal 'bast'—a pack-saddle—in other words conceived not in a bed but—in a barn, or along a road." I had started to say on a horse blanket. "But the folk belief that bastards are by nature base has really a sound philosophical foundation. They owe their very existence to a sin against Society and, we are taught, against God. They start out on the side of outlawry if not evil." Gerald was gazing at me with queerly lighted eyes, and I made an uncomprehended effort of will. "I'm the worst possible example, according to that. A woman of a criminal tribe, in most people's opinion—outcasts—and, in your own words, long ago, thieving—dirty. Imagine a Gypsy sitting down at the table with you!"

"I wish you'd cut it out."

"I keep forgetting he was your father, too. But Gerald—they dance beautifully—they're wonderful musicians—and they *do* survive. And it isn't so hard to imagine sitting down with them, by their fires, dipping in their pots. It doesn't make your flesh crawl nearly as much. That was what Papa did. He became a renegade for a while, but he didn't attack his own society."

"Are you sure of that?"

"Oh, my God! Yes, he did—three or four years later. But Gerald, he didn't mean to. He didn't think it was that. He told me the night before he died that, taking

134

me away from them so young, he thought I'd turn out an Englishman."

"Then he brought you to his own house. Rom, these are the cards that have to be turned face up. Understand, I don't blame you for any of it—for anything that's happened. By getting engaged to Sukey, you're not attacking your society—because it isn't yours. It's hers—and mine—and the Tatta Lancers'—and the Queen's. You have every right to try to survive and get ahead."

He drew a deep breath and turned white. The fear that blanched his face was for me, I thought. It was coming now—what he had come here to say—his great mission—the duty he must do—the climacteric moment of this meeting.

"It is yours and Sukey's business only," he went on quietly, "provided she knows what she's doing."

His eyes fixed on my face. They became like those of a judge before whom I stood on trial. They were not accusing, they were only searching.

"In other words—provided I haven't obtained her consent under false pretenses."

As I said that, there came a curious check, like a jerk, in the flow of my thoughts. I had a brief, dim intimation of something around the corner of my brain that I had missed—an ill-boded thing—but it flitted away before I could identify it. Perhaps I did not try.

"Gerald, I want to quote a couple of lines from *Othello*," I went on. "Sukey and I were talking about the play tonight. When Desdemona's father had confronted him in the Duke's court, one of the Senators asked:

" 'Did you by indirect and forced courses
    Subdue and poison this young maid's affections?
    Or came by it by request, and such fair question
    As soul to soul, affordeth?'

"That's what you're asking me, Gerald."

"That's a political version of it. I'd rather put it in plain words. Did you tell Sukey?"

"In plain words, I did."

He began filling his pipe, but his hands shook, and some tobacco fell on the floor.

"I'd better say this. I hope you won't blame me. If you *hadn't* told her—and wouldn't promise to, at once —I was going to tell her."

"I don't blame you."

"Not her father, but her. My brotherly office went that far, I felt."

He lighted the pipe, puffed a moment, and appeared completely composed. "It would have been best—this is just my hope—if you did it early in the game."

I knew now what I had just missed perceiving a moment ago. Its chill crept through every nerve and vein.

"I told her before she promised to marry me."

"Well, you see why I asked. There are people who'd say you had no right to court her until she knew, because after she'd fallen in love with you, she couldn't look at it straight."

The Colonel had said it in different words. If I knew something about myself that made courting her an offense, I ought to be horsewhipped. Gerald had expressed his own opinion without meaning to, I thought; he did not want me to know he agreed with the others.

Gerald rose and glanced at his watch. "We've still got time for a short wink before parade."

"I'm excused from parade, for being on watch tonight."

"Lucky devil. Nothing to disturb your sweet dreams. Well—" But he stopped, his head cocked, as though he had just thought of something. "Speaking of luck— would you mind showing me that coin the old witch gave you so long ago?"

"I'd love to show it to you, but I haven't got it."

His brow furrowed, and he stood so still that it gave the effect of a deep start.

"My soul, you haven't lost it?"

"No. I gave it to Sukey tonight."

I saw his mind work. He did not want me to think that he thought anything of that. He would not want anyone to know he could be so superstitious. I wished I could tell him my wonder and joy.

136

"That's jolly good," he said. "Now you'll both be lucky."

"She gave me something, too. A servant she was raised with—his name's Hamyd—a wonderful chap."

"My word! And he didn't mind?"

"Of course, but what she says goes."

"Well, you and she will be married in two weeks, and you can both have him." He paused, smiling. "I dare say there was some sentiment attached, wasn't there? Was he the go-between?"

"Not exactly, but he did help bring us together. I'll tell you about it, first chance."

"I don't want to pry into your romantic secrets, old boy. But it's been a wonderful *bukh*. I can't tell you how much better—how much it's meant to me." His eyes were luminous in the lamplight.

"Waisa hi." That was the Hindustani equivalent of "the same with me."

My eyes were shining the same. But I was glad I said so little, when I felt so much.

CHAPTER FIFTEEN

Gossip and Insult

IT SO HAPPENED THAT THE STREAM OF SWEET DREAMS
Gerald had foretold for me was once choked and fouled
by a horrid one. It came upon me through some channel of my brain that I thought was ten years dry; it was
like the walking of a ghost ten years laid. As far as it
went, it did not vary in the least particular from its previous visitation; indeed some wakeful watchman at the
door of sleep seemed to anticipate every shifting of its
movement and scene. Again Mamma's arms were
around me and her kisses warm on my face—her name
was still Mamma instead of the Woman. Again Gerald
called me—"*Rom!*" the call seeming to have actual
sound instead of being mute as a printed word, as is
most dream speech. Again Mamma spat in my face and
flung me away. But this time I wakened too soon. I did
not dream on to fight in the hope of winning. When
time and place returned to me, with the effect of an ex-
plosion, dawn was at the window, and I was wiping my
face with my hand.

The Woman is dead, was my first thought. No doubt
hearing the news last night had invoked the dream.

When, cap-a-pie, I reported to Major Graves, I could
hardly keep from grinning at his disappointment over
the will-o'-the-wisp gunrunner. I must have had a long
and tedious watch! Moreover, he had nothing exciting to
assign to me for the next fortnight—only reconnaissance
for the proposed extension of a military road. If I
turned in a good report, I could be almost certain of
immediate official transfer to the Survey.

When the sun began to slide toward the Kirthar
Mountains and the shadows had a cooler look if not

quite feel, I walked to the bungalow of Colonel Webb. Lieutenant Romulus Brook was going to pay a call on his betrothed as was fitting and proper! If Colonel Webb should ask what my business was, I would tell him so. But when the servant answering the door did not call him to attend to me, my relief was all-pervading and unashamed. Anyway—unlike, I supposed, my betters—I was never greatly ashamed of cowardice or any other weakness provided no one found it out.

The servant bade me wait, while he announced me. He returned with word that I would find the memsahib in the garden, with another guest. He showed me out a side door, and I followed a cobblestone path toward a dim glint of white through red-flowering oleander shrubs. Presently I caught sight of my beloved sitting on a stone bench by the garden rill, her hand in Henry Bingham's. It came upon me, in a dark, cold flood, that she was about to tell me that all that had happened last night was only a dream—at least I must believe it was —and she had decided to marry the *burra* sahib.

But the radiance of welcome in her face was for me.

"Rom, what were you smiling about as you came through the oleanders?" she demanded.

"I didn't know I was—"

"Well, you were, and it was a horrid smile, wasn't it, Henry?"

"I didn't notice. I dare say I was the butt of the joke. Old chap, why didn't you laugh aloud? The johnny who laughs last laughs best, they say."

He spoke in a good-humored tone, but in his eyes was a look I had seen in the eyes of men cruelly wounded while following a flag.

"Rom wouldn't dream of such a thing, Henry," Sukey told him, quickly and with a deep earnestness. "You know he wouldn't. But he does smile horridly sometimes, especially when he thinks he's going to be hurt. I'm going to get you over it, Rom."

"Henry, there's no one—"

"Let it go, old boy," Henry broke in when I stammered. "I know you want to say something comforting, and I'll take the will for the deed. Now I'm going to *jao jaldi* the hell out of here."

As he spoke, he moved with increasing speed. As he gained the oleanders, he waved his hand. Turned a little sideways from me, Sukey gazed after him. But there was no way of hiding those big hot tears, and in the end she did not try.

Chilled to the bone, as by an icy wind on a desolate moor, yet I went to her and kissed her eyes dry.

"I'm so glad you did that, Rom," she told me. "I was afraid you wouldn't."

"What made you cry?"

"About us, not about him. To think that knowing all this, we went ahead anyway. It's unbelievable that you and I—Rom and Bachhiya—could have been so brave."

"In the plays of the Middle Ages, the Gypsy was a stock character. Sometimes he was a knave and sometimes a fool, but he was always a poltroon."

"Sahibs—especially newcomers—think Indians are cowards. They're wrong."

"Is it worse than you expected?"

"Yes. It's not what the people say—it's what they don't say, and I have an awful feeling that it's the same when we're not in hearing. One person tells another, and neither makes any comment."

"Do many people know it already?"

"The whole post. That's my doing, of course. Papa came into my room early this morning, and asked me to send you a chit immediately, asking you to keep it secret for a few days. He hadn't closed his eyes all night, of course. His only possible reason was the hope he could break it off. I told him so, and that I was going to let nature take its course. I helped nature along by dropping over to see Martha Caldwell right after breakfast. The woman actually turned white. You should have seen her mouth, exactly like a carp's. She didn't bother about the details—the fact alone surpassed her fondest dreams. She couldn't get me out of the house fast enough, so she could set sail."

When I started to speak, Sukey kissed me. "Wait till you hear the rest. Mildred Ager invited me for tiffin, and of course everybody came by. Each had something fixed to say, worded as carefully as a prime minister's statement for the press. Nobody used the good old word 'congratulations.' Most of them said they wanted me to be happy—a few wanted both of us to be happy—not a soul said we would be happy. There was no cattishness, though—no glee that Henry's saved and I'm out of the running. The disaster was too great for jealousy to function—they were all united as women are when plague breaks out at a cantonment. None thought me fast or wayward or even foolish—their manner was much the same as though I had gone insane."

"Well, maybe you have. What did Henry say? Gerald told me last night that he'd proposed."

"Henry said, 'I might have known it!' and some sweet things to me. But what did Gerald say? Whatever he told you, you'd believe."

She was excited and somewhat flattered over Gerald's following and spying on her yesterday. Then she leaped ahead of my story.

"He knew all the time that you were his half-brother, and half-Gypsy," she said. "And of course he asked if you'd told me."

"Yes."

"Did he ask you *when* you'd told me?"

"Yes, and although he tried to conceal it, he was mighty distressed that I'd waited—"

"Until I wasn't in my right mind?" Sukey's eyes were indrawn and intensely bright. "Then you remembered what Papa said about horsewhipping. I wish I'd been there. I wish we'd eloped last night."

"I'd be in the clink right now, as a deserter."

"But we *are* married—aren't we? We haven't gone through the ceremony, but we belong to each other forever."

She was sitting very still, speaking in a low voice, but when I moved my arms a little in invitation or entreaty, she flung into them, her breast pressed hard as a child's against mine. Her quick, countless kisses covering my face seemed to tell me that she was frightened; they became fiercely hungry, my lips between her teeth felt exquisite pain.

"Show me, Rom," she gasped.

"Here?"

"Prove it to me again. Show me you're not afraid or

sorry or guilty. Yes—*here!* Someone might come—but the danger—is very little—compared to—"

The garden wall was high, but there were only oleander shrubs to cut off the view of the windows of the Colonel Sahib's house. There was no poetic tower to the desert stars or Gypsy bed to bless in the beauty of love. All our fears of the future, greater than we could understand let alone confess, and all our guilts which we must deny or defy, were transmuted into lust, or else were somehow exorcized by lust. It broke upon two people who loved each other, and in Sukey's case, love broke its chains, but even with her it was no function of the spirit, only of the new-wakened, stark, demanding flesh. There was no poetry in this mating. There was no time for tenderness as in rough haste we sought one assurance from each other and to ourselves, frantic lest it fail, our faces drawn, our eyes sunken and soulless, and lost to pride and shame.

Yet when Sukey's deep, anguished breathings ceased, and we were sitting side by side, we both knew that instead of being weakened by the savage experience, we were immensely strengthened by it. Its very commonness in the real meaning of the word—committed by countless thousands of lovers in a myriad holes and corners of the earth—reassured us of the broad humanity of our union, and hence of its honesty and hope.

"But it couldn't have happened," she told me, "no matter how much I loved him, with any other man."

"With any other man you wouldn't have been you—Bachhiya—but Memsahib Sukey Webb, the Colonel's daughter," I replied.

A high tide of happiness, different from bliss, rolled in upon us until the moment of my departure. Then her deep and tender concern for me, the like of which I had never known, raised mine to exultation.

"You won't care what anyone says?" she asked.

"No one will say anything—except perhaps Clifford Holmes."

"Don't be so sure. You put too much confidence in sahibs—look up to them too much, I suppose on account of Gerald. They can be wonderful gentlemen up to a point, but I've heard how some of them talk to natives when they're put out about something. I've seen how coldly contemptuous they can be to someone 'on the make.' They're not half as fine as women, in the pinch. Women are mean and spiteful up to a point, then they'll rally around like old troupers."

"I don't expect to have my back slapped—"

"Whatever they say—straight out or in cold little 'reallys!' or 'fancy thats'—let it roll off you like water off a duck. Will you?"

"Sweetheart!"

"Remember you're the most gifted man in the regiment, and you'll go farther than any of them, with me to help you. And Rom—no matter how they act—don't you ever be sorry, or feel guilty—"

"Fancy that!"

"Don't you dare give them the satisfaction of thinking you feel ashamed or beneath them in any way. If you do, I'd never forgive you. You're the man I love, and the one I chose."

"Well, I wish I'd told you about my colorful origins before you fell in love—"

"I wish Gerald had kept his damned public-school moralisms to himself. It's none of his damned business, anyhow. I wish we hadn't agreed to wait two weeks for a ceremony. There was no use of it—even if the vicar would put up our banns, he'd almost rather lose his living than marry us without Dad's consent. I'd much rather go to the Methodist Mission. We will, won't we?"

"Yes, or to a Hindu guru."

"Can't you persuade Major Graves to assign you duty away from the post for most of these two weeks? I'd get along with seeing you only occasionally—meeting you in town or anywhere—to save you from having to be around Papa and those pukka sahibs. Just so he doesn't give you dangerous duty."

"I think that may work out all right." I repeated what Graves had told me.

"You haven't got your witch's charm any more. Thank heaven you've got Hamyd—and me."

"Thank heaven!"

"Good night, my love! The moon won't shine—and

143

the music won't play—and the flowers won't smell—until you're in my arms again!"

Anything like a quarrel was unthinkable during regimental mess. The honor of the regiment demanded that no officer ever raise his voice to another during the rite of bread and salt. Long ago two captains had risen from the table at dessert and fought a duel to the death under the deodar trees; but not an angry glance had passed between them during the assembly. Indeed the least discourtesy toward me there seemed highly unlikely. Although Colonel Webb had announced that he would be absent tonight, and therefore the men could dine in undress uniform and would not toast the Queen, the ceremonious atmosphere induced by the trophies on the walls and the regimental plate on the board and the liveried servants behind their chairs would be hard to ruffle. A more dangerous time would be before and after the meal, if I joined my messmates talking and drinking in the lounge. I arranged to enter the rooms just as our *khan-saman* announced dinner, and intended to leave them when the second-in-command rose from the table.

Even this precaution seemed unnecessary as we filed into mess hall. Perhaps because he could not stomach dining with me this soon after my victory, Clifford Holmes was absent from his place. Gerald gave me a wave and a smile; there was no occasion for Henry or any of the others to address me. I thought that the men were quieter than usual and what talk there was, was carefully confined to shop. Indeed, only one person at the board gave me the slightest uneasiness—Lieutenant Winston Loring, the newest addition to our rolls. It was said that Colonel Webb had not wanted him in the Tatta Lancers, but could not get out of taking him, since his father had been an officer of the regiment and he himself a boy wonder at Sandhurst. In addition to a bad complexion and buck teeth—perhaps partly because of these handicaps—he had an unengaging personality. At times he was too anxious to please, at other times too quick to quarrel.

During the meat course he leaned across the long table and spoke to me in a tone I found markedly unpleasant. Perhaps, having been somewhat ground down himself, he was glad to find someone whom he might grind down. Perhaps he was merely nervous.

"I hear you've proven yourself quite a lady's man," he said.

I acknowledged the remark with half a smile and attacked my meat. The officers near me did not appear to hear; one of those beside Loring stiffened a little and looked away. The other said quietly, "Children should be seen and not heard."

Loring flushed, and when I glanced at him again there was a sullen expression on his boyish, unprepossessing face. He was staring at his plate, but only toying with his food. I wished that the dinner were over, so I could go.

The plates were removed and when the servants had filled our glasses with a sweet wine to go with dessert, they left the room. The men had begun to sip the drink when, to my great alarm, Loring rose to his feet.

"Sir, may I offer a toast?" he asked the second-in-command sitting in the Colonel's place.

Lieutenant Colonel Maddock eyed him up and down in cold, contemptuous appraisal—one of the most insulting acts I had ever seen committed at a dinner table.

"There is no rule against a junior subaltern offering a toast at dinner," he said, with that patently mock gravity more stinging than a sneer.

"I waited for one of the older officers to do it, but I dare say they either don't know the occasion, or it's slipped their minds," Loring went on. "Gentlemen, let's rise and drink to the forthcoming marriage and future happiness of the Colonel's daughter and our messmate, Romulus Brook. Let's show 'em we're happy in their happiness. Rom, you're a lucky fellow, and she's a lucky girl. Gentlemen, let's rise and drink—"

He stopped, because his voice could no longer flow against that dam of silence.

Gerald got quickly to feet, and so did Major Graves. A captain on the other side of the table whom I hardly knew, the only officer in the regiment who had come up from the ranks, rose and stood as stiff as though on the parade ground, his glass in front of him held with an

145

upright forearm as though it were his sword. But Henry Bingham, two places down from the pale, staring Loring, made a little sighing sound and gazed at the ceiling. All the other officers of the Tatta Lancers sat motionless with starkly expressionless faces.

Loring's hand shook, then steadied, and he raised his glass to his lips. Major Graves gave forth a low, deep-throated, "Hear! Hear!" and drank as though unaware of the reverberating silence. The captain opposite slowly drained his glass to the last drop. I saw all this out of the side of my eyes, it seemed, for the only one I gazed upon was Gerald.

He did not reach for his glass. Instead his clenched hands went to his sides, a position I had seen him take a few times in his life when he was furiously angry and trying to keep his self-control. Then he spoke in clipped, dry tones to Lieutenant Colonel Maddock.

"Sir, I beg to be excused from this board to write out my request for transfer—"

"Thanks, old man, but this is my affair," I broke in.

"Well, I'm not going to sit here—"

"Wait a moment, and perhaps the Colonel will be good enough to excuse both of us."

Gerald looked inquiringly into my eyes, and when I smiled at him, he moved around the table as though waiting for me, not far behind my chair. He was white but appeared perfectly steady. When the three toasters took their seats, I rose.

"Sir, I want to thank Major Graves, Captain Tisdale, and Lieutenant Loring for the toast," I said. "Also, I ask to be relieved for the moment from all obligations of military rule—"

"Permission is not granted," Colonel Maddock broke in. "But, in behalf of all who did not join in the toast, I apologize for a discourtesy to you that we felt we could not help. Gentlemen, this regrettable incident is never to be mentioned again, either among ourselves or to anyone else. I declare it closed."

"Hear! Hear!" someone cried.

"Lieutenant Brook, as far as your military career is concerned, we say *'Rung ho!'*"

"And as far as my social career goes, I say to all but three of you, *'Bosa mera puttha!'* "

There was no one here so deficient in Hindustani that he did not understand the vulgar invitation. Translated literally from English, the words themselves had an insulting sound when roundly and emphatically pronounced. I looked at the second-in-command, and my salute turned into the ancient gesture that meant the same.

One other gesture I made, half by instinct. It was to stop and give Gerald precedence in going out the door. That was his privilege by rank, but I let him know—and perhaps all the watchers too—it was also his right in my heart.

CHAPTER SIXTEEN

Fury and Its Handmaiden

I FOLLOWED GERALD TO HIS ROOM. Then he poured me a drink of whisky, diluted it with water, and handed it to me as though it were medicine I direly needed. No mirror was near by to disclose my face to me, but I felt its clammy sweat, my knees trembled, and I despised the fast, feeble beat of my heart. When I was seated in his big chair, he sat on the bed, his chin resting in his palm.

"Gerald, I ask you to throw overboard right now any notion of applying for transfer from the regiment."

"I don't see why. Anyway, I'm half committed—"

"You're not committed in the least. If necessary you can discuss it with the second-in-command—not Colonel Webb, who will have no official knowledge of the affair—and of course he'll ask you to stay on. For the good of the regiment—and your own good—you'll agree to do so."

My brain was working perfectly well, as it had often done before, despite my limp, spent body.

"I confess, Rom, that until tonight I couldn't have wanted more pleasant associations than with those fellows. Why, I liked 'em all—except Clifford—and thought they liked me. The regiment was my pick of the whole Army. But from now on—"

"From now on—at least very soon—I'm going to be gone. I'll have my transfer to the Survey—I'm breaking orders in telling you this—as soon as the recommendation can be sent through channels. Meanwhile I'll be away from the post as much as possible. Thirteen days from today Sukey and I will be quietly married by a missionary, and she'll join me, wherever I've been sent."

148

"Wait just a minute." Gerald wiped his cheeks and lips with nervous force. "Rom, are you sure—oh, damn it—that Sukey can stand it? She'll hear about it, no fear. You don't think, do you, that such extreme and bitter opposition by her father's regiment might break it up?"

Gerald was speaking with growing difficulty. His throat and jaw muscles worked painfully. I interrupted him.

"It might break up some engagements. It was open declaration that if she marries me, she'll be ostracized. But it won't break up ours."

"At least you'll postpone the marriage until the worst blows over? There'd be sense to that."

"No, neither of us would consider postponing it."

"Then she's a mighty strong-minded girl—as well as being head over heels in love—and you—but I admire you for it—you're a mighty strong-minded man."

"Others will say I'm a rotten cad. The decent thing would be to write a letter, resign my commission, and disappear. Well, that's not what's going to happen. We're going to marry, and strange as it may seem to the sahib world, we're going to be happy. My work in the Survey will take us all over India and will be exciting to us both. We can associate with natives and half-castes; and, after all, we may not be ostracized by the best society out here. If I accomplish enough, we'll sit at the Governor General's table with Colonel Jacob."

His eyes gleamed when I said that last. He got out his pipe, filled it with a steady hand, and lighted it with a friction match.

"I'd be much more hopeful if you hadn't told the mess to—" Suddenly Gerald sat up straight, growing excitement in his face. "*Oh, my God!*"

"I first asked permission to speak freely, and was refused."

"Well, you spoke freely! You addressed the mess in general and the second-in-command in particular. And what in hell will happen—"

"I don't think anything will happen," I broke in. "They're all Old School boys and Englishmen besides. I'm attached to the Tatta Lancers—I mess and serve

149

with them—despite some righteousness, they feel pretty sneaking about refusing the toast. As Englishmen, they wanted to see me stand up for myself. Also the second-in-command won't want any issue raised—perhaps for a screamer in the *Globe*. I'll wager he said again, as soon as we were out of the room, that the thing was to be dropped with a dull thud. I think all the men were glad to count it even and call it off."

Gerald considered, his hands clasped about his knee in a position that recalled his boyhood.

"I daresay you're right," he replied at last, "and I'll stay with the regiment."

It hardly seemed possible that I could shoot so straight and yet miss the mark. My reasoning was perfectly right and my general deduction completely wrong. Gerald's and my parting was quietly cheerful. That night I dreamed of a coiled snake that I tried in vain to kill—the sign of an enemy, according to our Berkshire farmer folk. But I could almost smile over the warning—days behind the Fair—and I meant to stay clear of his fangs until Sukey and I together could clear out of the country.

Yes, I would keep out of all thick grass. While congratulating myself on this wisdom, meanwhile finishing breakfast that Hamyd had served me in my quarters, a bearer delivered a chit. It was in bold handwriting and it read:

Romulus Brook:
If you are not on duty, I have business with you on the skittles green at once. I am sure you would rather have it done there than in a more public place. Do not appear in uniform because the lesson I am going to teach you doesn't concern the military.
Clifford Holmes

I felt my lips curling and straightened them quickly. It had been the start of the smile that Sukey had promised to break me of—the way I smiled when I thought I was going to be hurt. But I should be giving it in spite of her. As it was, the sorrow drowning my heart was unmitigated by pride. The smile had never been a sign of

150

pride, but being able to give it had somehow made me proud. It was not meet that anyone alive should see my face now as I groped about in my closet for clothes fit to wear to the meeting.

My legs walked me toward the skittles green, like two friends walking a drunken cupmate to sober him up. I should thank Clifford for choosing this place instead of a more public one. Surely it was as well suited to the present business as it had been to my first intrigue with Sukey. Here we had made plans for our first stolen intimacy; I was on the inside track even then, Gerald had told me later. I had told myself that the conspiracy was not against him—I could not possibly damage a love worthy of his winning—but perhaps I had damaged it then and there, in the unknown deep of his heart, and then he had found good reasons, absolving both of us from blame, for dropping out of the race. Despite its seclusion, I wished Clifford and I had met at some other place.

He was seated on the base of a piece of sculpture imaging a crouching, snarling tigress, probably an ancient symbol of the goddess Kali. He was dressed as though for tennis, and I had never before marked so well his broad shoulders, narrow waist, and smooth, long limbs. His muscular development was so symmetrical as to deceive the careless eye; to my now careful eye, it showed remarkably powerful. I had never before observed his short, tomcat neck.

But a strange thing happened during this observation. Not until this moment had I fully realized and conceded how large was his physical advantage over me, in what the tommies called a "stand-up" fight—perfectly obvious to anyone who knew us. In my mind, I had tried to dodge the patent fact—hoping against hope that the quickness and toughness of my body could offset his longer reach and greater strength. Suddenly admitting the truth, I felt that swift refreshment of spirit and quickening of brain, as so often when I faced reality, as though it were a broom to sweep away the blinding dust of lies. In that instant I had become a more dangerous antagonist.

He rose gracefully as I came.

"I received your note," I told him, "and I wasn't on duty."

"Good. We can get this over in jig time."

"You spoke of some business you had with me, better done here than in public. What is it?"

"I believe you know. I think you're putting on a little act, shamming innocence, to get off as light as possible. I fancy my chit was in perfectly plain English—it would have been to any real Englishman. But considering various things, I'll make a brief explanation first of what I'm going to do second."

He rather fancied the way he had put it. He paused briefly for me to appreciate it. I made no comment.

"To start with, I've nothing to say about you and Sukey becoming engaged. That's not my business. If I had been at dinner last night, I, too, would have refused to drink the toast, but that would have been on general principles. As it happened, though, I'd stayed away. And that proved to be a very lucky thing."

He paused, expecting me to ask him why. I merely waited.

"You did something there that the other fellows can't take any action on," he continued. "Colonel Maddock ordered everybody there to let it drop. But you see, Rom—I wasn't present. I didn't receive that order. I *can*, without disobedience, take action on it."

Again I waited, and the coolness, the nonchalance he was showing, that of an English gentleman *plus* a sahib —*burra* as well as pukka, as I jolly well saw—became a little spotty.

"I don't know how you got your hands on Sukey," he said, his eyes changing shape and glistening, "but I do know you insulted the second-in-comand and a number of my messmates. Because they wouldn't drink to your marriage with a memsahib—they'd see you in hell first—you used a vile expression and gesture. If you were a gentleman—of course this wouldn't have happened in that case—I'd feel it my duty to send you my card. As it is, I've got another duty, and it will be sterling pleasure as well. By now you must have guessed what it is."

"Is this a guessing-game, Clifford? You should have

told me in the beginning. But let's get it over, whatever it is."

"That suits me perfectly. Take off your coat."

"And then what?"

"I'm going to spoil your appearance for a few days, Rom. Sukey's not going to like the way you'll look, old boy, when I'm finished with you. You can account for it any way you like. If you want to complain to HQ, you can. I'll explain that it's completely unofficial—neither of us was in uniform—that I felt you needed a little treatment, and gave it to you."

"Of course you realize that you outweigh me by two stone." I was unbuttoning my jacket. "You're half a head taller with far more reach—"

"You should have thought of that, my lad, before you opened your dirty mouth last night."

"On the contrary, pistols, or even sabers, might fetch a reasonably fair fight." I was drawing my left arm from the sleeve.

"I'm not interested in a fair fight, or any other kind. You don't seem to be as clever as usual—and hurry up with that jacket! This is instruction. As I told you in the note, I'm going to teach you a lesson—"

At that instant I taught him one. I had not roamed the alleys of Trieste and frequented the dives of Tunis without accumulating a good deal of useful information in several widely diverse fields. I had now removed my coat and was holding it by the lapels, as though about to lay it on the stone tiger. My dazed-seeming movement in that direction had carried me within five feet of my impatient enemy, and at that distance I could not miss my throw. As the garment went over his head, I struck him with all my strength full in the belly.

He went down. The great James (Deaf) Burke would have done the same. It was necessary that he stay down until his dangerousness was removed. I knew how to effect that, also. I intended to be very thorough; and fury and its handmaiden, cruelty, caused me to love the work with a passionate love—even to give it fancy touches. After blackening both eyes, bashing in his nose, and making raw pulp of his lips, I recalled again what he had said about changing my appearance, and so went over the ground again to make sure I had changed his.

When he showed signs of returning to consciousness, I went to our clubrooms and without looking or speaking to any of my messmates there, I tacked Clifford's letter on our bulletin board. A glance over my shoulder as I was going out the door showed two men reading it. That they would visit the skittles green in the course of a very few minutes there was no doubt.

CHAPTER SEVENTEEN

Premonition of Evil

THEN THERE WAS JUST TIME TO GET INTO UNIFORM, and report to Major Graves's office for the day's orders.

He interrupted his talk with a General Staff officer to hand them to me. Our salutes were punctilious, but there was a glint in his eyes that did me a wonderful turn. I could not call him friend, but certainly he was not a foe. An observer on the world, inclined to keep clear of other peoples' lives, he had joined in the toast last night with more amusement than emotion, tickled to be standing with the self-made captain and the worm subaltern, and no doubt boundlessly delighted with the complete enormity of the ensuing outrage. Well, most friendships are a community of interests. Men who work alone make few. If I could have Sukey, I would not ask for even one.

When I read the paper in the orderly room, I knew he had stood up for me again. Of the many "boresome tasks" he could have assigned me, he had appointed me the very one that Sukey would desire for me—taking me away from the post for several days into an uninhabited sand-hill area west of Kotri where no tribesman had any occasion to raid. I was to locate its *dhands* and *sims*—kinds of desert ponds and springs—and especially to seek and follow the dry bed of a fabled river. It would be best for me to wear Moslem dress—if a caravan passed in distant view it would cause less comment —and to take only one servant. Our riding-horses and two pack ponies would furnish our transport.

With my native garments in a saddlebag—I did not want to be challenged at the gate—I rode along the Quarters to find Sukey. Hamyd had already informed me that Colonel Webb was in the field, and, by a little more rise in the new-turned tide of luck, my sweetheart was at home. Would I wait till she made herself presentable? Her ayah, big of eye, brought me the inquiry from upstairs, and carried back my reply—that I had to be on my way in twenty soldiers', not ladies', minutes. Thereupon, blushing at the grave impropriety, she appeared in a dressing-gown.

She stood in the door of the big drawing-room where we had defied Colonel Webb, and where I now waited with a kind of vision of him sitting tall beside a massively carved table. I was chilled by it, until her eyes shone upon me and her yellow hair made for me a palely beautiful sun.

"Come into the library, Rom. It's shocking enough to receive you there, undressed as I am. Here it would be *bloody awful!*"

I stood close to her and spoke in so low a tone that no big-eared servant could hear. "I've seen you dressed only in a mixture of moonlight and firelight."

"Do you think it's gentlemanly to remind me of it?" she asked, simulating primness so well I could almost think it real. I did not think she could have played the little game if her heart was heavy. It did not seem possible that she had heard what had happened at mess last night.

"Maybe it's not gentlemanly, but it might be comforting," I answered.

"It is! Isn't that strange? Maybe it isn't even strange; we only think it ought to be. Comfort comes from a feeling of security." She had taken my hand and was leading me into the library. "When people feel secure, they can make themselves comfortable almost anywhere. Look how comfortable we made ourselves with a couple of horse blankets and a bottle of arrack on a stone platform?"

"Do you think it's ladylike to remind me of it, Sukey?"

"No, but it's comforting."

"That's what I meant. The comfort's lasted all this while, because—two nights ago—we got some security. It doesn't look like that, does it? At least we won a better chance to stay together—we forged a bond that we'd fight like fiends before we'd let anyone break. Sukey, may I close the door?"

"Would you have that much cheek? We're in the Colonel Sahib's house, and I'm in a dressing-gown."

"That adds to the excitement."

"No, you can't close it. The servants would whisper their heads off, and some of the whispering might get to Papa's ears."

"I don't know if it matters any more. Anyway—that corner of the room isn't visible from the hall outside."

She went there quickly, fine sweat on her brow and a wistful expression on her face, more empassioning than lechery itself. But the lovely look became only more poignant, until suddenly she imprisoned my hand in hers, and the desire dreamy in her eyes changed to a gleam of ribald mirth.

"Rom, have you ever seen the fakir's rope trick? You know—throwing up the rope, and then climbing it?"

"I never met anyone who has."

"Parbati told me she'd seen it. Anyway, when the fakir pulls up the rope, where is he?"

"I give up."

"He's left up in the air. Well, that's where I don't want to be. I don't know when I could come down. We'll sit sedately on the sofa and talk."

All mirth defies the long-faced solemnities of life, and the ribald sort makes game of long-toothed, flat-chested, thin-shanked, many-petticoated Propriety herself. I was always delighted to have it crop out in Sukey. But I thought all mirth would pass from her when I told her, as it seemed I must, about Lieutenant Loring's toast.

I was wrong on both counts. When we were seated, she said cheerfully, "I hear the regiment gave us quite a sendoff."

"Can you joke about it, Sukey?"

"It's a tremendous joke, really. Those solemn waxworks around the table—fancying they were being so damned pukka—Rule Britannia—God save the Queen—all the time they were making complete jackasses of themselves. Can you imagine Lord Melbourne, or even Prince Albert, refusing to drink that toast? I wasn't a bit surprised though, except by—" Sukey stopped, her already high color rising a little more.

"By what?"

"Maybe I shouldn't have mentioned it, but, after all, we mustn't hide our thoughts from each other. Two things surprised me. One that Henry didn't drink to us, and the other that Gerald did."

"I don't understand that."

"Henry is an aristocrat, and just misses being a nobleman. The doctrine of *noblesse oblige* should have made him stand for the big things, not the little ones. In public at least he should have stood by you instead of by Papa—I can't explain that, but it's true. What they did was not only a silly but a vulgar gesture. I dare say he was so resentful that he couldn't see straight."

"I agree with you, I think. But why you should be surprised at Gerald—"

"I suppose I'm not, really. I told you before he's a lot deeper than he seems. He *seems* romantic enough to have sat with the other fools—even making a little speech that no matter how much he loves you and 'respects' me he couldn't drink to a wedding that he disapproved of. He's bound to disapprove of you, you know —that makes his support all the more wonderful. No, he couldn't refuse—the explanation would have been too difficult. Anyway I suppose he was so angry—"

"He was plenty angry. So much so, he never did— now that I come to think of it—actually drink the toast. He stood up with the others and announced he was going to apply for transfer, and then left the room without picking up his glass. I had to talk him out of any notion of leaving the regiment."

"What about Clifford?"

"He wasn't at mess."

"I know that, but he's bound to do something to get back at you. He's the one I'm most afraid of. He really hates you."

I decided not to tell her of my meeting with Clifford. She would probably not be amused by the mental picture I had of him this minute—plasters all over his face and raw meat on his eyes.

"What are you smiling about?" she asked.

"I have no occasion to smile, I assure you."

"Yes, you have. You've got me, who'll never quit hugging myself over what you told the mess. Mildred came to me with the story early this morning—first apologizing for disobeying Colonel Maddock's ruling—she wouldn't do it if it weren't best for me to know—I must never tell a soul—so forth and so on. Then when she got to where you stood up and spoke, she said she couldn't tell me the words you'd used, but they were coarse and insulting. I told her if she stopped there, I'd go to her husband. When she whispered them in my ear, I whooped with joy!"

Sitting beside her, I never saw anyone more alive. Her hair seemed to have light of its own; the color in her face was always in process of change; I watched the wonderfully buoyant rise and fall of her breasts.

"Gerald thought it might make you back out on the deal."

"What!"

"The whole thing was a sure sign you'd be ostracized. He was deeply troubled and thought we'd better postpone the ceremony until the worst blew over."

"Were you tempted to do it?" she asked.

"You know better than that."

"Well, you're so influenced by what he says. For once he was just weak in the head. I only wish I didn't have to be afraid of anything but being ostracized. What's this duty you're on now? I saw Hamyd in the compound, with four horses."

"It was just what you were hoping for. I'll tell you just before I go, to cheer us both up."

"Mildred acted surprised and pretty shocked when I let go that gleeful yell. I wonder if she was, really! She's a woman—she ought to know how I'd feel. There's a lot of very strange pretending going on. I wonder how she would have acted—and how much of it would have been faked—if she'd known the other feeling that came over me. It's a wonder she didn't see it in my face. Can you guess what it was?"

"No."

"Suddenly my pride in you made me want you un-

159

bearably. I wanted to feel your strength. She was sitting on the edge of the bed, and I wanted her to be you."

"I wouldn't have sat there long."

"Don't say that now. Not now." The pupils of her eyes became immense.

"Is there any place?"

"Not in the time you've got. You'd better go. All we're doing is tantalizing each other. Rom, have you ever heard this—Parbati told me—that at times of great danger people become more passionate? She says when plague hits an Indian city, the most carefully guarded virgins steal out to meet lovers—and lots of the women get babies. Rom, are we in worse danger than we'll admit or even think about? Not just being insulted—ostracized—but some real, terrible danger?"

I shook my head. It could mean "no," or "I don't know."

"I'm awfully afraid. Even the servants seem dangerous to me now. I would trust only one or two not to spy on us and then tell Papa—hoping for blood money. Although I the same as told him it had already happened, he'd say you ruined my reputation and heaven knows what he'd do. He's in a dangerous state of mind already —it wouldn't take much to make him run amuck. I can feel it in my bones."

"That's partly the reason you're staying out of my arms. What's the rest of it?"

"I don't—want—it to stop—hurting—until—"

She took both my hands and pressed them against her breast and then spoke evenly.

"I don't want it to stop hurting until after the ceremony. I want it to hurt so bad I can't even feel any other hurt that people try—or try not—to give me. I don't want to think of anything—any trouble or any danger—only of you."

She laid her lips softly against mine and kept them motionless while the tall clock in the corner ticked several times. Then its thin, black, evil-looking hands remorselessly moving told us that less than five minutes remained of our alloted time; and no doubt from some primeval impulse to propitiate the Dark Powers, we resisted the temptation to prolong it. As the sharp spear

160

on the clock dial transfixed and slew the little periods, I reassured her about my mission, to take me far from the rebel villages, far from the post.

"Maybe we've been seeing ghosts," she said in flushed hope. "Papa didn't kill that sergeant—he didn't deliberately kill Mamma. He'll never forgive us but he won't really do anything, unless he's gone crazy. Clifford could be vengeful—hurt you a lot if he can—but he doesn't hate you enough to commit some awful crime."

I might as well tell her of my meeting with Clifford —she would hear it soon—but I could not now.

"It would take a lot of hate, and it's not in the cards," I said. "Now tell me good-by in the loveliest way you can."

The next minute, it seemed, I was riding, followed by Hamyd, through the Quarters gate. I was aware of disappointment not with circumstance but with myself, an angry sense of what might have been had I been a little more perceptive—or resourceful—or bold. It was a very familiar experience, and three times out of four my lack had been courage. Today I had feared Colonel Webb's return, and some disagreeable aftermath of my business with Clifford catching up with me. What if I never saw Sukey again? What if on the day we had expected to be united, she or I had died?

I felt a great starving, gnawing all the worse for the feast just missed. I wished I had asked Sukey to ride swiftly to the tower, where I could have met her only a little way off my course. Let proper sahib lovers behave temperately with their betrothed! I was a Gypsy, doomed to wander over the face of the earth, and might never pass this way again. I must drain every cup held out to me along the road, and finish every crumb. Sukey, I am too far behind on kisses, ever to catch up! Bachhiya, you do not know how long and deep the dearth. Now the dust of the desert is on my lips.

CHAPTER EIGHTEEN

Ambush

HAMYD WAS A CLOSE, WATCHFUL, but so far not a very cheerful companion. This was his first sharp parting with his former playmate and forever delight; and no doubt he had the feeling of her needing him just now. All that day he rode punctiliously behind me, declining my tacit invitations to fraternize with me or to discuss the topic uppermost in both our minds. Partly this was his sense of propriety with a johnny-come-lately, and partly a kind of *pooja* against bad luck. When English people speak what the Devil may use against them, they quickly knock on wood. Indians try to button their lips before the risk is run.

Certainly I must not rush matters. My relations with Hamyd could be not only a great joy but a great strength, one of the three most important in my present life, if carefully promoted and cherished. At present it was in its most delicate stage. There was no jaundice in his eye; it seemed to me that he was highly disposed in my favor; and his profound brotherly love for Sukey was without a trace of even unconscious jealousy. But I had an appallingly great deal to live up to, in his eyes. If he were a general accompanying me, I would not have been more anxious to say and do what he considered the right thing, but with so little knowledge of his standards, I did not dare try to impress him. In the main, I relied on my instincts and in particular on the one main, certain fact of our bond—the joining of our hands by our beloved.

On the second day I ventured to speak occasionally of her beauty, her dash, or her wit. Though he made little verbal acknowledgment, always his eyes glowed.

Meanwhile I was discovering what a competent servant he was. A superb rider—meaning he could ride all day without undue tiring of himself or his mount—he had an expert's knowledge of horse handling and care. Our bivouacs were the most comfortable I had ever seen on the desert. Fires blazed up as by magic under his hand and directly became the right size and kind for cooking; what he needed to prepare a tasty meal was always in the first saddlebag he opened; the unhurried economy of his movements was a delight to my eyes. After our first camp, I never again concerned myself with our commissary or any impedimenta—knowing the horses would be watered, fed, rested, and ready to ride, and there would be water in the jugs, arrack in my flask, good clean food on the cloth, and a comfortable bed, all at the appointed time.

I felt that he saw, heard, and smelled much that I missed. These things were of no danger to us, or he would call my attention to them; later I hoped he would let me share them with him for the sake of companionship and our mutual pleasure. Our relationship warmed gradually during the first three days of our journey, and in the morning of the fourth. In the early afternoon of that day, when we had had to dismount and tie our horses in order to follow the big, dry bed of the unknown river through deeply gullied ground, it seemed that we had broken the last ice and were entering upon a new relationship akin to that established between sahib hunters and their gunbearers. Speaking very little, but aware of companionship, Hamyd and I were walking side by side.

Suddenly he lifted his head in a thoughtful way, and then came to a dead halt. His head was cocked a little to one side, as though he were listening to some faint, far-off sound, and he sniffed long.

"Sahib, I smell something—"

"What is it?"

"It is a stale smell, very faint, but bad. It is like—"

Then his eyes fixed on a steep-walled gully entering the river bed forty paces ahead of us. His position, a few feet from me, enabled him to look at it from a slightly different angle and behold what was still hidden

163

from me. A tremor ran through his body, leaving it rigid. Then he gasped out three Hindustani words.

"*Sahib, maut hai* [Master, it is death]!"

Then Death waiting in ambush moved, and I saw him plain. A carbine was in my hand, but I flung it from me as though it were a cobra, and in the same motion raised my arms high over my head.

These acts were prompted by hope so far below the level of consciousness that it was not much more than a blind instinct to struggle toward survival. A mountain climber falling from a high cliff would, perhaps, brace against the body-bursting impact with hardly less volition. It was a hope with which my ingelligence would not treat for the merest instant. It seemed that I beheld hopelessness as plain as day; the horror of death seized me in instantaneous cold grasp, but not its terror, which is the black umbrage of still glimmering hope. Even that would pass from me quickly.

Out of the gully sprang a score of 'wild-eyed, black-bearded Rind tribesmen. They raced with one another and with an equal number leaping from a near-by crevice, each striving to be the first to wet his high-brandished blade. They howled as they lunged across the little space of rough ground between them and their goal; and my ears, listening and interpreting with extreme precision—doing well by me, it might seem, in this last office—distinguished drunkenlike laughter as well as fanatical shouts of fury. The space narrowed, quickly according to watch time, while long I lived on according to soul time—measurable by the amount I saw and heard and thought. All this was exceedingly vivid but seemingly impersonal—as though it were being shown to a spectator. No doubt my emotional responses to the events, although of extreme power, were depotentiated and drowned in horror of impending death.

The race was but half run when I picked the winner. It was a tall, young, Arab-looking Rindi who had been the first to leap from the ambuscade. All but one of the rest scurried toward me in a wolflike pack, while a richly dressed graybeard, hopeless now of sinking his steel in living flesh, plunged mightily in the rear. Both Hamyd and I waited motionless, my arms stiffly raised,

164

Hamyd's stiff at his sides. In the several seconds of the murder race we could have run and dodged, surely prolonging it a brief, hideous while; but perhaps the flintlock muskets carried by about half of the tribesmen stifled the thought. Or perhaps we had other guidance. Actually if there was a grain of unknown, unrecognized hope in the deep of our souls, we were playing it, by instinct, in the same way.

If so, it appeared to fail. The winner bore down on me, the sword in his upraised arm pointed behind him beginning its long chopping sweep. By then the lagging elder had shouted something clearly audible above the uproar—no doubt a vehement command which might have changed my fate had it not burst forth too late. The sword flashed high over the killer's head and lashed downward in a shining arc, perfectly aimed at the top of my head. My upright arms jerked forward and bent backward as its shield, but the instinctive act had no effect on my soul's surrender to death. That surrender was not realized in thought. It was like a wind blowing out a flame.

It was not the obstruction of the flesh and bone of my forearms over my crown that caused the killer to change his aim. That powerful stroke would drive the steel through them as through the pulp of my helmet to cleave my skull. For some other reason, which if I lived one second more I would grasp, the glittering streak veered from its straight-down course—curving outward around my forehead and then slashing inward at one side. Then I was blinded save for darts and streaks of light as from bursting stars; but a second passed, and I opened my eyes and lived.

I lived strongly, with my feet under me and my head above me and my soul tight-grasped, despite my right cheek being sheared away from eye socket to jawbone. I felt that same hard-to-finish flame, fierce and bright as though from inexhaustible oil, that had kindled my flesh and bone at my father's deathbed. It burned me wide awake to the present instant, its time and place and event, and particularly to the sudden lull in the violent action. I became sharply aware that the lull was the consequence of my standing here with a

165

gushing wound which for some reason, involving both my attacker and the graybeard, had bemazed the others' minds. That I was wounded but not dead had caused a dilemma which they were not immediately able to resolve.

Excited to my highest powers of perception and action—in love with the breath in my nostrils and the light yet in my eyes—I seized upon the circumstance as offering the only immediate chance to prolong Hamyd's and my reprieve from the waving swords. I played that chance for all it might be worth.

Taking no visible notice of my wound, I turned to Hamyd and spoke in Urdu, not loudly but perfectly audibly in the momentary abeyance of loud sound.

"Hamyd, what command did the venerable sheik give the young hotblood who nicked me with his sword?"

Hamyd answered in a wonderfully level tone.

"Sahib, his words were, 'Fool, let them die slowly!'"

"Then repeat my word to him in his own tongue." I faced the elder, and touched my forehead with the fingers of both hands. "O Sheik, since I have lived this long, I ask to live enough longer to sell thee a good horse."

Of all the things that he might have expected me to say, evidently this was not even the last.

"Feigning madness will not save thee a flaying of thy dog's hide, O Lomri, inch by inch. Then when thou hast sat awhile in the fly-swarm in the sun, thou wilt kiss my feet, thou destroyer of my kinsman Kambar Melik, in prayer that I cut thy throat."

"Aye, I was the destroyer of my Rani's enemy, Kambar Melik. Before that, I was the decoyer of the Emir's *lashkar* into the ditch at Meeanee. Even now, my life in pawn to thee, and direly bleeding, I am still Lomri. Thus it behooves thee to be on thy guard when I would sell thee a horse. Thou must still take care against the fox's cunning, lest thou be cheated in the deal."

The old sheik stood silent for several seconds. Against his will, it seemed, he was puzzling over this strange thing—perhaps trying to master the curiosity glimmering in his fierce eyes. In that desperately crucial interval, my heart could only flutter without strength to

166

beat. Then he tugged his beard—always a sign of vacillation—and spat copiously.

"Thy four horses, including the excellent mare, are mine for untying their halters," he growled. "What fox's bark is this?"

"Aye, and I am thy carrion for the least thrust of thy sword, so there is no need of haste. The stallion of which I speak is to the mare as a king's charger to a fellah's donkey, and his buying and selling is not a business to do while water may run out of a broken jar."

This last was an Arabic expression, usually employed to designate the limit of time with which a woman may be closeted with some man other than her husband without presumption of adultery. I thought it might be familiar to these Arabic-blooded Rindi, and the slight change in several fiercely haughty faces told me it was.

A poorly dressed fellow, with the marks of a cobbler, made a remark that caused a low nicker of acrid laughter. No one interfered with my asking Hamyd to translate it.

"Sahib, his words were, 'No business is well done in so short a space, except a seven-year sailor's with a seven-year widow, which is the fastest in the world,'" Hamyd replied.

"Then, O Sheik, have I thy leave to sit? The young man's playful tickling with his sword was of less delight than a beautiful virgin's with a wanton finger, but, lo, I am as faint as I ever was with love."

"Thou mayst sit, O dog with a fox's tongue. Truly the business of cutting it out, and cutting off thy other members one by one, until only thy Christian shame dangles from thy limbless trunk, need not be hastened. Not only we will take more pleasure in the sight, after due and savory delay. So will our kinsman, Kambar Melik, and they who died in the ditch at Meeanee, looking down from Paradise. We, too, will sit, out of the wind of thy foxy smell, and hear of the wondrous steed thou hast to sell."

I knew then that I was dealing not with a minor chief, but a well-born, literate Baluch sheik, although as bloodthirsty as his most ruffianly follower. It was his own lust to kill, thwarted by the swifter attack of the younger hillman, that had prompted the command to spare me for a while, and it was his fixed resolve that I die by torture. I did not think about that now. It was not necessary, in order to make the maximum effort, at the utmost height of my powers, to live on. Such effort was native to me. I could not slack it if I tried.

Only to live on! That was my sole aim, now, and would be for any period of time I could contemplate. If I lived, Hamyd might live, but that was the only way I could help him; no heroism in his behalf would enable him to draw one other breath. I had no sahib pride to stand between me and bare survival. I had tossed it away with my rifle. I had become the lowest Gypsy of them all.

Sukey, would you rather I die like a man than live like a dog? If so, I cannot grant your wish, or heed it at all. In a moment more you will be no longer in my life, so reduced it is. The time may come, a dream beyond a dream, that I may take you back, but I cannot treat with it now.

Farewell, Beauty that would have walked with me. Farewell, sentient flesh glowing to my kisses, craving interflow with mine, the greatest joy I had ever known. Farewell, Bachhiya, who came to me as a free girl, unconcerned with my deserving, who became integral with me, so for a little time I stood so tall! I can't have you any longer. I have to let you go.

But whether I die soon or live on in chains, I charge you in this parting with a most solemn charge. Can you hear me across this desert of our dissolution? Yes, for wherever you are, my spirit stands in your doorway, demanding, not entreating, a final troth.

You may not know my voice, or be aware of it at all, but your spirit will remember the charge at the hour of requitement. Look well at the hand offered you in place of mine! Mine was swarthy from dark birth, but make sure his is not stained black and red. If you do not, you will break the troth I am keeping even now, and there will be dreadful retribution. I would save you from it, as the last office of my love.

BOOK TWO

CHAPTER NINETEEN

A Fight for Life

My CAPTORS WERE RINDI TRIBESMEN of Arab descent, among the most stalwart, proud, and warlike in all the mountainous land between India and Persia. They made a half circle before Hamyd and me, their woolen lungis worn gracefully, and seeming both poised and in repose. Directly opposite me sat the gray-bearded sheik, addressed by his men as Mustapha, more richly dressed than his followers and wearing the biggest turban. The others were of all ages, and their rank was roughly designated by the height of the stones on which they sat. At Mustapha's right hand, sitting only a little lower, was a young headman or melik with a bullet burn along his temple, quite possibly a memento of Meeanee. He seemed the most impatient of the band to get on with their bloody work.

Perhaps they expected me to sit on a tall stone, either in soldierly pride, or as a token of sahib power. Instead I sat on the ground, a sign of defeat that I felt would calm rather than excite them. They listened intently as I addressed Hamyd, and one of them who spoke Urdu scornfully translated the conversation for some of his fellows.

"We are both captives of the Rindi, and I have no right to command thee. But as my fellow in evil fortune, wilt thou look carefully at my wound, and tell me its severity?"

"Much flesh has been cut away," Hamyd answered,

169

after a close inspection, "and thou art losing too much blood."

"A little blood makes a great show. Are the teeth visible through the rent?"

"No, sahib. A tissue of flesh remains."

"They will show well, when thy skull is sent to thy Colonel in Hyderabad, with plums in thy eye sockets," the translator broke in.

"We mean to take thy life grain by grain, as though gnawing an ear of young corn, but surely the cob will be fit only for swine, at this hour tomorrow," Mustapha Sheik proclaimed. Hamyd translated this with fluency and dignity.

"Aye, if that be my kismet. But sometimes a young ear is better left on the stalk, to furnish bread in winter, or even seed in planting time. Have I thy leave to speak further to Hamyd about my wound?"

"Aye, and we will listen, and not interrupt thee with loud laughter."

"Hast thou a cloth to stuff into the rent, to quench the worst of the bleeding?"

"Aye, sahib."

"Do not pack it so full I cannot freely work my jaw. I have a horse to sell to the great sheik, and must sing his praises well." Saying this helped me hide the pain of the stuffing of a strip torn from Hamyd's face cloth into the raw wound. Hamyd fastened the wadding with a bandage across the tip of my nose and tied over my left ear, then carefully repeated our conversation.

"We have seen enough of thy skill," the old sheik responded. "Now bid Lomri tell us of his wondrous steed."

"To begin, he stands seventeen hands when stoutly shod, and is pale brown in color."

"Why, he is tall enough for an emir to ride in state!"

"Truly, he is fit for the finest stall in the stable of Nazir Khan, and worth all of the half-hundred horses who broke their necks in a ditch at Meeanee."

"By Allah, this fox has a bold bark. But truly we remember the lambs he has riven and the poultry he has stolen without reminder."

"The Koran bids thee do justice to Allah's least creature, whether fox or worm. Truly Lomri rived no

170

lambs, or stole no hens. He slew or captured only lions of the desert—enemies of his Rani."

"That be true. Speak on of thy horse."

"He too served the Queen, on whose corn he fed. If thou were to capture such a horse, loose on the desert, wouldst thou slay him on account of that loyal service to thy enemy? Nay, thou wouldst put a bit between his teeth and a saddle on his back, and give him as a gift to thy Emir. He has won fame for his feats in battle, not only in his own country but in thine. He is well taught in many branches of learning and can speak many tongues, among them the language of thy forefathers, spoken at very Mecca."

The sheik gave his beard a short, fierce tug and addressed his followers. "How would a fox know any bark but his own—or perchance the whinings of the jackals of Hind? To deal plainly," he went on, turning to me, "thy *giaour* [Christian] ears could not recognize Arabic if they heard it."

"Do you speak the truth, O Sheik?"

He sat still, save for an almost invisible tremor down his body. "No, I've spoken falsely, which is a shame even to a horse-dealer—or a captive about to be given to the flaying knife."

"Will your followers understand if you, a sheik, address me, your captive, and suffer me to reply, in the language of the Prophet and the Koran? For seeing that they had a hand in my capture, in all justice they should give ear to such buying and selling as we may do."

I thought I was answered by a slight lifting of the tribesmen's heads. The sheik spoke with great pride.

"My clan came hence from the North, even the Sarawan, and we're Qoraish Arabs of unmixed blood. It's true that in dwelling among and trading with the Tajik people, we have come to employ their language in common dealings, but there's not a man of us who doesn't know a base bastard Arabic, truly a memento of the noble speech of our ancestors. My followers will comprehend enough, to discover every trick of your *giaour* tongue."

"Truly I'm a Christian, and have served the Christian Rani. Mark you, I do not plead, as some captives have, I be permitted to forswear my faith and embrace Islam, that I may live. As you've answered most of them, you would answer me. 'The mullah's thumbnail would unmake you a Christian, or a gelder's knife would save you from fatherhood of Christians, but only my sword at your throat will empty your veins of Christian blood.' "

"It is our very saying." When he glanced at his clansmen, their beards wagged sagely. "Also we say, 'There are two things that when broken may never be mended—a virgin's maidenhead and a soldier's faith.' You wouldn't have lived this long, O Lomri, had you whined to become a renegade."

"You've lived too long on any score," the bullet-marked headman broke in. "You seek to parry our swords while your kinsmen ride to your help. Kambar Melik was my uncle and my steel thirsts."

"And mine," rose another voice. And then other voices in a deep-throated growl, "And mine!" Some of the tribesmen were rising from their seats of stone.

"Fools!" Then, when the killers paused at my shout: "Truly, you deem Lomri a fool, to think I look for any help save by your own benefits. Why should my kinsmen fear for me, when I've been sent to survey an empty desert far from your villages? Why, it was needless to bring a rifle, save to shoot a gazelle for the pot."

I paused for dramatic effect—playing the dreadful game at the peak of my powers.

"Are you gazelles?" I asked. "If not, what strange chance brought you here?"

All were listening now, their thin lips curled downward, and a bright glint under their black eyebrows.

"Yes, it's a strange chance that we, journeying across these wastes, should catch sight of a sahib and his servant," Mustapha Sheik remarked blandly. "Then to discover that our captive was none other than Lomri—" He paused.

"In that case, all your winnings so far—four horses, bridled and saddled, good gear, and rifle—are a windfall of clear gain. That is nothing compared to the profit to be made on the Arabic-speaking horse. What will you give me for him and his groom?"

"The fool should be answered according to his folly, said Suliemen the Wise One. What's the asking price?"

"One quarter *karwar* [150 pounds] of carrion flesh unfit for food."

"Dog flesh, perchance?"

"Fox flesh would describe it better. That you may have, if you choose, in lieu of the horse. After the skull has been sent to the English serdar with plums in the eye sockets, you may bury the rest, or throw it to the vultures at your whim. But you will have no noble gift to send to Nazir Khan, so to win honor and reward for your clan."

"You are seventeen hands tall, and pale brown in color, and speak many tongues. Could it be that the fox has changed into a horse?"

"It was my jest, Mustapha Sheik, at the point of the sword."

"It was a bold jest truly, and not a dull one. Perchance my master Nazir Khan will relish it, also."

"By my beard, Mustapha," cried the nephew of Kambar Melik, called Kamel by his fellows, "it's a better jest than the jester himself knows. For that very carrion, Ali Khan, Vizier to the great Khan, has offered a hundred cattle."

"The word reached me long ago," I broke in. "When I was a soldier of the Rani, it made me proud. But you, effendi, must jest broadly, to hint that he would pay more for carrion than my living hand and brain. Is a thousand cattle too little to pay for a peerless slave to his throne?"

So I spoke, sitting in the dust and a queer sort of red mud. Beside me, Hamyd, taller than I, gazed toward the hills, revealing his profile to the foe. The attitude signified great pride. The greatest of the kings of the East thus presented themselves to history in carven stone and painted papyrus. My mind did not stop its work to explain to me why Hamyd was so proud. If I asked, the answer might be that, since he was the grandson of a sheik, he would not cower before his conquerors. That answer would have been reasonable but wrong. The right one I need not seek anywhere but in my heart—it was one of those unreasonable truths that can abide only there.

Hamyd was the grandson of a sheik, but even so, even now, he was a servant of a captive sitting in bloody dust, trying to sell himself into slavery that both of them might live. I had lost everything, but he had not lost me, and proudly he served me still. That was what he was telling the insolent foe. Full well they understood.

I wished I could borrow a little of his pride. What I showed my enemies had become a counterfeit, which they might at any moment discover. Every human being obtains his sense of identity by it being recognized by others, and I had an eerie sense of having lost mine, the same as when I discovered my stepmother's hatred and my alienship in my father's house. It was still reflected in Hamyd's mind and posture, but although the tribesmen addressed me as Lomri, the dangerous foe associated with that name had ceased to exist, now that I was helpless in their hands. The least of them could put out my shadow by walking a few steps and jabbing once with his sword.

Indeed the least of them was the most likely to do so, I thought with growing horror. It would be beneath the dignity of the chiefs. It seemed now I would not be worth the trouble of elaborate torture. I would be killed when the game played out, but in careless contempt.

"Great Sahib," Mustapha Sheik was saying in a florid tone, "so esteemed by your fellows that one of them sent us word where we might cross your path and do you honor—"

I did not hear the rest, and the part I had heard I already knew. I realized now I had known it at the first glimpse of the enemy ambush, but had put it by, somehow, so I could breathe better. My breath no longer seemed any good, of any use.

"If you won't buy the horse, at least make good use of his groom," I told him.

"For God's love, be still," Hamyd whispered.

"He was born in a sahib's service and is of your own faith, and has never raised his hand—"

174

"If we send you into slavery to our Emir, we will send him also," Mustapha Sheik replied. "If we give you to the kites and the jackals, as our judgments and hearts decree, we'll give him the like."

"That became my kismet when Bachhiya put me in thy service," Hamyd said with great dignity, for all to hear. "Fight on, master, that we both may live."

CHAPTER TWENTY

To Live for Revenge

AN ARGUMENT AROSE ABOUT a bird in the hand against two in the bush. Dead, I was certainly worth a hundred cattle—that had been secretly promised by Ali Khan, Vizier of the Emir—while sent to him alive, the hillmen's reward might be enough rope to hang them, for getting him in trouble with the English. This seemed reason enough to most of the tribesmen for cutting my throat at once, but the old sheik chose to prolong the game.

"It does not wholly lack spice," he told his fellows. Then he turned to me and spoke in mock gravity. "What service could you do our master, whereby none of his other slaves would be your peer?"

"Doesn't the Khan of Persia covet Nazir's crown and kingdom? Is Lomri so lacking in guile and the knowledge of war that he could not serve him to the worth of a hundred cattle?"

The old sheik stroked his beard. "That is a little more than spice, and might have a grain of salt."

"The salt of the *giaour* that his own comrade betrayed?" Kamel held his nose and spat. "Would you trust any swine-eater to serve our Emir? But we needn't sully our swords in his dog's flesh. Let each of us pick up a stone that he has strength to throw, and at your word, hurl it roundly, and he who misses the mark is a cuckold to his very *cobah,* made so by a black groom! Thus we may end the sorry game in something like sport."

Then from the beardless lips of a youth sitting far back on a low stone there rose the high-pitched, horrid yell of *"Ala-la-la-la-la!"* A terrifying animation flexed the bodies and kindled the faces of the others, but before they could spring up, Mustapha Sheik arrested them with a ringing command.

"Hold ye a moment more." And then when his followers turned sullen or scowling faces, "I am Mustapha ibn Ismael, Sheik of Habistan, and it is for me to say when and how the game ends. If the Christian's head is broken in little pieces by your stones, how will we send it to his kinsmen?"

"Remember, my father, his head has been given us by his friend," Kamel replied. "Wouldn't it be ill-mannered to return the gift? But we'll throw only at his body—and if the stone of any one of us flies too high and harms one hair on his head, the thrower stands revealed not only a cuckold, but a eunuch masquerading as a man."

"Truly not more than one or two of us would be so shamed," said a waggish elder. "If I'm one, I shall shave my beard, talk a treble voice, and walk mincingly. Surely then the skull won't show more than one or two unseemly cracks or holes, and will still be a fine sight for his brothers-in-arms."

"Especially for the one who betrayed him into our hands," Mustapha said thoughtfully.

There fell a brief silence. I had the strange, harrowing inkling that it offered me an opportunity for a telling stroke if I could grasp one illusive fact— If I could remember something I knew well— My brain was not working as clearly as before. It seemed to hang on the brink of delirium. The chance was lost as Kamel spoke softly.

"And by our heaving only at his body, he shall die more slowly, as you yourself commanded, Mustapha Sheik."

The clouds thickened across my mind. It came to me that I might have won this fight for life, had I been captured fairly, in something like a fair fight, instead of being betrayed and delivered helpless into their hands. Thereby my worth was diminished in their sight, and—though I strove against the base yielding—in my own. All or almost all my fellow officers had counted me unfit to marry Sukey; one had made it at least an ex-

177

cuse for a terrible crime. Those thickening clouds were of shame and sorrow. My blood was turning cold and torpid. The very will to fight on was failing swiftly.

"Sahib?"

It was Hamyd's voice. Dizzily I turned to him.

"Hamyd, I've led thee to a shameful death," I said in low-toned Hindustani.

"It may be we both shall die, but not in shame." He began to speak in swift staccato. "But, sahib, both of us yet breathe. Thou art still Lomri Sahib, who captured Kambar Melik, overthrew the Emir's *lashkar,* and lay in the embrace of love with Memsahib Bachhiya! Be of good heart still."

While I stared at him in wonder, he began peering into a leather packet, in which he carried his amulet and some other small treasures.

"This will need strong *pooja,* Hamyd," I told him, remembering how to smile.

"I would trade much *pooja* for a little *dawa* [medicine] to give thee. I thought I might have a pellet of opium left, but the gardener, of unspeakable begettings, ate up the last." Pretending to tighten my bandage, he spoke in desperate entreaty. "Sahib, heed me, for the love of God! The despair upon thy mind is only a shadow cast by thy weakness of body. Thou hast bled enough to weaken a pony, let alone a man. Brace thy sinews for a little longer. They were all but persuaded to sell us into slavery only a moment ago. That be an evil kismet—all but life being lost—but better that than to die—"

"Are you two saying charms, so the stones may miss the mark?" Kamel taunted.

"Why, no, great Sheik."

I had replied that far, hardly knowing what I was saying. But my voice had more resonance than a moment ago, and somehow my accents had suggested self-confidence. There was a distinct glow of warmth throughout my body, and my face was no longer wet with clammy sweat.

"In truth, my follower Hamyd and I were pledging to each other our most faithful service to Nazir Khan, ere we pledged it to all of you," I went on.

"It's in my mind that only your death at our hands will satisfy the honor and assuage the hearts of my kinsman Kambar Melik and the others you slew." Mustapha Sheik spoke with noble earnestness, and the tribesmen listened for my reply.

"What sight would be sweeter to Kambar Melik and the others—my bones dry on the desert, or myself in lifelong slavery, serving their Emir with the very cunning that sent them to Paradise? To that I will take oath before my God, and Hamyd, my follower, will swear alike before Allah."

"If you eat our Emir's bread—"

"Give him stones in his mouth, instead," a ruffian broke in.

"Hold your tongue, you misbegotten, while I speak." The old sheik turned again to me. "Lomri, would you swear before your God to give our Emir lifelong loyal service in peace and war, and to fight to the death against all his enemies?"

Mustapha's face was impassive save for a bright glint in his eyes.

"O Sheik, I'll answer truly. Your Emir will be mine in council and in battle, save as regards my lost people. In all business concerning them, I will be as one slain."

I had dreaded this issue and, now it had been faced, I could not divine its effect upon the tribesmen. Their faces were as still as their lean bodies.

"Why, now, this is a hard riddle to read," Mustapha Sheik remarked. "Your people are indeed lost to you, but ere that, they betrayed you to our swords."

"It's my kismet, O Sheik. I was betrayed by one who hated me and lusted for my *cobah*."

"Do you know his name?" Then two score fierce-eyed tribesmen held their breaths.

"No, O Sheik. Do you?"

"Allah bear witness, we don't know who wrote the letter, but take comfort, Lomri. He won't lie long with your *cobah*, gloating in his victory. On the day of Jihad [holy war], we'll cut every white throat in Sind, his among the rest."

I heard his voice thin and strange, so loud was my pulse in my ears. My thoughts were surging under great

179

strain. An opportunity that I had missed a while ago had come again. I made an extreme effort of will.

"Bah!" So I answered Mustapha Sheik, then waited, certain I would not wait in vain for his remark—certain, too, that none of my enemies would reach for a stone.

"You don't believe that we will slay all the sahibs—"

"If it be your kismet, which I greatly doubt. I've heard whispers that the Rani and your Emir will make peace. What I scorned, Mustapha Sheik, was the comfort you offered me. What joy would it be to me if his throat were cut by any hand but mine?"

My throat had tightened a little as I spoke, and I felt my face flush. It was not strange help from heaven, only my heart bounding out of a cold, smothering fog.

"Do I need tell any of ye so?" I went on, looking about the circle. "What joy have you taken in capturing me, the destroyer of Kambar Melik, and the confounder of the Emir's *lashkar* at Meeanee, when it was worked by another's hand? If I'm sent into slavery to Nazir Khan, I will ask that when I have served him faithfully for some years, and proven my troth to his person and his throne, that he let me go from him for some moons, even into Hind, wherein, unknown to my former comrades, I may accomplish a joyous task."

The desert became as still as though we were not here. That stillness was broken by the clap of Kamel's open hand, first against his breast, then his forehead.

"In the name of Allah, the great, the glorious," he cried in a loud voice. "If I were Nazir Khan, I would give you leave!"

"Keif, keif," rose several deep voices.

"There is no God but Allah," Mustapha intoned, after a pause. "In him all might and all glory repose. Lomri, it may be Allah's will that you be taken into Nazir Khan, there to go into slavery unto him, or into the darkness of death. If so, it may be made known to me, when we have taken you to our pavilions, eight kos across the desert."

"Peace be upon you, O Sheik, and ye all."

"It is a long march for a wounded man, and we will see how you bear up. Truly Allah would not suffer us to

180

send a weakling unto his great servant, Nazir Khan. But we'll give you a lump of musk and abundant water ere we set forth."

"Allah will bless your charity to the fallen."

To live to reach Mustapha's pavilions would be my immediate goal. But some greater goal than mere existence is necessary to all men that they may have even that, let alone the miraculous gift of human life in all its blaze and wonder. Whether that goal is noble or base, wise or foolish, it alone can brace the sinews, quicken the brain, and heal the wounds of the battle.

CHAPTER TWENTY-ONE

A Gift for the Emir

BEFORE STARTING OUT I was given a lump of musk, a sooty substance found in the reproductive glands of a small hornless deer of the Hindu Kush, and a stimulant of great power. When its effect began to wear off, I was still permitted to drink from the ponds and springs.

The other mercies granted me were less substantial but large. They were not vouchsafed me by my captors, but by my heart and mind. One was the realization, kept ever before me, that the torture was only partly punishment, the rest being a trial of my worth as a slave to the Emir of Baluchistan. Another was the assurance, at times becoming eerie as a dream, that the sand hills between me and my destination were a definite number and their infinity was an illusion, and when, in extreme travail, I climbed another, that number was one less.

The third mercy could be called a last, saving grace. It was given me after sundown, after dusk, after it seemed the oil in the lamps of the sky must be about burned out. I had lost track of time and almost of specific pain. Half delirious, I dreamed of two long rows of sahibs, once my brothers-in-arms, raising their glasses in triumphant toast. The Colonel Sahib had returned to his place at the head of the table, Holmes Sahib occupied his chair, only Gerald was absent from the feast. All drank to the narrow escape of the Colonel's daughter, but to one the wine was the nectar of the gods. Sweet on his palate, heady in his brain, it made him like a god in his own sight.

The dream came and went, but during its visits my feet seemed a little lighter and the sand a little less deep.

Often the sand heaps and the rocks had taken the shape of palm trees and tents at an oasis. There came one moment in the night when there rose out of the starlit landscape a stranger shape—so grotesque that I could hardly believe it was either rock or sand, and so must be a fantasm. But it was more ominous than the rest—it appeared so solid. I was in an aura of nightmare, about to scream, when my bulging eyes gave a little jump, and only a picketed camel was gnawing thorn scrub. From behind a dune spread the wan glimmer of a hidden fire.

I was able to keep my feet, Hamyd proud not to lend me a hand, until Mustapha Sheik and Kamel dismounted from their captured horses. The elder spoke in low tones to his companion.

"Among the dog tribe, many are mangy curs, many are good shepherds worth their keep, and some are like wolves in mettle and strength."

"Even so, my father."

"It has come to me that this Christian dog has earned meat and rest."

Both men had turned away before I dropped on the sand.

Time that had crawled, ran. Hamyd had hardly rolled me upon and then wrapped me in a carpet he had somewhere requisitioned, when I felt his hand and then saw him by the frail light of the moon. In his hand was a wooden mug.

"Thou hast slept three hours, sahib, and it may be that thy stomach will now hold, and not cast forth, this milk. Drink it now, still warm from the teat, but in small, not lusty, swallows."

It proved to be strong-smelling camel milk. I had tasted it before and gagged over it, but now it was pleasant to my palate, and, God knew, welcome within.

"There be no milk in Allah's world as strengthening to man as that given by a young she-camel, newly fresh, save mother's milk itself," Hamyd went on.

In the minute or two before I slept again, I thought of the first camel I had ever ridden, and how together we had well weathered a sandstorm. Since then I had used hard words on the hairy, ungainly, foul-smelling, evil-tempered brutes, but I took them all back. My heart warmed to all milk-givers unto men, goats and cattle and mares and camels, and great shaggy yaks amid the pillars of heaven, the sky-climbing mountains of Tibet. It was wonderful to think of a she-tiger with pitiless fangs and bloodied paws, her ferocity in abeyance as she lay supine in the jungle, giving suckle to her cubs.

My lips curled a little, as though I remembered how to smile, at the oddness of my thought. It was that God's greatest handiworks were not galaxies of stars burning in infinite space and time, nor sun nor moon nor earth, but firstly, Eve and Adam, and secondly, a cow and bull. But I was often slow in recognizing wonders. Billions of Hindus living and dead had thought the same, and no doubt it had been mused upon by countless farmers in every land on earth.

Hamyd brought me another bumper after sunrise prayers, as well as some bread that the dawn-rising cook had prepared for me, baked, lest a curse fall upon his head, without salt. When my companion had dressed my wound with rags begged from our captors, one of Mustapha's servants brought me a riding-beast.

"My master bade me tell you that no mercy on a wounded fox caused him to lend you, for the day's journey, this whore of a she-camel, verily the most baseborn, evil-hearted, and rough-gaited in his drove. It so chances that he has urgent business, of ill-omen to you, at his village."

Hamyd was given a seat atop some bales on a big baggage camel. We set out across trackless sands, to intercept a dim caravan road that no doubt met the old Arab trade route between Persia and Sind. When we stopped for noonday prayers, I was tossed some Rindi-style raiment occupied by innumerable fleas, whose bites were not even a counter-irritant to my burning wound. Soon after we forded a wide shallow river that I took for one of the confluences of the Hab. No one spoke a word to me until, at sundown, we were winding down to a village of flat-roofed huts on what I thought was a larger confluence, from sixty and a hundred miles generally north of Karachi. Here I was told to wear my face cloth, and if I was spoken to by anyone, to answer only, "*Sall'ala Mohammed* [Bless the Prophet]." Apparently the stranger would then assume I was an Arab pilgrim vowed to muteness until my goal was reached.

At the caravanserai an elderly hakim with skillful hands carefully washed my wound and dressed it with some sweet-smelling ointment. "But mark you, Christian, it may be labor and good myrrh thrown away," he told me. "There is no incipience of fever in the cut itself but an onset of affliction to the whole man."

In the morning, a small caravan formed in the village road, in charge of a handsome Rindi who Hamyd told me was Mustapha's nephew, Hassan. The amount of baggage indicated a journey of many days. The sooner we set forth, the safer. Save for a few slaves, the village was made up of the clan of Kambar Melik. A mullah's vision in the night, or a jinni sent from Paradise in the form of a vulture to flick its shadow at my feet, might cause Mustapha Sheik to change his mind. When he appeared reluctant to order our departure, I took the risk of approaching him, salaaming deeply.

"O Sheik, have I your leave to address you?"

"'A cur has Allah's leave to whine, and a hog too squeal,'" he quoted.

"I shall do neither, master, only speak what's in my heart. If it be God's will that I go into lifelong slavery to Nazir Khan, be assured that my service unto him will be proud and joyful, not of the lip but of all my body and brain. I'll never forget it was for that I was saved from death by torment."

"Methinks this fox was taught to bark in very Oman," an elder remarked.

I thought a faint look of pride stole into Mustapha's face.

"It's in my heart to ask one more boon, great Sheik," I added quickly. "Is there, in your village, or hereabouts in easy reach, a despised and unblessed skull?"

"Truly, there is. There's some flesh on it yet, but the first kite who drops down upon it will clean it well."

"Has it a full set of teeth?"

"I'm of that opinion, from the good sound of their
185

gnashing. Their owner was in the prime of young man-hood."

"Is the skull of a size that it could, perhaps, be mis-taken for mine?"

"It could well be."

"If God wills that I go to Kalat, in slavery to your Emir, have you a slave who would draw from the upper jaw the rearmost wisdom tooth on the right side, and from the lower, the tooth next to and behind the dog tooth on the left?"

"Could it be that those same teeth are lost from your dog's jaws?"

"Verily, O Sheik, and one of my kinsmen in the regi-ment is well aware of the loss. I had reminded him of it only a few weeks ago, when a tooth doctor of great skill was sent from Bombay. Also I'd have your servant bore a small hole in the upper surface of first grinder on the right side of the lower jaw. It so chances that there's such a hole in a similar tooth in my jaw, for the gold that had filled it, placed there by an English doctor in my boyhood, was loosened by time and fell out when the bone was caused to tremble two days ago."

"If your kinsmen had wit to look for the gold—" Then Mustapha paused.

"Of a certain one will look, Mustapha Sheik, in love of him who was Brook Sahib—and one who stands by, watching and listening, will be sure to look, also. Both will think that the gold was gouged out, to be reset in the handle of a sword."

"Then it should not be a clean-bored hole, but roughly cut. Truly that will sharpen the edge of the jest."

"By your leave, O Sheik, I don't mean to jest."

There was a sheen on his eyes as they met mine. "So I see."

Actually I had meant only to play on the same tribal trait that had served me before—the mountaineers' abhorrence of treachery and their passion for blood re-venge, called *thar*. I had toyed with the skull trick to take my mind off terror and pain. It had seemed there was only one person whom I wanted convinced of my death, the one of whose love I was sure. I could not let

186

her hope for my return. I would not pay her in that spurious coin. However, it was best that Gerald have no doubt, lest he institute inquiry dangerous to me.

But when Mustapha's eyes glistened, the fantastic notion began to appeal to some Gypsy traits I had never tried to repress. It might work perfectly well on all who were still concerned with me, and give me more to live for.

"Master, will you appoint a slave to look well into my mouth, to make sure that the fallen head could counterfeit mine?" I asked.

"By my beard, I'll hold my nose from thy swine's breath and look myself!"

When I opened my mouth wide, he forgot to hold his nose. "In the name of Allah, I've a good view," he went on. "What little flesh remains on your right cheek is thin as silk covering a wanton's enticements, and almost as transparent. I mark the missing teeth—nor shall I forget which ones—and the hole in the grinder. In whiteness they're like the skull's, if I mistake not, but I'll make sure of their comparative size and shape. If that skull won't do, it will be no trouble to find another."

"Allah upon you, Shahzada!"

"Nay, I'm not a prince, only an old village headman, who hates treachery to the bread and salt. Since you do, also, in that like a Son of the Prophet, I'm of a mind to let you eat the bread of slavery to our Emir, and the salt of life. Perhaps you'd like to know whose skull may be sent your kinsmen, in lieu of your own."

"Aye, master."

"It was the bringer of the letter from your betrayer. He might have lived if he hadn't asked for twenty of the hundred cattle, as additional reward to the hundred rupees which—as he confessed before he died—had been tossed with the missive into the window of his house. But aside from his greed, it was not meet that he live. His name was Abdullah, and he had eaten your bread and salt."

I felt my lips drawing into something like a smile, but I did not know the meaning of it. I recalled Abdullah's seeming loyal service, and my regret at parting with him only the day before I started for the sand hills, to make room for Hamyd. He had appeared grateful for baksheesh and a letter of recommendation.

"We never dreamed you might live to kill the dog yourself, Lomri," Mustapha explained. "Anyway it would have been a trifling task, more trouble to you than joy."

"I'm grateful it's done. But I've a curiosity to see the letter that he brought."

"He had destroyed it, nor did he know what sahib had written it, it being drawn in capitals in Urdu."

"If by my kismet and my master's leave, I pass this way again, will you break bread with me?"

"Yeah, truly, knowing you've served him well. Also, if I have a horse to sell—a good horse, mark you, but the buyer hating all horses, and loving only camels—I'll appoint you the task."

I salaamed deeply. With a deeply thoughtful look, Mustapha waved his clansmen out of hearing.

"Truly you are Lomri," he went on. "But tell me, are foxes not allowed in the white man's heaven?"

"I don't read your riddle, O Sheik."

"The good Mussulman is in no haste to die, but he won't lose his *izzat* in order to live, perhaps because he knows—or at least believes—he'll drink inexhaustible nectar and break infinite maidenheads in Paradise. Have you no hope of some equal bliss beyond the grave?"

"The heaven of the white man is not as alluringly described, Mustapha Sheik. Also, I have a feeling I won't get in."

"Truly I never saw such struggle against death, with so little cause. The cunning of Shaitan was in it, and the stubbornness of a baggage camel. The prize was to go into slavery for many years, if not for your whole life, whereby your *cobah,* your friends, and all that men live for, are lost, and the most you can recover is revenge. Mark you, you are not as a soldier captured in battle and sold by his captors. Such slaves aren't honorbound to their masters; in full honor they may kill them and run away if they get the chance. You will live, toil, thrive—perhaps finally obtain freedom—by another's leave."

"Your words, O Sheik, are sharper than the young man's sword."

"It's your riddle, O Stranger, that's hard to read. No other Englishman I've ever seen—and I've fought them long—would do what you've done. Shouting defiance, he would have died beneath our swords."

"You shame me deeply, master."

"It isn't my intention. And I wonder, Lomri, whether you're really shamed within your heart, although you must pretend to be before me and your own soul. Even now I can hardly believe you are alive. Indeed, I'm not sure I didn't swear before Allah—happily my memory of the occasion is a little dim—to cut your throat with my own hand if ever the chance came."

The old sheik breathed a fervent, "Bismillah!" with raised hands, then spoke on. "I stood between you and others likewise bound, I being Sheik of Habistan. Even so they were glad, in the end, that I did. One reason you were spared was your refusal to fight your own people, which struck a responsive chord in their fierce hearts. Another reason was your blood debt to your betrayer, which you acknowledge, and which my clansmen, children that they are, desire to see paid. Truly it struck fire into my old, fierce, foolish heart, I being a blood feudist of no small fame. But there was another reason—behind the good show you gave us—behind our curiosity as to what you would do and say next, whereby we were eager to show you to our Emir. After deep meditation, I suspect the reason might be our respect for a special kind of courage you possess—to look upon the truth without flinching, letting no hope or wish dim or color it, and then acting upon it without thought for anything in the world but your own concerns."

The old sheik was so thoughtful he looked actually benign. Surely some little *pooja* lingering from my absent good-luck piece had caused him, instead of a less studious man, to be captain of my captors.

"The price of such clear seeing and unmitigated acting is great loneliness," Mustapha went on. "We pitied

189

it, I think, even as we honored it. And in our hearts we knew, since it was so patently in your own best interests, you would serve our Emir well."

"I know it, too, Mustapha Sheik," I told him, my eyes on his.

"What kismet awaits you in court I can't guess or dream. But there's one assurance I can give you, perhaps of some comfort in your solitude. Your betrayer in Hyderabad will never doubt you are dead."

"Dakkil-ak ya Shaykhe!" This stately Arabic expression meant, literally, "I am your protected, O lord."

"In that one matter, yea. Every soul who knows you're alive is under my hand, and no whisper of the truth will ever be carried on our desert winds. Instead, a fine tale of your death will be wafted to your kinsmen, the deed done by a band of wandering Yezedis from beyond the Koh Rud. Your betrayer will not lie awake beside your *cobah* in terror of your return, but his enjoyment of her, and his gloating over his triumph, will make his life all the more dear to him, and hence your revenge—if Allah wills it—all the more sweet. And if it be your kismet to steal upon him, with thirsty blade, you won't be cheated by a guarded and bolted door."

His throat worked, and a flush worthy of a young clansman in his first hate affair diffused his wrinkled face. Then he waved to his nephew, Hassan.

"Noble youth, you'll take our prisoner even to Kalat, presenting him, with the letter you bear, to my great kinsman, Nazir Khan." The old sheik turned to me and stood very straight, his arms folded on his breast. *Alhamdolillah* [praise be to Allah, Lord of Three Worlds]! You have my leave to go."

The last time I had heard these final words was by a low red fire, not far from an enchanted tower, when Sukey had given Hamyd leave to depart from her. It was as though I had been reincarnated in far distant time and place. But once more I was sure of my identity and could know a Gypsy pride.

Instead of clambering aboard the she-camel, I addressed her with an imperious, *"Ikh! Ikh!"* to make her kneel.

CHAPTER TWENTY-TWO

Fateful Scar

OUR CARAVAN, SWIFTLY MOVING, gained the ancient town of Bela at the close of the second day. Seated with the drovers beside a cooking fire in the caravanserai, I attracted no undue attention from other travelers; and the bandage covering most of my face excused the muttered, *"Al,"* an abbreviation of "O Allah bless him!" to every "Bless the Prophet!" sounded in my hearing. To the few curious, my guards explained that I was a pale-colored Persian, on a pilgrimage to Solomon's Throne, and I had been wounded by a bursting gun.

From this populous region, its deserts turned almost into swamps by irrigation waters, we headed up the valley of the Porali River toward Wad, an ancient highway to Kalat known as Kohan vat. Across unpeopled wastes, amid giant sand dunes marching before the wind, over passes silent save for screaming eagles, through valleys strewn with stones, we made our way to the mountainous wilderness below the Sarawan. Meanwhile I was finding out all I could about Nazir Khan. He had never forgiven the English for killing his father, Mehrab Khan, one of the worst bungles in the history of India. A real Oriental potentate, he had beheaded in one afternoon fifty followers of a rival claimant to the throne. However, in fear of attack by the Persian Shah, he had an open mind to Western arts and sciences, particularly those pertaining to war.

The wilderness gave way to rugged pasturage for fat-tailed sheep; then to a wide fertile valley with tilled lands, pretty villages amid orchards and mulberry vineyards, and herds of humped cattle. Then my heart was deeply moved, in strange, sorrowful wonder, at the sight of Kalat, where I was to live, and perhaps die, a slave, rising ghostily in the dim distance. Slowly it took shape and substance in the lucid mountain air. Crowning a low hill, ringed by rugged peaks, the whole city had the aspect of a fortress. Long before sundown we could make out the *miri*, an immense towering citadel containing Nazir's palace, reminding me of some of the great castles on the Danube, although far more austere.

The light was failing as we rode through the narrow streets lined with mud-walled, flat-roofed houses huddled in the vast shadow of the fortress above. The people watched us pass with only mild curiosity, but the keen-nosed dogs they kept, mainly hounds and pointers, barked savagely at me as long as they caught my scent.

We spent the night at the caravanserai, with hirsute Afghans, lithe Persians, and a band of slant-eyed Tartars from Turkistan. In the morning Hamyd laid out handsome garments, obviously from Mustapha's wardrobe, that I was to wear to the palace. Of course these indicated no respect to me, being merely wrappings of a gift intended for the Emir. Since by nature I was a *kusah*—a scant-bearded man—Hamyd shaved me clean save for a narrow mustache and a small tuft on my chin.

I told him that I had been troubled the last few days by a prickling tension of the skin all around my wound, from nose to ear, and from temple to chin; was there any sign of the extension of proud flesh?

"Nay, sahib, it's a clean wound, although far from healed."

Some peculiarity of tone caused me to look quickly into his eyes. "What ails thee, Hamyd? I would like to see for myself, if thou wilt buy a mirror in the bazaar."

"I have a small mirror, sahib, and will fetch it, since it is thy kismet."

I did not know what he meant until I looked into the glass. Nature's effort to restore the hacked-out flesh and to close the gash had drawn the skin and tissue from all the surrounding area, and was beginning to reshape that whole side of my face. Aside from the scab, only a rim as yet about a three-finger circle of proud flesh, it already had a distinctly different aspect from the other side. The right eye looked longer, with what seemed a different luster. The slight change in the set of the ear might be hardly measurable with calipers, but was markedly altering its appearance. My mouth, even now effected by the tensure, was beginning to appear longer and more sensuous, and my nose thinner and more hawklike.

The alteration had only started. To what lengths it would go I could not imagine, when the scar tissue had formed, and Nature had done her utmost to fuse the two diverse sides of my countenance into a harmonious whole. When before the great change I used to walk the alleys of Hyderabad in native dress, I used to fear recognition. If my steps should ever wend that way again, such fear would be groundless.

Until now I had often wondered how God had managed to make a million faces, with the same utilities, all different from one another. The reason was the incredible complex that makes up appearance, recognized by the eyes but unresolvable by the brain, in which the most subtle variation of line or shape or color or texture looms so large.

But I was not as shocked as Hamyd had expected me to be. If, in the usual way of humankind, I had harbored a secret motherlike love of my own face, I had certainly never admired it. Save for the disfiguration of the scar, I might be no better or worse looking. Indeed I felt a certain sense of fitness, almost poetic, in my appearance changing utterly with the utter change of my fate. My old life had ended; a new one had begun; it was causing great changes in the workings of my mind and the strings of my heart and the warp and woof of my soul. Perhaps the conflict between the two lives would be lessened by this public declaration.

It would come in handy in the pursuance of revenge, although as yet I was aware only of owing a great debt which someday I must pay. With this new face, itself a testament to the debt, could go an implacable hatred, a remorseless heart. It could become a wicked face.

When I looked at it in the glass, I would not see the face that Sukey had covered with kisses. I would become more quickly reconciled to the death that had parted us.

CHAPTER TWENTY-THREE

Trap for a Fox

HAVING SEEN THE ANCIENT PALACE of the Emirs in Hyderabad, my eyes were not dazzled by the gaudy glories of Nazir Khan's. During the business of our admission into an outer hall, and the putting of Hamyd and me in the charge of a eunuch seneschal, I looked only at the faces of those whose favor or disfavor toward us, and whose headaches in the morning, or sour stomachs at night, could loom so large in our fate.

When the time for the audience drew near, we were led into the durbar and stationed with some richly appareled Negro slaves, no doubt the gift of some pasha or cham out Africa way. The room filled with officials of the court, petitioners, courtiers, and visiting sheiks and headmen, mighty in their villages but small potatoes here. Then a hush fell, and with it all present fell to their knees, foreheads on floor. When the Grand Vizier bade us rise, Nazir Khan, Defender of the Faith, the Shadow of Allah on earth, Emir of Baluchistan, was seated on his gold-and-ivory throne.

In due course Hassan's name was called. Quaking in his lungi of many colors, he prostrated himself before the throne and was permitted to present Mustapha's letter. I thought there was a sparkle of interest in the royal eyes.

"Hassan Melik, the matter is to our pleasure, and we will send the letter writer a purse of silver rupees to the worth of—two hundred cattle," Nazir Khan pronounced.

Then to Hassan's glory, he permitted a scarf to be hung around his neck.

The Emir's pleasure might lie in the gift of a slave, or

with getting hands on an enemy of some note among his tribesmen. In the next few days I became no wiser than before. I was told brusquely by the seneschal to answer to the name of Paulos, which among the Moslems seemed to be a generic name for a Greek, and not to speak of my history unless by royal command. Such palace attendants as I encountered gave me haughty as well as curious glances, which were my due as a Christian. The slaves with whom I was quartered did not dare kick or be kind to me until my fate was known, meanwhile avoiding me like the itch. The younger of two Arabian physicians belonging to the court, Murad Hakim, treated my wound twice a day with what I sensed to be unusual skill and, fastening its vinegar-soaked compress with glued strips, dispensed with my awkward bandage. But English doctors treat wounded prisoners in their death cells, lest they cheat the hangman.

About ten days after the audience, an excited eunuch bade me bathe with Levitical care and array myself in my best clothes. Another attendant sniffed at them and at my breath, an assurance that I was going before an illustrious personage. Then I was led up dark, narrow stairs to a small, dimly lighted room, no doubt an informal council chamber. There, seated on a heap of cushions on a dais, was the handsome young Emir, richly arrayed and bejeweled, but puffing on a hooka and spitting fine as any camel driver in a coffee house.

When I had prostrated myself, I was given permission to stand.

"My servant Mustapha wrote me that you speak well the language of Oman," the Emir began bluntly.

"I have some small knowledge of it, exalted master."

"The letter stated a condition to your service as my loyal slave. It was that you could not raise your hand against those whose bread and salt you had eaten. Truly no Son of the Prophet could find fault with that. But I, too, am bound by bread and salt to some who died at your hand. Only if your service to me was of great value, greatly pleasing unto Allah, could it substitute for the shedding of your blood."

"Lord, is there not an indication of its value in your

Majesty's owning of that bond to so many lions of the desert?"

The Emir puffed luxuriously, but I was warned to be on rigid guard by the sheen on his bold, black eyes.

"It is a brave boast, Paulos—as you will be known us —but I don't say it's an empty one. If I were certain of your lifelong willing and loyal service as a slave to my throne and person, your counsel uncolored by self-interest, ever speaking the truth without flattery to me or to yourself, why, then the might of your deeds while serving your Queen might weigh the balance for, not against, my sparing your life."

"You may be certain of it, master, I swear by my God and honor, and Hamyd will take a like oath before Allah."

"The capture of Kambar Melik was a notable feat," the Emir went on. "It evidenced some bravery and much cunning. But it was a minor feat compared to the decoying of my *lashkar* into the ditch at Meeanee on that day of woe. Save for that, the charge against the enemy flank would have broken his lines and his spirit and given victory to our arms."

I did not immediately reply. Considering what he had said a moment before, I was confronted with an extremely dangerous decision. I made it on instinct.

"O mighty King, have I your leave to dispute the truth of your royal words?"

"The tongue of many has been cut out for less, but you have my leave."

"If you take comfort in the belief that your *lashkar*'s charge could have turned the tide of battle, it is false comfort. The battle was already won—although I was not then aware of the fact. At least that is the belief of the high command and every officer of the English Army and my own belief."

There was no decipherable expression on the Emir's face. "Some among my councillors say otherwise," he remarked thoughtfully. "Even so, you may keep your tongue for the time being. For that time, I accept your slavehood unto me, as you've sworn it by your God. You have my leave to go."

If I could have possibly known what I was going

197

into, I might have been so terrified as to implore his mercy. While backing, my head low, from his presence it seemed I had played my cards well. Perhaps, instead, I had disabused him of a cherished illusion. Yet in dreadful days to come, it remained one of my few reasons—excuses, for all I knew—for feeble hope.

If the degradation heaped upon me had been made public, a thing by no means rare in Central Asia, I could believe that the Emir was demonstrating for his people, with Oriental lavishness, his contempt for an Englishman who had chosen base slavery instead of honorable death. If jeering crowds had been permitted to watch me, I might have thought that the Emir, or one of his councillors, was trying to lessen their respect for the white race, heightened at Meeanee—an act of policy not unknown to kings of the East. Hamyd, working in the stables, was not permitted to visit me. Actually no one came near me but a handful of slaves, our foreman, and Murad Hakim, who, with a masklike face and as few words as possible, continued to treat my wound. Even these did not seem to know me as Lomri, only as Paulos the Greek. The foreman's whip was plainly laid on according to orders, the strokes counted carefully; although he never evidenced the least pity, neither did he show rancor or even scorn.

Every day was one which, in some dimly visioned future, I would want to tear from my life's calendar of days. On falling to sleep every night, I wanted to bury, too deep to dream of, all that had happened the night before. My food was almost as horridly garnered as that of the prodigal son before his redemption. The labors I did, and the goads that enforced them, could be longer endured by a native than most Europeans—the latter were subject to more rapid mental dissolution—and I dared not calculate how long I could live and stay sane. Perhaps someone in court, unknown to me, bore me malice too cruel to satisfy with one clean stroke. Yet I clung with bulldog teeth to the belief that this was an ordeal of strength and faith, inspired by the fame of Lomri and influenced by the religious frenzy called *malbus,* and at some unpredictable moment it would pass.

The drouth deepened, and the heat mounted day by

day; the cool nights became cruelly short. But the scant rains broke at last, and the night of the summer solstice brought a visitor to my den. He wore an iron slave ring, as I did, and both ears had been cut off; his yellowish skin and facial features suggested mixed European and Asiatic blood. Aside from those signs of his evil fate, he was almost meaningless to me. There was a dim glimmer in his eyes, but otherwise his face was as expressionless as a cadaver's.

"I'm called Langur [the Monkey] and I am—I was —a half-caste of Bombay, and born to the service of the English throne," he told me. "I must be back in my cell before the watch changes, so I'll waste no words."

I gave him a breathless nod.

"I bring you evil news, but also a bright hope. A great serdar of the court was boon-fellow to one, his name unknown to me, whom you slew; and the daughter of that one is the wife of your enemy's son. He could not cut your throat with his own hand, but the Vizier winked at this slow death for you, and the Emir, toying with a new slave girl, has forgotten your existence. There will be no easing of your labors, or lightening of the kurbash [hippo-hide whip] until you draw your last breath."

"Truly, it's evil news. What hope can you offer me, and at what price?"

"First, do you swear before God that you won't betray me, now or hereafter, to anyone in the Emir's court?"

"I'll never knowingly bring harm to a British subject who hasn't harmed me."

"There's a certain Persian with whom I'm in concert. In a certain number of days his caravan will take a certain road. It chances that a mad mullah was among his company, and no road guard, or *askaris* dare approach his curtained litter in fear of his curse. It so chances, too, that the mullah has lately died and his body been hidden."

"Speak quickly, Langur, and softly."

"If you are taken in the mullah's mahmal to a city of the Queen, will you take oath to reward him to the amount of five thousand rupees? Mark you, if you have

199

only one chance in ten of a safe arrival there, it is still your last and only chance to escape a dog's death here. But so cunning is this Persian, and so perfect his plans, that there's hardly one chance in ten of disaster. You've only to take my hand and follow me, by a safe passage, to the gate of a certain courtyard. There a camel driver will be waiting, and he'll convey you to a hiding-place, more safe than you can hope or believe. It was not well that you be approached until the last minute, for reasons of safety, but the Persian was certain you'd clutch at a straw, let alone a veritable lifeline thrown into the sea of your despair."

"Truly, a drowning man will clutch at a straw." The Arabic saying was almost identical to the English. "But what will be your reward, for carrying the Persian's message?"

"He's promised me one-tenth of the amount he receives from you, whereby I can buy a certain boon." Langur clasped his trembling hands. "Take your oath quickly, Paulos. Every moment is precious."

Happily I did not have to put my soul to trial. I need think only of my skin. Langur did not know how bright a hope he had brought me!

I shaped him a fine speech.

"It was said of old that there be two things which, if broken, can never be mended. One is a maidenhead, and the other a soldier's faith."

"By Allah, you can't be such a fool—"

"Perhaps I wouldn't be, if I were awake, but all this is a dream in the night. You haven't come here, you haven't spoken to me of escape, and even now I'm talking in my sleep. In the morning it will all be forgotten. But just now I'm dreaming that you are departing in great haste—"

"Truly your name is Lomri," the man broke in, in a quite casual tone. After eloquently spitting on the wall, he disappeared in the darkness.

In the morning my iron neck ring was removed, and I was made the third assistant to the Master of the Wardrobe of the Grand Vizier.

CHAPTER TWENTY-FOUR

Beautiful Slave Girl

IN A LITTLE LESS THAN TWO YEARS, when officially my highest honor had been the passing of tea and coffee cups, water perfumed with mastic, and tobacco pipes in the Vizier's chambers, I planned and brought about the execution of a *coup de main*. The opportunity arose from the trouble we were in with Persia.

I began sitting in the game when I recited to the Vizier all I knew of the Shah's military strength, as reported by the Survey only shortly before my capture. When the Vizier had me relate the information to the Emir, I seized the opportunity to unfold a plan for winning a strong ally. English hands were full of bloody war with the Sikhs, but it seemed possible to enlist Sa'id ibn Sultan, the great Arab king, whose former capital, Muscat, was only five days' sail from our coasts across the Persian Gulf.

Sa'id had begun his great career as a relatively minor prince, although with a vague claim to a vast African empire. He had conquered the upstart emirs of Mombassa and the shore towns, and for about ten years had made Zanzibar, off the African coast, his principal residence and really his capital. With his enormous revenue from slaves and ivory, he kept a powerful navy, and the Queen of England and the President of my native land had made him rich gifts. And it so happened, because of trouble in Oman, he was spending most of this year at his old palace at Muscat.

A small card in our Emir's hand was a legendary distant kinship between him and Sa'id. The great potential ace was the port of Gwadar, on our coast, which had been ceded to the Sultan of Oman at a love feast about a century before. Since Sa'id, like so many great men, had a weakness for ceremony, I proposed that the transfer of the territory be celebrated by a great fete. If he would attend in person, break bread with Nazir, and enjoy himself hugely, he could no doubt be induced to join hands with our Emir in sworn defense of his little Baluch sheep range of three hundred square miles on the road to Persia. Then there would sit a snarling and sick Shah on the Peacock Throne.

Nazir Khan agreed to the plan before I left the chamber. From that hour, I never served another cup of coffee in his or the Vizier's chambers, or deloused another lungi. It was not by chance that my hand could loom large in the preparations for the durbar. My greatest lingual accomplishment being a mastery of Arabic, and always ambitious to play a part in Arabian affairs especially in regard to East Africa, I had read carefully the Indian Survey's confidential dossier on Sa'id ibn Sultan and had discussed it with Major Graves. Thereby I knew some of his vanities, his tastes, and his strengths and weaknesses.

Since he prided himself on being a great nimrod, I proposed he be promised a lively chase after wild ass on the fleetest horses in Nazir's stables. I had heard Gerald, who loved hunting, pine for this sport. In the same letter there could be a hint of a gift unworthy of his receiving, yet which might afford him relief from the cares of state. He should be reminded that Gwadar, if small, was his only possession in Greater Asia, whereby his empire embraced two continents. In accordance with these ideas, the Vizier had me compose a suitable invitation to the fete, saying he might find suggestions in it for the official document, to be signed by the Emir. I spent the whole night on the composition, of course employing the stately Nahwi Arabic, as opposed to the *Kalam wati,* the vulgar tongue, which was the best that Arabic-speaking Baluch chiefs could boast. Naturally I did not shrink from floweriness, and the hint of the gift was conveyed in a voluptuous verse by Jamil.

What I thought would happen did. Explaining that he was not sure on some points of grammar, the Vizier showed me the finished letter in elegant Arabic script. Except for one added salutation, copied from the Koran, it was my composition word for word.

The ambassador who would bear it to Sa'id ibn Sultan set off on a fleet Umanian camel, the drovers leading several spares. From Gwadar he would sail for Muscat on Nazir's swiftest dhow. I burned and froze by turns, because if the invitation were flatly declined, or at the very least was not accepted in name, with his son and viceroy Thuevee to represent the Sultan, a scapegoat would be needed, and I could not imagine a more likely candidate than myself. Although we could hardly look for a reply short of three weeks, it arrived on the sixteenth day. I was on attendance to the Vizier when it was put into his trembling hands.

That night a syrup made of apricots that had stood too long to be an entirely safe beverage for True Believers, flowed freely in his chamber, and one of the chamberlains addressed me, after several cups, as Paulos Effendi. Sa'id ibn Sultan would attend the fete in person!

Anxious for the promised gift to please him, and putting more confidence in my own connoisseurship of beauty than that of anyone at court, I petitioned the Vizier to let me select it at the Kandahar slave market. No doubt a visit there would afford me easy opportunities to escape, but I was sorry for that, since it might militate against my being entrusted with the mission. Actually the notion did not appear to cross his mind.

"Allah bless your journey!" he cried. "Think you Sa'id would want her bones well padded?"

"His *cobah,* the Armenian Araxie, who was a power behind the throne until she died of small pox, was on the skinny side."

"Was she, in truth! Paulos, you are, indeed, a Greek in strange lore and cunning. Employ them mightily, while praising Allah, to pick a very moon of beauty."

Of the wares displayed at Kandahar, a good part were rich brown or polished black. Magnificently formed and animated, these were in brisk demand by the mountain chams, but surely they would be coals to Newcastle if fetched to an African sultan. I was looking for a delicate Kashmir bloom; and when a merchant offered a Sikkimese girl, called Cheetal, at first I was more interested in him than in his exotic merchandise. He was a pious-looking hadji, soberly habited and sternly bearded, and his solemn recital of the maiden's charms caught at my ribald ribs.

"Sikkim lies in the Himalaya Mountains halfway to China and the cost of bringing her here was scandalous," he told me. "However, I was prepared to lose on her, to humble the pride of one of my competitors who boasted a Kazak Christian not nearly as rare. Mark you, Paulos, in her heathen country one-third of the men become celibate monks. Thus only the most beautiful and fiery Sikkimese maidens ever obtain husbands, and that beauty and fire is intensified every generation until all the daughters of the land are golden, winnowed flames."

"In that case, I'll look at her."

"True, she's mild and demure-looking, but experience has taught me that is a recommendation. Maidens from mountainous regions under a tropic sun are almost always satisfactory. There is something about the warm days and cold nights of their habitat, the thin air, the heat amid the snows, that increases their value at least five hundred rupees each."

I gazed on Cheetal through a screen, and laughed no more. Surely here was a plaything to please a prince. Broad-minded, capable of writing pleasing verse as well as sound laws, Sa'id ibn Sultan would not fail to appreciate her charming oddity. The contour of her face was Mongoloid and had an eager, childlike expression. Her eyes and hair were brown; her skin the color of sandalwood; her miniature form was the kind that, in Arabic poetry, "waved like a tamarisk in the soft wind of the hills of Nijd." I have never seen so much voluptuous in so small a vessel.

I wished I could buy her for my plaything. After the deal was made, her spell was on me yet, and perhaps that was what caused me to utter words that should be kept in aching curb for years to come. Although my hearer was only a gossip-loving clerk called Jessa, and I spoke them in an idle tone over cups of coffee, the dusty alcove where we sat became weird as the scene of a dream.

From discussing the late-ended Sikh war, we fell easily into mentioning famous regiments and their commanders. One such Colonel—Webb Sahib by name—was a famed foe of my Emir. "It's said that his cruelties are caused by sorrow that he has no sons," I ventured.

"That's a great shame to any man, whatever his faith. The sahibs are allowed only one wife at a time, but why didn't he put the woman away, and take a younger one of richer furrow? The white men be many kinds of fools —but not all kinds."

"Did I hear that he has one daughter, wooed by many captains?"

"You may've, since she is much talked of, being born in Hind and speaking our tongue as one of us. But the news you had of her is no longer true."

I dared not lift my coffee cup lest my hand shake. "So?" I asked politely.

"The report of her wedding reached my idle ears more than a year ago."

He spoke in a casual tone. He was repeating trifling report heard at the teahouses, where the affairs of prominent sahibs were frequently discussed. He appeared to be a down-at-heels Rajput called Jessa, but instead he was a courier sent to me from a lost world, a builder of a bridge greater than any spanning the Indus, even one that linked the living with the dead.

"*Wah!*" Jessa's exclamation revealed astonishment and alarm. "Are you looking at a ghost?"

"Why? Was I staring into space?"

"Yea, and your face turned pale, and the great scar on your cheek showed like a brand."

"It is a brand. No, my friend, I was thinking of my own wedding, long ago, and a day of woe."

"May your gods be merciful unto you that you may forget."

"I've forgotten even now. My thanks, and pardon my wandering thought. You were speaking of the memsahib's wedding to—did you say to a Governor Sahib?"

"Nay, to one of the officers of her father's regiment whose name I did not hear. Truly the sahibs have

205

strange ways. Their daughters go unveiled in public, and choose their own husbands, and before and afterward dance unseemly with bachelors, their arms about their partners' necks. Often they are twenty and past before they make their choice. It is my own opinion that they must be cold as the snows of Solomon's Throne, or they would all be mothers before they are wives."

Had she married Henry Bingham or Clifford Holmes? Was she already great with child?

CHAPTER TWENTY-FIVE

Promise of Freedom

THE BRIDGE STRETCHING BETWEEN two worlds fell during the night. Mere thought was too heavy a load for its cobweb girders. Perhaps it had troubled my dreams, and I had brushed it down with a wave of my hand.

In the morning I went about the business of wrapping a gift for the Sultan of Oman. I bought Samarkand silk and cloth of gold, veils, shawls, heavy gold chains and bracelets, and necklaces of jade, sapphires, and amethysts. It was a great joy to me to present Cheetal with the treasures and watch her mouth and eyes grow round; then, placing a little image of Buddha on the chest, she knelt before it, in touching, childhood gratitude and joy. Little virgin from the distant mountains under Tibet, it is not meet that a slave should look upon you with such bright eyes! Have you guessed my guilty secret? A faint flush steals over your strange, lovely face.

We brought our prize, bundled almost to her eyebrows, to Kalat. The Emir's first comment, repeated to me by a fat eunuch sent panting upon an errand, was that the boldness of the choice appalled him. However, the small heathen's charms must have grown upon him, for finally he declared to the Vizier that he had made up his mind to present her to Sa'id ibn Sultan, and Allah have mercy upon him.

My slavish pride rose high at the reception given the Sultan in the durbar of the Sheik of Gwadar. A king of this stature was not to be found from the Turkish border to Cathay. Wearing no jewelry, in rich but rather simple clothes, he had a majestic bearing and yet a great deal of kindly warmth. I stood in the Emir's train, when, heavily veiled, Cheetal was presented to him along with other gifts. His gray eyes sparkled when he heard that she had come from far-away Sikkim, and they swept over her in full approval of what he could judge from her form.

The climax of the great fete was an impressive ceremony, performed over bread and salt, in which Sa'id ibn Sultan pledged his sword beside our Emir's in defense of Gwadar against all enemies. It was tantamount to putting all Southern Baluchistan under his shield, and the gnashing of the Shah's teeth would be heard afar.

It was Allah's curious will that the deserving do not always get their just deserts this side the grave. The sad fact has been remarked upon by every philosopher worthy of the name. Even so, I was to have a triumph of my own after Sa'id ibn Sultan had decorated both our Emir and his Vizier with scarfs at an informal farewell.

"My brother," he had remarked to Nazir Khan, "I've long known you as a great king and defender of the Faith, but I didn't know, until I received your letter, that you were so well-versed in our poets and in the language of very Mecca."

"Truly I am not, Sa'id ibn Sultan, and don't deserve your praise."

"I'm sadly aware that no ruler has time to obtain wisdom in all fields of knowledge. I, myself, am so deficient in mathematics, even algebra invented by our forefathers, that I can't cast a correct account of a day's spending. But verily, someone in your court has the erudition I mention, to have composed the letter to which you signed your imperial name."

"In the name of Allah, great King, it was composed by my slave, Paulos the Greek."

"Did he come hence bearing gifts?" Sa'id asked with a sly smile.

I was not sure Nazir understood the allusion, which certainly did not require a serious reply, Perhaps his exultation caused him to make one so royally generous, or he was overanxious not to be charged with deceit.

"Truly, Sa'id ibn Sultan, I've trusted him far, even in

that matter, according to the ancient saying that a faithful slave is part of his master's body."

"If he's among your train, I'd be pleased if you would ask him to stand forth."

I stood rigid until the Emir nodded to me, then prostrated myself before the Sultan.

"You may rise, faithful slave to my brother. In serving him, you've served me."

The Emir spoke quickly in the way of emirs when a chattel is admired by an illustrious visitor.

"Sa'id ibn Sultan, I aspire to the honor of presenting him to you, as a token of gratitude for the honor you've paid me."

The Sultan looked at me thoughtfully, stroking his grizzled beard.

"It comes to me you may have good use for him, as long as Mohammed Shah gazes hungrily eastward from his Peacock Throne. But if he should be taken to Paradise, you may proffer the gift again. It may be I would accept it, if, by Allah's will, I yet live and reign, and provided I could express my gratitude with a Grecian of another skin. I could promise you longer hair on the head, and a fairer hue, but regarding its contents—you could well be cheated in the exchange."

In the slave-trading argot, "Grecians" were bright blonds often from Thrace and the Danube countries. If superfine quality, they sold for as high as a thousand English pounds.

"O mighty Sultan, we've become brothers-in-arms, and my slave Paulos is yours whenever you will do me the ineffable honor of accepting him," Nazir Khan replied, bursting with pride.

"That is for the future, known only to the omniscient Allah. His peace be upon you, Nazir Khan, and upon you all."

He took his magnificent departure, and our jubilant Emir returned with his train to Kalat. My position in the court was from henceforth as high as that of the head eunuch's, himself a slave, and my influence with our master, although toward completely different endeavors, fully as strong. He worked through the women of the harem. No ambitious courtier could afford to offend him or not to grease him well. I operated mainly through the Grand Vizier, and it became my strange, happy fate to be able to serve both my king and Gerald's Queen.

It became my job to disabuse the Emir of his lingering dream of jihad. He must be convinced that no native state in easy reach of English armies could withstand a full-scale war. I cited, at such times as I dared, the long succession of English victories in India—Plassey, Buxar, Assaye, Argaum, Mehidpur, Kabul, Meeanee, and now Sobraon over the proud, warlike Sikhs. Although a mere spark might set off the powder of bloody and disastrous mutiny, I warned the Vizier never to fool himself that the English would abandon India. I knew the breed too well. If the Emir were wise, he would no longer countenance border raids and uprisings, and would make a strong alliance with the Indian Government against mutual enemies.

Other English-born in other native courts were giving the same advice. Some lost their heads; others—their names all but unknown in the council chambers of India—served the Queen well. But the time came, at the end of the fourth year of my slavery, that I might lay down my labors for a while, to serve my heart.

The Vizier arranged for me a private hearing by the Emir. When, in his chambers, I had kissed the hem of his royal garment, he dismissed all his other attendants, and gave me leave to offer my petition.

"Great King, before I was Paulos the Greek, I was Lieutenant Brook of the Tatta Lancers, and known to your people as Lomri."

"I know it well."

"You also know I was betrayed by one with whom I had eaten bread and salt, in every belief that I would be slain. Instead I was delivered into your most potent and merciful hands."

"Yes, in the chains of slavery."

"I ask to absent myself from your service and protection for half a year, with my former follower, Hamyd, to go into India, to discover the name and abode of my betrayer, by such proof as would stand in a court of law. I would go in the guise of a Tajik horse-trader and, by my bond with you, not make myself known to my former people."

There was a conflict of emotion in Nazir's face. "You would yet delay putting him to the sword?" he marveled.

"Yes, for as long as it might bring trouble to your throne." But I did not tell the Emir that if the proof were strong enough, I could, if I chose, find means to deliver it to the Provost Marshal of the English Army. I need not regret being absent from the trial—murdered men always are. The penalty might even be mitigated if I were there—a whimsical fact. However, I had no definite plan of action other than what I had revealed.

"Paulos, do you think your enemy is one whose slaying would make great stir?" Nazir asked thoughtfully.

"He may be a colonel of horse or a lesser officer. Doubtless his slaying—unless most cunningly done—would make great stir."

"It was whispered to me that evil lust for your *cobah* tempted him to the dire deed. Do you long to take her back, even though her furrow has been plowed by your most hated foe?"

"If so, it was in ignorance of the plowman's guilt. If she's rewedded in these years, by right of English law, her husband may be my foe, or some other. I long for her, but won't attempt to get her back as long as I'm your slave."

"I wish I could grant you leave to darken his eyes. I would, save that English law doesn't recognize blood feuds, and their police sahibs, tireless and unbribable according to report, veritable greyhounds with pointers' noses, might trail you to my court. But your petition to run him down and establish his guilt I gladly grant. If you would be content to let some hireling's hand deal him the stroke of death, I would give you leave and the wherewithal, although we both know your hate demands personal revenge and your *izzat,* a public atonement. That can be worked when you have completed your service to me."

"*Completed it, Nazir Khan!*"

"Yea, for the time has come to hold out to you a most fair hope. My enemy the Persian Shah, Mo-

211

hammed, balked in his evil designs, fades fast and, according to my spies, may any day drink the cup of death. But whether or not he has breathed his last, one month after your return from Hind, I will do even as I promised my brother Sa'id ibn Sultan—present you to him as a token of gratitude for his most prized friendship. I will trust your service unto him to be such as to help keep your giver green in his memory and our friendship warm in his heart."

"To hear is to obey."

"When the day comes for me to dispatch you to him, I shall say in the letter that I'd promised you, had I kept you, to retain you and your follower, Hamyd, in my service for five more years, then to set both of you free. So I will ask him, for such is not unseemly among us, that he do the same as though you had served me in the same wise. No doubt he will honor that request, he being truly a Son of the Prophet of kingly honor."

I knelt before the Emir, and there was no practice in that.

"You're a young man, not yet a score and ten," he went on solemnly. "When you're free, you may take your revenge, and, if Allah wills, and it be your yet desire, your *cobah*."

He held out his hand for me to kiss, and spoke in a voice harsh with the emotion that strikes so readily and deeply such off-white men as he and I.

"You've served me well, you who were born free and once a brave soldier of your Queen. Your cunning counsel aided me in balking my enemies and lengthening the shadow of my throne. You've kept your vow to me in every jot and tittle, as though we had broken the unleavened bread, and eaten the salt of God. Now go from me quickly, lest we both be shamed."

CHAPTER TWENTY-SIX

Letter of Betrayal

LONG AGO NOW, I HAD GROWN used to the face of Paulos, the Emir's slave. I could no longer call to mind what Lieutenant Brook had looked like. Indeed it had begun to seem as native to me as the other. Both sides had fused as I had expected, the right not much different from the left, save for its very large flat scar. Since this had weathered well, unmottled and more gray than red, it was conspicuous without being especially ugly. Looking in the glass it did not seem a wicked face, or one to go with implacable hatred.

Actually that fire had never caught, perhaps partly because of the completeness of the break with my former life. Only a few ghosts are harmful. They may haunt the scenes of their great wronging, but it is too far distant, too changed when seen through ghostly eyes, for them to avenge. Also my slavehood had been most profound. It was far more complete than for those carried away against their wills, who by dreaming and plotting escape remained merely exiles from their former world, with the umbilical cord never cut. Even my love for Sukey had become like a dream in the night.

When in my right mind, I had deeply desired her to be happy, and craved retribution on my betrayer. I had known for years now that if fate did not bring these about, I surely would, unless I died too soon. If it should be my lot to choose between Sukey's happiness and my betrayer's punishment, easily the case if she had married him and had children by him, the choice was already made. One was a small duty compared to the other. Indeed it seemed more duty than heart's desire as yet, when still I did not know his identity, so that he had no face. I visioned him as one of three officers of the Tatta Lancers, standing in the dock being sentenced to hang for heinous crime.

But the compulsion became more passionate as the caravan that Hamyd and I had joined drew nearer the Sind frontier. We were not far from the sand hills of my fall, and the scenes were reminiscent of some I had known before then. Since the merchants wished to touch Liari, I decided to leave them at Uthal, and go by Mustapha Sheik's village on the Hab. If he still lived, he might have news of my death, and I wished to gaze again into the old gray wolf's eyes.

In the street I recognized at least three of my captors, and felt as though I were waking from a dream. They stared at some pilgrims from Sarbaz with whom I journeyed, but did not honor me with a second glance. The waggish cobbler who had joked of the seven-year sailor's haste with a seven-year widow remarked that no doubt I had fought many battles, to boast such a fine scar. When I asked the name of the village headman, I feared he would answer, "Hassan," the elder having died in this long time. Was I such an outlander not to know it was Mustapha, Sheik of all Habistan?

When I found him at the blacksmith shop, only a little leaner and fiercer-looking than before, he readily agreed to speak to me in private. We went only a little way down the village road.

"O Sheik, has it been my honor to have seen your face before?" I asked.

"I think not, or I would have recalled yours. It does not seem one easy to forget."

"Look well, in Allah's name, lest you speak falsely."

He gazed at me long. "If ever I saw you, it was ere you came to manhood."

"Have you ever seen one with a wound that might have formed a scar like mine?"

Unbelieving wonder came into his eyes. "It cannot be," he said, his voice shaking. "There was once a captive, whose cheek was shorn away—the only wound I had ever seen that might cause such a scar, but—what can I say? Nay, I will not believe unless you give me a sign!"

" 'A fool should be answered according to his folly. What is the asking price?' "

"Allah! Allah! Allah!"

I saw him standing there, pale and trembling, and then he became dim. I had not thought such a thing could ever happen to me again.

"Don't be ashamed," he told me. "I won't think you *fatis* [literally, 'carrion,' but as thus used, one who dies in bed]."

"Father, is it such a wonder that I've lived to see your face again?"

"It wouldn't be, but we heard that the Emir put you to the sword the day after our departure."

"Have you heard no word of Paulos, the Greek slave of Nazir Khan?"

"Bismillah, blind fool that I am! By Allah, the Emir owes us more than the two hundred cattle he paid—"

I laughed then, and he bayed with laughter.

"Come!" he cried. "Let me spread a feast. There be many here—"

"By your mercy, O Sheik, not one of your village is to know that Lomri—"

I was stopped by the glitter in his old wild eyes. "You're even now going into Hind?"

"Yes."

"You're in great haste? But you should answer a fool according to his folly."

"Not in too great haste to ask the fulfillment of your promise."

When we had eaten, I asked him to sell me forty horses, to be paid for from the sum the Vizier had lent me, and which I had promised to repay at a premium. It was a by-word in the East that the bond of the bread and salt did not apply to horse-trading, but Mustapha charged me a bottom price and threw in a mare that he said was the equal of one he had captured amid the sand hills. "Belike she's worthy of being mounted by a stallion I bought the same day," he told me.

"But I have another gift for you," he went on, suddenly grave. "On that day of deathless memory I told you that the bearer of the betrayer's letter had destroyed it. That was a lie unto an enemy, permitted by Allah.

215

Truly, though, he had preserved it, perhaps with some notion of seeking out its writer and sucking his blood, and we found it hidden in his turban. Even then I yearned to give it to you, but since it named you as the slayer of Kambar Melik, our kinsman, I dared not risk its fall into the hands of the English, lest they suspect that we, not wandering Yezedis, had darkened your eyes. But we have eaten bread and salt, and also you have kept your vows to me and to our Emir. I will fetch it from its hiding-place and give it to you for anything you may read between the lines."

As I read the yellowed letter in faulty Urdu, Mustapha's eyes fixed on my face like a hungry hound's. The skin of my scalp was drawing because of a vision. It was of an officer of the Tatta Lancers thumbing an Urdu dictionary, and carefully copying on bazaar paper the words of treachery. He was a tall, fine, *burra* sahib, barely acknowledging the deep salaams of the dark conquered, cool under fire, pukka at all times. *Pukka Sahib,* I thought, my stomach churning, but that was faking of a kind I had done before; I was sick not with disgust but with horror. Never before had the black deed loomed so real.

"Mustapha, could there be any doubt in my betrayer's mind that I was killed?" I asked.

"None, my son. On the day that you departed for Kalat, a rumor blew across the sands toward Hyderabad that a band of Yezedis from the Jebel Bariz had murdered a sahib and his follower for his rifle and horses. Your betrayer knew we had accused them falsely to avoid reprisal, but he would let sleeping dogs lie."

"Truly, he would."

"Mark, now, our cunning. A little of it was mine, the main was the hakim's who treated your wound. Mostly it was to save our necks from the Queen's rope, but partly it was our heart's delight in a great blood feud. Well we know that an officer, wise in our ways, would follow your footsteps with a stout guard. It came to pass, and in due course he arrived upon the scene of your capture. What he found there was, first, a great stain of blood on the sand. Also, he found a welter of tracks as though a sahib had run about trying to escape

216

from a band of horsemen. Also he found some valueless articles that the Yezedi had dropped when greedily searching your saddlebags, such as a broken jar that had held ghee, a letter, and an English book, as well as a worn-out belt of the dressing and decoration peculiar to the Shaitan worshippers, doubtless discarded when one of the band took yours in its stead. But his greatest find was your turban, with a bullet hole through it. And fear not we revealed our trickery by bungling. Ere I fired the ball, I had put the turban on the skull, which was set up at man's height, whereby it pierced its fold and the thin bone of the crown as well."

"In that, you were as my father even then."

"Mark you, what more we did, half in earnest, half in jest. The bones of the message bearer, Abdullah, were already cleaned by the birds of death. The skull, bearing the bullet hole, with the teeth drawn and another chopped out, was brought to the place, with a few other bones—a part of the pelvis, the long bone of the thigh, and a broken rib. These were scattered about as by the beasts of the desert. Such beasts had indeed been drawn to the spot by the smell of spilled blood, so there were tracks in plenty. The other bones had presumably been carried away to the animals' dens. Lest the desert foxes and wolves make away with those we wished found, we placed them only the night before the searchers came, our watchers reporting they had taken your trail and were following it fast as possible, but slowly as needs must."

"Were you careful of your own tracks, those you made on the day of my capture, and when you returned?"

"They were followable only to the plain of Jalmud's cairn, where the desert wind effaced every mark."

"What would the searchers guess of the fate of Hamyd?"

"Perhaps that he was carried off into slavery, or that these bones were all that remained of two skeletons."

"Do you know whether they were buried or carried away?"

"We know full well. We had posted another spy amid the rocks we call Dar-id-Daniyal, a good kos from the

217

spot, with the double-barreled spyglass we took from you. While the guard of lancers stood back, two sahibs advanced to make close survey of the scene. One of them was taller than the other."

The taller sahib was, of course, Gerald. Colonel Webb would not fail to grant his request to take part in the search. The other was probably Major Graves, no taller than I. Of course the betrayer, despite a quite lively interest in the affair, had resisted any temptation to be present. Even so, his sleep might have been troubled until the search party's return.

"The two officers walked here and there, often bending to look close at the ground," Mustapha went on. "They picked up articles, and peered at them long. At last the tall one took the skull—so white now it glimmered in the sunlight—and sitting down, examined it with great care. He was no doubt satisfied, because at once four of the guard were called forth, and began digging a hole in the sand. It was a deep hole, to judge from the time spent. At last the bones were wrapped in a saddle blanket taken from the tall man's horse and gently lowered into the hole. Then, while the guard formed a long line, one who had waited with them came forward, and stood still beside the hole, the others remaining motionless likewise. Then the hole was filled in and covered with a cairn of stones. So it remains today save for a worked stone which a squad of soldiers brought there and raised at the head of the cairn some two months later. It has writing on it that I cannot read."

When I did not speak, Mustapha spoke on in a shaking voice.

"No soldiers came to raze our village, or even to ask cunning questions. That was full proof that your kinsmen were assured you were slain by Yezedis." The old man laid his hand on my shoulder. "Truly, my son, unto them you are one who has drunk the cup of death. It's in your heart now that it be true—that you're a ghost revisiting these scenes—but it is not so! You are yet Lomri, your eyes undarkened, your blood swift-flowing, your cunning unabated, your hand bold and strong."

"Keif, keif." But my voice would not resound.

"Since your countenance is changed past recognition, your guise that of a Mussulman in every word and sign, you may make your search for the evil one, unnoticed as a pariah dog in the street, and, if need be, go into his service to find proof of his guilt. Lomri, how many are there, who could have done this thing?"

"There are two who coveted my *cobah* and had fair hope of taking her, if death took me. Both had scorned me, and one at least bore me deep hate. My *thar* is against one of these, or with one of her close kinsmen."

"By Allah, I would slay them all, rather than let the guilty one escape. When you sink the steel, turn the blade strongly in your hand ere you draw it forth. In your place I would slit his body its whole length, laying him open like a cleft fowl."

After hearing this, and seeing his aged eyes fill with unholy fire, I marveled at the thoughtful expression that followed swiftly and his meditative tone.

"My son, it is not good to be a slave. The very soul is wounded, and a man sometimes forgets he is a man. How long has it been since you proved yourself one, not by deeds of brain or hand before the world, but in the common way that all young men must, lest they know secret shame—alone with a bringer of delights?"

"Since before I went into slavery."

"Then I have a farewell wish that may also bless you. In my household is a slave girl from the Kashmir, taken from a caravan sacked by my kinsmen. At sight of the maiden, I became heated and claimed her for my prize, but I had been deceived by a mere ray of sunshine through the gray clouds of the winter of my years. Now both she and I are shamed that she has borne no babe."

"I hear you, father."

"It is my wish that you spend the night as guest of my house, the honors that I pay you, and that you pay me, never to be revealed."

CHAPTER TWENTY-SEVEN

A Shred of Cloth

A RIFLE REGIMENT HAD BEEN stationed at Kotri, in lieu of the Tatta Lancers now barracked at Lahore. But the people of Hyderabad had not forgotten the tall, blue-eyed horsemen, and the third tea seller I would ask, if not the second or the first, would probably know which *Jangli sawar* had married the Colonel's daughter.

I did not put the question to anyone, because I did not, at this time, want to know. It would amount to nothing as evidence, but I might become persuaded that it did. If, for instance, it were Henry Bingham, the most likely winner, but to my best judgment by far the most unlikely suspect of my three, I still did not want to devote thought to him until I had investigated the others. This was a fine, large reason, a credit to my intelligence and honesty. The only trouble with it was, another peeked out from behind it. Perhaps it was a desire to stifle my imagination. The man in whose arms she slept, to waken often in the night, also had no face. And behind that reason there might be still another, its existence predicated only by my stubborn insistence on its nonexistence.

Having told Hamyd to avoid any mention of his lost beloved, I would not find out from him.

Downy-chinned when I had first met him, Hamyd had now a good growth of beard. In Tajik dress, he need not fear a second glance, save from three or four friends he had made in his brief stay at Hyderabad, and for this he was prepared. I appointed him to look into the life—we already knew of his death—of my former servant, Abdullah. In the meantime I was going over the letter Abdullah had carried to Habistan. If the man

220

who wrote it should write another using the same grammatical forms, he would probably make the same mistakes. One very exciting item was his use and misspelling of the word *abyas,* meaning "white." It was not the vernacular word generally employed by Urdu speakers, and had undoubtedly come out of a rather comprehensive dictionary. Apparently he had used it to avoid the word sahib, itself a very interesting sign of the bent of his mind. He would not pay that honor even to one about to die.

He had spelled it *abpas.* Perhaps he had misread it, but possibly the dictionary had misprinted it. There were many such typographical errors in native dictionaries compiled by Calcutta babus, and some English dictionaries had factual errors.

On a long chance, I visited a shop that had carried books, mainly native literature but a few textbooks for students in various languages. The intelligent Parsi shopkeeper told me that he had stocked several English-Urdu dictionaries to sell to the troops, one kind large and fine fetching two rupees, but they were all gone.

Hamyd's luck was much better. He had loafed about the teahouses until he encountered a babu formerly employed at our regimental headquarters who was readily led to speak of old acquaintance among the officers' servants. He recalled Abdullah's last name, and told the quarter where he used to live.

His widow had moved, and since our inquiries had to be cautious, it was a week's work to locate her. She was living with Abdullah's brother, Jansar, a clerk in a silk shop, who apparently had taken her as a concubine. Jansar reminded me of Abdullah and was probably of the same ilk. The latter had married above him, which is hard for any man not to do, but not far.

"Fatima, your husband Abdullah left the city four years ago about the time of our Holy Day of Delivery," I began bluntly.

"Truly he did, and I've wept—"

"Doubtless, but you live in a better house than the one you left on Chamar Rasta. Do you want him to return?"

Jansar and Fatima looked at each other.

"To speak truly—" Jansar began.

"The wretch deserted me," Fatima broke in, "and I was shamed before my neighbors, but, lo, his brother took me into his household, caring for me with brotherly tenderness. I hope I'll never see Abdullah's face again."

I bade Jansar close the door and windows, and Fatima remove her veil, for I had long ago learned how to take advantage of others' guilts, wishes, and weaknesses, blackmail being a fine art in Eastern courts. When, with sour, sullen faces, they carried out my instructions, I showed them a cheap amulet that Mustapha had given me.

"Bismillah!" Jansar breathed. The woman looked frightened.

"He is, presumably, happy in his present abode," I went on. "That was his reward for bringing a paper to the enemies of a great sheik. I want to know all that you know of the writer of that paper, in the pursuance of my master's *thar*. So far, your names are not on the list of those who must pay the blood price. If you take great care, they will not be written down. Shortly before Abdullah's departure a sahib came to his house."

"If so, I never saw him." Fatima started to say something more, then closed her mouth.

"Fatima, wife of Abdullah," I murmured, while moving my forefinger as though writing on my palm. "Jansar, brother of Abdullah."

"The woman next door—she has moved away and is counted dead—saw someone come here that night before Abdullah went away," Fatima went on quickly. "He wore what seemed a face cloth against the dust, it being a windy night, although clear with a waning moon, but the shape of him, made out plainly against the moon-bright wall, made her think he was a sahib."

"Was he tall, or short, old or young?"

"He was tall—and he must have been young to leap over the goat-pen gate. A packet he had thrown through the window of our sleeping-room had struck a charcoal pot, with a noise loud in the night, causing

222

him to run. Like a very goat he sprang, Miriam told me."

I had learned, by now, how to hide feelings. A harshening of the tone will give the effect of it being steady.

"Could a sahib with gray hair and grown sons have sprung over the gate?"

"Perhaps, melik, he being alarmed lest he be seen. Yet I remember now that Miriam, herself but newly wedded, spoke of him as a 'young sahib.' "

I was greatly inclined to take her word for it. Mohammedan women, looking out from little windows, learn to see quickly and gaze deeply. If so, my search was well begun!

"What night was this?" I asked. "Since it was your last night you lay beside him, you haven't forgotten."

"Nay, or ever will. It was midnight before the Holy Day of Delivery, four years and some days ago."

Hamyd and I had started for the sand hills the preceding morning. My deliverer to the Rindi swords had worked fast.

"It comes to me that you've spoken truly. If not, you've yet time to redeem the lie ere vengeance falls. For, mark well, the full keeping of a vow made at Solomon's Throne may take a little longer because of your names added to the list, but hardly one moon at most."

"Defend us from the fury, O Stranger," Jansar cried. "If Fatima has lied to you, I swear before Allah she lied to me in the same words."

"Why should I lie to either of you, in the care of one I hate?"

"Do you believe me, Jansar and Fatima, that if either of you speak one word of this, to your neighbor, or your friend, or in the bath or the teahouse, to a lover or beloved, when heated with wine, or befogged with bhang, at that moment both of you have been bitten by the hooded serpent?"

Jansar stared wide-eyed at my scar, then turned his gray face to the woman and spoke in a frantic mutter.

"Fatima, have you told him all? I know the death feuds of Zamandawar! Too well I know this is a great sheik, who's come to us in common dress. By my beard, you didn't speak of the sahib's fall! Is the bread I buy

223

for you so stale and poor you'd trade it for death apple?"

"I forgot, lord," she wailed, her hand over her mouth to stifle the sound. "O Sheik, springing lightly over the gate, the sahib's garments caught on a nail of a chicken crate beyond, and threw him hard. I heard the noise of it, and Miriam thought she heard him groan. Miriam said that he lay still while she could have counted ten, then rose slowly. When he ran away, she saw him limping heavily, and doubtless in heavy pain."

"Where are the blue shreds of cloth?" Jansar demanded. "If you've lost them, I shall find a stick—"

"I wound them on a spool, thinking to sew a blue flower—"

Fatima hurried out of the room. If she was like most native women of this class, she would not have thrown away a hand's length of good corded thread. Jansar explained that she had found the shreds on or near a nail on the chicken box. When she returned with them and gave them to me with trembling hands, I had no doubt they had been torn from a pair of blue twill breeches, part of the undress uniform of the Tatta Lancers. I put them carefully away in my wallet.

"Was there blood on the box?" I asked.

"Not on the box, but quite a little on the ground where he lay."

"It may be that Allah will bless you for your true speaking," I told them. "The list of the soon dead is no longer than before."

When I had returned to the caravanserai, the heat of the hunt turning wintry in my heart, Hamyd looked carefully at the shreds, and seemed to think they were a great find. "Note this one, more heavily corded than the other," he said. "It's from the seam of the breeches leg, on the inside. By their length, it's plain that the nail caught two handbreadths above the knee and tore along the seam to the boot top. If there was blood easily seen on the ground, its point did more than scratch the skin. And it comes to me that if the nail had ripped unresisted through the cloth, no shreds would have been found. I think it was hard drawn through flesh as well."

"How may we look on the inside of a sahib's bare

224

leg? Yea, his servant may be hired to look for us—but that's a long road. Even so, I have gained much. A man of the Colonel's years might vault, would surely not leap, over the gate."

"Sahib, I have known the Colonel Sahib all my remembered life. I'll swear by my mother's chastity he didn't do this thing."

But that was the kind of blindness I must fight—the kind caused by unquestioning belief. When someone *knows* but cannot tell how—will swear to it before a galaxy of gods—that knowledge is especially suspect.

"Take care, Hamyd, you don't make her out a whore. By the light of reason, the Colonel Sahib is the most likely murderer of the three."

"Will you, that I may see better, throw that light?"

"True, he didn't slay the sergeant who stole cherries long ago, or murder his wife with a tool that drew blood, but does the blood he didn't shed foul the water of his bath? Am I the sergeant come again? You are a good Mussulman. Veneration of your father was sucked in with your mother's milk. The Colonel Sahib is the father of your greatly beloved. But the grayer a man's head, the more wicked are his thoughts moving therein. A young man remembers his mother, honor to him is something more than pride, but to an old man who has climbed high—what is right compared to his exceptional importance? Hamyd, my brother, from now on let's believe only what is proven. Tomorrow and perhaps the next day we'll seek the woman Miriam, in hope of learning more of Abdullah's visitor. Then we will go to Lahore, there to dwell in the shadow of the tall riders, and to gaze upon all three sahibs with the same straight eyes."

Miriam had vanished in the Indian swarm, but it so chanced that Hamyd and I did not need to go to Lahore to gladden our eyes with the sight of the Colonel Sahib. Hamyd brought me the report of his arrival in Hyderabad for a visit with the Commissioner Sahib, at present dwelling in the very house the Colonel had occupied when the Tatta Lancers had been quartered here.

"Did you ask the Commissioner's name?"

"Nay, and showed no interest in the matter. Doubtless he is acting for the Governor Sahib, now in England."

I saw nothing to be gained by spying on his guest, for which I was deeply thankful. But Hamyd's handsome black eyes were alight.

"Hamyd, if we should look again upon the Colonel Sahib, could you read guilt or innocence in his face?" I asked him, smiling.

"I should like to try, sahib. Dwelling with great evil changes the countenance, because it changes the soul. It isn't remorse, but a defense of evil, sometimes growing to a love thereof. Great fear changes it likewise. Mark you, lord, I know his face better than the palm of my hand, from often gazing upon it to know his least thought and mood. Maybe a vision will come to me."

Well, I would go with him. At least I could help handle the chokidar. This decided, a curtain was drawn aside, and I knew why I dreaded going. The sharpest, most powerful experience of my life, save a kind of death I had met in the sand hills, had occurred in the garden where we must lurk; it was also the most triumphant. In that house Sukey and I had defied its master. I had come once before in native garb to the gate of its compound, there to learn why I had been spied upon, a dog for whom Bachhiya had no anna, only her spit.

The Commissioner and his distinguished guest would not dine till about nine. We approached the house half an hour before—the area was policed but no longer a military reservation—to find the windows open to the breeze. Since the border was quiet now, two chokidars instead of armed sepoys watched the gates, and before we could decide on a stratagem, none was needed. The rear fellow left his post, and strolled around the house to *bukh* with the other. We made haste through the portal and were instantly concealed in the dark garden.

Its ghosts let me pass. Excited now, I led the way to the lighted window of the drawing-room, where, in a previous existence now thrown strangely back, the Colonel Sahib had questioned a suitor for his daughter's hand. While still ten paces from the window, I made him out, seated on a divan against the inner wall, facing someone seated in a high-backed chair. I could see the blond head of the latter, one arm and most of his legs. Both sahibs wore the black-and-white evening dress of civilians.

Even before I gained the window, blood rushed to my head. I did not look into the Colonel's face, and was staring, incredulously, at his host. Even before he showed me his profile, that incredulity had died. The Commissioner Sahib was Gerald.

He had wanted to be Governor. He was esteemed by Sir Charles. He was on the way. He looked a good deal older, but his distinction was even—

The wild welter of my thoughts, crowding upon one another, was interrupted by the clutch of Hamyd's hand upon my arm. From his position beside me he had once seen killers lying in ambush a second before I did. By a like circumstance he was now the first to discover a new entrant to the room. But I saw her move across it, with long, light steps—bend at Gerald's chair—kiss the lips he raised to her. The lamplight glossed her naked shoulders and limned her ghee-colored hair.

I turned quickly and stole away, aware of having no more life or substance than the black shadows of the night.

CHAPTER TWENTY-EIGHT

Unmistakable Clue

ROLLED IN MY LUNGI, at a room in the caravanserai, I wished that I could wish for something. My heart would not signal me its existence, save by its silly beat. After a long time, I did. I wished that the beautiful Memsahib Brook would give me back a little silver sixpence, now that she did not need its charm of Gypsy spittle. Since I must not let Hamyd follow me through these gates, with their dreadful legend overhead, I would restore him to her, in its stead. No, I had forgotten; Bachhiya had died, and he could not find her in the Commissioner's lady. He would rather go in with me.

He became a more passionate hunter, as though sensing a lack of passion in me. "Be of good heart, master," he told me on our journey to Lahore. "Doubtless we'll find proof that the judge sahibs will believe, if you're of a mind to let the hangman settle the debt. But if the proof be sufficient to you only, in due course your hand, or mine in your service, will bring unto him the bitter cup of death. Then, being out of debt and free, you shall embrace your kismet."

"You're certain now of the innocence of the Colonel Sahib?"

"Yes, lord. The vision came upon me as I'd prayed."

"Which of the two officers is your pick?"

"I've made none, sahib. Holmes Sahib was roundly beaten that very morning, and who can measure the hate and fury in his heart? But Bingham Sahib coveted the memsahib as much or more, and being kinsman to the white Rani and with princely honor, how would he take his defeat at your dark hands? The English Shahjazas go about with small trains, and mostly without cymbals and sounding brass. They don't bid their subjects prostrate themselves before them, and they can be most gracious, and good fellows at the feast, when they've lost a polo game. Once Bingham Sahib bade you strike him with a cane. Was he surprised to be obeyed, and did the blow burn like white fire when you came to stand between him and his heart's desire?"

It was very plausible. "I still think it was Holmes Sahib."

Hamyd brooded a moment, his face deeply lined. "It is our kismet to know shortly."

We wouldn't know without a lot of difficult and dangerous spying. That was as plain as the scar on my face. I wanted to look at the doctor's records for the Moslem Day of Delivery more than four years ago, and for a few days thereafter, to see if he treated a nail-raked leg. If not, one of us must somehow look for the scar. I would like to listen carefully to Clifford Holmes and Henry Bingham when they spoke Urdu, and, if possible, read letters they had written in that language. It was important to know if either of them had an English-Urdu dictionary that had misprinted the word *abyas*.

We could not trust hired spies. At first I had intended to employ Hamyd's talents for the job, but ever collided with the fact that he was far more likely to be recognized than I. Feeling perfectly competent for it, dreading the idleness of waiting, suddenly I decided that I would enjoy it. The role of servant to the very regiment from whose rolls my name had been crossed would not appeal to an English gentleman, but we off-white people, Gypsies and the like, love to dramatize ourselves. At least I would have to stay awake.

Staying at the caravanserai, Hamyd set himself up as a minor horse-trader. I sought out the Mess House *khansaman,* who hired its servants and whose hand liked grease. Although there was a constant turnover of employees, almost always he engaged his relatives, from whom he could exact a good share of their salaries, so I had to take pains. I began with telling him that my mother was sick, and my father reduced to beggary. He hoped that Allah would have mercy upon them. I remarked that great sahibs in Karachi had given me eloquent letters of recommendation. He nodded politely, but did not ask to see the letters. I was not at present employed because—he listened attentively for what might be an interesting variation from the usual—because my scar frightened the ignorant city folk, who associated it with the evil eye, but since I had won it in battle, it would certainly be admired and appreciated by battle-scarred sahibs. He smiled his approval, and leaned a little closer. The main business could now go forward.

"By Allah's will, and your mercy, I seek personal service to the sahibs, with whom I have a way—only Shaitan knows why—of winning rich baksheesh. Positions of greater *izzat* would put less silver in my pocket, as bitter experience has taught me. Hence I am not particular as to the salary itself. If I am given good food and warm lodgings, I shall be glad to turn the bulk of it over—say six rupees out of ten—to my benefactor."

We closed the bargain at seven. I became a "boy" of the officers' canteen, on the jump in late afternoon and after dinner, and with long hours to wash glasses, polish tables and chairs, and *bukh* with my fellows. I saw neither Clifford nor Henry the first day of my service, and of the other officers I used to know, none saw me. I was part of the canteen landscape. I came swiftly to their calls, salaaming deeply, and they were conscious of my swift and accurate filling of their orders, but they gazed through me as though I were as unsubstantial as other ghosts that might haunt this spot.

The excitement I had expected at sight of their faces did not develop. Mildly interested in their aging and changing, the effects of promotion or lack of it, I remained separated from them by an unbridgeable gulf. I waited upon them without the least sense of its queerness. When a tall senior lieutenant with buck teeth came in and ordered whisky, I marked his resolute manner and confident carriage—so different than when as a junior subaltern he had offered a toast to an outcast—but my choosing for him the largest peg from my tray of poured drinks was only a little joke between me and the Devil. I looked about for Major Graves, a little fearful of his sharp eyes, but decided he had been transferred to some busier scene. The captain who had risen from the ranks ere he rose to toast me might be retired, or he might be one of us ghosts. Perhaps his lonely spirit was still knocking at the door that he, in life, had never quite entered.

I wondered why any ghosts ever bothered to walk, unless, like me, they could not help themselves.

Windy old Jam, head boy, would tell me of my very death, if I would take the trouble of leading him up to it. On his own hook, he mentioned Gerald's rise, while displaying a magnificent tiger skin he had won while on leave. But Gerald did not come here any more. Not even his wraith need haunt these scenes. He had come into his own.

After dinner the following night, my heart took a running jump. Four officers entered the canteen, one of them a subaltern I did not know, one Dr. Haines who had excused me from watching a hanging and quoted Shakespeare at me, and the others were my quarry running together. I had not expected to confront both at once, and I had dreaded the first drink I served either one, lest my hand shake and the liquor spill on the table; but in a moment the blood in my veins flowed slowly and felt cold.

Both men were captains and both looked older than I had surmised. The face of Clifford Holmes had coarsened, he had drunk too much wine at dinner, and his voice and movements were a trifle pompous. I thought he knew he was not as *burra* as he wanted others and himself to believe, and I should have known from the first that he never would be. Clifford bitched too much of his business. One piece he had tried to do with me had caused a bump on his once aquiline nose and definitely thickened lips.

True, he did not look equal to the crime of treason and murder, but that fitted in with his bungling it. I had lived to avenge it, and he had lost its main prize, Sukey. By foresight she had seen him as I saw him now —only a *chota* [little] sahib; indeed she had told me that above either Clifford or Henry, she preferred Gerald. Yet I felt intense eagerness to prove his guilt. It

231

would become him better than Henry, who had the look of a sane, happy, successful man, long reconciled to Sukey's loss, bearing with distinction his name and riches.

"Boy!"

It was Clifford's voice, a little thick, a little pompous. I ran to him and salaamed.

"Sahib."

"Whisky *lowh.*" Then he looked at me sharply. "You're new here, aren't you?"

When I stared blankly, Dr. Haines spoke in his old good-humored tone.

"The sahib asked if thou art newly come."

"Yea, sahib."

"Why can't that damned butler hire niggers who can speak English?" Clifford demanded.

"Personally, I'd rather have tough countrymen like him than those boot-lapping house dogs," Henry told him. "Anyway, don't be a jackass."

When I brought Clifford the drink, Dr. Haines gave me a friendly smile. "What is thy name?" he asked.

"Timur, sahib."

"Art thou of the blood of the Lame One?"

"What desert man is not, sahib—when he has drunk bhang?"

"Thy claim could be stronger than most, since it comes to me that thou, like Timur, hath fought many battles."

"Not battles, sahib, only dog fights with our neighbors. But sometimes their fangs draw blood."

"I would like to look more closely at thy scar of honor. I'm the Doctor Sahib, and take interest in the medicines of thy people. When thou art at leisure, and I am, visit me at the *shafakhana.*"

I salaamed and withdrew, pleased with my gains. Somewhere in the doctor's office were his records of mid-March, of four years before. Two days later, while the officers were having tiffin and the canteen was empty, I went there and gave my name to an orderly. The fat babu expressed doubt that the great hakim was in his quarters, or would receive me if he was, but waddled away to see. In a moment I was allowed to enter, and found him enjoying a well-lardered tray of lunch.

"It is given out that every day I go to my home for tiffin," he told me, grinning, "but truly I lie doggo here certain days a week, to gain time for some reading and thought. Art thou a mind reader?"

"Nay, O Hakim, but the mess servants have sharp eyes and long tongues."

"Timur, hast thou not come down in the world, to pour the forbidden drink for sahibs?"

"I've been higher than this, betimes, but also lower."

"It was a sword or saber cut," he said thoughtfully, looking at my scar, "and well treated and kept clean."

"The cloths were soaked in vinegar, sahib, whose sourness fights the sickening sweetness of putrefaction."

"It comes to me thy women hardly knew thee when thou hadst returned from the wars."

This ice was a little thin. "Truly, they ran from me modestly, but not as fast as might be, being fat from lack of exercise, and from my knowing them, they soon knew me." The pun was more pointed in Urdu.

I had made a friend of the doctor then and there.

"The shape of thy forehead, and the slight hollows under the eye purses, mark a thinker," he observed.

"I pray thee, do not say so to the sahibs, or they will think I look above my station, and cast me forth."

"I will not, and they won't notice it, fear not. The two among us who would have noticed it, and sat with thee and questioned thee long, are with us no more."

"Great serdars, I doubt not."

"One was a major who has gone North. The other was a junior officer known to thy people as Lomri. He was the capturer of Kambar Melik, and he decoyed the Emir's *lashkar* into the ditch at Meeanee."

"I have heard much of him, sahib. He was slain by the Yezedi. But it was not fated that he live long. There were many who coveted his head."

"He was my fellow, in certain ways, and he left without my telling him farewell, or being present the last night he dined at the mess—to my long pain and regret." A queer darkness filled the wise eyes.

Doctor, I wish you had been present! One more would have stood to the toast, and perhaps spoken

233

plainly. It might have made more difference than you can dream.

"I am haunted by his spirit this moment," the doctor went on. "Timur, when you leave the service of the regiment—for it will not content you long—will you carry a message from me to those kinsmen of Kambar Melik who coveted his head? Then I think they will no longer bemoan its loss to the vile Yezedi, and perhaps rejoice that their kismet deprived them of the prize. Truly, they might lay another stone on his cairn."

"I will carry thy message, Hakim Sahib."

"Tell them he captured the border raider at his Rani's command, but he could not watch his hanging."

"Keif, keif."

When he had mused a few seconds, I played a card.

"O Hakim, I have known few sahibs whose tongues are so wise and fluent in our speech. Would that mine were as learned in thine. Then I would not have been shamed before thy fellows."

"Thou has no cause to be shamed. It is our business to learn the speech of the people, not theirs to learn ours."

"It came to me that one of the captains, Holmes Sahib, knew naught of our speech or our ways, or he would not have called us 'niggers,'—one English word that every coolie knows. But the other captain, whose name I have not heard, looked to be wise."

"Nay, Holmes Sahib speaks Urdu incorrectly but with fair fluence. That day he was—a little—*matwalla*. The other captain, Bingham Sahib, is indeed wise in some matters—I know him well—but he knows not a dozen words of Urdu. Truly God did not give him the gift of tongues."

"Hakim Sahib, I spoke too freely and pray thy pardon. And taking advantage of thy courtesy, I have used much of thy precious time—"

The doctor looked at a ledger open on his desk, then glanced at his watch.

"I must go to the bedside of a sick one even now, but —art thou needed in the canteen?"

"Not for a time yet, sahib."

"Then if I am not gone too long, wait for me. I am

preparing a paper, for a society of hakims in London, on native medicine. And it so happens—and I myself speak too freely—I'm already well instructed in the noble game called polo."

He did not expect me to smile, so I did not, but he smiled wryly to himself.

"To hear is to obey," I told him. "But wilt thou instruct me, a newcomer, whether it be forbidden to look at the pictures in thy wise books?"

"Help yourself."

He went out, and I could hardly believe this chance had come so soon. The ledger on his desk had brown cardboard covers; on a shelf in easy reach was a stack with the same binding. I waited a crawling five minutes lest the absent-minded doctor return for something he had forgotten. Then I looked at the topmost of the stack.

In his bold hand he had written *1847*. I laid aside that one and two more. In the volume marked *1844* I was looking for the entries in mid-March when the entry *Lieutenant Holmes* jumped from the page to my eyes. But the date given was the day I had departed for the sand hills, not the day following, and he was not being treated for a long nail tear on the inside of his leg.

I read:

Lieutenant Holmes brought in with a badly bashed face, received in fisticuffs (the God-damned fool). Nasal bone fractured, both eyes swollen, severe trauma all over face. Prescribed hot compresses and rest.

I turned the page. The entry was for 8 p.m. of the following evening, some four hours before a packet was thrown into Abdullah's bedroom.

Lieutenant Holmes's face badly inflamed. Temperature 101, pulse 110. Considerable pain (serves the bastard right). Incipient delirium. Prescribed sedative. 10 p.m. Fever 103 2/5. Semidelirious and in severe pain. Prescribed 1/3 grain opium. 11 p.m. Holmes responded well to opium, sound sleep. Midnight. Same. No rise in temperature.

235

2 a.m. Heavy sleep. Temperature 102. 4 a.m. Temperature 100. Prescribed physic but can't wake patient. 6 a.m., and another day, temperature normal, Holmes still asleep, and I wish to hell I was.

I wished to hell that I was, too, and had dreamed all this. Instead I was feverishly awake, every nerve taut, and my brain turning over fast. I read on a few pages to see if anyone had reported a clawed leg. Of course no one had—its owner would have treated it himself, in breathless secrecy. The Colonel in his mansion? I had been a fool to take any stock in Hamyd's vision! The son of an English peer in his cozy quarters? How could Dr. Haines know for certain that he did not speak Urdu, or have some deeply trusted confidant who did?

I went back to answering "Boy!" I did not want to go back to the hunt for a little while, but the game ran all over me. Grizzled Jam, who had poured drinks for the Tatta Lancers before I was born, himself brought up the subject of the officers' linguistics, remarking to Fethi Nur that the new times were not like the old, when mere subalterns could speak the language of the country, and no orders were ever mixed up. Now very majors—save Graves Sahib, who had gone—did well to blather a little Hindustani of the bazaars.

"But what of the great Colonel Sahib?" I asked. "Surely he—"

Jam looked uncomfortable. "Webb Sahib speaks Hindi well, but his affairs have been too great for him to learn Urdu. When I forget and speak it unto him, I could as well chatter like a monkey."

"Bingham Sahib told me he could not write or speak in Urdu," I proposed.

"Nay, but he can be forgiven, since his silver poured into our purses sings a merry tune," Fethi Nur replied.

But if either had a comprehensive English-Urdu dictionary, as well as a work on Urdu grammar, he might, with great labor, piece out an Urdu letter. There might be such books in the Mess House library. The writer could have borrowed and returned them. Owning such books, he might have, in time, put them in the library, for it was the officers' custom to contribute to it, especially if transferred to another regiment. When the club-rooms were empty, I went in to see.

There were many more books than before, and the larger room was but faintly reminiscent of the cubby-hole at Hyderabad, where Sukey had wiped my kisses from her mouth. What appeared to be its most recent addition was a whole shelf of ponderous tomes, most of them dealing with Indian military and scientific subjects, with a few sober works on polo and big-game hunting. Wondering what ambitious and rather scholarly sportsman had made the gift, I opened a thick *Life of Clive* to look at the bookplate.

There I found Gerald's name.

How little I had realized his parts! He had never told me about his studies or paraded his learning; and Sukey had perceived him more clearly than I. That was why she had married him, and would soon be memsahib to the Governor of Sind. Sukey, the little piece of silver that I gave you brought you wonderful luck! But you should have never parted with Hamyd. Any luck you gave him has worsened since then.

I was turning back the cover of *Etymology of the Indian Desert*. Gerald's bookplate was in it, as well as in other volumes that passed half-seen through my hands. Sukey, I wish I didn't love you any more. Since it was written that he who lusts after a woman is an equal sinner with him who gratifies that lust, I am breaking two commandments in one fell swoop, and committing technical incest to boot! My brother's wife—but I thanked my Gypsy gods I had never doubted he was the best man. I ought to be glad he was also the lucky man. It does not always follow—

Among the big books was a little one, privately printed and beautifully bound, of Gerald's own authorship. It was entitled *Tiger Drives in the Tehri* and appeared to be a modest, informative account of a vacation spent with Sukey as the guest of a rajah in the North. I was not surprised by the offering. Most of the important sahib administrators in India took up big-game hunting in an extremely pukka way—mainly full-dress affairs held by native kings, in which tigers and other game were driven by long lines of beaters toward the guns. This was only another indication of Gerald's ambition and its swift advancement.

Thinking of Sukey's shining eyes as the tigers broke from the thickets, I had opened another book without looking at the title. After seeing Gerald's signature, the title page caught my eye. It was So-and-So's—with many letters—*Complete English-Urdu Dictionary, Containing a Full Glossary*.

I had never known before that a man's hands can move, and his eyes read type, when his heart has stopped beating.

I turned to the word "white." It gave several Urdu equivalents, but the last, *abyas,* borrowed from the Arabic, had been misspelled or misprinted *abpas*.

CHAPTER TWENTY-NINE

Proof of Treachery

WHEN A SENSE OF SPACE AND TIME returned to me, I was roaming narrow, crooked roads near the Mosque of Wazir Khan. I was properly dressed for the street, having taken off the Mess House livery and presumably left it in the servants' dressing-room. When I began going over certain matters in my mind, I discovered that I had already gone over them, perhaps several times, and to some of them I had found the answers.

It was now perfectly plain why my eagerness to convict Clifford—or Colonel Webb—or even Henry Bingham—had become a frantic, unreasoning anxiety. I knew now why I had not wanted to know who had married Sukey. I had been dodging these demons, denying their existence—myself the three smug little monkeys in a row, sillily covering eyes, ears, and mouth, for four years.

I turned abruptly, and went quickly to the caravanserai. I could not eat, but I smoked quietly and read a little from Avicenna until Hamyd returned. He glanced at me, then stared. I did not know what made him touch both hands to his forehead in a deep salaam; we had long ago dispensed with those tokens.

"What has happened, sahib?" he asked, his voice trembling.

"Sit down on a cushion, Hamyd, or if you want some tea—*timbak*—"

"Nay, I had a cup and a pipe at the horse market." He sat down, crossing his legs like Buddha. I cleared my throat and spoke with fair ease.

"Hamyd, have you ever thought that our betrayer might have been my foster brother Gerald?" I had

239

never before remembered using the plural possessive pronoun; I had thought about Hamyd's capture as an accident, chanced by his service to me. Actually, as my follower, he, too, had been in the service of the Queen. If we had both been killed, we would have both been murdered.

He turned gray, then slowly nodded.

"How long ago did the thought strike you?"

"It was so long I can't remember."

"When you saw he was the husband of Sukey, you became hot on the chase of Holmes and Bingham Sahibs. Was that for the love of the memsahib?"

"Partly for love of her, sahib, and partly for love of you." He spoke simply.

A lizard climbed up the walls. I watched him stalk and kill a fly. Then I told Hamyd about the dictionary.

"Mark you, Hamyd, that's no proof of Gerald's guilt, only a good reason to search for it." I went on quickly. "How do we know who might have borrowed the book? But we will search on, when and where we can, until it's found, no matter where it lies."

"If you die, and I live, I'll search alone. *Allah Akbar!*"

"If you die, and I live, I'll search alone. Hamyd, did Bachhiya's marrying my brother make you more inclined to believe him guilty?"

"Yea, sahib. Bachhiya loved you with great passion, and she married him because he was much more like you than you know. I remembered that, when I saw her give him her lips. He's a most resolute man. That moved my Bachhiya, who is like to the native women in her craving for a strong begetter of her babes. He's also a ruthless man, if I judge aright, and the servants' talk be true. Your ruthlessness fights with justice in your heart, or sometimes even with pity, but I wondered if his did. You'd both been through fire of a fierce sort—which drew her to him as to you, for she, too, had been through fire. But if the flame he carried from those fires was on the opposite side of yours—" Hamyd paused.

"Hate?"

"Yes, sahib."

"Did you think he hated me?"

"I didn't know. I knew only what Bachhiya told me —a secret you had told her—and what you babbled of, in your dreams, the night you had walked wounded across the desert to the pavilions of Mustapha Sheik."

"I must have spoken in English—"

"I had learned English, sahib, but Bachhiya and I spoke better in Hindustani, as do you and I."

"I told you I was his bastard half-brother, by a Gypsy woman, and raised in his father's house?"

"In his mother's house, you said. But you said something else. I remember the very words. 'Gerald wouldn't drink the toast. Mamma hated me, and he hates me, too.' And I wiped the tears from your face, lest the Rindi see them and deem them weakness."

"But Hamyd, you yourself never saw any sign of his hating me. Did you?"

"I saw cause for it, sahib, even before Bachhiya told me of his mother's hate. He was a pukka sahib, an Englishman of the English, of higher rank, acceptable as Bachhiya's suitor, richer than you, a product of great schools, while you were a half-caste. He looked the part of the pukka sahib, tall, handsome, and fine, while you were swarthy, with Asia in your eyes, and a hawk's nose. He was a great horseman and polo player and deadly lancer, while you cared for none of these things. Yet you always won. It was you who won fame with the enemy, whereby a price was put upon your head. It was you whom the wise doctor admired, and whom Major Graves was pushing toward high office, and whom Colonel Jacob, one of India's greatest, favored above all the officers in the Brigade. Didn't your brother see you snatch prize after prize from his hands? Nay, but he thought he did—save for you in his way, he believed he would have won them all. And the day came that you snatched—truly from his hands—the greatest prize of all. He had wit to recognize it—that much I knew from the first—and wit to know that, save for you, he would surely win it. Think you he cared for Bingham and Holmes Sahibs? They were cobwebs in his path. Bachhiya played with the idea of marrying first one and then the other. But you alone stood between his winning her, as both of them knew. And, sahib, he almost won."

"He did win, Hamyd."

"Even so, when the way was cleared. Was it by his hand or another's? But it comes to me now, I saw what might have been a sign of his hate. On the night of your return from the tower, you talked to him long. I was watching through the window, knowing even then he was the horseman whose hoofs I had heard at a distance when I had stood guard far from the fire. I could barely hear your low voices as you sat there, but I saw his face ere he came to the window and spat. You thought he had drawn bitterness from his pipe. I thought it was disgust, born of hate, that you had lain with Bachhiya."

"That night, too, he didn't drink to our wedding," I said, my voice flat in my ears. "He said he would soon —and I thought he'd forgotten—"

"I would pour you a drink of whisky—"

"Not yet. He said it, too—'not yet'—when I offered him the drink. Then he asked me if I'd told Sukey of my Gypsy blood. He acted relieved that I had—was he relieved?—then he seemed worried—trying to hide it and not being able to—that I hadn't told her before she fell in love. Was he *glad* I'd taken advantage of her, to ease his own conscience for what he was planning to do even then? Remember how short the time was."

"Not too short for someone to borrow a book from him, sahib, or to go into his quarters to use one."

"Thanks, but it's a little thin. I remember now that at our last meeting Gerald suggested the marriage be delayed. Did he hope that in the meantime he could break it off without killing me? Or did he know he had to kill me and just wanted more time to do a safe job? I'd like to think that if he waited until I got out of his room and then got his dictionary and a piece of bazaar paper—I'd like to think he'd decided there was no other way."

"You are weakened, sahib, even as by loss of blood on that Day of Woe. What do you care whether he did it in sorrow or fierce joy? The words are too pale upon your lips."

Hamyd rose, poured arrack into a glass, diluted it with water, and handed it to me.

"Yes, it was a weakness," I told him, as my cold body warmed a little. "But, mark you, Hamyd, where the train of thought leads. Not toward the likelihood of his innocence, but of his guilt. I told him neither Bachhiya nor I would dream of delaying the marriage. I was unmoved when he told me that all the sahibs and memsahibs of India would close their doors to her if she married me. By all that, I was giving him what he could believe was justification. Maybe he craved it to feed his hate, and hunted everywhere for it, but he was a man who had to have it, before he could strike. He prided himself on being a great sahib. He didn't have clear eyes to see the evil in his heart and soul—as I have to see mine. By his thinking, twisted by long, deep, and gnawing hate, he was justified at saving Bachhiya from me at any cost."

"And to take the prize thereof." Hamyd spoke quietly, without palpable irony, but that was enforced upon him, as I knew when I glanced into his face. He was in a scorn of passion such as I had never seen.

"I call to mind now his asking me if I'd lost the Gypsy charm," I went on when Hamyd had calmed himself. "Much seemed to hang on my answer. When I told him I'd given it to Bachhiya, he was either greatly worried—or greatly relieved. And then—" But the sweat burst out on my face and hands and my throat closed.

"Speak slowly, sahib, and evenly, and it will come."

"I told him she had given you to me."

"And then?"

"He asked if you had been a go-between between her and me, in our secret courtship. I said you had hand in it."

"Was he again relieved?"

"I think now that he was, Hamyd."

"I thank the great sahib for making sure I deserved death, ere he slew me."

"Don't convict him without a fair trial, my brother! Surely a nail tear deep enough to bleed well will leave a scar. Tomorrow we'll set out for Hyderabad to see with our own eyes. If we find one, on the inside of the leg from above the knee to the boot top, it still might have been caused by some other injury. But taken with the other evidence, it will be final satisfaction to me of his guilt."

We went there at a dogged pace. Taking quarters at a serai close to the Commissioner's mansion, with all the care and cunning we could muster we contrived a plot. Its very perfecting so occupied my brain that I had little dealings with my heart. By the time we had gone over it detail by detail, made our extensive preparations, and rehearsed its every move, we were as cold and steady in its confronting as though it were a trade at horse fair.

In laying the ground, I made use of some shoptalk I had overheard in the canteen at Lahore. It was that in case the Sikhs rose again, their general, Shere Singh, serving under Sir Harry Lawrence, might join the mutiny. No doubt Gerald, bearing heavy responsibility in his chief's absence, was worried about Shere Singh's loyalty, since trouble in the North was surely brewing. So Hamyd wrote, in the ill-spelled native-sounding English he had learned, the following letter:

Excellency the Commissioner Sahib.
Exalted Sir:
I have obtained knowledge that the Serdar Shere Singh plots with the Rani Jindan to slay all the sahibs in the Punjab. Only if it be proven, beyond your and other sahibs' doubt, will I seek reward, and then but 500 rupees. I will ask no earnest of the sum.

But I dare not whisper the knowledge to any ears but yours. I will trust no Sindhi, and no sahib under you, for while I know of your noble honor, my mother's uncle was once betrayed by a sahib. I am very frightened, O Excellent One. I would not have any but you see my face. If you will hear me, I will come tonight to the rear gate of the compound. I will draw the cloth over my face as I beseech entrance, but bid the guard search me for any weapon, lest I be an enemy seeking your death. I will say the word "jharu," meaning a broom, so he may know me, and when I stand alone with you, in the courtyard, I will drop the cloth in token of faith. I will take your most honorable word that you will post no spies. The token of that word will be your name signed on the back of this letter, and returned to me by bearer. I cannot give my name lest this paper fall into some other hands, and truly, if it be not returned, with your name thereon, I must flee the city. I love money, by which I live, but I love not Sikhs.

Your humble servant
Jharu

Hamyd told me that Sukey had never seen his handwriting in English, and when I compared it to his hand in Urdu, all the letters of which were shaped differently, there was not the least resemblance. Nor did I have much doubt that Gerald would take the bait. It would be a great feather in his official cap to discover treachery in Shere Singh, and, unless I missed my guess, he would be flattered by the writer's trust in his honor. I could picture him showing the letter to Sukey, but, in the same eerie vision, telling her she must not peek! The keeping of a promise made to a native is even more important than one made to a sahib. A great many administrators don't understand that, Sukey. That is why a good many of them fall down on the job. A sahib could understand how circumstances forced the breaking of another sahib's word, but natives only looked at the result. Sukey, you must promise not to peek. It's one of those little, but important things—

Hamyd sealed the letter with candle wax, marked it confidential, and entrusted it to a native chaprasi long operating at the bazaar. The bearer's instructions were to deliver it into the hands of the Commissioner Sahib, Brook Sahib by name, and to no other; otherwise he was to bring it back. On his return he was to wait at a certain corner. Hamyd watched from an alley to make sure no suspicious-looking strangers had collected thereabouts, then retrieved the reply, paid off the bearer, and brought it to me. Gerald had signed it in his bold hand.

Hamyd and I remained cool. About ten o'clock Hamyd approached the rear gate of the compound, I about thirty paces behind him, barefooted, and completely hidden in the gloom of the moonless night. The chokidar had a lantern, which was a good thing, since it would save me lighting the one I carried under my garment. As Hamyd drew into its light, he lifted his neck scarf to cover the lower part of his face. The chokidar ran his hands up and down Hamyd's body, felt under his arms and between his legs, and then had him remove his turban. I tiptoed along the compound wall to a jutting pilaster, not more than twenty feet from the gate, my face cloth raised, and a four-foot length of bamboo ready in my hand.

This was what was known as a female bamboo, as opposed to the much heavier male, and an ideal club for the purpose, since it would break short of cracking the skull.

A dangerous moment passed when the chokidar did not touch what seemed an envelope in Hamyd's hand. Actually it was a lead plate, a quarter of an inch thick, on which I had pasted white paper. Hamyd was then admitted, and, just as I had expected, the sentinel turned to gaze after him, his lantern held high, his body cutting off the light.

Hamyd was to stop about twenty feet from the gate, as though afraid, at a point shielded from view of the windows by an outbuilding. When I heard him say, "Art thou the Commissioner Sahib?" I began to count ten, and keeping the timing we had practiced helped me keep cool. I did not hear Hamyd say, "Protector of the Poor," so at the tenth count I took three silent, long, forward strides still in deep shadow, and then sprang toward the gate. The chokidar heard my footfall in the sandy alley, and had no time to turn or cry out before I had stunned him with a hard blow atop his turban. He was reeling as I struck him in the jaw with my free hand and snatched his lantern.

When I lifted it, it showed Gerald hanging in Hamyd's arms. At once he threw him over his shoulder and carried him to the appointed place close by the wall. I dragged the chokidar—who was certainly out of the fight for all the time we needed—away from the gateway. Then I looked at Gerald and saw that Hamyd had done his work well.

He had planned to strike with the lead plate, laid flat on his hand, the instant that Gerald whirled at the thwack of my bamboo. His victim was groaning a little and evidently half-conscious, but that served our needs better than if he had been knocked insensible. Hamyd had raised his face cloth and was fixing him a gag; I began turning his pockets wrong side out and jerking open his shirt as though in search of something.

"I cannot find it," I said in a low voice to Hamyd in Urdu.

"Cut his braces, and take off his trousers and jacket. It may be sewed in the lining."

Whether he heard us, there was no way to know, but the garments I hauled off of him would have every appearance of a minute search, after Hamyd had split or cut away their linings. He was busy at it as I pulled down Gerald's stockings and held the lantern over his bare legs.

The lantern light was soft and yellow, but such light will sometimes pick up variations in color and texture invisible in a glare. The narrow scar ran from the calf to just above the knee on the inside of his right leg.

I had a knife in my hand, with which I had just cut his braces. I looked at his neck, a length of it bared by the sideways lop of his head glimmering in the lantern light. I could do it now, because my heart was cold. There was not enough heat in it to kindle any thought or feeling or memory; they were all stone-cold. My pledge to the Emir mattered no more than if I had died. I did not crave the steel's soft plunge or the red geyser or anything else; I was only a tool of some great necessity above or beyond me. I had no desire to be used, or any reluctance. And it seemed unless I did it now, it might never be done.

It had to be done and the sooner the better. Then I was bothered by the light changing subtly and the feeling, very faint, that I must find out why. "*Jharu!*" Hamyd murmured in quick warning, and his remembering not to call me "sahib" waked me more than the sound. The light's changing was caused by there being

247

some where none had been before. From around the corner of the outbuilding a yellow glimmer slowly grew and spread.

I had drawn an unloaded pistol when its source came into view—a candle flame, unflickering in the windless darkness. Sukey was wearing a white gown that reflected well its thin yellow shine, and our lantern light reached out through the gloom to glimmer on its silver stick. Hamyd held the lantern in front of him, and the big shadow of his body blacked out most of Gerald's body and made other lines and shapes incomplete and indistinct. Even so, if she had been much alarmed to start with, she would have seen enough in her first glance to cause her to take some action—to run or scream or both. Evidently she expected to find Gerald talking to a native, and had in the dim glimmer mistaken one of us for him.

I spoke instantly in a low tone.

"Don't make a sound, memsahib, for thy own and thy lord's life."

Her eyes fixed on my pistol, and she did not make a sound.

"He will waken in a moment, and we will be gone. We were sent to get a certain paper, supposed to be on his person at all times. Walk a little nearer."

She did so, with a slow, steady step.

"We bear ye no ill will for our fool's errand, but will surely kill ye both if one word is disobeyed. Be seated, memsahib, on the cobblestones. Jharu, guard her closely with this gun."

I passed it to him and had her clasp her hands behind her back. With a thong worn handy on my belt I tied her smooth, strong wrists. They throbbed a little in my hands.

"Thy pardon, memsahib," I told her as, pretending to stay out of the line of fire, I tied another thong about her ankles. Lastly, I started to stuff a cloth into her mouth.

"Do not, melik [lord]," she said quickly. "I will puke, and it will go down my windpipe and strangle me. I am—I was—Bachhiya, daughter of the Colonel

Sahib, and I swear by Siv and Kali I won't utter a sound until the servants come."

My palms remained a second or two on her silken throat. Then I beckoned to Hamyd, and we ran through the gate and away into the darkness.

CHAPTER THIRTY

Worthless Captive

HAMYD AND I HAD CAREFULLY CHARTED and kept open our line of retreat. It was rather elaborate and had dramatic aspects that somehow crept, without my conscious bidding, into so many of my projects; at the same time it offered an extraordinarily high margin of safety. Making to a busy native road near by, and picking up a bundle on the way, we entered a darkened *Kasbighar*, where two good Mussulmen could well hide their faces behind their neck cloths until each would be alone with his bringer of delights.

To the chokidar we explained that we were pilgrims from beyond the Kohidistan. By the tenets of our sect, we must perform certain ablutions and ceremonies before we sinned, as well as afterward, for which we needed some hot water and a few minutes' privacy. I already had in my pocket a razor, scissors, and some shaving-soap; in jig time I shaved Hamyd clean, helped strip him of Musselman clothes, and stuffed him into those of a Hindu of the tradesman class. When the hall was clear, he sneaked out into the street. Then I summoned the chokidar.

"My brother, when we gazed into the *mirayat* [magic mirror] the auspices were bad," I told him. "Truly we've been tempted by Shaitan. My fellow was so frightened that he has fled. Sadly I will go forth also, my base flesh hungering but my spirit soothed by a dream of Paradise."

"Who will pay me for—"

"The hot water and ten minutes' rental of the room? That you may give in charity to two pilgrims, but the number three came into the dream, perchance meaning

250

three annas, which I will give you lest unknowingly I've incurred debt."

The chokidar salaamed and then shrugged. He was used to all kinds. In the dark entry I changed my blue lungi and turban for much finer white ones carried in the bundle. I was sure now that we had eluded immediate pursuit, and had no serious doubt of safe flight soon from the city. To calculate our best chances, again I had to devote thought to Gerald and Sukey—a team now, one always involved with the other—despite my intense desire to ignore their existences until some years were done. Neither of the pair, nor the chokidar, had seen my scar. Only Gerald had seen Hamyd's face by dim light, masked by his beard, and our low voices changed by nervous strain would be hard to recognize after a few weeks' absence, let alone from under an old cairn of stones, a landmark now in the sandhills.

Hamyd and I went back to trading at horse fair. After two weeks I thought that the watch of departing caravans must be growing slack, the Sind police being shorthanded, anyway. Still our safest route would be the peaceful South, where spies had little business now, and hence a long, roundabout way home. Indeed, I was grateful for the excuse for a big horse-trading jaunt through regions of India I had never seen. Not half of our six months' leave had expired, and we need not, like old, lame dogs, head straight for our kennels in Kalat.

So we joined a company of merchants and travelers making for the Rann of Cutch. A sepoy guard fumbled our bales for stolen rifles, and his scanning of our faces —perhaps in search of notorious spies—was officious but halfhearted. At Badin in the desert we changed to a caravan making for Bakhasar, and there we traded some tall scrubs for shorter but better stock. We carried coals to Newcastle at Jodhpur, but had had an interesting journey at no great cost; and at Bikaner, all India became our oyster to open and search for pearls. This old, walled desert city was the home and headquarters of the Marwari, the great traveling traders who dealt from the Chin Hills to Persia. If we wished to buy civet in Katmandu we need only wait for a caravan going that way. Hamyd and I planned a fascinating ramble by way of Multan to the very Khyber.

It so chanced we went wide of that road also. The trouble in the North was turning into a full-scale war against the mutinous Sikhs. It did not concern me now, so with the scared Marwari we made for Dera Ismail Khan on the Indus. Hamyd and I, falling in with a party of armed Rindi, went through the bandit-infested Gomal Pass.

We thought to visit Kabul before circling southward to Kalat. Travel was far from safe, but neither of us had as much to lose as long ago. Bravery is curiously related to riches, whether of the purse or the heart: he who is rich in both must be brave to mount a fractious horse, but he who is poor in both need not tremble overly in the mouths of cannons. Hamyd and I had each other, a drove of good horses, half of which belonged to the Grand Vizier, and a distant hope. But we never reached the ancient capital, on account of guarding a trifling prize which, I had been told, was not worth two hundred rupees.

We had crossed the Kabul River at Jalalabad, to trade in the horse markets northward, when on the caravan road from the Kunar we came suddenly on a band of Pathans who had every earmark of robbers. I had never seen a more villainous-looking crew, and except for knowing the stout hearts and the good aim of my companions, we would have showed them clean heels. Their number was almost the equal of ours, but they knew the Rindi of old, and I was not surprised when they gave us Allah's peace.

We had met them in a defile between low hills and were at close quarters. Noticing their ill-hidden eagerness to hasten on, I feigned interest in their camels, meanwhile wondering what in the Devil they had been up to. Two or three had recent wounds, and two of the worst ruffians in the lot remained in the background, blocking my view of a third camel and its diminutive rider. The latter was dressed like an urchin of the tribe, but the little strip I could see between face cloth and cap looked definitely lighter-colored than the dirty brown hides of the rest.

"Yonder is a very young soldier, to go harrying the Unbelievers," I remarked to the headman.

"He's the son of one of us, but don't go near his camel, for the brute is the most vicious-tempered of our drove. I bade my men keep his teeth out of the reach of yours."

"Are all the grown men afraid to ride him?" I replied, approaching closer. Then the short hairs rose on my neck, for the big, frightened eyes between the rift of the cloth were unmistakably blue.

"Have you slain many of the foe, little soldier?" I asked.

I received two replies, both eloquent beyond the power of words. One was in the child's eyes. Until now I had supposed that very little could be conveyed in this way, without expressions of the mouth and the movement of facial muscles. Yet their glance into mine was a fervid prayer for help. The other reply from beneath her face cloth was a faint wail, not only of terror and woe but somehow of blind faith in me.

"The boy is afraid of strangers," one of the two watchers said, laughing loudly.

"But not of a vicious camel?" I turned and beckoned to Abu Melik, the chief of the Rindi. When he rode up beside me, we talked quietly in the bastard Arabic that I did not think either of the two Pathans understood.

"These great warriors have raided up the Kunar," I told him. "Allah be praised, they got the worse of it, to judge from their small baggage and the scars of battle, but they managed to snatch up one little girl."

"They be jackals parading as men," Abu Melik answered stoutly, and spat on the ground.

One of the Pathans scowled and touched the hilt of his knife, then slowly drew away his hand.

"Abu Melik, they shame their turbans, and it comes to me that this day we should strike a blow for Allah, the great, the glorious, and the compassionate."

Abu gave his beard a fierce tug. "You are not of our tribe, O Timur, but if that be the vision before your eyes, by Allah, we will cut every throat."

"Yea, if need be to deliver the helpless one, but it

253

may be they will surrender her to save their dogs' lives. Will you draw your Rindi into battle line, to give weight to the words I shall speak?"

"Even so, O Sheik of horse-trader mien, and be not too gentle of word or hand, for my sword has thirsted long."

As the Rindi were grouping, I spoke to the Pathan who had touched his knife, the more formidable of the pair.

"This small one is not the son of one of your number, but a fair-haired girl of Kafiristan, whom you are taking to sell in Kabul."

"Who shall question what we do with the spoils of war against the vile Unbelievers?" he answered loud and fierce, again clutching his big knife.

"Draw the steel, if you can, before the quickest of the Rindi can shoot you off your camel."

"Why, now, we came in peace and would go in peace. You, too, be of the Faith. But truly—"

"What other use would you have for her? She has seen but ten snows."

"What would she bring in the slave markets? A hundred rupees? Two hundred at the most? Is it for that we have fed her many days among her devil mountains? What is even two hundred rupees, divided among us all?" He was speaking loudly, for his companions to hear. "Truly we've been accursed by many devils ever since we rode forth on holy war. But I was the one who slew her parents, and it so chances that my eye is taken with her fair hair and blue eyes. If they will award her to me, I will give them certain other spoil I have, worth well over a hundred rupees, and take her to my bosom, where in time she may bear free-born babes."

I turned and called to Abu Melik. "Will you look to your muskets?"

"Yes, Timur Sheik."

"It may be you'll have need to use them, but I think not. The child stealers aren't spoiling for a fight. But the jackals would get their fangs into some of us ere they died, so whatever happens between this dog and me, I ask that you don't fire unless they attack you."

"Even so, O Hakim."

I turned again to the scowling Pathan. "Aren't the Kaffirs peaceful dwellers of their mountain ranges, never raiding your villages?"

"Aye, but they worship strange gods."

"I would on no account buy her, to reward with silver your evil deeds, but I ask you to give her to me."

"What kind of a fool is this?" the man asked his companion.

"You say you slew her parents. Was it in a great fight?"

"If Omad says so, he lies," one of his clansmen answered angrily. "Then he would have spoil-right to her. He came upon her, with her parents and little brothers, herding their sheep far from my village. Truly, they fought the best they could with their shepherd's crooks, even the little boy trying to defend his sister, but he shot the man, drove his sword through the woman, who was uncomely, and holding the boy by the foot, like a cockerel, cut his throat. If you are a hakim, as your followers say, does that merit him more than his share of her market price, divided among us all?"

"I think it does." I turned to Omad. "I ask you for the last time. Will you give her to me?" I think my face was pale, it felt so cold, and he misunderstood the sign.

"Nay, and be glad I don't answer a fool in the way—"

My right hand was under my lungi, on the butt of a pistol I sometimes used to kill poison snakes.

"I have something else than the maiden for you to take to your bosom," I interrupted him.

He saw death in my eyes and reached for his knife, but he was far and away too late.

In utter silence he tumbled from his camel, and his clansmen watched his fall without a sound. The Rindi, with ready rifles, listened in vain for the "*Ala-la-la-la-la!*" shriek of battle. When the hush had held long, I spoke to the leader.

"If you have kinsmen close by, call them out and follow us. Your spavined camels aren't worth much, but we have poor kinsmen who'll find use for them."

"Nay, for the evil eye is on us yet," the chieftain replied. "Bismillah!"

I lifted the child from the rude litter and put her on my own,

CHAPTER THIRTY-ONE

Willing Slave

WE HAD ENCIRCLED KABUL and were on the big caravan road to Ghazni, our protective tax paid, before our
little charge stopped giving frightened glances over her
shoulder. Traveling fast those two days, I could provide
her only with creature comforts, not one word of reassurance that she would understand. Actually she did not
seem to need it as much as I thought she must. She
stayed as close to me as possible and ran after me when
I went on the most private errands, but never whim-
pered, ate ravenously the food I gave her, and slept
peacefully on the rough bed I made for her at my feet.
Hamyd remarked that she was of stout spirit. When we
climbed or descended dizzy slopes or hung on the brinks
of precipices, she was the calmest of the lot, but I took
it she was used to such since she was born.

Not until the third night, when we rested at a walled
town below the white peak of Shutangarden, did I get
my first, long, good look at her. She was playing gravely
with a wooden doll I had bought her at the bazaar, and
speaking to it from time to time—quite likely the first
breach of her dreadful stunned silence since her little
world had been destroyed in horror and bloodshed. I
was wondering that a blue-eyed child, whose hair, if
washed, would probably be light brown, and whose skin
might be rather fair under its coating of dirt, could look
so unlike an English child. Still scant of flesh from her
ordeal, the bony structure of her face was Oriental-look-
ing to start with, and her long eyes, brighter than I had
seen them yet, appeared to slant. At the same time there
was something very engaging in her delicate features
and her beautifully molded head.

257

Seeing her scratch, I was reminded of another purchase I had made for her—new raiment to take the place of her dirty, vermin-ridden Pathan dress. So I sent for a sort of chokidar in charge of the serai, and bade him bring me a charcoal brazier to heat the chill room, a kettle big enough for her to stand in, and two big jars of hot water.

The kettle proved to be copper and of ample size. I thought it must be used for rendering mutton fat. The girl put her doll to bed and then watched me, big-eyed, as I got out towels and liquid soap. Evidently she had no inkling what this process was. Then I pointed to the water and made gestures to suggest swimming. I knew that the pagans on the remote borders of Kashmir bathed in their rivers in summertime, and thought that the mountaineers of hell-and-gone Kafiristan might do the same.

She did not smile, but her eyes brightened, and she nodded to show that she understood. But she looked baffled when I pointed to her and again to the water, making the same motions. Then she said something, and I would bet a pony that it was, "It's too small."

I called her to me and took off her cap. Then very slowly and gently, so not to frighten her, removed her boots, a woolen coat, and then a shirt tucked into her big woolen breeches. I thought I might have trouble with the latter. Hindu and Moslem girls are taught shame almost before they are weaned. Instead, catching the idea, she pulled them off.

Although gray with dust and dirt, her body proved to be beautifully chiseled, and not quite as immature as I had thought. Although much smaller, it would correspond to that of an English girl of about twelve. Pouring water in the kettle, I tested it with my bare elbow, and then had her put her hand in it. But when I asked her to put her foot in it, she appeared bewildered and a little frightened.

Smiling at her, I picked her up and stood her in the makeshift tub. I felt her body tremble, but she looked at me trustfully, and presently, as I began to bathe her chest, with childish animation. To get her clean required a lavish use of soap, repeated rinsing, and brisk

258

scrubbing with a woolen cloth, but my labors were being rewarded in a quite wonderful way. As layer after layer of dirt washed off, I could hardly believe my eyes. It reminded me of a picture-restorer removing one layer of paint after another from an ancient panel, to find beneath the creation of an old master. The drab little mountain waif was turning into a diminutive but perfect mountain nymph. Not until I had washed and rewashed and dried her hair was the transformation complete. Then I felt like an artist myself, in a kind of romantic exultation that poetry lovers know. It was as though, in the middle of the nineteenth century, I had indeed found and captured a nymph who had seen Apollo.

Of course, every traveler of Afghanistan had heard of fair-haired people dwelling in the Hindu Kush. Indian legend was full of references to "white Huns." But all the mountaineers on the border of Islan were of mixed blood with the hill tribes, and even in the heart of Kafiristan, terra incognita and the ultima Thule, I had thought that the people would be merely pale-colored, with brown hair and old-ivory-colored skins. Instead, my little charge was blond as a blond Swede. Her hair was the hue of a new hemp, and her skin snow-white.

She seemed aware that I was pleased with her—little she knew my delight—and gave me for the first time a small crooked smile.

I was loath to have her dress, when she was such joy to my eyes, so I poured in more hot water and let her bathe her doll. During that time, I did not worry with thoughts of her future, only sat and watched her with a lifted heart. When finally she yawned, I dried her silky skin, let her find her own way into the big-sleeved white shirt that was the nearest thing I had found to a nightgown, and pointed to her bed. She climbed in, gave a happy sigh, and went straight to sleep. But I sat an hour, over my *timbak*, wondering what I had let myself in for. It was unthinkable that I could carry her into Kafiristan, find her kinsmen, and turn her over to them. It seemed to me almost certain that her family had come from its distant fastnesses down to the frontier, perhaps with a flock of sheep to sell at Kunar, and had

259

fallen foul of the raiding Pathans. I would know better about that when I could teach her to talk to me, but certainly a journey into her native mountains was impossible now.

If the Pathans had sold her for two hundred rupees, they would have swindled themselves. In a few years more she would be worth many thousands at Samarkand. In the same few years she might become the *cobah* or even the wife of a noble Moslem or Hindu, but how could I protect her in the meantime? I, too, was a slave. At this moment she belonged, technically at least, to Nazir Khan. Happily, he had never pined for blondes, or immature girls of any complexion, but many natives did so, and a sword hung over the head of every Oriental prince. There was nothing to do but be her guard and companion for the remainder of the journey, and hope to cross the bridge when I came upon it.

In the morning I wakened to find her blue eyes on mine. She gave me another smile, then grew round-eyed when I signaled that the pile of new, gay-colored garments were for her. "Rajah!" she burst out, when she picked one of them up—the first word she had spoken to me. Then she laid the garment carefully down and, pale with happiness, knelt at my feet.

I picked her up quickly, laughing in a way that she knew was not scorn, only a sign of friendship between us. "Not Rajah," I told her, pointing to myself and shaking my head. "Timur."

"Tarmarr?" she echoed.

I nodded my head and, poking myself in the chest with my finger, repeated the name. Then I pointed to her with a look of inquiry.

She caught on at once and said something that made my head swim. Positive there was nothing to it, I decided to let it go for a few heart-thumping seconds while I took another tack. I pointed to myself, showed her my ten fingers twice, then eight fingers. Her deep-blue eyes sparkled as she grasped my meaning.

When I pointed to her, she replied with a gesture and expression I knew well—a slight hanging of the head and a faint smile, universal to the Orient and indicative of helpless shame over a deficiency. Then she held up ten fingers once, and two of them again.

I had thought she was eleven at the most; plainly the maids of high, cold Kafiristan matured much more slowly than the girls of the plains. Once more I pointed to myself, said, "Timur," and pointed to her. And again she answered as before. It sounded like "Sith'ra."

Now it was written in the days of Homer that when men first began to worship Aphrodite, a thousand years before she became Venus on the seven hills of Rome, she was frequently called Cytherea, because she had risen from the sea near the island of Cythera.

"Cythera?" I said distinctly, pointing to her.

She nodded happily.

Still, Sith'ra might be a Kafir name meaning almost anything and of only local interest. Most Indian names, especially Moslem and, in a lesser degree, Hindu, have religious origins, but the Kafirs were pagans and I had no real reason to believe—

I put my hands together as in prayer, raised them, looked high over my head, and said, on the wildest impulse, "Zeus?"

If I lived till every mystery of India was explored, I would never forget the expression on her face. I was suddenly more than her protector on this distant road; I became the link between it and the old roads of Kafiristan; I had bridged the awful chasm that had ended her old life, so that she could go on to a new. A high color glowed in her face and she became in one marvelous moment much more alive. I could see that she wanted to express this in some way—was bursting to, but did not know quite how. Crouching down, I held my arms out. With a gasp she ran to me and pressed her body hard against my chest, but she did not kiss me, as I had half expected. Instead she gently sniffed my cheeks.

She did not know what she had given me in return! I did not know either, yet; but I felt a glow of enthusiasm permeating regions of my heart and soul that had been cold for years. At the very least, she had given me an exciting new interest that would surely enliven and enrich my remaining days in Baluchistan and my mind for as long as I lived. No European in modern history had ever penetrated Kafiristan, a land of mighty mountains five thousand square miles in area in the highlands of the Hindu Kush. Marco Polo had spoken of it as Bolor, and the history of Tamerlane made the earliest known mention of the people as Kafirs. Throughout centuries they had guarded their passes against invaders, slave catchers, and traders. Quite possibly I was the first student from the West to have contact with an "unmixed" Kafir from the unknown interior. When we could communicate freely, I could certainly discover much of the customs of the people and particularly their language, perhaps be able to trace its connection with the other languages of India and Central Asia, a task for which I was not ill-fitted. A monograph of interest to the Geographical Society in London would be its finest fruit; but the mere inquiry, with its manifold interests, would stand me personally in good stead.

If it so proved, as I wildly believed, that I had brushed against the last worshippers on earth of the gods and goddesses of Homer and Achilles, my heart would glow with a poet's fire on many a cold day.

I raised my folded hands again and named Zeus's consort, Hera, who to the Romans was Juno. But I could tell by her face the name was unfamiliar to her. I had no better luck with Pallas Athena, and was getting worried, when I invoked Apollo. Instantly she put her hands to her forehead and bowed her head. To my surprise, Sith'ra did not, after all, respond to Cytherea, except with a big smile. I took it that she might have become a mere household spirit, as great gods and goddesses have been known to do, to be named after, and loved, but not worshipped. She responded slightly to Hestia, looked blank at Ares and Demeter, but showed excitement over Adonis, who was not a great god, but rather the source of a cult.

It was time to take the road, which all that day was at once richly long and tirelessly short because of her. I had her wear a face cloth through the Afridi villages and in sight of travelers, but she rode unveiled and bareheaded through the lonely mountains, and while she saw the big and thrilling wonders of the vast land-

262

scape, I looked at little, lovely ones in her small, strange face. But when steep cliffs overhung the road, I worried a little about her flowing, flaxen hair, it would shine so far in the sun.

She remarked to me on many interesting things. I never understood what she was saying, any more than she my replies. Several times she said, *"Kim?"* when I had spoken, an ancient Sanskrit word meaning "what." I was puzzling over that, when it dawned on me that she used *aham* for "I" and *vam* for "you." These were certainly Sanskrit pronouns, that had disappeared from all modern languages save the strange, ancient Dardic spoken in and about the headwaters of the Indus.

An eagle's nest she called *nilah,* Vedic Sanskrit. Pointing excitedly to a bear crossing a long slope, she yelled *"Bharami!"* Plainly a large proportion of Kafir words were unadulterated Sanskrit, indicating that her people had been isolated from the Indian civilization for two or more thousand years. But a greater linguistic surprise was in store for me.

She had asked me a question in what was, no doubt, her mother tongue. I shook my head. Then she scratched her head and repeated the question in a language as utterly different as English from Eskimo. Indeed it sounded like no language I had ever heard, or heard about. It contained vowel sounds that I could not possibly imitate and, for me, did not exist.

I leaned over, put my finger on her lips, and then held up two fingers with a questioning expression. Her alert mind instantly caught the symbolism—she nodded happily and repeated the question in both languages. Then she tried hard to tell me something. Happily I had the key in the word *man,* the Hindi term for "mother," forms of which were found all over the world including our own "mamma." *Bab,* like the Hindi *Bap,* I took for "father." Saying one, followed by words in Kafiri, and then the other, followed by some in the completely different language, she finally made me understand that one was her mother's and the other her father's speech. Obviously they came from different tribes and probably far distant regions within Kafiristan.

There was no doubt that I had before me a study of

no small importance to the sciences of etymology in general and linguistics in particular; and one that would be a joy to me as long as I had access to this little, beautiful pagan from Kafiristan.

That night she gave me a key that might help unlock many mysteries. I had continued my search into her pantheon of deities, discovering that she acknowledged most of the Greek gods and a few of the goddesses who were in fullness of glory about the Age of Pericles. The others she might know under other names—or even pronunciation of the same names—that I did not recognize. But when I had gone through all these that had resounded through classic history, she had seemed troubled, and I got the curious impression that it was on my account, not hers. I had left something out. I was falling short in some comprehension she thought I should have. I had the feeling she wanted to say something she hardly dared. Did she have a god so mighty that the speaking of his name was forbidden? That was not usual among primitive peoples."

To encourage her, I again pronounced, "Zeus," and went through the motions of worshipping him. She did the same, and then, with an anxious expression, employed sign language in a brilliant way. Saying, "Zeus," she raised her palm as high as possible. With the same gesture she said, "Buddha," who obviously sat with Zeus on the Kafir Olympus. Then she stood on tiptoe and pointed straight over her head, her lips moving.

"Kim?" I asked gravely.

She turned pale, but with high bravery she crept up to me and whispered in my ear.

"Lak-zandar." At once she dropped on her knees and touched her head to the floor.

Not for nothing had I read and thrilled over the campaigns of the greatest conqueror the world had ever known. It came to me now, with a great joyful surge of my brain, that he had twice crossed the Hindu Kush, and at the very time he had begun to array himself as a Persian sultan and to demand from his stout legions the worship accorded Oriental despots deeming themselves gods.

"Alexander?" I asked, when she had risen.

She gave a frightened cry and clapped her hand over my mouth, but there was not the slightest doubt of my shot. Probably some of his legionnaires had deserted, rather than prostrate themselves before a fellow Greek, and hidden away in the fastnesses of Kafiristan. From now on I could look for Greek influence, not only in the child's religion, but in all that she could teach me of her people's language and ways.

Sith'ra, are you, yourself, an Attic nymph, born two thousand years after your time, in lovely mortal form? Truly fate has dealt strangely with me once more!

Her living presence in my life would, no doubt, be brief. Since I could not hope to learn her language in that short stay—anyway my pleasant elementary studies of Kafiristan would not justify the labor—I decided to teach her one of mine. I chose the Hindustani vernacular of the bazaars, bound to be useful to her, and the easiest to learn at least in the way of fluent conversation; and since she used a great many Sanskrit words, she should pick it up as we went along with no trouble to either of us. Thereafter on the road, I addressed her in this tongue only, and every time I recognized one of her words, told her its equivalent.

Her mind was eager and quick, her tongue lively, and before we made Kandahar, she knew more Hindustani than several officers of the Tatta Lancers. Here we parted with our Rindi fellows, and staying at the caravanserai, Hamyd and I horse-traded for a fortnight, ere we set out with some camel dealers on a roundabout route to Kalat. Three weeks we spent on that ramble, two months in all since our meeting with the Pathans, and when we came in sight of the fortress looming against the limpid summer sky, Sith'ra and I could discuss any matter under the sun.

I would have sworn she was an inch taller than when I had first seen her—she was a remarkably hearty eater for her size—and two inches more in chest measure. She had learned Moslem manners of eating and dress, and added Allah and Mohammed to her galaxy of gods. That she had not learned to bathe herself was the thinnest pretext for my doing the job for her, but my role of *gusal-walla* did not offend my dignity and, indeed, I dreaded the time when I would no longer have her silken, warm, beautiful little body between my hands.

"Will we stay here long, Timur Rajah?" she asked. I could not break her of using the title.

"Perhaps always," I answered.

"Why is your voice sad?"

"I didn't mean it to be."

She had a question to ask. Finally she shaped it.

"If you stay here always, will I also?"

"If it be your kismet."

"I mean—if you go, have I your leave to follow you?"

"You have my leave, but it may not be your kismet. Be of good heart, *chota mithai* [little sweet]. There are great wonders to see."

I left Sith'ra in my old quarters, when I went to pay my obeisance to the Emir. He gave me his hand to kiss, and a glance of passionate curiosity.

"We have missed you from our court," he told me graciously, "but if the time was well spent—"

"Truly it was, master."

"You learned the name and abode of the evil one of unspeakable begetting?"

"Praise be to Allah, I did."

"I'll receive you in closet shortly."

In the story I told him I managed to omit two pertinent facts—one that Gerald was my half-brother and the other that my *cobah* was the daughter of the Colonel Sahib. In the first instance, politeness as well as policy was a factor. The murder of half-brothers was a frequent occurrence in Far Eastern courts immediately the King breathed his last, and was regarded as a necessary evil by ambitious princes. Most rulers had four wives permitted by the Koran, each ranking as a queen and vying with the others to bear him sons, any one of which was eligible to the throne, had he the power to seize it. Occasionally the sons of mere concubines, their number unlimited, became strong contestants and bloody fratricides. At least two of Nazir's half-brothers had died by violence, ere his seat became secure.

I got out of revealing Gerald's name and office by calling him Serdar Nalla—a literal translation of Captain Brook—and by saying he served the Governor Sahib. Licking his chops over the tale, Nazir Khan was satisfied to hear that my *cobah* was a moon of beauty called Bachhiya. His black eyes glittered when I told of holding a knife within arm's length of my fallen enemy's throat.

"By Allah, Paulos, I wish now I'd given you leave to end your *thar* then and there," he cried.

"To hear was to obey, great King."

"It was obedience deserving of Allah's taking you to Paradise, *giaour* or no, when your cup of death is brought. But be of good heart, Paulos. It comes to me that Allah won't allow your enemy to die save under your hand. When the time comes, you shall again search him out, even across the black waters. After the fullness of your revenge, is it your purpose to take back your *cobah*, despite your very enemy's drinking of that fountain?"

"If Allah wills."

"And on no account to cut her throat?"

"Lord, she didn't conspire against me, or know that her taker was my betrayer. Among the English, O King, widows are suffered to rewed."

"That I've heard. Paulos, the time of waiting won't be long. It's my pleasure to give you tidings of great joy."

"Allah upon you, master."

"In your absence I bespoke the Ambassador of Sa'id ibn Sultan, ere he set out for Zanzibar. That speaking is now answered by letter. He accepted, with many expressions of pleasure, my gift of you to him along with your follower Hamyd, and above his hand and seal, he declared that if you served him faithfully for five years, he would indeed assume the promise I had made you, and set both of you free."

Nazir permitted me to kneel and kiss the hem of his garment.

"If the Destroyer of Delights comes to him ere then, he declared that his heirs will honor the contract. So after you have remained a month at my court, to take leave of me and your many friends, you shall take ship for Zanzibar."

I could hardly hope to find him in better fettle and fonder heart than now, so I held out my hands in token of a petition.

"You have my leave to speak."

"Lord, isn't it the Law of the Prophet that no man shall lie with a maiden ere nature betokens her of age to bear young, even though she be outside the Faith?"

"Verily it is."

"A Pathan murdered the parents and little brother of such a one, wantonly with his sword, and when he would lie with her, I quarreled with him, and in her defense, slew him."

"By my beard, it was well done!"

"It so chanced I couldn't return her to her kinsmen, and I have brought her here, into the shadow of your throne. Also, I'm seeking to learn from her all I can of her people and their land, whereby to transmit to the hakims of all the world a writing thereon, to increase their wisdom. Of you I entreat protection for her until she is of an age to marry, and then a pronouncement of her freedom, even as though she were a daughter, by a concubine, of a Moslem, so she may never be sold into slavery."

"I'll do better than that, Paulos. I'll put her in the charge of my eunuchs, you to talk to her when you will, until you depart from my realm. Then I'll ask Mazad Serdar, who is old and kind and without children, to pass her through his wife's shift, in the rite of adoption. If the child be comely, and of pleasant manner, he will gladly agree. Then, when the time comes, she will be a lady of good estate, fit to marry a Son of the Prophet of good name."

Nazir Khan was as good as his word. The following day the venerable Mazad spoke to me, asking to see the child. I had her brought from the haremlik, and when she had knelt before him, he kissed her between the eyes in token of his pleasure in her, and then confided to me he would adopt her as his daughter, and have a mullah teach her the Faith as soon as I departed for Zanzibar. I could think of no safer disposal of her, and, indeed, she would come to prosperity undreamable in the fastnesses of Kafiristan. But my preparing her for our parting was even harder going than I had expected. The truth was I could hardly stand the thought of it myself.

She was not in the least afraid of the old soldier, and I painted a rosy picture of life in his palace, from which in time she would go to be the bride and *saki* of a noble youth. I had not yet told her that the arrangement was already made, or that I was soon to leave Kalat, but it may be that she read between the lines. Her face was never sad in my sight—as Hamyd had observed, she was of strong spirit—but she racked her brain for things to tell me about her people and country that she thought would interest or amuse me. Tirelessly and, it seemed, eagerly, she kept to the tedious task of translating into the unknown language the Hindustani words I put to her, so I could write them down phonetically. Indeed, she volunteered a great many, and always, when we parted, she asked me to be sure and summon her on the morrow, for she had heaps more for me to draw so queerly on the paper, more interesting than anything she had yet revealed. To save me I could not help but think of Scheherazade, stopping her tale midway at dawn, so that the Sultan would let her live to see another.

The morrows came and went in plagued haste. I toyed with the idea of asking Nazir Khan to postpone my departure a month or two more. Little Sith'ra was the best informant as to Kafiristan I could hope to find, far better than a grown-up to whom the sights had gone stale, and the customs become such second nature that he did not notice them. Of more importance were my studies of the utterly unknown tongue. I could not trace the slightest relation between it and any other language, and its grammar and construction were bewilderingly complex and thrillingly new. Always, though, I had to forego the appeal as futile and dangerous. I was not a freeman, but a slave, and I knew better than to take lightly the word of kings. I would find new and thrilling interests in the great African capital of Zanzibar.

When only one week remained of my stay, I broke the news, as gently as I could, to my little schoolteacher. Not until then did I perceive the full strength of her spirit, as revealed in courage and in pride. She had me

269

tell her again of the richness of Mazad's abode, and of her happiness when she would be married to a handsome young sheik, but I knew she did not hear one word. Then she asked to go on with the *sabaq* [lesson], but I could not stand seeing her swallow and gulp, and the effort she made to speak with her old *élan*. So it came to pass that she spent most of the hours we had together sitting in my lap, listening to the fairy stories of my own childhood and tales from *The Arabian Nights*, patting my face, and teaching me nothing strange but the exceeding strangeness of her beauty and her pagan heart.

She had asked, and I had granted it, to serve my meals. She would eat only my leavings, but of course I saw that they were bountiful. When I had time for a smoke, she skillfully lighted my water pipe. On the night before my farewell audience with the Emir, she asked me to bathe her for the last time. I did so, in great joy, although fully aware that I should not, now that she was developing so rapidly, for running through that joy was a subtle excitement against which I should have guarded myself, and which might possibly be conveyed to her. However, I saw no sign of it in her face or actions. I craved to kiss her long, pink, beautifully molded lips, a natural thing enough, but I could not keep it innocent in my own perception, and would not accept the guilt. Then she asked if she could sleep with me tonight, and I had a hard time refusing her, on any grounds she could understand. When I saw her big eyes fill with tears she could not stay, I readily granted another request, on the condition of the Emir's consent. It was only to be present at the audience with him, since she had not yet seen the court, and she wanted to watch her Paulos Rajah, as she called me now, receive farewell honors.

An old woman, the mother of one of the Emir's favorites, provided her with proper and beautiful attire. I discouraged the elaborate and often uglifying use of cosmetics prevalent in the harem, and when I saw the child arrayed, her flaxen hair flowing, her fair skin in such striking contrast to that of the swarthy attendants, I was ready to bet my new lungi that the Emir would notice her. Indeed, I wished for an Arabian poet of the classic school to describe her entrance to the divan, unveiled as was fitting for a slave girl, and almost unaware of the eyes upon her, so busy were her own eyes with the sights. When we had prostrated ourselves, she stood at one side and a little behind me.

Not knowing any better—or so I thought—she trailed me when I was called before the throne. The court caught its breath as one man, but Nazir Khan did not glance at her yet. Having a fine sense of ceremony, like so many kings of the East, and his share of the Oriental gift of eloquence, he addressed me in classic Persian, in words to be recorded by the scribes, and for the whole court to hear.

"Truly thy cunning and wise counsel have served well my throne and person. Thy wit and merry, ready tongue have given me much laughter, diversion, and instruction. I will miss thy brain and hand at my command, but since I have decided to link my arms with those of the white Rani, and word has come even now of the end of Mohammed Shah, it has become my kismet to part with thee, and thine to serve my exalted brother Sa'id ibn Sultan. But in bidding the sarraf make a gift to a loyal subject on the southern border of my kingdom, the thought came to me to make one to thee likewise. To him—his honored name is Mustapha, venerable Sheik of Habistan, I send one hundred cattle. Partly it is to honor his yet sturdy strength, for he sent me word that his new *cobah* is great with child." The Emir paused.

"Be it a bouncing son, who will serve your Majesty when Mustapha Sheik goes to Paradise."

"*Keif, keif.* Partly it is to atone for an inadequate reward I made him long ago. And I've bidden the sarraf deliver to thee, as a token of my esteem, a purse of two thousand rupees."

"May Allah bless you for your munificence, Most High."

Then he bade me rise and kissed me between the eyes, causing a great exulting in the heart of the slave.

"And who is the moon of beauty in your attendance?" he asked, reverting to the vernacular.

271

"She is Sithy, the pagan girl I took from the Pathan."

"She is a young moon yet, but so is the most beloved of all—even the Moon of Ramadan, new hung in the west, after the holy fast. Truly my good servant Mazad is blessed by Allah—" He turned and pointed his scepter at the old serdar, who immediately came forward. Then and there the ceremony, that on the spur of the moment he intended to perform, was set awry.

With a pounce fast as a terrier's, Sithy sprang to the foot of the throne and flung her arms about the Emir's lower leg. It was almost an unheard-of offense, lese majesty to the point of sacrilege, for even a noble to touch the royal person, without his consent, and the whole court was stunned. But truly Nazir Khan rose to the occasion, like the deeply human yet illustrious prince he was. Without turning a hair he spoke gravely.

"Allah bear witness that this maiden has touched the hem of my garment, and hence, by the ancient law of the Sublime Throne of Osmanli, to which my forebears bowed, she is now under my protection." He threw over her a fold of his cloth-of-gold ihram according to a ceremony old in the days of Tamerlane. "Is there any here who can speak her language?"

"O King, she speaks Hindustani," I answered, "which several here understand."

"When a petitioner can't speak for himself, it's the law that one neutral to his interests, speak for him. Nanda," the Emir went on, addressing a Hindu attendant, "bid the mercy seeker rise and make her entreaty."

I was afraid Sithy might not understand Nanda's Hindustani, accented differently from mine, but I could not see that she missed a word. Not once did she break into his translation, and although quivering with fright, she looked the Emir in the face.

"Master, Paulos Rajah promised me if you would let him, he'd take me with him to—to the place he's going. Please, master, let him!"

"Why, it's a long journey across the black waters," the Emir answered, his eyes gleaming. "Wouldn't you be afraid?"

"No, master."

"He's going among strangers, and no one knows his kismet. If you stay here, you'll be as a free-born daughter of the Faith, but there you will be a slave."

"I want to be his slave, great master."

"True, I've heard of slaves who have slaves, although both are subject to the same master's will. Paulos, what say you to this?"

"Great King, I may soon die or be slain, or be sent away by the Sultan, and so be parted from her, friendless, and unable to speak to the people, in a strange, far-distant land. Your Highness knows the dangers that hang over a slave, and the weakness of his arm. But if you consent to her going with me, I'll keep my promise to her, for truly it was my heart's desire, although in conflict with my judgment."

"Mazad, I spoke with you of the adoption of the Kafir maiden, which gives you claim upon her. Will you renounce that claim, in case I give her leave to go with Paulos?"

"Yea, O Majesty."

"Then hear my decree. It's your heart's desire that the Kafir go with you, and she has made very plain to us it's likewise the desire of her stout, if small, heart. What claim I have upon her, from her being your captive, I now bestow upon you, subject to the will of your new master. Until this hour I'd heard but didn't believe that the pagans of the Hindu Kush had daughters such as these, not unlike the sahibs' daughters, save in countenance, which is strange even to us and most lovely. By my beard, I, myself, would like to visit Kafiristan."

"Lord, I aspire to the honor of sending you a draft of the paper I shall write on the strange land, when I'm more instructed in it."

"Doubtless it will be worth reading. But it comes to me that your fair-haired slave will serve you, in due course, in other ways than as your mufti. If I mistake not, she will be your bringer not only of learning, but of delight."

CHAPTER THIRTY-TWO

Unwilling Master

THE VIZIER PRESENTED ME WITH ALL THE HORSES I had obtained from trading, which I sold that day in the market for twice the amount he had lent me. When Hamyd and I had said farewell to our fellow slaves, we set out bearing our chattels on a well-equipped caravan for Sonmiani on the Arabian Sea. Although our way passed less than two days' ride from Habistan, our haste did not permit us to go there. I was sorry about that, on account of two people I should like to visit, or, if I could tarry long enough, three.

Life had changed for me in subtle but powerful ways, now that I had Sithy. We were both slaves of Sa'id ibn Sultan, but neither of us seemed to remember on the journey, for somehow, for a little while, she had set me free. I saw the wildly beautiful country through her childish eyes. There was promise around every bend of the road. Since she was not afraid of anything when she was with me, I refused to borrow any trouble from the future. I had again become capable of joys along the road.

In regions of my mind far back of these present occupations, there remained a matter that did not concern her yet, and perhaps that was partly the reason it did not oppress me more. I thought about it with astonishing infrequence, and did not recall dreaming about it at all. It was implacably in my kismet, if Gerald and I both lived long enough, but this was a lull between its two phases, its two great operations, its beginning and its end. The interval might be five years long—if the Emir's plans for me were carried out. However long the term, I intended to make the best of it, and the most.

With my two companions, I intended to live with all my might and main.

At Sonmiani we boarded an Arab dhow en route to Muscat. On the first day out we fell afoul of the monsoon, and with our rolling and wallowing about, and the rank smell of our dirty cabin, I thought surely that Sithy, who had never before seen salt water, would be miserably sick. She was not, for no reason I could imagine other than her practice at balancing herself on goat paths amid her native mountains; and, instead, I was. It was I who lay green and ghastly, while she crouched beside me, holding my hand, bringing and emptying the bucket, patting my face, and prescribing witchy medicines. The drastic nature of some of these indicated that she thought I might die. When assured it was only my stomach trying to ape the churning of the waves—the explanation for seasickness still believed by the crew—she tried to take my mind off of it by giving me a dramatic description of the beauties of Kafiristan. I caught only snatches of it—later I would have her repeat it—but I would never forget the way she looked, her strange face so animated, her gestures so lively, and her voice so lilting, and I could swear it did me good.

For the rest of the voyage we had good sailing, and on the fifth day put into the ancient capital city of Oman. This was the first big, busy seaport Sithy had ever seen, and, as though the afreets living in its ancient towers made a game of it, all its main attractions turned out for her. As we came to anchor within a stone's throw of a Salem trader, Muscat Tom, a finback whale who had visited the cove every day for many years fed and frolicked, blew and breached, in her plain sight. The seventy-foot monster was famous on seven seas, and since he scared out all the sharks, the populace was not only proud of him, but loved him. After dark, the harbor waters lighted up in such a display of phosphorescence as I had never seen, living up to their fame in this regard, and where they splashed against the foundations of the shore-line houses, the effect was of climbing flame.

We spent three days in the walled city, staying at a big, white-walled fenduke, before finding a ship to our liking bound for Zanzibar. For comfort I would have preferred a Yankee, but was afraid my little blond companion would attract too much attention from the crew, so I finally settled on one of the Sultan's own armed merchantmen. At dawn of the fourteenth day we raised the island, blue from a distance, low-lying and dreamy-looking. As we drew nearer, the shore showed every shade of green, with a bright-yellow ribbon of sand between the tropic foliage and the profound blue of the sea. In midmorning we made out the Gurayza, the fort fronting the city, with its watchtowers and low battlements, and soon Bet el Sahel, the Sultan's city palace, surrounded by lesser mansions occupied by various of his three dozen sons and daughters and officials of his court.

As soon as we had docked, Hamyd, Sithy, and I made straight for Bet el Sahel. Since no one knew that we, too, were slaves, breechclothed blacks were permitted to carry the Effendi's and the M'sabu's baggage. I was glad to have my hands free of it, so I could hold a small hand. My eyes, nose, ears, and, in this interval, spirit, made strangely free. I did not have to borrow excitement from Sithy; her pulse jumped to mine. I had seen streets in Tunis something like these, although not quite so wild and winding, and heard similar noises in Cairo and Bikaner, although not quite as staccato, but I had never smelled such smells before, at least in such synthesis. One of its elements was the aroma of cloves, the main crop of the island. One was the stench of human carrion, no doubt blown in from the beaches, where the bodies of slaves were thrown for the kites and crawlers up from the sea. One was the ghastly reek of the slave ship and the barracoons that had permeated the walls of the buildings and the very cobblestones of the streets, and which forty years of fresh air might never expunge. But one was the smell of excitement. It called to mind the opening charge at Meeanee. It had hung in the desert air of the sand hills, when I had sold a horse, and over the table of the Tatta Lancers, when a subaltern offered a toast. I think it is given off by man and beast, when they are preternaturally alive.

The city of Zanzibar was one of the meanest, dirtiest,

and, no doubt, wickedest I had ever visited. Its streets were tortuous dark alleys, five yards wide; we had to press against a damp-smelling wall, besmeared with red betelnut juice spat by passers-by, to pass a file of naked Negroes, chained to one another, and each bearing on his shoulder a great, glimmering elephant tusk. The best houses, with dark, narrow entrances and yards littered with livestock in the way of slaves, donkeys, dogs, and poultry, and with wood and reeking hides, all looked like jails, with heavy-timbered padlocked doors, small, barred windows or with plain plank shutters; all were of hodgepodge design. In most Moslem cities the mosques were of glory to Allah. Here they were miserable one-story barnlike buildings. But at the present moment, at the beginning of the middle year of the nineteenth century, this was one of the most significant cities in the world. All Africa danced, the Arabs said, to a flute played in Zanzibar. Actually it was the gateway to an undiscovered, unconquered half of a continent. It was the key to a treasure house that was the last great prize of history.

Already the merchants of Salem were getting rich on their cloth sold in Zanzibar. England, France, and Portugal were crouching to spring on the vast domain; as yet their hands were busy with other adventures in the New World and in Asia, but the lights burned late in their war offices and council rooms; their explorers were drawing maps; their adventurers were marking trails. For a moment I forgot the little warm hand in mine.

Sithy, I wish you would not look at me with such big eyes. Why are they not busy with the sights of the town? I am afraid you are going to be very lonely—

Bet el Sahel proved to be a considerable palace, with a lofty veranda supported by tall pillars, and a twelve-foot sea wall. We made our way through the courtyard, busy as a bazaar, with cooks baking whole cattle and giant fish, beasts being slaughtered, water carriers, black nurses with children of all complexions, and slaves loafing or being goaded to their tasks by big Negro eunuchs. I asked to be taken to the seneschal, who proved to be a small, alert Armenian named Kozerhn. He was expecting me, he said—he was glad to have another Christian

277

at the court—and my orders were to set out at once for Mtoni, the Sultan's country palace, about five miles north of the city, and his favorite residence. Kozerhn spoke of Sithy as "the Circassian" and of Hamyd as "your servant," and did not seem to know that all three of us were slaves. I did not enlighten him, and he provided donkeys with big Swahili *sais* for Sithy and me.

I thought that Kozerhn was glad I was to serve at the country palace, lest I impugn his authority and reduce his *izzat*.

Mtoni was a much larger, finer palace than Bet el Sahel. I was told that its two main structures and out-buildings housed a thousand of the Sultan's dependents, including kinsmen, court officials, and slaves. There were a dozen open-air bathing-basins at the end of the courtyard and two Persian bath houses of considerable elegance. Orange trees with golden balls surrounded a huge *benjile* overlooking the sea—a circular enclosure with a tent-shaped roof and handsome balustrades, large enough to drill a troop of cavalry. We climbed a steep stairway, asked for the head eunuch, and were presently received by him—a towering Abyssinian called Hannibal. An expert on women, he did not make Kozerhn's mistake in regard to Sithy.

"What is she?" he asked in elegant Arabic. "I've never seen anything quite like her."

"She's a Kafir from the Hindu Kush."

"We have Kafirs in Africa, so-called, but they are as black as she is white. Has the sun never shone on her, that she is of such snow? And is she a gift for the Sultan?"

"No, she's my own slave, and I pray that you quarter her with me."

He agreed without a second's hesitation, to my unutterable relief. We were given a bedchamber opening on the balcony, an anteroom for Hamyd, and a small parlor—a plain sign that I was to have a respectable office in the court. The woodwork was ornamented with brass studs, inscriptions from the Koran were carved over the doors; a shelved niche in the wall displayed some China dishes and a couple of gaudy swords; and a tall mirror, with only one crack, stood against the inner wall. There were no chairs, which wealthy Arabs had begun to show, but not sit in, in their houses; and the chests were plain, but the big, elaborately carved bed, no doubt brought from India, was worthy to be slept in by a visiting sheik.

As our various larders had not been assigned us yet, Hannibal sent us, by a black slave, a dish of kimah [chopped meat] and abundant fruit. When Hamyd had gone to his anteroom, Sithy removed her sandals and looked at her feet.

"I'm very dirty," she pronounced, "and need a bath bad." She used *bimar* just as children use "bad" in England, which I could not explain, since it is not a Hindustani idiom—unless she had caught it from me.

"You can have one in the morning."

"I need one tonight, and you haven't bathed me for a long time. I don't get clean when I bathe myself."

"You're too big to be bathed any more, Sithy."

"Then surely I'm big enough to sleep with you. A girl no older, and only a little bigger, slept with her master on the ship. She told me so."

"What else did she tell you?"

Sithy flushed a little. "Only what I already knew, and which I'm not old enough for, for a little while yet. I'll only lie close to you, and waken you if you have nightmare, and if you're thirsty in the night, get water for you."

"You're too old to sleep with any man until you're married. You shall have a nice bed of cushions on the floor, the like of which you never dreamed in Kafiristan."

"I wish I'd stayed a little child."

The sultan received me in his chambers immediately after breakfast, and I was permitted to kiss the back of his hand. After a very brief inquiry into the health and prosperity of his "brother," Nazir Khan, and a short word of welcome, he went straight to business. My official office was to be the palace librarian. My first duties were to catalogue the books, with notes on their quality and the lives of their authors, after which I was to buy more both old and new. I was to recommend, after careful perusal, important volumes for his own

279

reading, as well as for his councilors, his serdars, and his *Reis* Effendi [the admiral of the Imperial Navy]. If I ran across books with which his sixty concubines might while away time, I could turn them over to the eunuchs, but they were not to be of an inflammatory or titillating sort, for reasons that I would understand when my beard, like his, was gray. His sharp-pointed beard waggled as he chuckled.

"But since you're some sort of a Greek, all of whom are famed for subtlety, and since too the durbar at Gwadar was doubtless your invention—by the way, I saw through it from first to last, but gladly acquiesced in it, from despising Mohammed Shah—you're to have a confidential post under the Grand Vizier. He'll want to know all that you know of the political aims and power of the Western kings and their councilors. He's completely loyal and reasonably honest—which is a very great recommendation among my tribe—and if only shrewd, not brilliant, he's broad-minded enough to recognize the fact and not refuse counsel even from a Greek slave."

"To hear is to obey."

"Mark you, Paulos, I'm the last of the great Arab monarchs. My grandsons will do well to have rag-and-bobtail courts in the Arabian deserts. England has already put her vast foot down on my slavery export, a business from which I derived one hundred thousand dollars [22,000 pounds] a year. I can see the writing on the wall, and so have but one great policy. It is that in my old age I'm not made a bone for England and France to fight over. I must join the camp of one or the other."

So now I had one great policy myself—to help persuade him to join the English camp. England had set her face like flint against slavery. Her selfishness was usually intelligent; her rule over backward peoples, whom some European power would control if she did not, was the most enlightened in the world. By that policy, any power I could wield would be to my pleasure and good conscience. In the years before my chains were loosed, I might do worth-while service to the non-white races who were most in need, and a little for the off-whites, my own kind.

I went to work, and the rushing days began to be counted first in weeks, then in months, and then in turning seasons. I wanted no public *izzat*, for it was dangerous here, but could not entirely avoid it. It was no longer a secret that the Grand Vizier listened to me ere he advised the Sultan. There were great sheiks in the court who opposed his policies, and had expert poisoners and back stabbers at their beck and call. I stayed out of palace intrigue, and took measures for my own and hence for an innocent bystander's defense. Happily, Hamyd had been immediately appointed to and quartered with the palace guard, and since only the Sultan, the Vizier, and a few other trusted officials knew that he was my intimate, he proved an invaluable spy. Once he brought me a whisper of a plot which, if it had not died aborning, with the beheading of a mere dozen conspirators, might have rocked the throne.

Since Sithy had the run of the haremlik, she had playmates in plenty. Her "best friend" was the somewhat younger daughter of a mameluke who had been passed through the Sultana's shift, almost as blond as herself. Between her hours spent there, and in school to a eunuch mufti, and learning to play a dulcimer and other female tricks and accomplishments, I caught mere glimpses of her in the daytime, and was usually in the antechambers too early and too late for the risings and settings of what was once my little sun. But I marked how fast she was growing. The rich food and the hot climate were shooting her up like a bamboo, filling her out like a yearling doe. The process was a joy to my eyes. She was going to be as tall as most Arab girls, but not as plump, which would spoil her for many an Arab sheik, not to my regret. The tough tensure of her muscles, hardened in Kafiristan, abided in her still.

Late one night, I found her looking at one of my books of Arabian poetry. I laughed at her, saying that she could not understand a line, but our year and half in the Arabian court had schooled her more than I realized, and she read aloud, without much trouble, one of the verses.

"What does it mean in Hindustani?" I asked.

"The Sultan said to his *cobah*, 'In my kingdom are tall red hills, where my white sheep graze, but the hills of my delight are round and white, where my red lips graze.' Then he said—"

"That's enough." For I recalled the verse now, one of the most ardent in the collection. Some of its transposing of color was shocking even by Arab standards. "You've learned to read Arabic well."

"I go to school four hours a day. What else have I got to do with myself, except play dolls with Julnar?"

She sat awhile with her chin on her palm. Her long, deep-blue eyes looked some queer sort of Chinese.

"There's a lady of the harem who knows you," she remarked.

"So?"

"Her name is Cheetal, and she's one of the Sultan's greatest favorites. A long time ago she told me that a Greek named Paulos bought her at Kandahar, and asked me if you were the one. I told her I didn't know. Since then she peeked at you through a window, and today she told me you were."

"Is she happy?"

"Very happy and proud. She's given the Sultan a man-child."

"Do you think she's pretty?"

"I don't like her features much, but she looks beautiful because she's so happy." Sithy herself looked sad.

"You look very pretty, too, Sithy."

"Paulos Rajah, do you know how long it's been since you asked me about Kafiristan?"

It had been a very long time. The wild country was of only passing interest save to geographers; it would never be a prize of empire. At least I would like to continue my studies in the unknown language before she forgot its words. I got out my notebook and looked at it. At our last talk I had discovered that the word for "five" was the same as for "hand," "ten" meant "two hands," "eleven," "one at the foot," and "twenty, "the whole man." Who cared? The language might be utterly unrelated to any other and so primitive that it would throw light on the history of language.

"I suppose it's been about three months."

"It has been seven months, Paulos Raj."

"If you'll come here every day immediately after the noonday prayer, I'll study it some more."

"I'll come, but soon you won't come. Master, shall I light your pipe?"

"Not now."

"Sit on both these cushions, and then I'll sit on your lap as I used to do—unless I'm now too heavy."

"Why, you don't weigh half a tomand."

"That, and five rattel more [99 pounds]. But if you don't want me—"

I made myself comfortable, and then her. Her weight seemed very little, since she leaned against my shoulder, but my eyes attested to her having told the truth. Her face and form were girlish but no longer childlike. She was taller than Cheetal, and of the same sinuous molding.

"Do I find favor in your sight?" she asked. She spoke Hindustani, but the form was Arabic.

"You're a joy to my eyes, Sithy."

"Then why don't you put your lips against my lips sometimes, and press them with a little drawing movement, as Julnar's cousin did to her, when her uncle brought him to see her? Do you think my lips would taste bad?"

"I think they would be like *al-sharifi*." This was the delicious white grape of Arabia.

"I will do it to you, and then you do it to me."

We did so, and Sithy's eyes appeared to grow longer and more slanted and shone between the thick eyelashes.

"I am glad you don't chew betel nut and have black teeth," she told me.

"I'm glad you don't either." I was a little uneasy about my quickened pulse.

"Now let's both do it to each other the same time."

"Did Cheetal tell you about this?"

"No, I saw it."

"Well, we'll try it once."

After that she caught her breath and there was more color in her face than I had ever seen. It was a strange little face, not beautiful by any standard that I knew, but I could not keep my eyes off it. I managed to keep my lips off hers only by an effort of will.

"Did you know, Paulos Raj, I can no longer go back and forth to the haremlik unveiled?"

"Who told you so?"

"Hannibal. He said I might meet a young man in the corridors, and I would be shamed."

"Was it a shame to go barefaced in Kafiristan?"

"Kafiristan isn't Zanzibar. He said that Julnar's cousin mustn't see me unveiled when he comes to visit her, nor her brother. The eunuchs may see me, but you are the only real man who's permitted."

"I think Hannibal should leave the matter to me."

"He said you're a Greek, who didn't understand the hot blood of the Arabs. Paulos, I think my blood must be very hot, too, although I was born amid the snows. It feels like it now."

"You're much too young—"

"Do you know how old I am?"

"Thirteen and something—"

"I'm almost fourteen, but I might as well be ten, the way you treat me."

"Arab girls of fourteen are much older than you. They develop much faster, being daughters of the sun. You're like the memsahibs in developing slowly. But that is better, because you'll still be young when they're old."

"I'm more developed, as you say, than you think."

When I looked at her quickly, she dropped her eyes but her face was lit with ineffable pride.

"Why, you'll be fit to marry in two more years."

"Paulos Rajah, am I not your slave?"

"I let the people think so, to protect you, but when you're old enough—"

"Do you know what the women in the harem think?"

"I can imagine."

"Paulos Raj, I'm not a child any more. They think that for three months now, I've been your *cobah*." Suddenly she sat up straight. "I've let them think so! Even though you treat me like a Shenzi [black savage], I won't be shamed in their sight."

"Sithy, have you said so in so many words?"

"No, but I've hinted of your passionate love for me, and if you're angry—" She started to say she didn't care, but she bit her lips.

"I'm not angry, Sithy, but you must tell Julnar the truth. Hasn't she a tall handsome brother, someday to be Serdar of the Guard? Someday soon, you may become not his slave, but his wife."

"He's very handsome, truly, and hot-blooded I don't doubt." She stole a glance into my face.

"Even in six months—"

Half-crying, Sithy threw her arms about my neck and kissed me. "Paulos Rajah, I don't want to be anyone's wife. I want to be your slave. You can have others, but I want to be your *cobah* until you tire of me. They whisper that you go to see the nautch dancer at the fenduke. Is she prettier than I? Are her lips on yours more sweet? You can continue to go to see her, for all I care, but don't shame me any more before the women. I know you liked to kiss me, because I felt it in your lips. I felt your heart beat fast, as did mine. Wouldn't you like to do to me as the king in the book? What I read to you, and the part I didn't read? If tomorrow you turn me from your door—"

I drew her face to mine and held it there too long.

"Get my pipe and light it for me, Sithy," I commanded.

She did so, with a still face, and she did not try to get back into my lap.

"I see now you don't love me even a little."

"I do love you, Sithy, and that is the reason you can't become my concubine. If you were a girl I'd bought in the market, you could become so tonight, to my great joy, for my blood is not as cold as the waters of the Karasak. Because I love you, you must remain a maiden, so you can marry Julnar's brother—or some other noble youth, and bear him sons and daughters, and hold up your head among all the women of Zanzibar."

"You say," she said, drawing a long breath, "that if you'd bought me in the market, I could become your concubine. But not your *cobah?*"

"I didn't say that."

"That was what you meant. Is the nautch girl your Morning Star?"

"No. She's only a bringer of delight."

"Have you a *cobah* somewhere?"

"Not now."

"But you had, and you long for her still. You love her a bucketful to my thimbleful." A thought struck her, that made her eyes shine again. "Perhaps she's drunk the cup of death?"

"I am to her one who has drunk the cup of death."

"Are you going to try to get her back?"

"I want her back, if I can have her."

"And for that, at some far-off time, and because she won't let you keep me, too—"

"I can have only one *cobah*, Sithy."

"For that, which may never happen, and for wanting me to stay a virgin to marry some other, and despite what I felt on your lips and in your body, and despite the way Julnar's brother gazed at me, a most unseemly gaze—"

"That I don't doubt."

"Do you remember how I looked when you used to bathe me?"

"Very well."

"Would you like to see me now?"

"I wouldn't dare!"

"For those silly reasons, and despite all that, you won't even try to find out if I'm fit to be your *cobah*?"

"That's what it amounts to, I suppose."

"Then by Lak-zander—and I say his name aloud, if I be struck dead—by Lak-zander, Paulos Rajah, you're a fool!"

CHAPTER THIRTY-THREE

Dire Temptation

THAT LAST, I THOUGHT WEARILY, was quite true. But I was no piddling fool; my follies had always been of a large and, sometimes, noble sort. The supreme one was for me, Rom, to fall in love with Bachhiya, who was also Sukey Webb; if I had not done that, I would now be somebody in the Indian Government, smiling with Colonel Jacob over the overpowering pukkahood of the Tatta Lancers, but greatly gratified with the battles that they won. In that case, an extraordinary-looking blonde, such as pukka sahibs had never dreamed of, would not now be throwing cushions on the floor with a good deal of violence because I wouldn't let her sleep with me, the latter being a consequence of that same great folly. Even a fool, who later had to live with himself, could not take to concubinage a girl whom he had defended and supported since before her bosom swelled, for whom he was responsible to God and man, when he was in love with another and scheming to get her back. Unfortunately I was not an Arab, who might find a way to have both.

The fact remained that I was under dire temptation. I could find so many arguments for doing what I desired. What real chances did I have of getting Sukey back? If I yielded, tomorrow or some other morning, I might find myself forgetting her and in love with my little pagan. And since when, Gypsy Man, had I been a psalm singer? A bird in the hand was worth two in the bush, a Persian poet, named Omar Khayyam, had sung in much more flowery language seven and a half centuries ago. Having revised the Moslem calendar, he was no doubt well-versed in the trickeries of time.

To one Devil's argument I would not listen—that what I wanted to do with Sithy would be best for her, too. She could stand a year or two more of being "shamed before the women." Very young girls can fall very deeply in love, as did Juliet at fourteen, but I did not think that I, more than twice her age, would be much of an obstacle to her falling in love with Julnar's brother, say, and he, a Thracian Christian, would be no stickler for the Islamic doctrine of purdah, provided she was yet an actual virgin. For that matter, rather high-up Mussulmen were known to wink over their concubines and even their wives having been "compromised," as long as the goods were delivered intact. Anyway, I did not want her to marry into a harem. There was no real reason why she should not marry a perfectly good Eurasian or even European dwelling in the East.

No, I did not feel sorry for Sithy for the spurning of her first love, only for myself.

Yet in the following months I did not sail the straight course I had charted. I was simply not equal to it, with Sithy so near, so lovely, and so willing. Thoroughly ashamed of myself, I argued that she was entitled to the kind of courting that young girls enjoy and thrive on throughout the Western world and in vast regions of the East where purdah is not rigidly enforced. The difference in our ages was not the obstacle it would have been counted in the West; this was Africa, not England; I did not doubt that little Cheetal was deeply in love with the graybeard Sultan, love differing with different minds and ways. I did not believe that restrained wooing would hurt her chances for future happiness, and might, strangely enough, save her present pride.

So we played kissing-games such as English youth enjoy. Happily, no one saw us, and I saw the great delight she took in them, as well as the witchery in her face and manner when the play became a little more in earnest. To save me, I could not help but think of a terrier when his master poises a ball, so bright were her eyes when the game was in the offing. I had known high exultations in my time, but I could not remember such complete, carefree happiness as she gave me, titillated just enough by a sense of danger, warmed just enough

288

by the intimacies. I had no care for my dignity, since it had never been great when I was alone, and she considered me a fool only for being what I thought wise. I behaved with her like a young bumpkin to his village lass. Actually I had missed that wonderful springtime that most men could look back on; I had been briefly a child, then had had to be a man.

I could not hold her on my lap for very long without pain. Not yet wakened, only stirring a little, she did not understand. She could not possibly know shame, being a pagan of a curiously Pre-Homeric sort, and of late inculcated in the doctrine that girls had only two reasons for existence, one of them to satisfy men's carnal desires, and the other to bear them children. It was a devastating combination of wild nature and unholy cult. One dark afternoon of wind and blown rain. I was undermined by our warmth and closeness, and our kisses became too ardent. Her eyes grew luminous and then darkened, and she whispered something I could not quite hear.

"Did you say, 'I want all of you?' "

"I shouldn't have said it, Paulos Rajah. What I meant was, if I can't be your *cobah,* I would be your bringer of delight. The Emir said I could, when the time came."

"The Emir gave you to me."

"Then why don't you take me?"

"It wouldn't be fair dealing, Sithy."

"Why? Because you love the other woman too much?"

"To the other woman, I'm one who's drunk the cup of death."

"No, you'll get her back. I'm sure of it. You get everything you want, in time, and take nothing you don't want."

When she had said the "other woman" I could have smiled, considering Sithy such a child. I had no inclination to smile over it now.

"If I took what I wanted now, I would undo this little clasp—" But its very saying weakened my will.

"I'll undo it, and these cords, but there's one knot that only you can untie. Why isn't it fair to me, Paulos,

289

when I know now I can never be your *cobah?* When
you wish I was her, I'll try not to be jealous. When she
comes, you need never tell her about me. A week before
then you can give me to Julnar's brother, Theodore. He
sends me letters through her. He wants to marry me. He
the same as told me that he'll take me no matter what
you've done to me, because he doesn't believe—none of
the people do—that you've lived with me all this while
without making me your woman."

"I don't wonder. I can hardly believe it myself."

"He's a petty capudan now, and soon will be a serdar. He's a Christian and will have only one wife. I'll
be very happy with him, never fear."

"Would you like to marry him at once?"

"No, not until you get back your *cobah.*"

I undid the clasp at her throat, slipped off her jacket,
and bared her young breasts to my lips. The great
glance of wonder that she gave me, and then her arms
flung tight around my chest, broke all but one of my
barriers—which was my heart still enlisted in her behalf. It was under strong assault, but to give it brief
respite, I rose and went to the window. There the turmoil of the windblown clouds and the driven rain only
heightened my own turmoil.

"Are you ashamed?" I heard her ask, after a long silence.

"Yes."

"What of, Paulos Rajah?"

"My weakness."

"Your—weakness?"

"I'm going to yield to it, and be happy with you
until—"

"There's no happiness in weakness, master."

It was such a strange thing for her to say. I might not
have understood it, if she han't sprung to her feet.

"I don't want your weakness, Paulos Rajah. I want
your strength."

"What do you mean, Sithy?"

"The strength whereby you killed the Pathan who'd
killed all my people. The same I've always seen in you.
Yes, the same strength with which you'll get back your
cobah. I would take that strength until you get her, and

290

afterward have as much of it as you'd give me, as your slave. But I won't take your weakness. I won't have anything to do with it."

I could hardly believe that the strange, long, glimmering eyes so steadfast on mine held only yesterday the candid innocence of a child. She saw the incredulity in mine.

"I'm no longer a little girl from Kafiristan," she told me. "I've been with the women, and learned much from them, and have been with you, and have learned more from you than you can ever believe. All at once that learning weaves together like threads in the loom, and I can see what it means. Also I remember the men of Kafiristan. They're strong men, who hunt markhors along the ledges of the mountains, and stand up to the bears in the thickets, and plow the little up-and-down fields, and cut down the great trees for winter fuel. I love your strength, but I hate your weakness. I'll go now to Theodore."

I was not able to reply for a moment, and then only with a question.

"Would you want to marry Theodore when you don't love him?"

"I will learn to love him, if he's a strong man."

"Then let's stay together another year. You'll be only sixteen—no older than the Arab girls at fourteen. There are great things on foot here, and if plans work out, I'm going to ask the Sultan to set Hamyd and me free. If then you want to marry Theodore, you can, but if not —and I don't think you will—I'll take you anywhere in the world you want to go. I know many places where you'd meet many young men and have a fine time being courted, until you pick out the right one to marry."

"And after that, you'll go and get your *cobah?*"

"I think I'll have her—or have given her up for good —before then."

"You'll get her. I know that. If you want me to stay with you until then, I will, but I don't want to sleep in the same room."

"I'd miss you, Sithy."

"I'll miss lying awake, aching to get into your bed— or dreaming that you waked and came into mine. But it isn't well that I tempt your weakness, or you tempt mine. And you needn't feel sorry for me, Paulos Rajah, sleeping in the anteroom. I'll dream of the snows of Kafiristan, and sleep well."

"Won't you kiss me any more, Sithy?"

"Yes, as I did before today, and you did to me—if you still want it so."

"I won't feel sorry for you, Sithy—only for myself. You see, men are not given the wisdom of women, and the clear eyes. Often what we think is strength is weakness in disguise. But sometimes it's the other way 'round."

CHAPTER THIRTY-FOUR

A Cunning Plan

I MARKED A GREAT CHANGE IN HER from that day. She was no longer childish, but a lovely young woman of great grace. Something came into her face, so subtle that I was not sure I saw it, that I was never quite able to name. If it were not beauty, it was beauty's image in such a magic mirror as *mirayat*. She was quieter, I thought, and sometimes gave an impression of shyness. We played no more bumpkins' games, but she loved to have me kiss and caress her in accordance with our relationship, and often, when I was reading, her small, smooth hands could cover my eyes from behind me, and her exquisite lips press mine.

I tried to make the time pass as pleasantly as possible for her. Well greased now by court hangers-on with axes to grind, I bought her body-length headkerchiefs of Samarkand, pantaloons of Oman silk with tasseled cummerbunds, beautifully worked Persian coats, chemises of Bengal satin, and silver anklets with little tinkling golden bells. She smelled wonderfully of musk and rose water, and could, if she wished, walk with a pleasant jangle of bracelets, anklets, and gold chains. She spoke and read Arabic long since, so I introduced her to the wondrous lore of the desert. Few Circassian maidens, bought for the Seraglio on the Golden Horn, were more cultivated than my sweet Kafir maid.

That year I strove mightily to strengthen the throne, and became the Vizier's right-hand man. In the third quarter of the year he sent me as commander of a big safari up the old Swahili Road beyond the headwaters of the Umba River, there to deal with a black king who was raiding his caravans. When I had done the business, half appeasing, half scaring the huge savage, I established landmarks and blazed some trails in case I passed this way again on my own affairs. This was a wonderland surpassing my every expectation and wildest dream.

When I returned to Zanzibar, a great hour was about to strike.

Through Captain Hamerton, the British Consul, the Grand Vizier received a polite but strong protest against the continued export of slaves by runners to the coast towns. The Governor General of India demanded a guarantee from the Sultan that the ban be enforced—saying in diplomatic language, "Sa'id ibn Sultan, if you don't stop your subjects from shipping black cargo, we will." If that happened, he himself might become a "rag and bobtail" king, almost before he knew what was going on. On no account must the agreement leave a legal opening for the landing of English troops on that part of the mainland where the Sultan had established factories under the flag of Oman. To the Vizier I proposed that the business be no mere sitting down with a consul, who would have received instructions as to terms, and had "no authority to revise them." Instead it should be a full-dress affair, with a minor notable from India representing the East India Company and hence the Queen. I argued that the Sultan's *izzat* demanded such formal procedure, and thereby, having demonstrated his self-respect, we could make a better deal.

Thus far I was working only for my master. Pointing out that the writing of the letter to India would be tricky business, too, I requested the Vizier to do a turn for me. It was a big turn to say the least—to approach the Sultan now, and get his promise that if an agreement satisfactory to him was reached, on the very date it was signed he would set Hamyd and me—and of course my Kafiri—free. After a leave of six months, I would serve him faithfully for two more years as a free man, if he desired.

The Sultan replied that he would give the petition his cordial consideration. I had every reason to believe he would grant it, and shaped my plans on the assumption that he would. On my next audience in his chambers, I proposed that he should request that the ambassador chosen should be known to him by reputation as one friendly to Islam and with sufficient experience in administration to understand the problem of law enforcement over a wide border. Indeed, as a great king, he had every right to nominate various sahibs acceptable to him.

"You've kept a record of the great ones in Hind," the Sultan replied. "Name those who would deal with us justly and well."

"There are none more illustrious than Lord Gough and Sir Charles Napier." Actually the former was in England, and that the victor of Meeanee would come to Africa to negotiate a minor treaty was unthinkable. "Also there is one whom your kinsmen Baidu-ibn-Jabala of Oman praised for his just dealings with the Faithful in the matter of transport from Karachi to Mecca."

The truth of that matter was that Baidu had mentioned to me some official supervision of the pilgrim ships from Sind, but had credited no particular administrator. He was now safe in Oman.

"This sahib has had wide experience in the Northwest," I went on. "Also, he is a great nimrod, and if we promise him a lion hunt on the mainland with his memsahib—for he never goes anywhere without her—he will be in a good humor while making the treaty."

"I recall that I was in such humor, in making a treaty with Nazir Khan of Baluchistan." The Sultan smiled faintly. "You may compose the letter which the Vizier will sign, naming him and the others as acceptable to me. And you, Paúlos, have been a more than acceptable servant for three and a half years. On the day that the agreement is signed, whether or not it is all that I would wish, I will gladly manumit you to freedom, with your follower Hamyd and your *cobah*, the Kafiri. Then, after you've taken six months' leave to visit your country and kinsmen, I'll welcome you to my service as a free man."

The pertinent passages from the letter read as follows:

My master the Sultan requests that your Excellency

send as your representative to his court a sahib whose honor and fame has reached his august ears. There is none more illustrious in his sight than Lord Gough, Victor at Gukarat, or Sir Charles Napier. Of another one less known he has recently heard, because of his just dealings with his brethren in the Faith, in the matter of their ships from Karachi to Mecca, as reported to him by his kinsman Baidu-ibn-Jabala of Oman. The personage is Brook Sahib by name, a man young in years but old in wisdom, and is your Excellency's Viceroy in Sind.

The Sultan's nomination of a much lesser light should not astonish the Governor General, because according to the workings of the sahib mind, any act befriending the Faithful was bound to loom large in the Mohammedan mind, obsessed by religion. *"Isn't that just like a bushy Arab? But it goes to show how little things count, and how careful we have to be!"* The fine Greek hand showed again in the concluding paragraph:

If your illustrious ambassador wishes it, he may see for himself how law-abiding are my master's subjects on the mainland. If he wishes to visit there, after the treaty is made, within those territories immediately under the Sultan's rule, the Sultan will provide him with transport and proper convoy. It has come to him that Brook Sahib loves shikar and has written a book on the sport. If your Excellency chooses him as your envoy, the Sultan can promise elephants, lions, and other game in untold abundance. Pavilions will be raised for him in the wilderness, where he, his memsahib, and his servants may be comfortably and safely housed.

The only trouble with that was it was almost too enticing. The Governor General might offer the plum to one of his friends who had leisure for a wonderful holiday. In fact, the main trouble with the whole plan lay in what was the trouble with me. We off-white people are too given to self-dramatization. Indeed we have a passion as well as a flair for dramatizing all our affairs, great and small. True, there was a certain logic in my lurid plot. Long ago I had seen the necessity of getting

Gerald and Sukey off together, away from everyone who could interfere with our transactions. Such fulfillments as I dreamed of were impossible otherwise. Indeed, I could not find out what I wanted of them until I did so.

Any lonely place might do, but when I had visited the African highlands, I had found the perfect place. It was not only the most convenient, its appeal to my poetry-haunted imagination had been too strong to resist. Beyond the uttermost tenuous shadow of the Sultan's law, where no white man had ever gone, where the lions came roaring forth at dusk, and hyenas howled, and the wild elephant moved on silent feet, three people could meet their kismet. The very scene would ennoble that meeting, and bear upon its outcome. There the law of the wilderness could be my law. There the tusked bull, terrible in fury and revenge, the lion seeking prey, and the subtle leopard, might be my teachers. At least, between illimitable horizons, I could see plain.

In hardly two months the answer to the Vizier's letter arrived by dhow. The gist of it was, after amenities and platitudes, that His Excellency Gerald Brook, Lieutenant Governor of Sind, had been appointed to represent the Indian Government in the matter toward, and would sail from Karachi four weeks from its date. In addition to servants and a secretary, he would be accompanied by his lady, who likewise wished to avail herself of the Sultan's invitation to hunt big game in the interior.

As though Sukey would miss a chance like that!

I immediately crossed to Pangani to make arrangements for the safari. There I talked long with the district sheik, to discover the acknowledged border between the Sultan's ruled domain and the native kingdoms beyond exercise of his law. The north-and-south line zigzagged east and west. For instance, the Sultan could protect his caravans along the road clear into the Kimbu: on the other hand a mountainous region lying south of the river, to be gained by three days' journey in log canoes and a day's climb, was an unpeopled wilderness, save for a few Shenzis, beyond which the Sultan had no semblance of control. Was it a good hunting country? Fairly good, and in three days' march there were grassy uplands, with rocky hills and mimosa forests, where the game was thick as fleas in a Swahili's wool.

This meant that the safari could be much shorter and less difficult than the one I had planned to the Usumbara. If the hunters ventured from under the Sultan's flag, beyond the reach of his law, he could not be held responsible for any accidents overtaking them. A guide or guard might be blamed for negligence. If it were the criminal sort, or the accidents looked fishy, he might never dare return to Zanzibar. But not even the British Foreign Office, with an eye ever open for "incidents," could find an excuse for a military mission into the wilds if they occurred in the pursuit of dangerous game.

I spent a fortnight making arrangements for the visitors' accommodation. Perhaps I was somewhat negligent in choosing for safari captain an Arab ivory-factor named Bismilla, pompous, brave as a black-maned lion to hear him talk, but who had vowed to kiss the Black Stone of the Ka'ba before he died, and always took great care that the vow would be kept. He was an able handler of Swahili slaves, and would, no doubt, provide comfortable camps along the route. But these blacks were almost as terrified of Shenzis as was he.

When I returned to Zanzibar, I had quite a thrilling story to tell Sithy, of a rhinoceros that had chased me up a tree. But I got the impression that she was doing more watching than listening. She was wondering what I was covering up. I knew part, but not all.

"It was very lonely while you were gone," she told me gravely.

"I missed you greatly, Sithy."

"Twice you've gone for long stays among the wild people and animals. I hope you'll stay here awhile now."

"It so chances I must go again within a fortnight. Two great ones are coming from Hind, to hunt in the mountains, and I must see they are well guarded and attended."

"Have you ever told me about them?"

"You've never heard their names. They are a Governor Sahib and his memsahib."

Sithy was quiet a few seconds. "Paulos, aren't you, too, a sahib of a kind? Julnar spoke of her grandsire, who was a Greek, as a sahib."

"The Greeks are Europeans, and can properly be called sahibs, in Hind."

"Have you ever seen the sahib and memsahib, who are coming?"

"Yes."

"Tell me how they look."

"From the roof tops you've seen the Yankees and the English. They look much the same."

"They are young?"

"The sahib is my age, the memsahib younger."

"Is she dark or fair?"

"Very fair, but not quite as fair as you. She's also quite tall." I caught my breath. "But Sithy, don't say to anyone that I've seen them. I don't want anyone to know I was ever in Hind, because of trouble overtaking me there. And don't say that I'm going to help them with their hunt, as I may have to do. As far as you know I'm going only to Pangani."

"I won't tell a soul. But it has been a long time since I've seen mountains, and wild animals. I used to see the markhors and the bears, and sometimes the rams with great horns. Will you take me with you to the mainland, Paulos Rajah?"

The stream of my thought became divided in two. One of the branches, swift and clear, carried a matter I had not weighed before. After my visit to the hunting-grounds, what if I could not return to Zanzibar? What if I had to disappear into the wild interior, or work my way up the coast to find passage to Europe? I had to make some sort of arrangement to have Sithy join me. It would be very difficult unless—

The other branch of the stream moved slowly as the tidal rivers of the Waseramu. Like them it had deep whirlpools and seemed to flow in a dim, blue haze, as though it, too, had thickly jungled shores. I could not see into its depths and know what lived down there. I was conscious of its patient but indomitable sweep all the time I was thinking of Sithy's safety.

"There are lions and mad elephants and wild men where I'm going," I said.

"Master, I was once captured by a Pathan, who had slain all whom I loved."

"In spite of them, you might be safer going with me."

"Then have I your leave?"

"Yes, you may go. It's your right to go, and it's right that you should go. I want you with me."

CHAPTER THIRTY-FIVE

Forbidden Fruits

MY MIND WAS GREATLY PERPLEXED over what part
Hamyd should have in the enterprise. It was a much
weightier problem than it seemed. There were prac-
tical considerations and moral ones. Although boast-
ing a fine beard, he could not come into the game
too soon, lest he be recognized; his countenance had
changed greatly in the last nine years but had not been
transformed. His voice had not acquired an entirely different timbre from his mind's immersion into Arabic, as
had mine; his mannerisms seemed different to me but
they could well remind Sukey of long ago. However,
there would be plenty of work for him, if I could appoint him to do it.

He, too, had been betrayed to the enemy swords. If
Gerald ever gave thought to his bones, he might count
one or two of them—or three, perhaps—under the cairn
of stones with one or two—or perhaps three—of mine;
the rest had been carried away by the beasts of the dessert. Moreover, his offense had been small compared to
mine—the kind of love he had given Bachhiya was not
against the sahib's law. He had furthered our love affair
mainly at her command. Truly Gerald had had to beat
the Devil around the bush to justify his slaying at my
side; perhaps, to his credit, he had regarded it as a regrettable accident likely to happen in all punitive actions. Hamyd did not have nearly as much to win as I
had, and fully as much to lose.

He had, of course, heard the palace rumors of the
soon arrival of the Governor of Sind and his memsahib,
and had put two and two together. I got word to him
to come to my parlor; he came in gravely, wearing Arab

dress instead of the red-and-blue uniform of the guards, so not to attract too much attention. We were alone, so we lighted pipes as of old.

I told him about Gerald's official errand and my program, as far as it went, to meet him and Sukey in the interior. I explained that he and I would be free men, then, and we would not on any count cause trouble for the Sultan. I made it clear that after the stage was set, I had no settled plans for the ensuing drama other than the establishment to the satisfaction of any court, if he should come to trial, of Gerald's guilt. Though I did not tell him so, I did not even know which one of many motifs would dominate the action, or what great issues would arise.

He listened without comment.

"Hamyd, will the palace guard be called out in honor of such distinguished visitors?" I asked.

"Yes, sahib. The order has already been given. We are to be drawn up, and present arms, in the *benjile*."

"Before I ask you to join me on the mainland, I want you to look again into the face of my brother and his wife."

On the morning of their ship's arrival, the court made great stir. It was my right to stand in the Vizier's train, but I forewent the honor, and when the palace guard was arrayed in two lines, I took a stand immediately behind Hamyd, beside subordinate officials, mirzas, stewards, poor relations of the great, and hangers-on. Gerald and Sukey were being conveyed from the city in a luxurious launch presented to the Sultan, oddly enough, by the Government of the United States. From where we stood we saw its arrival at the Sultan's dock, and their greeting by the Grand Vizier. Then both entered palanquins to be borne on the shoulders of burly Swahili to the entrance of the *benjile*. Presently they came walking on the red carpet that had been laid to the main door of the palace.

I looked at Sukey first, escorted by our elegant English-speaking *Reis* Effendi, and followed by her ayah. Actually she was walking ahead of her husband and the Grand Vizier, which was not scheduled in the arrangements; plainly Gerald had upset them, as well as the

302

order of precedence of the court, to show he was an English gentleman before he was either a diplomat or the Sultan's guest.

She was wearing the scarf with which the Grand Vizier had presented her drawn gracefully over her butter-colored hair. Her gown was of white silk with a middling-long train. I knew that her beauty had not begun to wane in these years; I was not sure that it had stopped waxing. It was impossible to tell whether this was a consequence of happiness, or a deeply inward, hidden sadness. The lovely sensitivity of her countenance was as profoundly touching as ever.

I, Rom, Lomri, Paulos, sometimes Timur, stood and watched her pass. I did not see through a mist—my eyes felt dry and hot—but my throat cords were rigid, and nothing was in my chest but one, great, smothering ache. Hamyd quivered a little. Although she glanced at times at the statued guardsmen and bowed to their capudans, her eyes never met his. That she had caught the merest glimpse of me, peering between the pickets of that human fence, was unthinkable.

Gerald wore English formal court dress with knee-breeches. He looked considerably older than I had seen him last by lantern light and, oddly enough, taller, perhaps because his rather spare body had filled out. He had always been handsome; now he was an impressive figure of a Governor Sahib, immensely dignified, aloof, perhaps a little cold-looking. I wondered if he felt superior to this gaudy show, even while gratified by it. I thought that the two conditions could have coexistence in his mind, without conflict. My taut throat eased as I gazed upon him, and the painful congestion in the region of my heart quickly passed away.

Again Hamyd and I met in my parlor. Big-eyed Sithy brought us tea and, apparently without glancing at either of our faces, went out.

"The memsahib looked very beautiful," I began.

"Truly she did."

"Is she happy in her lot, do you think? I don't see how that will change anything kismet has in store for her, but I'd like to know."

"She's not unhappy, sahib, if I judge aright. It might

303

be that she still loves you—it would be hard for her to stop—but the pain of the wound of your loss has passed."

"Is she yet Bachhiya or wholly Brook Memsahib, wife of the Lieutenant Governor of Sind?"

"The Shahzadi of Hind, whom we both loved, abides in her still."

"Hamyd, do you wish to go with me to the mainland for the completion of the *thar?*"

"Has the sahib forgotten Bachhiya's words of long ago? She bade me cross with you the rivers and the deserts of your kismet. Thereby that became my kismet."

He did not say it was his wish to go. Plainly his wishes to go or to stay did not matter one jot or tittle.

"Will you come as my servant, or as my kinsman in the *thar?*"

"By your leave I'll come as both your brother in vengeance and the servant of the once-beloved husband of Bachhiya."

"Then, between now and our departure, make such preparations as would be fitting in the case we never return to Zanzibar."

He set about them, and I to the business of the new treaty. I had told the Grand Vizier it would be awkward for me, a Christian, to be seen as the Sultan's servant in dealings with another Christian, but I would remain in an anteroom to the council chamber. If the Vizier wished to take up with me any point in the contract, I would be available at all times, and I would do any writing of difficult passages that he desired. Only a latticed door was between me and the treaty makers. I could always hear the murmur of their voices, and almost always the suave but forceful voice of Gerald as he dictated to an English-speaking interpreter. It was never raised, but as, at this moment, it represented the voice of the Indian Government, and hence by a large vicariousness the Queen's, it carried well.

I did not need a Swahili's fan to cool my brow.

At the end of the first day, Gerald abandoned hope of any loophole in the new agreement permitting English policing of the slave coast. Like any good envoy, from then on he worked for the strongest possible enforcement of the previous agreement, banning the export of slaves from the Sultan's territories. I was his unknown ally in this enterprise. It would save many thousand natives from chains, and in the long run serve the throne, for Sa'id ibn Sultan would not sit there long unless the hellish traffic was wiped out. In the meantime he could expect trouble from the local sheiks lining their pockets from black cargo, Bismilla of Pangani being one of the worst offenders.

On the day that the agreement was to be signed, I proposed that the Vizier consult the Governor Sahib before appointing any escort of honor for his journey into Africa. The presence of such officials would demand formal behavior and ceremony in the upholding of their own and the guests' *izzat;* and it might be the two English would prefer a holiday from all court etiquette and cares of state. Gerald replied exactly as could be expected. He thanked the Vizier for his consideration, but he preferred to make the expedition with his memsahib not as the Lieutenant Governor of Sind, but as a private Englishman on shikar.

"He asked for plenty of porters, but as small an armed convoy as possible," the Vizier remarked to me. "Doubtless he is a very brave sahib, and a great shikar. But truly, since he is going no farther than the highlands of Kifaru, he has nothing to fear, save from the very beasts he willfully pursues."

"And that was a narrow escape from having our daily tiffin with a smelly Arab," I could hear Gerald telling Sukey.

It was a convenience for me, also.

The treaty was signed by Gerald, representing the Government of India, and by the Grand Vizier, as viceroy of the Sultan. It did not curtail the Sultan's power in any great degree, and was satisfactory to Gerald, although it was not much more than a postscript to the agreement made a few years before. Sa'id ibn Sultan celebrated the event with a fete at his city palace, for which the whole court wore its brightest plumage. From a balcony I saw my brother Gerald, in the full-dress uniform of the Tatta Lancers, receiving his due of honors, and then watching, with a slightly pained expression, a performance by nautch girls. He had shaken hands with the Sultan and made him a formal bow, but of course he had not knelt, let alone bumped his forehead on the floor.

The memsahib was, of course, absent, as was proper from a Mohammedan fiesta. But Gerald sped away to her, making short shifts of ceremony, the moment his host left the Divan. *Make haste, my beloved, and be thou like to a roe or to a young hart upon the mountain of spices.* I was having trouble with my imagination.

Within the next hour Sa'id ibn Sultan received me in his *gulphor*. As I knelt before him, in what seemed a dream woven onto a long pattern of dreams, I heard him declare my freedom, with that of my follower Hamyd and my handmaiden from Kafiristan. In the presence of the crown prince and a few officials, he praised briefly but highly my services to his person and his throne, and had the Vizier hand me a certificate of manumission bearing his royal seal. If I so desired, after my six months' pilgrimage to such shrines as I wished to visit, he hoped for my service as a free man in a post of honor. To facilitate my journey, his sarraf would furnish me with five thousand rupees. As a memento of my years in his court, he himself handed me a ring, on which were engraved his initials and the symbols of a blessing in Allah's name.

I did not weep when he shook hands with me, too, and instead I kissed the hem of his garment. My heart had a resonant beat, but it did not sing, for although I had been delivered from slavery to the Infidel, I was not yet free. I was still bound to the past. I bore a grievous wound that was not healed, and owed a mighty debt.

When the Sultan gave me leave to go from him, I went into my quarters and showed the certificate and the ring to Sithy. She wept, hardly knowing why—one of the few times I had seen tears in her strange, blue, slanted eyes—and I held her a long time on my lap, sometimes kissing her beautiful lips and girlish throat, but aware only of a profound tenderness toward her tonight, and of love of that kind which, asking nothing in return, can never die. I did not know what she was feeling toward me, although its depth and force was plain in every throb of her heart against mine.

"There's a new moon hung in the west," I told her, "beautiful as the Moon of Ramadan."

"What will it bring me, Paulos Rajah?"

"What do you think?"

"It will bring us both to the end of a road we've traveled four suns. I don't know what lies beyond, other than great change."

"There's a little change even now," I told her, to take that sibyl-look out of her face and cause her eyes to sparkle and not dream. "You must address me for a while as Timur and never speak of me save by that name."

"It's easy to remember. I called you Timur Rajah when I was a little girl of twelve. It must be great dangers we are going into, Timur," she went on, pretending to look off, but watching me out of the corner of her eye.

"Of many kinds."

She brightened wonderfully when I touched upon some of the sights and adventures we could expect on the journey, and thinking of those, with her to enjoy them with me, for a while I gave no thought to its main issues, and perhaps my face became bright. The hour was long past her bedtime, and, after several yawns, her eyes closed, her breathing became deep and rhythmic, and I felt that glow from her body that young humans and animals give off in peaceful sleep. I laid her on my bed while I made hers in the anteroom. When I started to waken her, so she could undress, I was reluctant to disturb her, partly because her face was so lovely in repose, and partly because her deep sleep showed that she had been overwrought. I could, of course, let her sleep in her clothes. Most high-class Arab women did so, a perfectly clean custom, since these and their bodies were kept scrupulously clean. But Sithy liked to sleep in a kind of winding-sheet of silk, which she wrapped around herself and turned in at the throat. I could, of course, disrobe her and put it on her.

So far, there was male ribaldry coarsening my thought. Also I felt a cheat, when I began to spy on

307

what I would not pay for to have for my own. Not that she would have thought about it in that way. No doubt what I was doing was running through her dreams, and had she resented it, she would have wakened. My frequent, often unnecessary touches on her luminous skin were pleasant to her, unassociated with danger, and perhaps acutely felt, causing an intense dream. I took a long time to unfasten clasps and undo sashes, partly because my hands were trembling and partly from design. Even thinking like an Arab, I thought that a very high price would not be too much to pay. Sithy was sixteen now, and the change from the dirty little waif who had stepped into a copper kettle four years ago, appraised by her stealer at only two hundred rupees, amounted to a transfiguration.

Awake, O North wind—blow upon my garden, that the spices thereof may flow out. Let my beloved come into his garden, and eat his pleasant fruits.

These were forbidden fruits, since I was not an Arab. So were those in the guesthouse tonight; the door to that garden was barred for some days to come. Still it was Sithy's right to go with me to the rendezvous in the wilderness; it had been more strongly established by this present scene; it was my right to take her there and right for her to be there. Sithy, I desire you as no Arab ever could, having a different concept of beauty, and as much as any memory of desire returns. I wish there was room in my heart to love you as much as any memory of love returns. If I did, I would keep the rendezvous with an untroubled and exaltant spirit.

I thought surely she would waken as I rolled her, arms free, in the winding-sheet. She only stirred a little, and sighed. I wiped off my brow, turned the lamps low, and went to bed in the next room.

In the morning I dressed in my mameluke-style to say farewell to palace intimates. But I meant to go into full Arab habit before I set sail to the mainland. I had done so on my previous trips to the mainland, as the Grand Vizier had bade me, so I could deal with the local sheiks and the native kings as a high official of the court, not as a Christian slave. Bismilla had no doubt that I was born to the Faith, nor did Na'od, the Somali chieftain of the Swahili village of Sa'dani, whom chance had let me defend from a false charge of ivory stealing, and who had gone with me into the Usumbara.

It was Na'od who had told me of Bismilla's slave-running against the Sultan's edict, and that was only one of several reasons he would be useful to me now. My mild worries that Gerald might take his secretary on the safari proved groundless; the bookish fellow had no taste for big game, and chose or was ordered to remain in Zanzibar, perhaps to prepare a report of value to the Indian Government. From a high window I watched Gerald and Sukey set out in palanquins for the dock, accompanied only by Sukey's ayah, Gerald's Sindhi body servant, and an English-speaking Malay, no doubt hired as an interpreter. At Pangani, their port of entry on the river mouth, Bismilla would have servants and porters for them without end.

All three of us in Arab dress, Sithy, Hamyd, and I set sail that night for Sa'dani. We were going to the Kifaru Mlima by a shorter but rougher route. We disembarked at dawn, and at noon were ready to set out with Na'od and fifty Swahili porters lightly burdened with stores, a couple of sun-faded pavilions for Sithy and me, enough muslin to protect two tender-skinned travelers from mosquitoes in the lowlands, two camp beds fit for a sheik and his *cobah,* an old litter for Sithy to ride in when she would, several flintlocks, and two heavy double-barreled rifles as good as any, although not as pretty as Gerald had brought from India. In addition to these necessities, we had what might be called "properties," the use for which I did not yet explain to Na'od. One lot I had bought from a Zanzibar curiosity shop frequented by sailors. Another lot I had run across in Sa'dani, and had decided to take them only on the spur of the moment. I had the same smattering of Swahili picked up by most Arabs of the court from hearing it every day, but Hamyd, who commanded Swahili soldiers, spoke it well.

Instead of taking up the Wami River, we set out over a wood path leading northwest, no doubt used for running slaves to the coast. This was rather heavy going through real jungle, too dense for sight-seeing, and, aside from elephant tracks in the wet earth and crashings in the thickets, we would have thought the land unpeopled. But in two days' march we were in the Wazeguha, where the country brightened. Here we saw elephants with small tusks, huge dewlapped elands reminding me of Brahman cattle, bushbuck, tiny dik-diks, and once our way was challenged by a herd of sullen slate-blue, wide-horned buffalo, among the most formidable of beasts. That night we heard low bumps in the dark that were the rhythmic grunts of walking lions, two furlongs from our fires.

Two days more took us to what the Swahili called Kifaru Mlima—Rhinoceros Mountain. Here we made camp, and the following noon Hamyd and I climbed to the crest. Gazing northward through my field glasses we took turns searching the grassy slopes. For more than an hour nothing crossed them but a few antelope herds and two lonely-looking elephants, then Hamyd, grinning, handed me the glasses. Over the crest of a hill there turned and twisted a line of black dots. Through fifteen miles of crystalline air, moistureless at this season, it was perfectly identifiable as a hundred or so porters walking in file.

Between surveys of the country, we watched them off and on throughout the afternoon. Long before they pitched camp, we distinguished three litters borne by four men each, no doubt containing the sahib, the memsahib, and the worthy Bismilla. An hour before sundown they stopped beside a donga containing springs, not more than four miles from our pavilions. From the care with which the tents were raised and the baggage sorted and distributed, we judged that they intended to stay here several days.

The field glasses brought the scene within a half mile. We could not confuse long-robed Bismilla and the two brown-clad aliens with the black, busy, loinclothed porters, but sometimes we confused Gerald and Sukey, until they removed their white sun helmets and the head of one showed yellow-colored in the setting sun. Through the glass of imagination I saw her, tall, with a beautiful carriage, her eyes lifted to the hills. She did not know she was being spied upon across a gulf of nine years, a gulf like death's.

I was heavy of heart and silent when I handed the glasses to Hamyd. He gazed awhile, his face expressionless, then laid them down.

"How far is their camp from the Sultan's border, sahib?"

The businesslike question waked me from dim dreams.

"There's a valley to the west not a day's march. Beyond that, the Sultan claims no sovereignty and sways no power. Bismilla will not want to venture there."

"They will have only fair hunting here."

"I doubt if it will be even fair, since the Swahilis are not hunters like the desert men, only seed planters."

"Your hunting, too, will be less than fair."

I felt a pleasant tingle across the back of my neck.

"True, the game can be only spotted and watched, for it's protected on these grounds. But later it may move into the wilderness."

"I think it will so move."

"Hamyd, it will be good sport to start and drive it, or better yet, decoy it, to the wonderful western highlands where there are no game laws."

"That could well be."

"But if the quarry becomes alarmed, it will seek safety with the wardens in the east. Picture me, Hamyd, as I was on the night Bachhiya bade you follow me, and compare that picture with the one before your eyes."

Hamyd gazed at me long and from every angle, his mind in a deep repose.

"Sahib, there's no reminder of that day. If Bachhiya sees your face by torchlight when all else is hidden, she might say to herself, 'He reminds me of Rom.' But she would not know why, so altered is your countenance by the wound and its healing, by the death you died, and by eight years of thinking, feeling, and acting as a slave. She won't wonder what's under your beard. She won't toy with the thought that you might be Rom; her wildest imaginings can't vault that far, with your bones long dried in the desert sands. And what little resemblance to him remains there is canceled out by your general aspect. In that, you're an Arab of the Arabians.

Your intonation is that of an Arab, so is your very least gesture and mannerism, so is your garb, and you are met in Arab country."

He paused, musing, and with my gazing at his thoughtful face, and considering his words, it came to me how greatly he had changed and grown from the beardless callow youth who had followed me into the sand hills more than eight years ago.

"Now it may be, sahib, that Bachhiya will know me at first sight," he went on. "Therefore she mustn't see my face until the hunting is over and the game's in the net. But you she won't know, nor will the sahib, until the door is unlocked between the present and the past."

"She's never seen you bearded or in Arab dress. I doubt if she'll know you until some gesture or tone makes known your love of her. It's best you get now into the habit of addressing me as 'Seyed Na,' as a good Arab should call his master."

"We both be good Arabs, Seyed Na—unless it be in our hearts."

"Are they Arab hearts, Hamyd? If they are, at once stony and on fire, implacable in *thar*, assuredly the hunting will be good."

He waited for me to answer my own question.

"They are not, Hamyd, and the love of Bachhiya dwells in them both. But I can speak for mine now. It's neither an Arab's, nor a Greek's, nor a sahib's, from now to the hunt's end. It's a Gypsy's heart."

"Kismet," Hamyd murmured.

"I see now it's my kismet. It throws back to a Gypsy tent, in which I was begotten. For that, it was my kismet to go into slavery, and, finally, to come here. Do you know anything about Gypsies, Hamyd?"

"No, O Mullah [teacher]."

"They're very lowly people, dirty and thieving, but they are good dancers and musicians. Also they're quite cunning, in a barbarous, sometimes childish, way. In their quarrels—for they are too lowly a people to have *thars*—they are vindictive, scheming, and cruel. They love to play cat-and-mouse with their victims. I believe they're given to elaborate plots and to strange torments. They are also very ingenious in their inventions."

312

"Bismillah [Grace]," Hamyd said softly, and moved his hands as though washing them.

"They're subject to rhapsodies, whether of love or hate, in which they are no longer in their right minds, but their dancing and their music is then most wonderful. It's said they belong to the Devil, not without cause."

"It comes to me that they do."

"A Gypsy is going dancing, and the Devil will play the tune. A Gypsy is going hunting, leaving behind him all restraint and all the good un-Gypsy things he learned among the sahibs. If you'll go with him, you'll have good sport."

"It will be excellent sport, surely, and Allah have mercy on my soul."

CHAPTER THIRTY-SIX

Safari into Peril

HAMYD AND I ENJOYED OURSELVES, merely seeing what we could of Gerald's doings, and piecing out the rest. Without the slightest danger of discovery, we kept within a mile of him, losing him and finding him again, throughout his first day's hunting. He and Sukey were being guided by Bismilla, who had, no doubt, boasted of his slaughterings about the evening fires; behind them were the interpreter and three or four porters to carry home the trophies. Actually it was hard to imagine a poorer hunter than the slave-smuggling sheik. He was too fat to climb, too careful of his skin to enter high grass or heavy thicket, and too heavy-footed, if not strong-smelling, to stalk wary game.

That day each of the two hunters shot a bushbuck for camp meat, and Gerald a middle-sized wart hog. None of these counted as trophies, and their best chance of the day—a small herd of buffalo led by a heavy-horned bull—was lost when Bismilla, becoming excited, fired a musket at one of the cows. On the second day they left the sheik in camp—probably to his great relief—depending on a pair of Swahilis to cary their comforts and to find their way back to camp. No fault could be found with their boldness, but Gerald had had no experience in locating and stalking game, his shikar in India having been stand-shooting at animals driven by long lines of beaters. To our amazement none of the party saw a huge rhinoceros not a furlong distant in scrub forest, and a herd of eland flushed before he and Sukey could approach in rifle range. Another bushbuck shot within the camp environs was the day's only kill.

Early the next day Hamyd and I had a fine view of

him and Sukey stalking two lions by a brushy donga. The animals crept past them and dashed out the upper end, unseen. They spent the remainder of the morning combing the thickets, and made the best of a discouraging foray by Sukey's shooting an immature buffalo bull that wandered across their path. It was their first trophy in two and a half days on the shooting-ground, and not worth hanging in the Residence at Sind.

Hamyd went to our camp and sent Na'od and two Swahili bearers to meet me a mile or so from Gerald's camp. As he and Sukey were having tiffin at the table their *fundis* had erected, we appeared on the open slope of the hillside. They glanced up at us, and Sukey started to rise, but Gerald knew how to handle natives, so she resumed her seat and both went on with their meal. Bismilla came to the door of his pavilion, but had not yet recognized me. Only when we approached within forty paces did Gerald lay down his fork and move his stool to face us. My heart was beating strongly but not overly fast.

"Timur Effendi!" Bismilla cried, obviously glad to see me.

"Bismilla Sheik! *Sall' ala Mohammed!*"

"*Alla umma salli alayh!*"

"We saw the smoke of your fires, and would wish you good hunting."

"It's been poor enough, so far. I think one of the cursed blacks has made *uchawi* [black magic] against us. I'll present you to the great sahib, guest of the Sultan."

On approaching Gerald, I bowed low and clapped my hand to my forehead and my heart. He responded with a nod and a lift of his hand. There did not come to him, and I had never imagined that there could, the slightest inkling that he had ever seen my bearded, scarred face before. Not the dimmest memory stirred in the deep of his brain, if his candid glance told true. So far I had not glanced at Sukey's unveiled face, as was good manners for an Arab of *izzat*. But I saw it out of the corner of my eye and I thought it revealed lively interest.

"Tell your master," Bismilla addressed Gerald's

315

Malay interpreter, "that this be Timur Effendi, an honorable servant of Sa'id ibn Sultan."

This was duly translated into a pidgin English.

"Salaam, Timur Effendi," Gerald said.

"Alicum salem, sahib."

"Ask him if he speaks any European language," Gerald directed.

When the question was put to me, I lifted my arms, palms outward, and shook my head.

"But I've learned a little Hindustani from the shopkeepers of Zanzibar," I ventured to the translator.

"He says he speaks some Hindustani."

Gerald spoke in a casual tone to Sukey. "That might be useful."

"Gerald, did we meet him at the Sultan's court?"

"I'm sure we didn't. I'd have remembered that fine scar."

"I would've, too, I dare say. But I thought at first there was something—"

"These johnnies all look alike to me, I'm afraid." Gerald turned again to me, and spoke in informal Hindustani. "Are you on safari, Timur Effendi?"

"Yes, sahib—to take ivory."

"From the size of the elephants around here, I wouldn't think you'd find much."

"No, sahib, they're very small. The game has been shot out or driven out of this area, it being too close to the coast. I'm only passing through with my porters, on the way to the farther wilderness of Wasegua." It was not difficult to speak Hindustani with an Arab accent and to employ simple forms.

"Why, I was led to believe this was a wonderful hunting-ground."

I started to answer, and then appeared to think better of it.

"You may speak freely, Timur. No one here but the memsahib and I and our servants know Hindustani."

"Sahib, the honorable sheik, good servant of the Sultan and my brother in the Faith, is not a hunter."

"I've found that out."

"Also—although he's a *ghandur* [brave] *bahadur* [officer]—"

316

Gerald turned to the Malay. "Tell Bismilla that Timur says he's a very lion in bravery." When this was done, and Bismilla stroked his beard, Gerald spoke in Hindustani again. "Now, Timur, you may omit the flattery."

"The sahib understands. Truly, since you were a guest of our Sultan, it's my duty to speak truth. The great sheik is a famous slave catcher. For that, some in the farther highlands bear him a grudge."

"I don't wonder."

"They are only Shenzis, but they might make bold to attack him, when he's not protected with your guns. For that reason, he chose this secure place. And truly, with better luck you may take a fair bag."

"What game is there on the highlands besides elephants?"

"Sahib, I could more easily tell you what game is not there. The buffalo you've slain—if you'll pardon me, sahib—wouldn't be worth a glance. The lions are black-maned and, having endless herds of zebra and wildebeest to prey upon, are numerous and, to speak truth, dangerous. But, sahib, the land lies two days' march beyond the Sultan's domain. It's an unpeopled part of the realms of a black king."

"I can't imagine him molesting an Englishman."

"Nor I, sahib. But the Shenzis might make trouble for the honorable sheik."

Gerald turned to his wife, who was listening to him with wifely concern. Her hand raised, with her long fingers against her cheek, revealed to me for the first time her bizarre bracelet, fashioned in India of gold and enamel, to which was fastened a small, bright silver coin. What luck will it bring you Sukey, at safari's end?

"I wish we could get there," Gerald was saying. "I'll be damned if I'm going to stay here. It's either that, or go back to Zanzibar—"

"Take care, Gerald. I don't think we ought to go beyond the Sultan's domains—"

"Nonsense, darling—if the sport's good enough. These blacks know what happens if they try any tricks on a sahib. Of course, this fellow would expect baksheesh, and plenty of it, for any help he gives us." He turned to me. "Have you a camp near by?"

"Yes, sahib, but we'll break it in the morning. We rested today because it's a day of feasting in my faith. If you wish to break camp, my men and I could go with you to the border valley, about four hours' march. Surely the hunting will be better than here. There you may have a day with my great tracker, Na'od."

"I accept with pleasure."

"But pray you, sahib, don't speak of this to the sheik until I'm gone, and then cunningly, lest he bear me ill will for my intrusion in his business."

"I will, Timur, but it's my business, not his. Are you, too, a hunter of renown?"

"No, sahib. I depend on Na'od to lead me to the game, and to fell it when the shot is difficult. I was once clawed by a lion of the desert."

"Sukey, that's the first Arab I've ever met who missed a chance to boast."

"I'm not sure I like that, either."

"Oh, come, Sukey. You've got too much imagination." He turned again to me. "Will you bring your outfit this way tomorrow? We'll be ready to march, and fall in behind you."

I salaamed to Gerald, bowed my head in Sukey's direction without looking at her, gave Allah's peace to Bismilla, and walked away swiftly, to conceal a sudden weakness in my knees. When I returned to our camp, Sithy looked at me inquiringly, and although I did not know what to say to her, I saw her with the most clear and open eyes I had ever turned on her. Until now, it seemed, I had always seen her in comparison with Sukey. Now I saw her in contrast with her. Her ashen hair was no longer rememorant of my love's. Sithy was a child of the snows of the Hindu Kush, Bachhiya a daughter of the sun. I was glad I had brought her, now that she stood on her own. I saw the witchery of her face, and knew that save for their haunting, my eyes could find a unique beauty there.

I was suddenly taken with a sharp awareness of her strength. Perhaps her costume of hard-woven wool, the kind worn by the Bedouin women when herding their flocks, revealed what had been concealed by the silken draperies she had worn in the palace. I had cause to remember her atop a camel, when I had brought her across the dizzy mountains from the Kafiristan frontier. Strong muscles and stout hearts are either native to human beings, or are acquired in early childhood; they can rarely be won in late years, or quite lost. I had persuaded Sithy to ride in the litter only half the first day, the final hour of the second day, when I, too, had been lame and weary, and not a moment since. She looked only a little leaner but a great deal lither. The scanty flesh on her facial bones appeared more spare and tighter-fitting, which was lovely-looking under her eyes, and gave the effect of planes between cheekbone and lower jaw. She wore her hair in two hemplike ropes encircling her head, which was the way I fancied Attic nymphs might have worn theirs.

"Have you seen the sahib and the memsahib?" she asked, as though idly.

"Why, yes. How have you spent the day?"

"I climbed many hills with Bazizi." This was a high-spirited Swahili about Sithy's age. "I took one of the guns, should a lion try to eat us."

The gun was one of the ancient muskets, no match for a lion.

"Do you know how to fire it?"

"Truly. My father was a good hunter of markhor and bears. He taught me how to load and fire a gun. I was so little then that every time I fired it, it knocked me down. He laughed, but he didn't laugh the day a wolf came to kill our sheep, and I shot him dead."

"That was a better trophy than any to be taken by the sahib and the memsahib, better than a black-maned lion or an elephant."

"If I can, I'll shoot some deer for us to eat."

"They're antelopes, not deer, and very good eating. But go wide of lions, if you see any, and most of all, stay out of the wind of rhinoceros. If one sees you or smells you, climb a tree, and wait till he goes away."

"All that I'll do, but, Timur Rajah, have no thought of me, until this business you are on is done. I'll be very

319

happy in the mountains. It's the first fresh air I've had since long ago. When the *shauri* is over—"

"Why, you use Bazizi's talk already!"

"When we go back, I'll entreat you to set me free."

"You're free already. The Sultan made you so."

"That's not enough. But I'll speak of it later, when my master is at leisure." She gave me a big smile, as though in promise of good news.

That night we split the outfit, I to take about two-thirds of the porters and the stores, both pavilions, and one of the heavy guns by way of Gerald's camp to the border, Hamyd with the rest to stay on our flank about ten miles distant, out of sight and sound. We arranged signals, if such would be needed, and made plans. Some of the latter would require Hamyd and a few of the boldest Swahili to leave the fires at night. He must be very careful.

"There will be a fine moon, Seyed Na, and I'll keep out of the thickets. Truly I'll stay in the open grass, where the lions will see me plain, and not mistake me for a buck, and unless they be man-eaters by custom—which Na'od says are rare save about the villages—they'll go their way in peace. I'll walk wide of rhinos and buffalo and elephants, be sure. But if one does attack me, I'll have one of the strong guns. Also, if the danger were ten times as great, this be *thar*."

In the morning we broke camp, and Hamyd and I, with our outfits, took different paths. Following me were a white and black mountaineer—Sithy and Na'od. Both had instructions not to mention Hamyd's safari to any new companion. Our appearance was highly reassuring as we neared Gerald's tents—breechclothed black porters of a humble, peaceful tribe, honest-looking baggage, only two guns, one of them a musket, and the master's slave girl walking sedately behind him. An Arab chief would not take his wife on safari, of course; in case of necessary travel, she would go veiled. Sithy's head cloth concealed her wheat-straw hair and her face was pink from sunburn; probably Gerald and Sukey were not aware of her native hue until we were almost in sound of their voices. Their gaze returned to her now, with ill-hidden curiosity, and Gerald spoke to Sukey in low tones.

"You arrived earlier than I expected you, Timur Effendi," Gerald remarked pleasantly in Hindustani, when I had salaamed.

"Good Mussulmen must rise at dawn, sahib, no matter their sleepy heads."

"And no matter their good companions," Sukey added with a sparkling glance at Sithy. No, it was Bachhiya who said that, or rather let it slip out. Within the pukka memsahib, wife of the Lieutenant Governor of Sind, whose aspect was almost always correct, Bachhiya still lived!

The effect on Gerald of the joyous, slightly ribald remark gave me wicked glee. Annoyed and acutely embarrassed, he could freeze his face but not erase its dark-red flush. He thought that Sukey had lost *izzat* before a native, and since she was his memsahib, so had he. Probably this had happened before, when Bachhiya broke loose. Of course he did not and could never know that a touch of nature makes the whole world kin—that the proudest Arab would relish the sprightly thrust, be flattered and warmed by it, and admire him for winning such an affable memsahib. I made a daring reply.

"It's a wonder, sahib, that you rise before noon."

Gerald's flush deepened, and his mouth looked as though he were biting his tongue. Yet when he spoke to Sukey in English, he managed a casual, trying-to-be-pleasant tone.

"You see what we get when you make remarks of that sort to a dirty-minded native. If you hadn't given him the opening, I'd have to punch him in the jaw."

This man who had plotted and apparently accomplished the murder of his half-brother in order to take his wife was not a hypocrite in giving her this bitter rebuke, and instead of gleeful I was suddenly dizzied and appalled.

"Don't strike him, Gerald," Sukey answered quickly but in an easy tone. "He's not a coolie but an Arab chief, and he'd have his knife in you before you could say, 'Scat.' It was my fault, and I'm sorry. Don't say anything more about it, please."

321

"Forgive me, darling. But you must remember to be dignified around natives." He turned again to me. "I'm glad you've brought a companion. If she's used to safari, she may be able to assist the memsahib, who's visiting Africa for the first time. May I ask if she's a Circassian? Since she's not wearing a veil, I see she's very fair of skin."

"I know only that she's from mountains far away."

Gerald turned affably to Sukey. "I don't believe she's Circassian, with that Mongoloid countenance. I think she must be what was called a white Hun from Kafiristan, but there was a runaway Swede in the woodpile, to make her that white. Look at her throat and the edge of her hair. She'd be quite pretty if—"

"I think she's beautiful."

Gerald again gave attention to me. "We'll be ready to start in a few minutes. May my cook offer you a cup of tea?"

"Not now, by your favor."

While the men were finishing loading, Sukey addressed Sithy pleasantly in Hindustani, and received shy replies. Evidently she was delighted that the little heathen knew the language, and looked forward to her company on the journey. Since the master's tent and its contents were always the last to be packed, she offered to show them to Sithy. Gerald heard the proffer.

"That's nice of you, Sukey," he said in English, "but watch her little fingers."

When we were under way, Na'od and I led the file in the role of guides. Bismilla was enough impressed with me not to ride while I walked, and, for reasons of her own, Sukey abandoned her litter at the foot of the first steep hill. "I want to stretch my legs," was the reason that she called to Gerald.

"I'd like to stretch mine, as you jolly well know," he replied, being swung along, "but it happens something rather important is at stake."

In three hours we made the valley bordering the Sultan's domains. We halted before crossing it, but Gerald gave no orders to pitch camp. Instead he searched the countryside with his field glasses.

"I see one herd of eland and some bushbuck," he

called to Sukey. "The country looks a little better than Rhino Mountain, but not much."

"Let Na'od look," Sukey proposed.

"I don't suppose he knows how—"

However, Na'od did, and found what he thought was a herd of buffalo on a distant hillside. "There's also a lion on the rock heap on the opposite slope of the valley," he told me.

"Timur Effendi, how far beyond the border would I find plenty of game?" Gerald asked.

"The game increases with every hour's march, sahib. But if you care to camp here, Na'od will devote the rest of the day to your service. You'll surely get a few shots."

He addressed Bismilla through the Malay interpreter. "I'm of a mind to go on a distance with Timur Effendi."

"Your Excellency, the Sultan can't guarantee your safety beyond this valley. Nor can I take responsibility for escorting you there."

"What is there to be afraid of, Bismilla Sheik?"

"The Shenzis have been known to come almost this far, in their hunting. They're very bad men, sahib."

"I wouldn't have you disobey your Sultan. But I've come a long way to enjoy the sport, and although I'm his friend and admirer, I'm a subject of my Rani. If you feel dutybound to return, I would miss your pleasant company, but with my interpreter, no doubt I could manage without you."

"The Swahili porters wouldn't dare enter Shenzi country without me, sahib."

"Ask them, sahib," I murmured in Hindustani.

"Have Na'od ask them."

Na'od did so, and they grinned and nodded. "We aren't afraid of Shenzis, *bwana*," one of them said.

"In that case, Bismilla, I've decided to go on."

"But I, too, am a subject of the Sultan, sahib," I said quickly. "I'll gladly show you the way in, and if you decide to go as far as the land of the big white ivories, I'll make camp close to yours until you know the country, but I can't be responsible for your safety. It be true that Shenzis sometimes cross the land, and are responsible to no king."

"Are the Shenzis friendly to the Arabs?"

"They don't love us, sahib, but they've no special grudge against me, and I go and come where I please."

"So does a sahib worthy of the name. And I fancy they've heard enough of sahibs to feel responsible to a regiment of tommies, if something should happen to one. Timur, you won't get in trouble with your Sultan if you show me the way in?"

"Not if you relieve me of all responsibility for your safety."

"I do, and tell Bismilla so."

I repeated the conversation to Bismilla in Arabic.

He gave his beard a big tug, and then stroked it.

"I'm Bismilla, Sheik of Pangani," he pronounced. "Although I, too, take no responsibility for his going beyond the border, I'll go with him and give him the protection of my scimitar." He turned proudly to the Malay. "You may tell your master so."

The news was not all bad. If he returned now, conceivably he might go straight to the Sultan with word of my guiding the royal guests into Shenzi country, and raise the possibility of a company of askaris being dispatched for their protection. Later, if all went well, the danger would be averted.

So we pushed on, and that afternoon I told Na'od a rather elaborate lie. It was that I wished Bismilla to lose *izzat* before the Sultan by quitting his post; therefore it would be well to penetrate the country farther than he would dare go. To that end, the sahib should not be shown too much game along the road, and ever be led on to greener pastures. Knowing that the danger from Shenzis was trifling, and despising the highhanded sheik, Na'od was only too glad to agree.

We trekked all the next day with only occasional protests from Bismilla who was lordly hiding his inward quakings. Much to my relief, Sukey did not raise the slightest objection, perhaps because she was as wonderstruck with the adventure as was my Sithy. We laid over the next day, so that sahib and his memsahib would hunt with Na'od. The pair came in exultant with the skin of a fine leopard which Gerald had felled from a tree at a hundred paces. They had seen a rhino, and

324

found stale tracks of elephants large, he said, as barrel hoops, but these and the lions had shifted westward. No one could account for the comings and goings of the great tusked *Timbu*, Na'od had told him, but the lions were following the antelope and zebra herds into the spring grass of the uplands.

Na'od told me that he had had a hard time keeping the pair from seeing a "mob" of seven lions, all males, around an eland kill in a brush thicket.

"Tomorrow, Bismilla, I will push on to the land of the giant white ivory, to be gained around noon of the second day," Gerald pronounced through his interpreter.

"It's against my wishes and my judgment, sahib," the sheik answered, "but if we're attacked by Shenzis, I shall die fighting."

On the morning of the second day we gained a wide plateau, encircled by purple-colored mountains. The cool air was wonderfully limpid, and throughout the morning march there was not a moment that a perch on an anthill would not disclose game. The striped hides of zebras winked like dim mirrors in the sun. They were dozing or grazing almost everywhere we looked. Wildebeests moved across the grassy plains or loafed in mimosa shade in countless thousands. Again and again we flushed them from their rest, to run in half circles, bound, and stampede off—horse-faced, big-shouldered ugly beasts but, next to zebras, the lion's favorite prey. Fine, plump, goatish-looking topis were everywhere, with their silly-looking kinsmen, the kongonis—both hartebeests in the Dutchmen's lingo. Mild giraffes strolled decorously by, each bearing a tower too tall to have entered the Ark; how then had they been saved from the Flood that very Jehovah had promised would drown the whole earth? Could it be that while archangels trembled in the pale dread of it, even He broke His word in pity on their innocence and grotesque form, and found them a refuge atop a secret mountain higher than Ararat? Ah, that was why all their generations since had been born mute, never the slightest outcry raised in joy or sorrow from their sesquipedalian throats! Otherwise they might tell their companions of the Heaven-rocking sin.

"Na'od, does the sahib want to shoot a *twiga?*" I asked.

"Yea, he's very eager to do so, having a place in his durbar where the mounted head and neck will look well, and he wishes what remains of the dappled skin to cover the seats of chairs, or so he has told Bismilla."

"He's not to be allowed to shoot one."

"*Sifahamu?*"

I did not know the word, though it seemed to indicate that he did not understand.

"He can't shoot one, Na'od."

"But, Timur Effendi, one can't say to a sahib—"

"Scare the *twiga* away, or jog his arm as he aims. It's not right that he should kill an animal that can't cry out in anger or in pain even in his death throes."

"Why, now, there be salt in that, yet—"

"It's an order, Na'od. From now on, although only you know it yet, the sahib is no longer in command of the safari. When his wish or word opposes mine, mine is to be obeyed."

The tall Somali considered briefly, his black eyes shining in the sun. "It comes to me there's more to this matter than your desire for Bismilla to lose *izzat.*"

"Truly there is, and I'll enlighten you before long."

"In the meantime, to hear is to obey."

The beautiful land continued to reveal its myriad and diverse dwellers. Small, pretty gazelles with vigorously whirling tails, as though ever winding themselves up for a mighty leap, grazed about the ankles of their towering companions. But they merely galloped away, and the mighty leaping was done by antelopes with long, thin horns, and skins of russet brown, called *m'pallas.* Their long, light-looking bounds seemed to be in direct defiance of the law of gravity. Gerald started to stop and stalk a big, sable-colored antelope with a harlequin face and scimitarlike horns, but it darted away. Na'od called it *palahala,* and truly it was one of the most beautiful of earth's creatures. Equally large, handsome and impressive rather than beautiful was a reddish brown antelope with white stripes and very tall, spiraled horns, which Gerald identified as the great kudu.

This was the world as it was before Adam. We saw no lions, they lying up this time of day, but no doubt no few saw us. Hyenas waited in the rocky caves for the sun to set; leopards became invisible in dappled light and shadow; buffalo sought shade in the labyrinthine thickets, to emerge in the cool of the afternoon. The only elephants we saw had small ivories—the rule rather than the exception here, Na'od confided to me—but twelve-foot monsters often wandered in from Ukimbu and the Masai. Amazingly, we met no rhinos, to Gerald's disappointment and Na'od's great relief. The evil-tempered, hard-to-kill brutes were more than half-blind, but six score scampering porters afforded them too much scope. However, their diggings and their dung heaps were everywhere.

At noon we pitched a comfortable camp beside a clear spring. While Sukey rested in her tent, Gerald made a short sally with Na'od, to return in great triumph with the news he had shot a rhino! His boyish enthusiasm worried me a little, recalling me to old days in Berkshire; but the distress soon passed, and the memories changed. He turned quite cold when Na'od told him that the porters could not retrieve the three-hundred-pound head and neck skin until the following day. Night would fall before they could gain our fires, and they had no protection from such as crept forth at twilight. But lions and hyenas would not attack the carcass until it softened in the sun, the two-inch hide being all but impervious to their claws and fangs.

"If the porters will go, and you'll provide me with torches, I'll have it in camp tonight," he said.

"You are very brave, sahib," I told him, "but remember the Swahili are not sahibs, only black men."

This mollified him, and he recounted the day's adventures to Sukey. "I'd 've got a giraffe, too, Sukey—he was eighteen feet tall if an inch—if Na'od hadn't tripped against me just as I fired. He's a good stalker, though, and I think I'll try to bribe him to stay, when Timur moves on."

"Do you expect to stay on after that?" Sukey asked.

"Why, I told his nibs I might be gone two months."
Which was good news to me, in its way.

"I don't think Na'ob is bribable. He doesn't look like it."

"You've some mighty romantic ideas about natives, darling," he instructed her fondly. "I've yet to see one who won't sell his own daughter for a big enough price."

How about his own brother, Gerald?

But my tongue was still, and my face told him nothing.

"I don't think it would be quite the thing, to try to get him to leave Timur," Sukey remarked.

"Perhaps not, but, mind you, Sukey, the Arab you mean—we'd better not mention his name too many times, for these johnnies have long ears when sahibs are talking—he didn't help us for love."

Not entirely, Gerald, true.

"He's got his own little pidgin—baksheesh probably, or maybe *izzat* with the Sultan."

It is very big pidgin, Gerald.

"Well, if Na'od goes, I'll have to hunt with the boys. That means I'll have to grind on Swahili. It's a lucky thing I got that little dictionary from the Methodist Mission in Zanzibar."

Gerald, be careful of misspelled words. Fate, you neednt have gone this far, to stir my memories.

I had supper with Sithy in the larger of our two pavilions, erected side by side about a hundred paces from Gerald's tent. If he or Sukey wondered what need we had of two, they never mentioned it in my presence. At my suggestion, Sithy came with me when I went to the small fire his servants had built for him there, by which the *fundis* had already erected benches made from empty store boxes. It was obviously a private fire for him and his memsahib—far enough from the porters' camp for them not to be disturbed by their noises and smells. Sukey's face brightened at our visit, but Gerald's appeared to stiffen at our intrusion. Truly he should be used to that sort of thing by now. In his official position he had to put up with a great deal of cheek on the part of native officials.

328

Usually such officials make important-sounding excuses for their call, to try to take a certain look off the sahib's face. I think Gerald expected me to do so and was somewhat surprised at my sitting down on an empty bench, without explanation or waiting for his invitation. Then I smiled at Sithy, and indicated she could sit beside me.

"Makes himself at home, doesn't he?" Gerald said quietly to Sukey. Then to me: "Where does Na'od think we should go tomorrow?"

"It's the very business I came on, sahib. Na'od said that this place has as many varieties of game as any farther on, and you may take as big a bag here as your heart desires. Only the elephant hunting is better farther on—and there are enough giant bulls here for excellent sport. But we be ivory hunters, sahib, not sportsmen. Na'od said also that you're very quick to see game and have already established landmarks, so you may no longer need his guidance. If so, we should be tomorrow on our way to Ukimbu."

To me this was not much more than pleasant time-killing. However, I was interested in finding out if he had the least uneasiness about our intentions, which I had seemed to sense in Sukey. In that case, we might have to change some details of our plans. Gerald did not know where to look for rare game, and had been able to see it only when Na'od had pointed it out.

I watched his face carefully. There was not the slightest expression of relief over our going conflicting with its anxiety.

"Na'od gives me too much credit, Timur Effendi. I'd hoped Na'od—and yourself, too, of course—would be able to stay several days at least."

"There are a few Shenzis not far away. Na'od saw their tracks. If Bismilla knew of it, he might insist on returning to the border, in which case most of his porters would follow him. Some of them were with him on his slave-catching *shauris* and would fear the wild men might include them in their mischief-making. For that reason, sahib, as well as your most honored company, I'm somewhat reluctant to leave you. Truly the wild men won't attack a sahib, but without enough porters

329

you couldn't hope to transport your trophies and baggage to the river."

Gerald spoke to Sukey in English. "What do you make of that?"

"I don't know."

"Well, we'll see." He turned to me. "Timur Effendi, I wouldn't want your kindness to me to cost you any of the profit you would make from going on at once. I'd be very glad to make up the difference to you, if you can see your way to remain here until I take a good bag."

I showed him my palms and twisted my head, bowing, in the Arabic polite gesture of refusal. "I thank you, sahib, for your consideration, but I couldn't possibly take payment or baksheesh from one who has been a guest of our Sultan. Even if I were poor, I could not— and it chances that Allah has seen fit to bestow upon me many worldly blessings. But tomorrow my scouts will follow the tracks of the Shensiz and see if they've left the country. If so—which is very likely—Bismilla Sheik and his porters won't be afraid to stay. If they are still in the country, Bismilla Sheik won't discover it for a day or two, for which time Na'od may hunt with you, and show you as much game as possible, in case you have to depart with Bismilla for the coast."

"That is most kind." Again he spoke to Sukey. "Do you think this chap is all he pretends to be?"

"At least, and maybe a lot more."

"He may be a pretty high-up Arab—if so, he's that much more responsible to the Sultan. His nibs certainly made a fine pick for us, in sending Bismilla. That's the way with native shows—they always break down somewhere along the line. There's nothing to do but—"

Bismilla, seated on a log near the natives' fire and watching me enviously, had apparently heard his name mentioned. In any case he came strutting up, as though he had been called, gave me Allah's peace, and seated himself on a food box. However, since Gerald did not call the Malay interpreter, he was unable to address the sahib.

"I hear a lion," Sithy told me in a low tone.

Dusk had fallen, and *Simba* was moving from his

lairs. Listening intently, I, too, heard a dull, rhythmic grunting away in the darkness. Then all of us listened to the wild, wonderful nocturne between interludes of intense silence. A lone hyena broke into demoniacal laughter. Another answered far away with an eerie howl, and presently a legion of lost souls were chorusing to the moon, with shrieks, wails, great sobbings, and horrid chucklings. The pandemonium ceased as though by a director's baton, and every little crackle of the fire resounded. Then there was a long-drawn, high-pitched, ear-splitting squeal not two furlongs from the fires. It sounded like a pig dying in agony, and that's what I thought it was—a young wart hog in the talons of a leopard or lion.

Gerald's face twisted a little at the sound. He pitied the poor swine.

Far off, a lion did something more than grunt. He began to roar, full dress, one deep-throated reverberant blast after another. Perhaps he was trying to stampede game for an easy kill; possibly he was merely declaring his kingship hereabouts before he went hunting. When he thus spoke, no little jackal barked. All of us were listening with firelit, alert eyes, and the noise from the porters' camp stopped in the middle. I rose and kicked some sticks into the fire.

The lion had stopped roaring, and a jackal was yapping a last word to the king of beasts, when we heard a soft but startling sound close to our ears. It was neither a whistle nor a whish but a medley of both, very brief in duration, but seeming quite long, followed by a sharp crack of board. Bismilla sprang up, one hand clutching his knife and the other, wildly palsied, pointing to the box that had been his seat. From one side of it thrust several inches of thin wooden shaft, with a feathered tip.

"Bismillah! Bismillah!" The sheik seemed to be shouting his own name, but actually he was imploring the mercy of Allah.

"What does it mean, Timur?" Gerald asked, in the calm, low voice of a sahib.

"It's a Shenzi arrow, but it missed the mark, and the

bowman's springing off by now." I was retrieving the arrow.

"How soon will he attack again?"

"Not until he has an easy target. Probably not again tonight, if we show no fear." I retrieved the arrow and showed it to him. "Be careful of the point, sahib." The whole head was smeared with a bright-yellow gum.

"It's poisoned," Bismilla gasped. "Timur, I told you—"

"One of us will stand close to you, Bismilla," I stepped between him and the outer ring of shadows.

Gerald had not understood the words but instantly comprehended the action. Just as I had foreseen, he came quickly beside me. It was as inevitable as a trained dog's jumping though a hoop at his master's signal, Gerald being a pukka sahib. Sahibship is an interesting and a highly admirable condition; it had been perfectly developed in India. Suddenly I realized that it was instinct with self-dramatization, but unlike me with mine, the sahibs did not know it. Gerald had been carefully instructed ahead of time that the Shenzis sought Bismilla's life only, but he could not be sure the savages would not let loose at him. If he had stood in extreme peril, still he would have spoken in his calm tone and, perhaps, the same words.

"Timur, tell Bismilla I'll shield him until he's out of danger. I dare say the beggars won't take a chance on me."

"Where can I go, to be out of danger?" Bismilla cried then. "I'd defy them in the day, but to be murdered in the dark—"

"You may go into your tent, Bismilla Sheik, when we've out-faced them awhile," I said. "They won't waste arrows shooting at the cloth. At present we need your counsel."

I did not know how, so soon, the porters had learned of the arrow from the dark. They broke from their fires and clustered like bees between the fire and the tent.

"Timur, how can he get back to the Sultan's domains?" Gerald asked. "It would be wretched luck if I have to escort him—"

"We will see, sahib. Something may be arranged so as not to spoil your hunt—"

The murmuring Swahili fell dead silent then, for a drum began to sound in the same direction from which the arrow had been shot. It was not the frantic fortissimo of war; three beats, of different timbre, were repeated over and over. Then Na'od burst into the firelight, followed by an old Swahili called "K'wiro."

"It's the *dundo-maneno* [drum talk]," Na'od told me.

"Can K'wiro reply?" I asked.

"That's why I brought him."

The *fundi* was carrying a stout shoulder pole used for balancing loads. Using it as a drumstick he tested a fuel log and a near-by tree for resonance, then was satisfied with Gerald's table, stoutly made of hewn board with stump legs. He repeated the three beats, with slightly different accent.

At once the *dundo* in the darkness became varied loud and soft beats, fast and slow, with pauses between the measures. K'wiro listened, his lips slowly moving, and there was no other sound in the night. The message lasted two full minutes. Then the drummer spoke in Swahili to Na'od, who at once turned to me.

"The Shenzis say, Sharafa and his slave catchers go home."

"Sharafa?"

"Woe upon me, it means Bushy Beard, the name I'm known by among the tribes," Bismilla cried.

I translated this quickly into Hindustani.

"Ask if they'll be given safe passage," Gerald directed.

When this had reached the drummer, he pounded long and with a kind of eloquence on the table. The reply came back at once, and seemed interminable. Na'od gave me a quick, narrow glance. Sithy and Sukey had something in common now—the eyes of both were popping with excitement.

"The Shenzis say," Na'od pronounced after the *fundi* had translated the message, " 'we be few.' Now that's true, from the count of their tracks. 'But Sharafa go, or we will get more. If K'wiro go'—that's the drummer— 'all go safely.' You see, Timur, K'wiro has had *dundo-maneno* with the Shenzis many times. They trust him to see that Bismilla Sheik doesn't double back."

"Ask them, if Bismilla and his men go, whether they dare molest those who remain," Gerald directed, when I had translated.

Again K'wiro telegraphed to great length. When the long-winded reply was received, Na'od relayed it to me.

"The Shenzis say, 'The white face and Kova-upande' —that would mean Scar-cheek—'are not slave catchers. They and Kova-upande's men may hunt here.'"

"Cheeky little devils, to say where I can hunt and where I can't," Gerald remarked to Sukey. "But you can't blame them for being terrified of slave catchers." He turned to me. "I dare say we've got to decide at once."

"Fairly soon, would be best. But there's no great haste."

"That would mean all our porters, but what about our interpreter?"

"It would probably be safe to keep him, but he would be no use to you, sahib. Since he speaks only Arabic and English, you can't address my Swahilis through him."

"Of course you realize that unless you stay, I'll have to go with Bismilla. We'd be helpless without porters. And how would I get my trophies and goods to the coast, when you move westward?"

"Sahib, the difficulty is not great. It so chances that one of my caravans will pass this way in seven days, to join me at the Ukimbu. I had them delay until I'd collected ivory for them to bring back. You could hunt till then, whereupon they'll transport you to the river while I go on to the Ukimbu. They will lose but ten days, and for those you may pay their actual cost to me, a sum not exceeding three hundred rupees. The week I spent here, with Na'od and my men, I'll consider a holiday in most honored company."

"Why, that's splendid."

"It's also a tiny bit glib," Sukey said in English, with a troubled face.

Gerald was a little annoyed by the interruption. "Listen, my love. Can you imagine an intelligent Arab holding the Lieutenant Governor of Sind for ransom?"

"No. And I don't suppose he has designs on me—"

"Really, Sukey, this *is* the nineteenth century." He turned to me. "I think it's a wonderful arrangement."

I spoke to Na'od. "You know the Shenzis. Will you guarantee Bismilla against attack on the way to his village?"

"All the way, Timur Effendi. So will K'wiro, who knows them well. To make secure, he may sleep in a thorn *boma* impervious to arrows, but there will be no need. But I couldn't promise him one day more of life, unless he sets forth at sunrise."

"By my beard, I'll leave as soon after dawn as my porters can load. I may not remain and defy them, as is my desire, for that would bring all of you—and my friends the great sahib and his memsahib—into peril. But truly, an evil eye has been cast upon this safari."

"It could well be true, Bismilla Sheik! And for that, say nothing of this to the Sultan, lest he believe the Shenzi lie that you catch and run slaves." I turned to Na'od. "Bid K'wiro send word that the terms are met."

When the message had been sent, it was answered with a dozen or so mighty thumps on the Shenzi drum. I thought that another drummer, who could not quite control his wicked mirth, had taken over the drumstick.

CHAPTER THIRTY-SEVEN

Attack by Lions

NA'OD HAD HALTED at the door of my pavilion.

"Timur Effendi, though it be a small matter now, the poison of Shenzi arrows is brown in hue, not yellow," he told me.

"I'll remember that, in case of future need."

"Also, all I've seen tonight was but a lion's shadow on the ground, not his mighty form. The *shauri* was not to have Bismilla and his men go, but the sahib—and his memsahib—to stay here without them. For that the Effendi went to no small trouble."

"Why, Na'od, it was no trouble—only a few hours' employment of a few hands—and didn't you enjoy the sport?"

"In all truth, I did. But what of the sport to come, Timur Effendi? For a child standing where I stand could see this is but the beginning, not the end."

"Na'od, why do the proud and crafty Somali leave their deserts to toil in the swelter of the Azanian Coast?"

"To make and to save money, wherewith to return to their deserts, there to live as sheiks with many women, fine raiment, and rich food."

"You've been in exile for ten rains. How close have you come to saving the sum needed?"

"Seyed Na, I'm still a long way from my goal. A matter of six hundred rupees."

"Will you, for seven hundred rupees, obey my every command for a matter of seven days, the silver to be paid on the seventh day, in case you must go straight from here to Somaliland, without touching Sa'dani? You won't be asked to stain your hands with blood."

"They've been red before, I remember. Timur Effendi, is this *thar?*"

"Even so."

"We're far from the Sultan's domains—the sahib is a great sahib but yet a *giaour*—and I've a fondness for good sport. To hear is to obey."

On entering Sithy's pavilion, I found another who had something to say. Sithy was sitting up in bed, a lighted candle on a box limning her bright braids, and causing interesting surface lights on her eyes.

"I heard the lions tonight," she said, "and also I heard you."

"Were you afraid of the lions?"

"Not very, with you there. But if I'd been the sahib, I'd have been afraid of you. He doesn't know you like I do."

"He's a very brave sahib, Sithy."

"So I saw, when he stood beside Bismilla Sheik. Likely he's braver than you, most of the time."

"Why, then, should he be afraid of me?"

"I don't know. At first I thought it was only because he'd stolen your *cobah.*"

She spoke calmly, not with the trained calmness of the sahib, but from natural composure. I had trouble employing the same tone.

"You think the memsahib is my *cobah?*"

"A babe in arms, knowing what I know, could see that. It was long ago that she lay with you, and it comes to me she was your very wife. You, too, were once a sahib, being some manner of Greek, and she was your memsahib, not his. For that, you've changed your name and have become an Arab, but Shaitan must have changed your face."

"But you think there's even greater reason he should fear me?"

"I'm sure of it, Timur Rajah. You told me that unto her, you were as one who'd drunk the cup of death, and it's true. She's so certain that you are dead that any memories of your look, your voice, and your smell crop up and wither."

"I smell like an Arab, Sithy."

"No, you don't. You smell of *timbak* and sometimes

garlic or frankincense, but under those smells is one I'd know in the dark. Haven't the memsahibs good noses?"

"It isn't good manners, among the memsahibs, to have good noses, God knows why. Since they don't heed them when they cry, 'Wolf,' they soon don't believe them."

"Anyway, it seems to me certain that the sahib killed you."

"Do you mean, he tried to kill me?"

"I think he who was in your body then died at his hand."

"He did, Sithy, in a way of speaking, but he's returned from the Land of Shades. And if you tell the memsahib any of this, my task will be harder."

"Harder, yes, but it will be performed just the same. I'm not such a fool as that, Timur Rajah, or you'd have thrown me out long before now. What is to happen, will happen. I'll wait and see."

"How will you pass the time tomorrow?"

"Pass it, my lord? It will pass me, running and jumping like *m'palla*. But Bazizi and I hope to get meat for the porters."

"I'm glad you came with me, Sithy, all the way from Kafiristan to here," I told her, bending to kiss her childishly eager, womanly lovely lips.

At sunrise Bismilla Sheik, his Swahili, and the Malay interpreter set out for Pangani. Some porters were sent to bring into camp Gerald's rhino head and some of the hide, valued for making cruelly beautiful, amber-colored whips. I informed Gerald that, by his leave, Na'od would guide him and the memsahib along the dongas in search of lions, I following to act as interpreter when they could not make out with sign language, and in charge of porters and skinners to care for the trophies. Gerald was agreeable, but rather to his surprise, Sukey announced that she was lame from the long trek and would spend the day in camp making friends with Sithy. Thus Gerald could carry his trusty percussion-cap rifle, Na'od a pinfire breechloader made in France, which Gerald had bought for Sukey but which was a little too newfangled for his liking, and I my own elephant rifle with a camel's kick.

Vultures were hovering or lighting down on lion kills all over the plain. The birds of death perched in the trees about the first kill we visited, scores of others circling overhead, but the fact that they had not yet attacked what remained of the carcass indicated that the killer was still close by. Indeed one of the skinners told me he thought he caught a glimpse of a tawny hide in a near-by thicket. That Na'od had seen the animal I had little doubt, yet I was not surprised when he immediately led Gerald off toward another kill. Na'od had instructions to be particular to a degree of finicality in choosing a fitting antagonist for the sahib.

There was a low hill less than a furlong from the next kill, but Na'od left Gerald at its base while he surveyed the scene. The porters and I climbed the rise, and there I could well believe that Na'od had overdone the business of furnishing him good sport. There were three lions lying down in a clear space in the thorn thicket, and two standing up. The loafers were a big male, a young male, and a very light-colored lioness. They did not begin to compare in importance, I thought, with the two alert and on their feet, which were another darker lioness, and a collie-sized cub. Gerald had not seen any of them yet, but I thought that he would, in a very few seconds more.

Na'od was walking on Gerald's right, ready to snatch his emptied piece with his left hand and thrust forward the spare with his right, and so was a few feet farther distant from the thicket. Both were far too close for safety. I had closed within fifty yards on their outer flank when the old male and his young companion broke from the opposite end of the cover. Gerald heard them and sprinted forward for a glimpse of them.

When he stopped and threw up his gun, the two beasts were about thirty yards distant, bounding off at top speed. It was not an easy shot to stop and take, but Gerald made it magnificently. The lion uttered a short roar, and dropped motionless.

At this point I had more than half expected the mother lioness to charge either Gerald or Na'od, the porters needing no telling to stay back. This very frequently happened under similar conditions. Gerald would, of course, be the most likely target, as he was the closest. Instead she stayed out of sight, and it was the tawny lioness that suddenly bounded into a break in the thickets, her big three-cornered face drawn in a snarl. Later I was to learn that this was not uncommon behavior by the queen of the beasts. Apparently, sticking closer than a brother, a barren lioness appoints herself protectress of a companion with cubs.

Gerald had fired his right barrel first at the running lion, as was his custom. Plainly he remembered he had only one load left in the gun, for he aimed deliberately. But when he pressed the trigger, the gun misfired.

He whirled to take his extra piece from Na'od. But breaking the first law of gunbearers, Na'od had not run forward with him and was now ten yards on his flank. At that instant the lioness charged.

With the terror of death upon him, Gerald still functioned intelligently. The lioness rushed in a terrier-like scuttle that is perhaps the fastest four-legged gait on earth unless it be the kill-rush of a cheetah, her head low, her tail stiff as a broom. If Gerald had wheeled and fled, he would be overtaken and pulled down within twenty strides. Instead he dropped his useless arm and cut toward Na'od, shouting, "Rifle! Rifle!" at the top of his lungs. But Na'od did not dash forward to meet him and he surely knew he could not possibly grasp the gun in time.

What he did not know was that Na'od himself was a deadly shot. However, he seemed to be taking too long to raise the piece. I had fired and missed when under the smoke cloud I saw the barrel level and blaze. The lioness crashed to earth as though under a massive weight not four yards from Gerald's feet.

Gerald's chest heaved once, then he snatched the weapon from Na'od's hand. "Damn you," he said. "Damn you." His face dripped with sweat.

"Sahib?"

"Mind your tongue, sahib," I called. "Is that how you thank him for saving your life!"

"He wouldn't have had to, if he'd been where he belonged."

"Why, sahib, when you ran forward you bade him stand."

"What? What do you mean by telling me a lie of that kind?"

"Load both guns, sahib. You've only one barrel, and I've only one. There may be other lions in the thicket."

His hand shook as he busied with the task. As quickly as possible, I rammed powder and ball into my empty barrel. When the gun that Na'od had carried was ready, Gerald picked up a stone and hurled it furiously into the thickets. Evidently the mother lion and her cub had stolen out on the opposite side, for there was no answering charge or growl. Then, still white, he strode toward me.

"What did you mean, Timur, by saying I bade Na'od stand when I ran forward for a shot at the lion?"

"Shaib, you said '*Kaa!*' Both of us heard you." I turned to Na'od and spoke in Arabic. "Didn't he say '*Kaa*'?"

"Distinctly, Timur Effendi," Na'od replied blandly. "I took it, he wished to battle *Simba* alone for the glory of it."

I repeated this to Gerald with an addition. "Also, he's indignant that you should have spoken to him in such a voice. He's no porter to be browbeaten, but a Somali chieftain, of ancient family and name."

"Why, I don't even know the word. If I said, '*Kaa*,' I was only clearing my throat."

"Then it was a mere mistake, sahib, that turned out well. You shot a lion—and will live to shoot others."

"By a black man's saving my life!"

"It comes to me, sahib, you owe him a great debt, as well as an apology for your harsh words."

"He ought to have known I don't speak Swahili."

"How could he know, sahib, when he's seen you sit with the little book? A dictionary, is it not? The missionary sahibs in Zanzibar use the like."

"I do owe him something for shooting the devil of a lioness. I'll give him a hundred rupees—"

"He would refuse one rupee, sahib, let alone such a munificent gift. What he wants is your word of contrition, due a chieftain from a great sahib."

"You may tell him that if I made a sound like '*Kaa*,' I repent my cursing him, and I thank him for his good shot."

I repeated the message with punctilio.

"But I still don't understand why that cursed barrel didn't fire." He retrieved the gun and examined it closely. "Why, the cap's gone."

"Doubtless it fell out, sahib."

"It couldn't have fallen out."

"Then it must be that when you loaded the piece, before the tent this morning, you failed to put one in the nipple."

"I've never made such a mistake before."

"Allah forbid you make another like it, since we were all endangered."

He did not appear to take this in the right spirit. When the porters came up to the big lion, grinning, holding out pink palms, and saying, "Baksheesh," he gave them the customary coins with bad grace. "*Simba mbili*," one of the boys protested, holding up two fingers, at which all extended their palms again.

"Tell these black pests that the lioness is Na'od's kill, not mine."

"But Na'od will gladly give it to you, sahib, to swell out your bag."

"I don't want it."

"Perhaps you've not looked at the skin, Sahib. The fur is nearly as soft as a leopard's, and would be pleasant to the memsahib's bare feet, when she steps rosy as the dawn from the bath."

"Confound you—" Gerald controlled his anger. "Timur, I don't discuss the memsahib's bare feet with anyone."

While the boys were skinning, he walked stiff-backed and alone into the woods. Despite the gunfire only a few minutes before, I saw him catch sight of a big kudu with a breath-taking set of horns. It was a standing but long shot, and he was too high of dudgeon and taut of nerve to hold steady. The fine trophy bounded away.

"Surely you didn't miss, sahib," I told him, overtaking him. "I was certain I heard the *twack* of the bullet. Doubtless he's run a little way, heart-shot, and now lies in the thickets. I would send the boys to see, if they weren't busy with the noble lion."

"I'll see for myself, thank you."

He was gone nearly an hour. "You didn't find him, sahib?"

"No, and it was a Devil's own place to search for him."

"Perhaps it was the echo of the report that I heard, often very like the thud of a bullet. Doubtless you were still nervous from the lioness's attack and jerked off."

"I'm not in the habit of letting anything make me nervous," he replied.

A grinning skinner gave him the good-luck bone, barely larger than a chicken's wishbone, from the brute's neck. Its charm failed, however, when, a mile farther on, he and Na'od had about completed a long, hot, arduous stalk through thorn thickets on a magnificent bull buffalo. Hurrying to overtake them after sending two of the porters back with the lion skin, I came in upwind of the beast, causing him to snort and thunder off. When I joined him, Gerald was flushed and strained.

"Timur, didn't you see that buffalo?"

"Truly, sahib, and one of the finest I've ever seen. It's a pity you couldn't put him in your bag."

"I would've, if you hadn't let him get your wind."

"How was I to know you were stalking him, sahib? You and Na'od are most adroit stalkers, for I neither saw nor heard you, and supposed you were farther on. The fortunes of the chase, sahib! The misses are half the sport."

"I have some fine scratches to pay me for my trouble." He turned on me, took his lunchbox and water jug from his bearer, and sat down for a lonely tiffin.

We waited patiently until he had finished, then Na'od led him down a donga to a water hole, always a resort of game. Here was a welter of tracks including those of a small herd of buffalo, containing at least one huge bull, leading into swampy ground below. Although they were sun-dried, Na'od pronounced them fresh. Would the sahib care to follow them? They might lead into thick country, where there was great danger of surprise attack. If the sahib was too shaken by the lioness's attack, Na'od would go in alone, outflank the herd, and try to stampede them whereby the sahib could have a shot in the open.

When I had repeated this, Gerald's temper was slowly tried.

"Tell that precious fellow of yours that I'm not afraid to go anywhere he goes."

That was no doubt true, but there were many places he could not pass with the same ease. I followed the pair through ever denser thicket to the first pile of dung. Gerald had not stuck his finger in it, but I did, to find it stone-cold. Then I returned to the high ground and was smoking a clay pipe, such as were sold these days in the bazaars and frequently used by Arabs if their hookas were not handy, when the two hunters emerged. Na'od's bare legs were wet and mud-smeared, but he moved with characteristic Somali *sang-froid*. I could not see a single scratch on his shiny black hide. Gerald's breeches and boots were plastered and dripping, his shirt ripped, and a score of livid scratches set off the pallor of his face and hands.

They won't leave scars, Gerald. They do not tear deeply like a nail on a chicken crate.

"You made a quick trip, sahib." They had been gone about an hour.

He did not answer.

"Timur Effendi, we heard buffalo all around us—but saw only one calf," Na'od told me.

I was not surprised. The morass was no doubt alive with buffalo, but Dutch and English big-game hunters in the tried grounds of South Africa learned to avoid blind thorny thickets of this kind.

"I found more tracks, perhaps fresher, entering farther down," I proposed, sure that there would be some. "Would the sahib care to venture in again?"

"I thank you, but I'm ready to go to camp."

Only one unpleasant incident occurred on the homeward march. Although we had seen giraffe off and on all day, Gerald had passed them by in his quest for dangerous game, once saying that he would leave the taking of this trophy for the memsahib. He changed his mind

344

when, almost in sight of the tents, we saw a giant specimen peacefully browsing from a treetop. He could use two giraffes, he said. One would go well in the high messroom of his old regiment at Lahore. The animal was upwind from us, and the stalk would be child's play. Indeed, giraffe were the most easily approached of all big game in Africa.

"The sahib says he'll shoot the giraffe," I told Na'od.

"Tell the great sahib that he may not, the animal being sacred to the Shenzis, whereupon they may attack our camp," he replied.

I repeated this to Gerald.

"To hell with the 'Shenzis." By his use of *Dozakh*, this was good Anglo-Indian Hindustani.

"You must not, sahib. You may challenge the most dangerous beasts at your own risk, but our Sultan would be enraged with us, if we permitted you to anger the wild men."

"This isn't the Sultan's domain."

"But we're his subjects, sahib."

"Of all the insufferable—" he began in English. He stopped with a start. "Timur, I told you how he reeled against me when I fired at the other giraffe. I know now he did it intentionally!"

"He meant no harm, Protector of the Poor! He had no way to tell you of *Twiga*'s sacredness."

When we were entering camp, Sukey ran out of her tent with a bright face.

"What a wonderful lion—" Then she stopped, her eyes widening. "What's the matter, Gerald?"

"I'll tell you later. He sat down at the table and ordered hot tea.

"You look a sight—but it's not that—"

I was seeing to the stretching of the skin, well in earshot of the table, when Gerald had drained the cup.

"Sukey, I've had a perfectly rotten day." He began to recount its misfortunes.

"You don't think—" she stopped.

"Think what, Sukey?"

"The two who were with you did their best, didn't they?"

"I suppose I can't find any complaint with their

hunting. They certainly didn't show the white feather. What seemed insolence at times was, of course, nothing but stupidity—"

"The Arabs aren't a stupid people, Gerald, as you well know."

"All the colored races are stupid, when the shoe pinches."

"The Arabs aren't exactly a colored race, either—are they?"

"Oh, cut it, Sukey. Neither are Madrassi almost as black as your hat—if you want to be technical. Fact is, the out-and-out colored races suit me fine. I like those Swahilis—they're pretty dull-witted, but they're straightforward and don't put on airs. I get along with them very well indeed—they understand me, and I understand them. It's these off-white people—neither one nor the other—"

Sukey had turned her face a little from Gerald's and in a roving glance I saw it. It had a strained look, and she spoke quickly.

"It couldn't be studied insolence. They know you'll report the whole hunt to the Sultan. It was probably the barrier of language—different ways from the Indians—"

"I could get along all right with one of the guides— the black one—if the yellow one would stay in camp. Na'od belongs to a tribe that's part Arab—he was a little top-lofty when I cursed him today—but if I had him alone, he'd be just plain nigger and we'd—"

"You cursed him?"

"Yes. Why?"

"Had he done something bad?"

"He'd done something stupid, thinking I'd said, 'Kaa,' like a bally crow. Oh, I told him I hadn't meant to hurt his feelings."

"I wonder if his feelings were hurt—"

"What's the matter with you, Sukey?"

"Well, they don't seem easily hurt to me. Both he and the other act very sure of themselves."

"That's just what I'm saying. The black one's a good hunter, and nippy, too. I made too much noise going into the swamp—otherwise we'd had some buffalo shooting par excellence—at just about arm's length, with the odds evened up wonderfully. But I'd get along without him to get rid of the other. We could make out well just with the Swahili in a game heaven like this. The other did act sure of himself, bordering on insolence. Maybe it wasn't intentional, but to my mind he definitely crossed that border with his dirty remark about the lioness skin. That's why I say the near-white people—"

Again she broke in quickly, although with a carefully casual tone.

"What was the remark about the lion skin? You didn't tell me."

"I find it very objectionable to repeat. If I'd thought it *was* intentional—not just the nature of a foul-minded Asiatic—and you know they've all got that under the skin—"

"What was the remark? I can stand it. Just be careful that in repeating it you don't indicate you're referring to it."

"He said the lioness skin—which I wouldn't take— would be soft to your bare feet when you stepped rosy as the dawn out of your bath. He acted as though he were paying me a compliment. I swear, Sukey, he came nearer to having his jaw punched—"

"Then you came nearer to having your chest slit open."

"Rubbish. Give a native an el, and he'll take a mile, but he's jolly well not going to put his neck in a rope. He won't go too far with a sahib, unless it's twenty to one. If I'd knocked him down, he'd have got up a sadder and wiser man."

"What would the other have been doing in the meanwhile? Gerald, you're not in Sind now. If you can't control your temper—no matter what happens—we'd better get out of here as soon as we can. The black one is the other's man. Well, about that remark. I shouldn't say this—since the blame comes back on me—in fact you've already said it, about the el and the mile. I gave him an el, so to speak, by that little joke about the slave girl. Just the same, what he said about the skin isn't typical of natives. I've never known any Arabs, but I know Mohammedans well."

"Then I should've hit him."

"Don't talk like a fool. You're not in a position to hit anybody, Gerald. We're too far from anywhere."

"Well, darling, you've heard the old saying. 'The Queen has a long arm.' And that fellow knows it."

"Take a look around. Except for two Hindu servants, every person we started with is gone. We're in an entirely new crowd. It happened very naturally, I know."

Don't start seeing ghosts!

"Well, I won't. The reason I won't was what happened about your rifle. You think it's mighty queer you forgot to insert the cap—you hinted that the gun had been tampered with before you left. But when the lioness was almost on top of you, the black one shot her. If the plan is to hold you for ransom, they wouldn't have stolen the cap. You were too likely to be killed by an animal. If they want you dead, they wouldn't have shot the lioness."

"Why in God's name would they want me dead?"

"They don't. That's been proven. The two actions counteract each other, so there's nothing to either of them. You've had a rotten day. That's all." Her hand moved, and she touched the silver sixpence worn on her bracelet.

"That's all, plus an Arab too big for his boots. I think he resented my not inviting him to sit down last night, so he did a little strutting when I cursed the black one and wanted to shoot the giraffe."

"No, for some reason they don't want you to shoot a giraffe. That was shown when the man disturbed your aim. It couldn't be the reason that I don't want you to —pity on the poor ungainly things. Besides, Gerald, you should have asked him to sit down. He's your host. It was unforgivable rudeness."

"A sahib has to draw the line somewhere—"

"Gerald, I'm afraid I haven't been a good wife to you."

"What do you mean?"

"You had the sahib attitude pretty strong when we were married. It seemed to me the one serious obstacle to your becoming a great man. I thought, knowing natives as I do, I could get you out of it. I haven't. It's grown steadily worse. You seem to rely on it. It's turning into a kind of horrid religion."

Gerald's face had a gray cast, but I did not think he knew it.

"I haven't done so badly, Sukey."

"Gerald, if ever in your life you need taking down a peg, it's right now. Your very life may depend on it—and mine. Colonel Jacob and Dad got you the post of Commissioner of Hyderabad District. They both wanted to see you Governor of Sind—you definitely had the abilities. The reason someone else got the knighthood and the post—"

"Was because Colonel Jacob stabbed me in the back. That's what I could expect from a half-caste."

"I wish you'd stop talking about half-castes and half-whites and off-whites, with that expression on your face. Your own brother was an off-white—of the kind you mean—and he's dead."

Sukey sprang up and ran into the tent.

CHAPTER THIRTY-EIGHT

The Broken Gun

GERALD HAD NOT SLEPT WELL. The purses under his eyes were dark as mine. But his gray face appeared to brighten when I expressed my regret for inability to accompany him and Na'od on their day's hunt. In truth, I had promised my slave girl Sithy that I would go forth with her today, to show her the sights of the country. I would miss the great sahib's company, but as it happened, Na'od wished to pit him against *Timbu*—the great tusked bull—and since he had ears like a watchdog's magnified one hundred times, the fewer who went into his thorn deserts, the better.

"Truly," said Na'od for me to translate, "there would be no steps in the thickets but the sahib's and mine. But I will carry the sahib's comforts, and the ivories will take no harm until the porters can come for them."

"What of the memsahib?" Gerald asked.

"There are not enough guns for her to go, lord, *Timbu* frequents dry bush land, without much game, starting four miles from here, and if he charges with his brethren—truly he's the most dangerous of Allah's creatures—I must have a strong gun in my hands. Since Timur Effendi will be carrying his own—"

"Sahib, you've plenty of time to hunt *Timbu* another day," I added, after translating this. "If today you wish to go after buck or buffalo, I'll postpone the excursion with my slave, and go with you. In that case, Na'od may borrow my gun, in times of danger."

"Thank you, but I'll go with Na'od."

"But you'll not be able to talk to him, sahib."

"We can always make signs and I've learned many Swahili words. Tell Na'od, that if I say *kituo* [camp],

I've had enough, and wish to return. Also I'll hunt *Timbu* only till noon, returning to have tiffin with the memsahib."

"Then I'll follow you, with my slave, only to the escarpment where you shot the rhino."

From that point the two hunters moved into what the natives called *mkwamba* country, being of dry, sandy soil unable to hold moisture and hence grown to low bush and thorny scrub. The track was not more than ten miles long and half as wide, and was frequented by elephants, rhinoceros, great kudus, one variety of zebras, lions, and a few other bucks agreeable to a desert habitat. Na'od carried two water flasks and Gerald's French breech-loading rifle. Sithy and I, followed by her friend Bazizi, flanked the long escarpment that bordered it, mainly to see the game, but hoping to shoot a leopard, and, if possible, to lay low some of the wild dogs that were numerous and harrying the game.

As though it were the light in her own eyes, I saw Africa in quite a different light when Sithy was with me. At other times, I was obsessed by its naked, vivid cruelty. Such sights were shown under the blue crystal sky—the vultures ever soaring or dropping down on the kill of lions, leopards, and wild dogs; the late-gorging hyena, loath to retreat to his den; the blood-daubed water holes; even the vast herds of antelope and zebras that seemed kept by the killers for their bloody fare and spared only while themselves slept. When Sithy was with me, I saw it as Adam might have seen the garden, after God gave him Eve. She reminded him, when she ate the apple, that the theme of the universe was birth, not death. We crept nearer and watched the animals, in wonder at His world. Staying carefully downwind we saw a matronly cow elephant's angry rush at a lion who had roved, innocently perhaps, too near her calf, and laughed at the king of beasts' inglorious flight.

I almost wished to declare an intermission in my *thar*, this pleasant morning. I could not, and listened for the distant sound of Gerald's and Na'od's rifles. One of them fired about midmorning; immediately afterward we heard two quick shots from a slightly different direction. About half an hour later there was another single shot, perfectly audible across at least three miles of silent plain.

"The sahib is having good hunting," Sithy remarked, gazing in that direction.

Then she whirled, for I loosed my big thunder-roarer into the thickets.

"What did you shoot at, Timur Rajah?" she asked, unable to see any game alive or dead.

"Didn't you see that wild dog at the edge of the thorn?"

"No, I was looking the other way."

"I didn't hit him."

About half an hour later, we heard the boom of a rifle much nearer than before, and then another, faint in the farther distance.

"The sahib and Na'od are not together," Sithy remarked.

"I dare say they've separated, so Na'od may run game for the sahib to shoot."

"They are too far apart for that."

"I'm sure Na'od is running game."

The next shooting that we heard was one lone shot at a great distance, then two shots not far away. So it went, at long intervals, up and down, and back and across the *mkwamba*.

"They've been signaling each other a long time," Sithy ventured.

"Perhaps the next time I hear a shot, I should reply to it."

She made no answer, and I could hardly get her to look at the herds of game. The next report was from far away in the blue. I fired in the air.

"I notice you didn't fire when the shot was close," Sithy remarked.

"Didn't I? That was stupid of me."

"No, it was very cruel."

"Perhaps, if the sahib's lost, he would lose himself worse trying to find us."

"In Kafiristan, the men run markhors into snow drifts and kill them, but it is a cold, quick death."

"You hadn't told me that."

"I didn't want to see it. Has the sahib any water to drink?"

"Now I stop to think of it, Na'od was carrying his flask, as a servant ought."

"It's a dry country, you said, with no water in the dongas."

"The elephants must have some place to drink."

"Away in the thorn, perhaps."

Sithy did not speak for nearly an hour. During that time we heard three lone shots, without reply.

"There's an ostrich," I told her. "You said you wanted some of the beautiful feathers, and the meat is very good."

"I don't want the feathers, but it's all right to shoot it for the meat."

I shot, but deliberately missed. She came and slipped her hand into mine.

"Why did you spare him, Timur Rajah?"

"He's never harmed me, and we can get meat closer to camp."

We climbed a hilltop and had lunch. Sithy listened in vain for any more shooting in the *mkwamba*.

"Do you think they've found each other?" she asked, when we started on.

"Perhaps, or perhaps the sahib has found his way out and is on his way to camp."

But when we were creeping up to watch a family of giraffes, we heard a single shot hardly a mile away, and two others far off in the blue.

"They've not found each other, and the sahib hasn't gone to camp to eat with the memsahib," Sithy said.

"I believe you're right, Sithy."

"Aren't you going to do anything to help him?"

"Not now."

"You have gray eyes and they're very bright."

"Are they?"

"I wouldn't want to kiss your lips, the way they look now."

"Maybe you'll never want to kiss them again. I wouldn't in your place, perhaps."

"Will the sahib die of thirst, or be killed by an elephant in the *mkwamba?*"

"He may be killed by an elephant. That's the fortune of hunting, sometimes. He won't die of thirst. Na'od will surely find him before dark."

"Timur Rajah, I've heard much of that from the harem women. They speak of this one or that one, among the Arabs. But the Arabs kill quickly, and get it over with."

"I'm not an Arab, Sithy."

"How many days will pass before he dies?"

"Why, he might outlive both of us. We might both be killed by a rhino in the next hour."

"I'd like to go back to the camp."

"We'll circle homeward slowly, looking for wild dogs."

I missed my only shot at one. Sithy said that she heard a distant report, a mere dot of noise, far away in the distance in answer to mine. We reached our pavilion in midafternoon. I was carving whips from the two-inch hide of the rhino when Sukey, carefully dressed, but with a white, strained face, came with her ayah to pay me a visit. I rose and salaamed.

"The sahib didn't get back for lunch, as he said he would," she told me. "Have you seen anything of him?"

"No, memsahib. No doubt he was having such good sport that he felt no pang of hunger. We heard several shots from the direction he'd gone."

She wanted to say something more. "What are you making, Timur Effendi?"

"Whips, memsahib. They are called 'kurbash' by the Arabs, 'kiboka' by the Swahili, and one will outlast two made of the skin of hippos. I thought that the sahib might wish to take several with him to Sind. They are wonderful teachers of obedience."

"I think they must be very cruel."

"So is Life, the great teacher. But, then, I can make him a cane, which looks less cruel. He may walk with it, or, when need be, use it on those who fail in their duty toward him."

"Timur, I'm uneasy about the sahib. Could you send some of the porters to look for him?"

"Memsahib, alone they could never find their way
354

into that country, let alone come out. It all looks alike. But I'll go with them."

"I'm afraid he might be hurt, or lost. I'm sorry to ask you to go—"

"It's my pleasure, Moon of Beauty, to serve the sahib. And I'll take one of the litters and many bearers to bring him in if by some great woe he's been hurt. But it will be dark before we return, and I would not want to leave you and my slave girl in camp with no arms."

"Can we both go with you?"

"It will be a ten-mile trek—perhaps much longer." Actually, if the schedule arranged by Na'od was fairly well kept, the round trip would not be more than three or four miles.

"Ten miles is nothing to me."

"My *cobah* is also a strong walker, memsahib. And it's necessary that she go, for your honor's sake."

Sithy and Sukey's frightened ayah both wanted to go, and we were under way in five minutes with eight porters. But we had barely encircled the first brush-grown nullah when we caught sight of the two hunters, walking side by side over a long veld. At nearly a mile, their gait seemed very slow, and I could never see any light between the two.

"He's been hurt!" Sukey cried. "He's hanging on to Na'od's arm."

"Not badly hurt, memsahib, or Na'od would carry him. I think he's only very tired."

"Tired!" But that was Sukey's last word to me, as we sped at a fast walk to meet the laboring pair. Apparently they did not see us weaving between the thickets, and as soon as my voice would carry to them, I hallooed and shouted to them to stay where they were. At once Gerald lay flat on the ground.

When we were at a stone's toss from him, he sat up. My brother, the Lieutenant Governor of Sind, was not now in the dress uniform of the Tatta Lancers receiving his fill of honors at the Sultan's fete! His clothes hung in rags. His face and hands and the skin showing through the rents were lacerated and bloodied by the long, needle-sharp African thorns. His face, unlike mine, was still recognizable as his own, but it was a

355

ghastly white under his tan and drawn from extreme fatigue.

"Be careful what you say, Gerald," Sukey warned.

He did not reply. I opened a flask and handed it to him.

"It's a drink forbidden to us of the Faith," I told him, "but I had some for medicine, and it will refresh your jaded spirit."

"Be careful, Gerald," Sukey said again.

Gerald took a long pull at the flask. Then Na'od helped him up and into the litter. We started at once for camp.

He did not speak until he saw the smoke of the fires.

"Na'od and I became separated, and he had the water flasks. We kept signaling to each other, but missed each other in the hellish brush. Once or twice I mistook the Arab's shots for signals and went the wrong way."

"You don't believe that. Why do you say it? It was a put-up—"

"Shut up. I'm in no humor to hear any romantic nonsense. Na'od was out of breath from running when he finally found me. He'd built a smoky fire to guide me, but I didn't see it in that blue haze. He saved my life. I'd have died of thirst in there—I was losing my mind, I tell you, when he ran and caught me."

Gerald, why are you so eager to believe the best instead of the worst? Are there whisperings in your ears to which you don't dare listen?

But I did not speak aloud.

Na'od spoke to me in Arabic. "The sahib didn't know that when I answered his signals with two shots, it meant for him to stay where he was."

I repeated this in Hindustani. "It's the signal used everywhere in the bush," I added.

"You should have told me, Timur Effendi. I'm a newcomer, you know. But thank you for the drink and this litter. I was at the end of my rope."

"To hear you *thank* him—" Sukey bit her lips.

"Didn't you say to be careful?" he demanded, his voice hoarse with anger. "Don't sing one tune one minute, and another the next. Anyway, I told you there's nothing to it. Na'od is just a nigger trying to do his best.

The other broke his safari to show me some game. It was my fault we got separated—I misunderstood his directions. He gestured for me to take one side of a dry nullah while he took the other, and to come together at the *'kilima'*—hill. I thought he said *'kisima'* and looked up in the dictionary. *Kisima* means water hole."

It is astonishing, Gerald, how one wrong letter in a word may invite disaster.

"Don't try to talk," Sukey said.

"I don't need any advice, and if I can stand to tell it, you can stand hearing it."

"I was only thinking you weren't able—"

"I know whether I'm able or not."

"You're speaking in a very harsh tone. They're listening to it, and we don't know positively that one of them doesn't understand English."

"Bah! I'm not as easily taken in as all that. Anyway, if either of them knew a hundred words, he'd be parading 'em before the sahib. *Kisima—kilima*—it was a natural mistake. But I made signs besides, though he didn't read 'em right. I followed that damned donga for three miles, thicker thorn all the time. Then I started back, thinking I'd missed the hole. It was absolute hell. Then I kept trying to get to him, and he to me. Hour after hour under that baking sun, without a drop to drink. When I found a stinking hole full of it—but I can't tell you without getting sick. I had to run and hide from a cow elephant with a calf. I didn't have enough ammunition left to dare shoot her. Elephants and rhinos were everywhere in the thickets. Trying to avoid them made me miss Na'od again and again. A few hours more, and I don't know what I might have done. Maybe gone crazy and blown my head off."

"Sahib, will you have another sip from my flask?" I asked.

"If you please."

"Sahib, I can feel for you," I went on, after he had lifted the flask. "On the day I was wounded by a lion of the desert, I trekked for many hours across sand hills."

But he looked at me bleary-eyed, and in the next five minutes fell asleep. At his tent, I proposed that one of the Swahilis remove his torn and dirty clothes, and anoint the tears in his skin. Sukey replied in an even tone that if I would have the boys bring plenty of hot water, she would see to his care. She addressed me as Timur Effendi, and was punctiliously polite. I had never before been more aware of her inward resources, and of how they were reflected in beauty. I had the strange impression that now she was less afraid than was Gerald, and if she did not know why, I did. It was not because she was less conscious of danger. She was far more so than he; she had enough imagination and knew the Orient so well that she did not weigh events with the scales of the Government House in Hyderabad. She dismissed nothing because by those scales it appeared improbable; all Central Africa was one vast improbability. But in this trial she was forsaking Sukey, the Lieutenant Governor's memsahib, and reverting to Bachhiya. As Bachhiya, she had the comprehension and thus a kind of protection of kismet. She was looking that strange spirit in the face.

In the morning I began to carve a rhino-hide walk-ingstick. Shortly after sunrise Gerald's Hindu body servant brought me an invitation from the sahib to come to his tent. There I found him and Sukey finishing breakfast. Gerald looked haggard, and although he smiled, he could not conceal his extreme tension.

"*Alicum salem, sahib!*" I said, salaaming.

"Good morning, and excuse me for not coming to your camp. The truth is, my feet are so sore I've delayed getting them into boots." He raised one of them, clad in a mat slipper.

"Then you won't be able to hunt today, sahib!"

"I'm afraid the blisters won't heal and I won't feel refreshed for several days. I certainly can't hunt in a litter. But I could travel in one, Timur Effendi, toward the coast."

"Truly you could, sahib, if you've had enough hunting."

"After all, I've a fine leopard, a lion, and a rhino, three of the best trophies obtainable. I wouldn't be happy lying around camp and the memsahib was so disturbed over my experience yesterday that she, too, has had enough. Of course, we must call on you for trans-

358

portation. Since you planned to be delayed until your other caravan arrived, the loss to you would be no greater, and perhaps less, if you lend us enough porters to make the trip. We would like to break camp today and get in a good day's travel."

"You'll need many porters, sahib, to carry food and water, litters, and your tents and belongings. But surely I could spare enough, if you think best to go."

"I do, Timur Effendi, to my great regret. Since I can't hunt, I may as well return to my labors."

"I'm rather loath to have you start out with only two guns. We were very lucky not to be attacked by rhinos on the outward journey—always a bad thing, since so many porters running about in terror often result in one or more being killed. But both you and the memsahib are good shots."

"We're fair shots, and will both shoot at once at the first sight of a rhino."

"Do you think your guns are to be trusted, sahib? One of them misfired at the lioness—"

"That was because of a lost cap. It didn't misfire once yesterday, nor did my spare piece."

"You're mistaken, sahib. Na'od told me that he had to cock and pull several times to make the breechloader go off. If he'd been firing at a rhino, he would have been carried away on the beast's horn. But perhaps he didn't know how to work it well. Or perchance a bit of wood got into the breech—"

Gerald bade his servant bring the French breech-loader. "I'll shoot at the big tree, below camp," he told me, thrusting a copper shell into the right barrel. Bracing his shoulder against the recoil, he cocked the hammer and pulled the trigger. The hammer did not fall.

With a white face, he pulled it again, in vain.

"Be careful, Gerald," Sukey said quietly.

Gerald drew a sharp breath and held hard. "I don't suppose it's anything serious. Kushri, bring me my kit."

When it was brought, Gerald began to remove the breech plate. His hands shook, and his face was drenched with sweat before he could take out the screws. Then he unhooked the spring and stretched it in his hand. It extended but did not spring back.

359

"Oh, my God," he breathed. Then he made a powerful and partly successful effort to rally. His voice barely trembled as he spoke on. "Timur Sahib, we will have to make out with one strong gun. But if you can spare us a musket—"

"To fire at *Kifaru* with a musket is only to anger him, sahib. Certainly you'll have to wait until my caravan captain arrives and can guard your passage with his gun."

"I'll take the chance, and so will the memsahib—won't you, Sukey?"

"Yes, since our fortunes have been so ill."

"Don't invite worse fortunes, memsahib! After all, you've had only two unfortunate days. Truly, sahib, I'm responsible for the porters' lives. Also, my Sultan would be wrathful, perhaps having me throttled, if I were so remiss in duty as to permit his late honored guests to set forth five days across the deserts with only one gun."

"We *are* his honored guests, Timur, and we wish to start at once for the coast."

"You *were* his honored guests, sahib. When you left his dominions, you became my guests. You're newcomers, as you say. I couldn't permit you to undergo such danger. But you'll be able to hunt in a day or two more. I myself will hunt with the memsahib, if time passes heavily on her hands."

"I will speak to the memsahib," he said after a long silence. Then he asked quickly, "Shall I tell him you and I and the two servants will start out alone? We could carry water enough."

"Don't say it. It would sound too desperate. Anyway, we'd have to keep fires going all night—get lost—starve. That's the last resort—and then he won't let us go!"

"It doesn't make sense, Sukey!"

"It doesn't make sense, but there it is."

"What in the Devil can he want?"

"We went over that last night."

"It must be ransom for both of us. Huge ransom, to make him an Arab prince who can defy the Sultan."

"That deliberate torture yesterday—"

"Control your voice, Sukey."

"What good will it do? I only hope it is ransom—all

the money we've got. I'd pay it right now to see Zanzibar again. But maybe what happened yesterday was to prove to you how helpless you were."

"Well, that would show they're afraid of the Queen—or the Sultan. They're not as sure of themselves as they'd like to have us believe. I feel like threatening him—"

"Not yet, Gerald."

"How about the letter?"

"It might only make him work faster. But—if you think best."

"Timur Sahib, what day do you expect your other caravan?"

"In five or six days, sahib, if not before."

"I dare say we can pass the time pleasantly until their arrival, and it may be they won't have to escort us to the coast. I'll confess now that I was rather frightened by the Shenzi arrow, and wrote a letter, in Hindi, to be delivered by Bismilla to the Sultan. In it I told him of the attack, and requested that if it was against his pleasure for me to hunt beyond his frontier, to send askaris at once."

"He will think only of your pleasure, sahib, and won't be in the least afraid of Shenzis attacking your Excellencies." Actually Na'od had seen to it that no letter passed from Gerald's hands to Bismilla's, but I was in a state of mind to enjoy the belated invention.

"Don't press it," Sukey said quickly. "Let him think about it."

"I think he'll send the askaris regardless, Timur, and save your men a trip," Gerald went on, heedless of her good advice. "You see, if anything should happen to a sahib envoy, it might cost him his throne."

"Why, sahib—but it isn't meet that I say it."

"If it's important to this matter, please do."

"It was the talk of the court that the treaty to be made was a trifling one, merely the satisfaction of a request from your consul, and the Sultan's naming great sahibs—the General Sahibs—as fitting ambassadors was merely a matter of form. Then he named one fit for the office, of whose fairness to Mussulmen he had heard talk from a visitor to Sind. Truly I was told you were the second to the Governor of a province. But if my guest is a great personage, I've been remiss in the honors due you. Shouldn't I address you as Prince?"

Gerald's pale face grew livid. "Don't say a word," Sukey cautioned him.

"You don't answer to that title? But certainly, sahib, the higher your place, the more care of you I must take. I can't permit you to depart for the coast without stout convoy and strong guns."

"Don't say a word," Sukey warned again. "He may want you to start a fight, so he can kill you in self-defense. That's as reasonable as any of the rest."

"It's a nightmare."

I had nightmares, Gerald, on the night of my march from the sand hills. In them I wept, and Hamyd had to wipe away my tears to hide the shame. Does the shoe pinch a little, my brother? I can feel for you, for my feet were exceeding sore that night.

"Memsahib, may I escort you to the game fields, so you may fill the sahib's bag?" I asked. "You may be followed by your ayah, in case I'm overcome by your beauty in the fastnesses."

"Sit still, for God's sake," Sukey cried.

Gerald shivered and sat still.

"Why, what took the memsahib so?" I asked. "You sounded alarmed."

"Timur, a sahib is greatly offended when his wife's beauty is mentioned in that light. I told him that you didn't know our customs and meant no harm."

"Surely, memsahib, he should regard it as a compliment. Moon of Beauty that you are, still I would safeguard your true husband's rights to your favors against all coveters."

"Still I'll stay in camp with my husband."

"Then I'll go back to making walking-sticks—and whips."

Sithy went meat hunting near camp with Bazizi. I had the impression that she wanted to avoid my company. Gerald and Sukey spent most of the day in their tent. Yet they must have kept a sharp lookout, for they saw almost as soon as I did a file of porters, led by an armed man in desert dress, emerge into the open grass

362

from the eastward. Both were standing in the doorway when I started to meet the newcomers.

"It's my caravan arriving a few days early," I explained. "We'll see presently what's to be done about your return to the coast."

I hurried on, and being in plain sight of tents, Hamyd salaamed deeply.

"I'm sorry you sent for me so soon, Seyed Na," he told me. "I was enjoying the sport from a distance, and I fear it must end, with only grave business to do, when the memsahib sees my face."

"I don't think she'll know you, Hamyd. Your bones are hidden under rocks in the sand hills and much of your face behind your admirable beard. Lower your head band a little, and the game may go on awhile longer, ere work begins."

"Has it been to your liking, master?"

"Yes, but when the mouse can't run any more, the cat eats it."

"I would like to see some more running, and have thought of a good trick. I would hint that I might be bribed, then start away with them after nightfall and have sport with the great sahib in the dark. It may be he'll become separated from me, and without gun or torch, amid the lions." Hamyd looked at me with terrier-bright eyes.

"Not for very long, Hamyd, or the running might quickly end."

"Does it matter? Then you'd take the memsahib to your tent tonight, making it your harem for both your wife and your concubine, and tomorrow we could depart for Somaliland. But if his shouts frighten the lions, I could lead him on a long circle to a view of a fire. At a distance he won't recognize the scene, and I'll tell him it's a camp of askiris, sent from the Sultan for his protection. When he comes running, in great joy, you may give him a pleasant surprise."

"By my beard, Hamyd, it's worthy of a Gypsy! But—"

"If you tire of the game, master, it may be the last chukker. If you wish, I could arrange to separate him from the memsahib soon after we begin. Then you can find and reveal yourself to her, and make a bed like to

363

that beside the fires, near the Tower of Silence by the Indus long ago. If you entertain her well, I doubt if she'd make a sound when she hears him calling."

"It's not quite as simple as that, Hamyd, we not being Arabs. As for the game you propose, it would cancel out only a moiety of our debt, and so is hardly worth the time and trouble. That was the fault I found with the other games."

"Is it pity, sahib?" Hamyd asked, his eyes on the ground in shame.

I considered the question a long time. "No, but it may be respect for humankind in general. It comes to me we've played enough jokes on our brother. It was good sport, and it fed my heart, but let it be on the lap of the gods from henceforth."

"Truly, the Great Ones may play more cruelly than we, sahib. In any case my heart won't go hungry."

We paced by Gerald's tent, Hamyd looking straight ahead. When all the fires began to blaze in the lowering dusk, I returned, with Hamyd in attendance, to find him and Sukey sitting on wooden benches, trying to give every impression of self-assurance. Hamyd wore his head cloth and stood with his face in shadow.

"I've talked with my captain, Akbar, about escorting you to the coast," I began, after salaaming.

"I thank you, Timur Effendi," Gerald replied with an agony of strain in his voice.

"I have good news for you, sahib."

His wan face brightened horridly. "I'll be glad to hear it."

"Akbar served for some years a Hindu merchant in Zanzibar, and can speak the vernacular of the bazaars even as I do."

Instantly he went white, and his hand gave a nervous jerk.

"Yes?" he breathed.

"I was under that impression, but dared not promise it until I spoke to him. That means that you and the memsahib can communicate with him, for the convenience of all."

"Yes, that's good news. How many porters, Timur, do you think we will need?"

"Akbar, you heard the question. Will you answer it?"

He turned his face a little nearer the light. "Not more than forty, Seyed Na."

"Can you be ready to start at sunrise, Akbar?" Gerald asked.

"No, sahib. The porters are weary from forced marches. They must rest all day tomorrow, and perhaps the next day, also."

Gerald started to rise from the bench, a frantic expression on his face. Sukey caught his hand. There was no sound but the fire's crackle and the distant bark of a fox.

Gerald's thwarted fury slowly passed, and I think despair came in its wake. But although his countenance was an interesting study, I was watching Sukey's. Hamyd had turned his firelit face to her. Her eyes rounded, then became expressionless as she seemed to be straining at some elusive memory.

"Of course the men must rest, Akbar," she said. "I would speak to my husband about the matter of delay."

"Yes, memsahib," Akbar answered.

"Gerald, have you ever seen that man before?"

"I don't know. I have the vaguest impression of hearing his voice—"

"He doesn't look Arabic to me. I think he's an Indian and—"

"He may speak English, then."

"What does it matter if he does? Whatever it is, it's going to be brought into the open very soon. Timur was only waiting until this man came. I don't know why he played those little jokes—maybe he just hates Christians on general principle. But there won't be any more jokes. Our jig may be up—we may know in the next two minutes—but there's no use prolonging the suspense. I'm going to try something."

Gerald seemed numbed. "Nothing will do any good—"

"Akbar, have we met before?" she asked.

"There is something familiar about your face—"

"I believe you remember it well. I believe you're not an Arab, but a Mohammedan from India. Have you ever heard of Bachhiya, the daughter of Webb Sahib?"

"It is possible, memsahib, but so long ago—"

"I remember a scene of four years and more ago. A man decoyed my husband into the compound of his house in Hyderabad, and there he and another man felled him and searched for something he was supposed to have on his person. I saw them, their faces covered, by lantern light. They were merciful to me, in the matter of a gag, and in sparing both our lives. I heard the voice of him who came first speaking to the chokidar, and later I heard the voice of the other. It comes to me that you are one of the two men, and Timur is the other."

"Rubbish," Gerald muttered hoarsely.

"I'll answer that, my husband, so these two may hear. I don't know what mission they were on that night, or who had sent them. In any case it was a failure—they didn't find what they were looking for, because you didn't have it, or even know what it was. But they found out, I believe, that Bachhiya could keep a promise. They didn't put on the gag, and I didn't make a sound until the chokidar revived. Perhaps it was because of that delay they were able to avoid capture, flee from Hyderabad, and finally seek safety—or riches—in Zanzibar."

"Oh, you fool!" Gerald cried in English. "They're not the same pair." His voice began to rise. "I tell you they're not! Shut your silly mouth, or I'll—"

"What are you afraid of, Gerald?" she demanded, her face drawn in terrified amazement. "Keep your nerve, for God's sake. If they are the same, they're no more likely to kill us because we know it." She turned her wonderful eyes on mine. "I think that in Zanzibar you heard of the sahib's arrival. You remembered how you bested him before—although without winning your prize—and you thought to best him again for a still greater prize. You intend to hold us both for ransom. Perhaps when you've forced us to write the letter and the money has been sent, you intend to cut our throats. But you believed me that night—will you believe me again tonight?"

"Truly, memsahib."

"If you'll let us go to the coast, I, Bachhiya, swear by Shiva and by Kali and by very Brahm that I'll deliver the sum agreed on at any place you name, and no askaris will ever be set in your pursuit."

A dim hope stole in Gerald's face.

"I believe you, memsahib," I said. "But Akbar and I aren't seeking ransom."

"Please don't lie to me. There's no use of it now."

"I don't lie, memsahib."

"Then it must be—though it doesn't make sense—you're on the same business as before."

"It's connected with it, truly."

"But I didn't have anything hidden on my body," Gerald cried. "I haven't now."

"Could it be that the great sahib is also a great liar?"

"I swear I didn't ever know what you were looking for. Some stupid spy gave you the wrong information—or gave it to some native king who sent you on a fool's errand. Sukey, did I ever know—"

"He didn't know, Timur. You believe me, don't you?"

"Perhaps he lied to you, memsahib."

"I didn't—"

"Have you never lied to Bachhiya, sahib?" Hamyd asked.

"Bachhiya—" Sukey was staring at him, her eyes the only color in her marble-white face.

"Why, so you gave your name—"

"Bachhiya! You—you—" Then while her breasts swelled, some heart-throttling thought struck her, and her eyes darted to mine.

Then she screamed a long-drawn scream hideous in the silent night. Gerald leaped up toward her, his hands open to silence her, and I sprang between them.

"What's the matter, Sukey, for God's sake!" Gerald cried.

"Don't you know? Can't you see? One of them's Hamyd." She broke into wild sobbing.

"It isn't true. You're out of your mind—"

"Do you think so? I wish to God I was. Look at the other. Don't you know him, either? He can't be—but he is. They've both come back from the grave. *They came back for you.*"

CHAPTER THIRTY-NINE

Trial in the Jungle

THE NIGHTMARES OF THE DAMNED are those in which monstrous things, denied by the soul, stand by the side of common, familiar things. On a bench made out of crates by a stump-legged table, Sukey sat with her hands pressed against her temples, uttering naked screams and sobbing yells. They carried far and excited the hyenas drawn in about the camp by the smell of fresh meat, and these began to howl and wail and chuckle. The fire crackled in the brief intermittent silence, and then I heard Gerald's voice. He did not shake or slap Sukey or throw water in her face. Instead he leaned over her, his hand on her shoulder, saying, "There, there."

I knew that for the moment he was out of his mind. It was as though he had gone out of it on purpose, as though he had left it, to function the best it could without him. Thus he gave the nightmare impression of being dual—his soul, his inward being, flying from the scene, and his shell in dreadful combat with it.

I thought that his soft, maudlin tone reached her finally, and that extreme grotesquery shocked her into some sort of consciousness. Her cries died away, and her hands gripped the table. Then she turned her head very slowly, her lips thrust out and rounded, her eyes bulging, empty save for firelight, to look at him.

"You may be right, Sukey, about Hamyd," he told her in a calm, convincing tone. "We never had proof of his death, you know—I'd often thought he'd been carried away by the Yezedis. No doubt he's been in slavery all these years to some Emir in the North. Somehow the Emir got the idea I had a priceless document, and since

Hamyd told him he knew me, he was sent with another man—just a spy—to get it. As for the spy, there are many Arabs on the coast—and maybe he's a Persian."

Gerald, your brain forsaken by your spirit has worked fast!

Sukey sat rigid. "You said you saw enough of his body—"

"I did."

"How much of it?"

"It was only his skull and a bone or two, but I found the turban he'd worn, with a bullet hole through it, just where it would enter the skull. The teeth he'd lost were missing. The one with a gold filling had been chopped out. You see, darling—"

With her face horridly drawn, Sukey pressed her hand to her mouth as though in extreme nausea. Instead she was only trying to check a scream. All we heard was a long, high-pitched moan.

She dropped her hand and said quietly, "I won't yell any more, Gerald. I won't laugh, either. Just go on talking. It doesn't matter what you say."

"Surely you realize how foolish—"

"Foolish, Gerald? It all makes sense now."

"Don't say that! Hear me, Sukey! If you say that, I'll slap your face—"

"Hit me hard enough to knock me out. That's what I want. But I'd have to wake up sometime—and so will you."

Gerald's hands fell, but he quickly lifted them again. His face that for a moment lost all expression, seemingly all vestige of personality, became desperately resolute. He gasped and spoke on.

"There was no mistaking the skull, Sukey. There was a lot of blood on the ground—"

"He'd been wounded by a lion of the desert—in the face. He told us about it—don't you remember? He'll tell you again if you ask him. He's standing right there."

"Stop it, Sukey. Be calm and sensible. The tracks showed he'd been surrounded. The people living there heard how he was killed—a good deal of detail got back finally to Hyderabad. There's not a chance of his being alive, and if he was—would we meet him here? Why,

369

we're in Central Africa. I was personally recommended by the Sultan to make that treaty, on account of—"

"You've forgotten one thing, Gerald. The thing that began it all. It's awful hard not to laugh—but I won't."

"Don't try to talk. You're still half out of your head. Just listen to me—"

"No, you don't want to hear it, but you've got to. You've forgotten the most important point. I don't see how you could, Gerald, when you remember so much more. Rom's a Gypsy."

He slapped her across the mouth—a sharp blow. Then he whirled to face me, in mortal terror. I did not look at him but at Hamyd.

"Take your hand off your knife, my brother," I told him quietly.

"I shouldn't have done it," Gerald cried in Hindustani. "But I'm terribly worked up by her screaming— my nerves are all on edge."

"It ill becomes a great sahib, sahib," I said.

"You'll have to forgive me, Sukey. But you see now he isn't Rom. If he had been, he'd—"

"Knocked you down? No, he's a Gypsy. You know he wouldn't knock you down, and maybe out. He isn't ready for anything like that, for a good while yet. There won't be anything like that. It would half spoil the fun. It would hurt his show."

"Sukey, for God's sake—"

"There's no use calling on God."

"Look at him. You see there's not the slightest resemblance—"

"Look at both of them. What did they come for, Gerald, the night they came to the compound? Had they found out they'd been betrayed? They knew that in one minute when they were about to die. But who'd arranged for them to be murdered? At last they came back to find out—they came to our house. It was a strange place for them to come, wasn't it? Rom idolized you, Gerald. He'd have to find absolute proof—"

"My own brother, Sukey—"

"Your half-brother, a half-white man. Did he find it that night? Or is he only finding it now, in your desperate effort to believe him dead? Oh, that might be just

370

because of me. You just want to keep me. Gerald! You didn't do it! You hated him with all your heart, but you couldn't—"

"Sukey, you know I couldn't—"

"No, I don't. I've got to know you didn't. He's certain that you did—but if you've got any proof of your innocence—"

"If Rom was alive he'd know—"

"If Rom was alive! Look at him standing there. He and Hamyd—and you and me. You can speak to him, if you want to. I—can't."

Gerald turned to me, his arms quivering at his side. "Timur Effendi, do you understand English?"

"I once did, sahib, but I haven't spoken any for eight years."

"Eight years?"

"And some months. A very long time, sahib."

"Ask him when his face was injured, Gerald," Sukey said.

"Eight years and some months ago, memsahib."

"Well, Gerald? What shall we say now?"

"Timur—I'll still call you that—if by a miracle you're my half-brother Rom, and you were betrayed to the Yezedi, you might conceivably suspect the man who married your sweetheart, even though he's your half-brother. You might have tricked us out here to find proof, as Sukey says. What you've put me through might be an attempt to break my nerve and make me confess. But tell her, if you've got a drop of kindness in your heart, that it's only a suspicion—that you haven't any proof—"

He stopped talking, and both he and Sukey stopped breathing.

"There's no kindness in my heart, sahib," I replied.

"Well, you haven't any proof. It's an utterly unjustified accusation. I don't even believe you're Rom—"

"Long ago, sahib, before I drank the cup of death—as the Mohammedans would say—I was Rom."

Gerald took two slow, halting steps around the table toward me. Then he stopped and braced his hand against its edge.

"I must ask you to identify yourself," he said clearly and distinctly, "before I'll believe it."

"Don't, Gerald," Sukey pleaded.

"Well, if he's Rom, he understands it's my duty to ask for identification. I don't see how a stranger could hope to—"

"Stop it! You needn't make his show better. Don't you see you're doing just what he wants by talking that way? Like a sahib gone crazy? Such awful terror, Gerald. I've never dreamed anything so awful. I'll go crazy, unless you stop. Sit down. I'll play any game you want if you'll stop. You're just afraid he'll take me away from you. You're just afraid he'll do something to an innocent man. If you didn't do it, I'll stay with you, Gerald. He won't harm you, if you're innocent. Please sit down."

When, very ceremoniously, he sat down on a stool by her, she said a dreadful thing. It was, "There, there."

"Sukey, how could you have any doubt I'm innocent?"

"Wait a minute. Rom, will you sit down on the opposite side of the table? You, too, Hamyd, please. *It's all right to sit down with the sahib—*" Her eyes tightly closed, and her face drew, and her mouth opened wide, but she let out her breath in silence.

I took a stool, but Hamyd remained standing behind me.

"It's not meet that I sit down with my sahib, in the presence of others, memsahib," he said in formal Urdu.

"Very well. Rom, you loved me once. Maybe you still do. Will you get this over with, just as quickly as possible?"

"Yes. Hamyd, wilt thou get the book out of my tent?"

"Nay, sahib, by thy leave. But Na'od is in call, and will fetch thee the book."

"Bid him do so."

Hamyd called in Arabic in the direction of my camp. I had not noticed Na'od, standing about fifty paces out of the moonlight, but as he went on the errand a far-flung glimmer of the fire glinted on his naked back. He brought the dictionary, and laid it on the table in front of me.

"Did you notice if my slave girl is in her tent?" I asked in Arabic.

"No, Timur Effendi. The flap was open, and I didn't see her."

She had no doubt started this way when Sukey had screamed. The porters who had heard her and gazed in wonder had gone back to their cooking, although more quietly than usual. I wondered where Sithy had gone. I could be sure she would not have ventured far into the darkness. My Kafiristani mountaineer kept a remarkably level head.

Na'od withdrew. I took one of two papers from inside the book and handed it to Sukey.

"This is a carefully traced copy of the message carried by my former *sais* Abdullah to the Rindi tribesmen, kinsmen of Kambar Melik," I told her.

Sukey held it to the firelight and read it carefully.

"Gerald, will you print some Urdu words on a page from your notebook?" she asked. "I'll read them aloud."

"I certainly won't. You've no business asking me to, Sukey. If Rom charges me with this crime—if he's been that much affected by his awful experience—I'll stand trial in an English court."

"I'm afraid it won't get to that, Gerald. You're being tried right now. If you're innocent, you'd better do everything you can—"

"I won't submit to it. I refuse."

"Note the spelling of the word for white?" I asked.

"I don't know the word well, but I think it's misspelled."

"Here's a dictionary I stole from the Tatta Lancers' library in Lahore. It was on a shelf of books presented by Gerald, when he resigned his commission."

"Is this your dictionary, Gerald?"

"How would I know?"

"It has your bookplate in it."

"I dare say it's mine. I had one. Everybody borrowed it."

"Look up *abyas,*" I said.

Sukey did so. I could see no change of expression on his face.

373

"It's misspelled there, too, the same way."

"You call that evidence?" Gerald demanded. "The whole mess had access to that dictionary. I'd have thought my brother would have blamed one of his enemies—"

"Sukey, I never even suspected Gerald until I saw this dictionary. Until then I'd had only three suspects, Clifford Holmes, Henry Bingham, and your father. I had to eliminate Henry, because he didn't know enough Urdu to have written this letter."

"Of course Henry didn't do it. But Clifford—"

"It was delivered to Abdullah, at his house, late at night, on the day I left. That night Clifford was in the hospital drugged with morphine. That left only your father—"

"I could have eliminated him for you. I couldn't close my eyes the night after you'd left. You'd told me there wasn't any danger, but I was afraid—"

"Second sight, no doubt," Gerald broke in.

"I suppose it was. I was still—Bachhiya. Maybe I am yet. Anyway, Dad didn't leave his room."

"So I'm to be convicted by a process of elimination! Sukey, why don't you stand up for me? Great God, it's as though you're trying me, too—my own wife. You say Henry couldn't have done it—your father couldn't have done it. I don't think they did, but don't you know this man is mad? My brother's mad. He's been through so much—this is his obsession. Don't listen to him any more, and don't say anything. By helping him accuse me, you may lead him on to some insane act—"

"He doesn't seem much different than he ever did. You may be mad, and I may go—"

"He never was sane. This whole thing is mad. The very cunning he's employed—"

"Rom, is there anything to what he says?"

"You know how mad I am, Sukey, and how sane."

"I think I do. The way you've done this—where the hyenas howl—is your kind of madness. But there's awful coincidence in it, too. It's affecting me a little, Rom— for the worse. At least it keeps clouding my mind. When we were lovers—when you knew me as Bachhiya, and I was—we both believed in kismet. You didn't follow us

374

to Zanzibar—you were in Africa long before we came. That we should meet here—"

"Don't let that worry you any more, Bachhiya. I sent for you."

"That's not true, Sukey," Gerald broke in frantically. "It's proof that he's out of his mind. The Sultan asked for me, because of my helping the Mohammedan pilgrims get ships—"

"He sent for you, Gerald, and you came. He said you could bring me, to go on safari, and you did. He invited us beyond the Sultan's borders and to stay when Bismilla was scared out, and here we are. There weren't any Shenzis. Hamyd shot that arrow. His own men beat the drum. Well, I can think better now. It isn't mad, or it isn't kismet, it's just Rom. Go ahead, Rom."

"I found out your father was innocent. Hamyd looked at his face and said he was."

"And that eliminated all three of your suspects," Gerald said with seeming intense bitterness. "Did you think of some half-caste woman who might hate you? You always had plenty of women, and threw plenty of them over. She could have found out your orders from some babu at Headquarters—"

"I was starting to say, Sukey, that I had other evidence to acquit your father. The man who delivered the message to Abdullah was seen. The woman said he was a young sahib. I have a copy of her statement, sworn to before a cadi. The man came there, tossed the note and a hundred rupees into Abdullah's bedroom. It made a lot of noise, and he ran and in jumping over a gate he caught his breeches leg on a nail. Some shreds were ripped out, including some of the seam. There was quite a little blood where he'd fallen and lain a minute—obviously the nail had raked deeply the inside of his leg along the seam, and it had bled through the rent. The shreds had pulled tight and broken at the boot top, and from their length we could tell that the rip would be between there and above the knee. Such a deep tear—"

I stopped, because of what I saw in Sukey's eyes. Very slowly she turned them on Gerald.

"Then you did do it!"

"What?"

375

"Don't hit me. I'm in my right mind. I dreamed once that you did it—I didn't remember the dream until now, it was so awful. That's why they came to the compound. They took off your trousers, do you remember? It wasn't a fool's errand. They found what they were looking for. They saw what I'd seen one day when you were asleep. What can you say now, Gerald, God help you?"

"I won't say a word. I won't listen to another word." He leaped to his feet. "My own wife believing cock-and-bull of that kind. I might have known—you've always loved him, not me. I'm going to my tent. You can go to his, if you want to. I'm willing to stand trial in England, but I won't submit any longer—"

It was only a few steps to the tent door. He took them in swift, lithe strides, but the darkness of the entrance concealed him hardly a second. When he reappeared his muzzle-loading rifle was at his shoulder.

In two more strides he was at the edge of the firelight glimmering on his sights. His face was a horror of hate, but he was perfectly steady. Sukey did not make a sound. She did not dare.

"It's my turn now, Rom," he said quietly.

I did not answer.

"I'm going to send Kushri to collect every gun in camp. You're going to tell your men to give them to him. You're not to speak in Arabic. Say, *'Toa bunducki.'* That, too, is out of the dictionary, Rom, the kind that missionaries use, you dirty Gypsy. They're to be put in one litter, where I'll ride. You're going to tell them to take Sukey and me to the river."

I heard him but with a small part of my attention. A dim figure had appeared from behind Gerald's tent. I wouldn't have discovered Sithy in its shadow save for hair called flaxen picking up the distant glimmer of the fire, and for the faint gleam of a musket barrel already leveling. Sukey had not seen her, because her gaze was riveted on Gerald.

"Do you hear me, Rom? Work fast, if you don't want your guts shot out. Call Na'od. Just his name and nothing else."

"Na'od!"

"Seyed Na!" he replied, and came bounding to me.

Still there was no roar of a gun. Obviously Sithy had pulled the trigger in vain. And now she came stealing along the side of the tent, the gun grasped wrong-end-to like a club. If she had but known it, the barrel end would have made it a much more deadly weapon.

"What shall I say to him, Gerald?" I asked. "He can't speak English or Hindi."

"Then make signs. Salaam to me, to show who's boss. Better yet, get off that stool and kneel down. He'll understand that well enough—"

Sukey saw Sithy now, only a few feet behind Gerald and lifting her club. She need only scream and point to warn him. But her only movements were her fingers slowly spreading.

"If you intend to kill me, Gerald—and of course you do—will you tell Sukey—"

A twig crackled under Sithy's foot. As Gerald started to whirl, she leaped forward and struck. The blow caught him on the shoulder, knocking him down. Screaming, she dropped the musket, jerked the rifle out of his hands, and darting out of his reach, she whirled and flung it to her shoulder.

"*Bandkey* [Stop]!" Sukey yelled, leaping up.

Instead Sithy aimed the big rifle with deadly speed at Gerald's breast and pulled the trigger.

There was not even a flash in the pan. Quickly she pulled the other trigger with the same result. Then she flung the weapon down and turned to me, her face flushing and her eyes blazing with fury.

"Don't be disappointed, Sithy," I told her in Hindustani. "We unloaded all the guns in fear of accidents."

"Why didn't you tell me, you *barnshoot!*" *Barnshoot* was the most comprehensive and possibly the most obscene insult in all Hindustani, and I had no idea she knew it. "Why did you let me hit the sahib, when he couldn't hurt you? I wish it had been you. You made a fool of me. You can have your memsahib that he's had, and you can think of him all the while. I'm going to our tents, and don't you come there all night, or I'll kill you."

377

I did not hear a sound from her as, musket-straight and head high, she walked toward our pavilion, but she collided with a food box, and I took it she was half blind.

CHAPTER FORTY

A Gypsy's Mercy

Na'od helped Gerald to his feet and back to the bench. There was no indication that his shoulder was broken or that he was in pain, but his blank face and dim eyes portended deep stupor. Sukey waited motionless for the event of which all this was the shadow cast before. The hyenas were answering Sithy's cries. If we listened carefully, we would soon hear a lion.

Gerald revived and looked at Sukey.

"It's plain now whose side you're taking," he said with genuine and profound bitterness.

"Because I didn't warn you when Sithy was creeping up behind you? I didn't know your gun had been unloaded, Gerald."

"She might have killed me."

"Yes, but I didn't think so. Anyway I couldn't warn you, so you'd shoot and kill Rom. You see, he is the one who has the most right to live. You are the most guilty."

"Then you believe him, not me."

"It's not a question of belief any more. You've been tried and convicted. If I'd needed any more evidence of your guilt—which I didn't—you gave it while you were standing up there with the gun."

"I wasn't going to kill him—and now he's going to kill me."

"I'm not sure of either one."

"Go ahead and kill me, Rom. Why don't you do it and get it over with? I'm not afraid any more."

Strangely, I believed him. "Do you confess? It won't help me, but it might help you."

"Yes, I did it. I did it to keep a Gypsy bastard from

379

marrying a memsahib whom I loved. There was no other way to keep her from marrying you. I hated you, of course—I always have. Mamma taught me to hate you so long ago that I can't remember anything before then. You might as well kill me now. I'd rather you would than have it come to trial—or to have anybody know."

"Well, that's not as easy as it looks. What about Sukey?"

"What about her? You get her whether I live or die."

"Sukey, do you still love me?"

"I'll always love you, Rom, and I need you."

"Do you love Gerald?"

"Yes, because he needs me."

"Whom do you love the most?"

"You, of course. Do you still love me, Rom?"

"I love you just the same."

"Do you want me back?"

"Yes. Do you want to come back?"

"Of course I do. But Rom, if you kill Gerald, I won't come back. You can't ever have me."

"What if I let him live?"

"I'll come back to you now. My marriage to him wasn't lawful. No man has a lawful right to anything, let alone a wife, he gained by crime."

I wiped the cold sweat off my forehead.

"I thought it would be a hard decision, whether to kill Gerald or not. It turned out easy, as far as I'm concerned."

"I don't know what you mean."

"He's just playing another game, Sukey."

"No, the games are over," she answered.

I turned to Hamyd and spoke in Hindustani. "It comes to me, Hamyd, that the sahib's deed against us was one of a madman. He'd been driven mad by hate. The law wouldn't excuse him on the ground of that kind of madness, but considering it came on him through my father's sin, I can forego any further vengeance. The evil he's done since has been trying to defend and conceal that great evil. But he didn't hate you, Hamyd. In spite of that, he sent you to your death. You debt against him is much greater than mine—I see that, now my eyes are open. It's for you to say whether he lives or dies."

"In the madness of his hate of you, sahib, he sought to slay me," Hamyd answered instantly.

"I told you I'd rather be killed than brought to trial," Gerald cried.

"If brought to trial, you'd be hanged. I swore I'd bring you there, as a debt owed to all men, but I can't keep a straight course. I can't even see straight for very far. I'm going to ask forgiveness for my inability to do my duty to society. I don't know what my duty is to God. I do remember the last entreaty in the Lord's Prayer."

Weeping, Sukey put her arms about my neck and kissed me with great beauty.

"I don't want any credit for standing in the way of the law," I went on. "I've no right to assume that I understand the case better than the court-martial. I may be sparing you so I can have Sukey. Yes—I'm sure that's the reason. I was covering up nicely, as usual."

"In spite of that—the mercy or the weakness of letting him live—I think you're going to be a great man," Sukey told me.

"That's what you wanted," Gerald said.

"I won't be a great man, but I'll be remembered, and serve well. Gerald, there are one or two conditions. Sukey said you'd made a religion of the sahib business—of course she knows why now—and it's gone too far to stop. For that reason, you'll have to give up public service. You can go back to England and live on your money and not do any work except running your estate. I want back the money that came to you when I was declared dead. My father, who like me attacked his society, left me that."

"Oh, my God." Gerald dropped his head into his arms and wept.

Sukey laid her hand on his shoulder, removed it, and turned to me.

"Rom, you said you want me. Are you sure?"

"Yes."

"You heard what Sithy said. He's been my husband

for—eight years." The pause was perceptible, and her expression changed. Perhaps it reflected guilty fear.

"That long?" I asked.

"I didn't wait very long, did I, Rom?"

"Were you with child?"

"No. But he was like you in so many ways—at least I thought so—and how could I doubt you were dead? Wasn't the skull you'd fixed—you did that, too, of course—to convince me of it as well as the person who betrayed you? That wouldn't have been like Gerald, to set me free, but it was like you."

"Yes, I set you free. But I remember now that as I was waiting to be killed I tried to send you another message. I tried to put a thought in your mind to take care whom you married in my place. I wanted to warn you that if you chose the murderer, some awful thing—"

"Retribution? Well, it came, didn't it, Rom? Maybe there's more to come."

"The warning didn't reach you. How could it, clear across the desert? It couldn't occur to you that anyone could have sent word to a band of Yezedis—"

"I didn't let it occur to me. And I told you that I dreamed you'd been betrayed—" she paused and drew a sharp breath—"and by Gerald. The dream came several nights before I married him. I should have believed it. I was false to Bachhiya—and so to you."

"Why, you didn't even remember it until tonight."

"Maybe I forgot it—on purpose."

"Even if you had remembered it, how could you believe it? You couldn't even imagine, any more than I could, Gerald—doing it. I won't let you feel guilty. Forgive me, Sukey—I was a little out of my mind. I love you and want you."

"If there's the least doubt in your mind and heart, I want to stay with Gerald. I'm the only one who can help him now. I'd have that much to live for."

"There never has been any doubt."

"If there is, let me go. It wouldn't be fair to me, Rom —it would be going against this"—she showed me the silver talisman—"to have me stay. You gave me your sixpence, and I believe in it still."

"I'll stand by it, Sukey. And if you're troubled about

Sithy, it isn't necessary. She's never been my concubine, she has a great deal of spirit, as you know, and she's only sixteen. I won't go near her tonight—I'd just trample on her feelings—but tomorrow I'll talk with her about her future. She's got the stuff to have a very happy future."

Gerald heard me and looked at me ashen-faced. "Tonight," he gasped. "Rom, are you—going—to—"

"Yes, I'm going to occupy your tent tonight with Sukey. Right here is the appointed rendezvous—tomorrow we'll be starting back. For a moment I was a little troubled about—well, what you used to call good taste. After what we've been through I don't think we need regard it. I could wait for Sukey, but of course I won't, when I've waited so long already. That will mark for all three of us the full turn of the wheel."

"But the Swahili! For Sukey's sake—not mine—I don't want the white people in Zanzibar—"

"That will be taken care of incidental to another arrangement I'm going to make. This has happened so suddenly you might have another breakdown. You've never spent a night in a *boma*. It's a great experience on a moonlight night, and not nearly as dangerous as hunting. A dozen of the porters will take torches and build you one, where Bazizi shot and hung a kongoni for camp meat. It's only about a quarter of a mile from camp. Hamyd and Na'od will stay with you there, and they'll have blankets for you, and Hamyd will have one of the rifles. The lights will go out and a chapter of your life will end, and after a while there'll be tomorrow."

"Yes— Yes." He did not look at me or at Sukey.

"I don't know what arrangements we'll make for traveling. Anyway you and Sukey had better say whatever needs saying to each other now. Do you want to go in the tent?"

"I'll walk with him to the *boma*, and come back with the porters," Sukey answered.

"All right. I'll give the men their orders."

I left them, and in a few minutes the men had prepared an armful of *mwenge*—the slow-burning reed torches. Two of them flared weirdly in the cold light of the waning moon as the party set forth. I stood by the fire a little while, every sense and feeling numbed, then wandered into Gerald's tent. There, in the lantern light, I set about a task that occurred to me a while ago—nothing important—at most just a symbol of return to a long-lost world—perhaps something that Sukey would like—perhaps an act for memory's sake, and to help lower the barriers bound to have risen between us in these long years. Using Gerald's tools, I was hardly aware of what I was doing until by lantern light I looked at my face in the glass. Still I did not look the least like Romulus Brook.

I tidied up the tent a little, then blew out the lantern. Perhaps I was thinking that Sukey would rather come to me in the dark, but all my thoughts were slow and dim. I lowered the flap of the entrance so the porters would not see me here on their return, and then, deeply weary, undressed and lay down on the tick-covered grass mattress of the big bed the *fundis* had built. Building a stout *boma* might be a two-hour job. I wished I had asked Sukey not to go. I wished my wide-open eyes would stay closed.

But they must have shut a few minutes without my knowing it. There was a brief, blissful dream still weaving slowly in my brain when the curtain of the tent was drawn aside. I caught a glimpse of dull red glowings from the dying fire, and these flickered wanly until quick hands tied fast the strings. There were soft sounds close to me—the rustling and, I thought, the fall of garments. One side of my blanket was lifted. Then there ¬ a small, warm body pressed against mine, fragrant, ˥utiful to the touch, and strong; and there were lips, ˥nteous of love and life, pressed against mine.

˥ was wide awake now, utterly awake and living; still I remembered my dream of a moment ago. I had not known that it was my dearest dream until Sithy had entered the door to make it come true.